W.G. Grace's Last Case

'William Rushton has been a familiar figure on the scene for over twenty years as an actor, satirist, illustrator and occasional writer. Now he put his first appearance as a novelist . . . It is a h rolling burlesque of the Victorian era . . . humour really comes in the recklessness with wh Mr Rushton lays on his jokes. He is not a writer play around with trowels, if there is a shovel within reach. But there is also an excellent wit in some of the asides, which come and go so quickly that the reader has to remain on his toes to catch them all.' Auberon Waugh *Daily Mail*

'The plot is a hilarious phantasmagoria, but where Rushton really scores is in the creation of W. G.'s character . . . Rushton's extrapolation from the folklore figure of Grace is a triumph of the comic imagination.' *Times Literary Supplement*

'Mr Rushton plays fast and loose with many of the better known personages, fictitious and actual, of the Victorian Age . . . the author's illustrations, two dozen of them, are extravagantly imaginative and very well drawn.' *Sunday Telegraph*

William Rushton

W.G. Grace's Last Case

or

THE WAR OF THE WORLDS – PART TWO

with drawings by the author

METHUEN

A METHUEN PAPERBACK

First published in Great Britain in 1984
This paperback edition first published in Great Britain in 1985
by Methuen London Ltd, 11 New Fetter Lane, London EC4P 4EE
Copyright © 1984 by William Rushton
Set in IBM 11 point Journal by 🅕 Tek-Art,
Croydon, Surrey
Reproduced, printed and bound in Great Britain by
Hazell Watson & Viney Limited,
Member of the BPCC Group,
Aylesbury, Bucks

ISBN 0 413 57860 7

A question of graver and universal interest is the possibility of another attack from the Martians. I do not think that nearly enough attention is being given to this aspect of the matter. At present the planet Mars is in conjunction, but with every return to opposition. I, for one, anticipate a renewal of their adventure.

H. G. Wells
(In the Epilogue to *The War of the Worlds*)

I have nothing to do today. My practice is never very absorbing.

Dr John Watson

I began to perceive more deeply than it has ever yet been stated the trembling immateriality, the mist-like transience, of this seemingly so solid body in which we walk attired. Certain agents I found to have the power to shake and to pluck back that fleshly vestment, even as a wind might toss the curtains of a pavilion.

Dr Henry Jekyll

How can you expect to make runs, when you are always reading? You don't catch me that way.

Dr W. G. Grace

To my two grandfathers.

To William, the Welsh one, who was at Bart's Hospital
in the Nineties and told me much of that and how
he went to Buffalo Bill's Wild West Show in Cardiff as a lad.

And to Bertie, the Lancastrian, who was far larger than life,
but would probably like most to be remembered for
bowling Gilbert Jessop second ball.

I hope there's a Hatchards in Heaven. And gin.

Contents

Lord's Cricket Ground.

The Marylebone Cricket Club XI
versus
XXII Gentlemen of Philadelphia.

1   Foul Play at Lord's Cricket Ground

Doctor William Gilbert Grace, the Great Cricketer, felt anything but great. He should have been in roaring form. It was Lord's, it was June, the sun was shining, the Nineties were Gay, God was in his Heaven, the Queen was on the Isle of Wight, and he was putting the Gentlemen of Philadelphia to the sword in no uncertain manner in front of a first-rate crowd. Nonetheless, Dr Grace felt extremely low.

A small man with bright red whiskers and a spotted shirt bowled him another short ball on the leg, and with a casual heave of his shoulders the Doctor despatched it full-toss into the Popular Stand, which enthusiastically cheered his fifty runs.

Why isn't the spirit soaring, thought W.G.; am I growing old? He slipped a hand under his right leg-guard and rubbed his aching knee. That knee and, of course, the invasion, had only allowed him some twenty innings the previous summer and he had averaged but nineteen, the absolute nadir of his career. He had heard the rumours, that he was past it, overweight and over forty. This little fellow is a fool to himself, thought the Doctor, as the elfin Philadelphian lobbed up a full pitch outside his off-stump. He smacked the ball to the picket fence under the shadow of the pavilion.

It was gratifying to be fully in command but then again so he should be. They were, after all, only Americans, so he had no excuses not to be. Still, in fairness to himself, there were XXII of them, and the gaps were few and far between. The Marylebone Cricket Club, the Royal and Ancient of Cricket, had decreed from their offices in the Lord's Pavilion that the Philadelphian team could contain twice the number of players 'in order to make a game of it.' This, despite the fact that they had whitewashed the Gentlemen of Sussex, Ranjitsinghi included. It had also to be admitted that whatever talents they lacked in the batting and bowling departments, they certainly made up for with their fielding. They were quick as lightning with prodigious throwing-arms, particularly those who had played at baseball.

Between overs he met his fellow-opener halfway down the wicket. A.J. Raffles enjoyed a chat. Usually, he drew your attention to some pretty creature in the crowd. Today it was a sporty little thing in pink. W.G. merely grunted, and silently harboured grave doubts about Raffles' relationship with that young Bunny Someone.

'Cracking form, W.G.?' said Raffles, flattening a wormcast with the bottom of his bat.

'More like it indeed,' replied the Doctor.

'A goodly crowd, too,' continued Raffles, 'and still a-coming.'

'Yes,' said W.G. Carriages ringed the ground. Top hats and parasols bobbed and weaved. 'I shall delay my century until the gates are closed. Foolish to pass the hat round at less than capacity.'

'There's certainly money about today, Doctor,' said Raffles, not inexperienced in these matters. 'Hello, I think you are about to enjoy yourself.' He beamed happily and winked. 'A change of bowling.'

So there was — and high time too in the Doctor's opinion. *And* the new bowler was Castor Vilebastard, no less. Oh, it will certainly give me great pleasure, he thought, to make mince-meat of this fellow. W.G. expressed very few intense dislikes, but in his view, C. Vilebastard was a fully-qualified *bounder.*

'The italics,' he announced to a startled umpire, 'are my own.'

Undoubtedly it was this rotter's presence at Lord's that lay at the root of his melancholy.

A.J. Raffles turned the first ball of the over neatly to leg, and they walked a sedate single. Vilebastard was still quick, W. G. reflected as he flexed his shoulders, adjusted his beard, tweaked his red-and-yellow-striped cap and spun his vast bat in the air as King Arthur might have whirled Excalibur aloft on such a Saturday afternoon centuries earlier, when battle was to be joined. He revolved slowly on his heel, searching for suitable gaps in the massed ranks of white-flannelled Philadelphians. Suddenly and violently the ball whistled through the Champion of All-England's voluminous beard like a grenade, fizzed past the unsuspecting wicket-keeper and all three long-stops and exploded against the sight-screen.

'None of us was ready, Vilebastard!' boomed the Doctor, scarlet with rage.

'Villibart!' cried Vilebastard, 'It is pronounced "Villibart", as you bloody well know! As in "Cholmondleigh".'

'It is pronounced Vile Bastard,' pronounced the Doctor, 'as in totally unacceptable and unsportsmanlike behaviour!' And he added for good measure, and to the mystification of all about, 'Not to mention disgusting practices in a Holy Place!'

Vilebastard marched back towards the Nursery End, seething. Behind him in the Pavilion, W.G. could hear the outraged snorting of the claret-faced members.

'He's no Gentleman of Philadelphia,' said the wicket-keeper apologetically.

'He *is* a member of the MCC,' replied the Doctor, 'or *was*.'

'There's a rotten apple in every barrel,' said the wicket-keeper.

'Ready *now*?' called Vilebastard from the distance.

'Get on with it!' roared W.G. and Vilebastard began to approach at pace. The Doctor raised his bat in readiness, and tapped his left foot impatiently on the wicket. He was going to smite this ball into the next county, where it belonged. Essex that would be.

As Vilebastard reached the crescendo of his unnecessarily long run-up and rose into the air, arms flailing, preparatory to unleashing the thunderbolt, he emitted a shrill shriek, began to fall, and, falling, was propelled by his own momentum into a series of cart-wheels and somersaults towards the middle of the pitch, where with a final jerk, a quiver and a bubbling moan, he lay still. A breathless hush fell over the ground, as the ball dropped from his hand and trickled across the grass until it halted at the Doctor's feet.

'Fore!' he cried, and banged the ball away towards the Tavern to the evident delight of the drunken Thespians and Men of Letters quaffing there.

'Come on!' he called to Raffles and set off for a quite unnecessary run as the umpire was already signalling a boundary. However, it gave W.G. the opportunity as he returned to his crease to tread on the recumbent Vilebastard's outstretched right hand.

'He's not budging sir,' said an umpire. 'He don't look at all perky.' Anxious Philadelphians were gathering about the fallen bowler. The umpire turned towards the Pavilion.

'Is there a doctor in the House?' he shouted.

'I'm a doctor!' boomed the Doctor. 'Let's have a look at him.' As he was about to leave his crease, he insisted that the umpire shouted 'Dead ball!' as he certainly would not trust young Castor further than he could throw him. W.G. pushed his way through the ring of fieldsmen and prodded Vilebastard vigorously with his bat.

'Get up!' he prescribed sharply. There was no response. W.G. turned the body over with his boot. Diagnosis was quite simple.

'Aha!' he said, nodding wisely, 'Here's your problem!'

There was an arrow embedded between his patient's shoulder-blades.

'Ye Gods, Doctor,' gasped the opposing skipper, George S. Patterson, no less. 'What, in Heaven's name is that?'

W.G. Grace knelt and broke off the end of the arrow. He peered knowledgeably at the feathers and looked slowly round the circle of bewildered faces.

'Apache,' he announced.

'Is he dead?' asked one of the umpires, the colour of flannels.

'In my book, as a doornail,' vouchsafed the Doctor.

'I tend to agree,' said a large, smooth-faced man of fifty in a top hat and frock-coat, kneeling beside him. Opening a black bag, he produced a stethoscope and began to listen to Vilebastard's chest. Twice during this operation he was obliged to straighten up, once to blow his nose with a noise that would have been music to the ear of a passing goose, and again to give vent to a racking cough.

'This is one of the Vilebastards surely?' He dabbed at his nose with a silk handkerchief.

'Castor, in fact,' replied W.G. 'You know them?'

The top-hatted gentleman sneezed violently over the seat of Vilebastard's soiled trouser.

'Not really,' he said. 'They had expressed some interest in my work. Now there's one less.' He sighed and began to pack his instruments away. 'Doctor Grace, is it not?'

'You have the advantage of me,' said the Great Man.

'Henry Jekyll,' said Doctor Jekyll huskily, 'Doctor Henry Jekyll, pronounced *Jeekyl*, a fact of which laughably few seem aware.'

'Haemorrhoids?' enquired Dr Grace.

'Try again,' said Dr Jekyll, closing both of the corpse's bulging eyes at once with a tidy two-fingered movement, and then expelling a gout of green phlegm onto W.G.'s boot.

'I've read something of yours in *Lancet*,' said Dr Grace quickly.

'Schizophrenia, perhaps,' suggested Jekyll.

'I'd have laid odds on haemorrhoids.' W.G. shook his head. You could tell a rectum-man, usually.

A Third Opinion was pushing its way through the throng, black bag in hand. A short, sturdy man in bowler hat and tweeds, a military moustache and a game leg, acquired at the fatal battle of Maiwand during the Afghan Wars, that had prevented him from arriving sooner. He lowered himself with difficulty into the space between Dr Jekyll and Dr Grace.

'Watson,' he said, 'Doctor John D. Watson.' He held his left arm in a stiff and unnatural manner. Another souvenir of Maiwand and the hectic retreat to Kandahar.

'I am Doctor Grace,' said Dr Grace, 'and this is Doctor Jekyll.'

'*Jee*kyl,' corrected Dr Jekyll.

'Well, if two practitioners as distinguished as your good selves pronounce the fellow dead, then dead he most certainly is.' He took a mirror from his bag and held it to Vilebastard's chill and curling lip. 'You're absolutely right. Rum case.' He ran the feathers of the arrow reflectively through his moustache. 'Never seen a rummer. Is there perhaps archery being performed at the Nursery End?'

'That is an Apache arrow,' said Dr Grace.

'Quite unknown, one imagines, to the toxopholites of St John's Wood,' added Dr Jekyll. Dr Watson looked sadly into the distance towards Primrose Hill, on top of which the wreck of a huge Martian War-Machine stood, as a Memorial to all those Londoners who had perished during their recent visit.

Watson shuddered at the meaning of it. What a beastly business that had been! The first cylinder that fell on Horsell Common, and was thought at first to be a meteorite. Was it only a year ago? Then more cylinders disgorging dreadful war-machines, great armoured tripods that destroyed everything in their path, Weybridge, Woking, Ottershaw, Artillery Batteries and Regiments of Foot, men, women and children. They were merciless, those Martians. God, however, in his wisdom struck them down. They were unable to cope with something in Earth's atmosphere and in the end only London and the Home Counties had suffered. How they had suffered, though, from the Death-ray and the appalling Red Weed the Martians spread where'er they walked. Quite the finest reports on the Invasion had been those by Mr H.G. Wells, serialised in *Pearson's Magazine*. It was soon, he had heard, to be a book.

Watson shook himself. He must put the past behind him. The distressing events of the past eighteen months.

'Very, very rum indeed,' he said, 'Would that Holmes were still with us!'

'Who?' asked W.G.

'The Greatest Detective the World has ever known,' replied Watson, 'but alas, as you may have read in your *Morning Post* —'

'Won't have it in the house!' snapped Dr Grace.

'Ah, then you won't have read of his tragic death last year,' continued Watson, 'at the hands of Professor Moriarty. Do you read the *Strand Magazine*?'

'*Wisden's Almanac* and *The Lancet* are quite enough for me.'

'Sherlock Holmes was a genius,' Dr Watson stated simply.

'How did he die?' asked Dr Grace, who still retained some interest in matters medical.

'He fell off the Reichenbach Falls,' Dr Watson bit his lip glumly.

'Bloody stupid thing to do,' said Dr Grace, unsympathetically. The trouble with genius, in his view, was that it always let you down in the end.

'He'd only just finished the definitive work on Tattoo Marks,' Dr Watson added sadly.

'If you must know, Dr Watson,' said W.G., gesturing to distant groundsmen that the wicket could now be cleared of corpses, 'this case is none too rum, not if you know the full story.' He turned away to direct operations. He could sense that the crowd was restless and, with the collection in mind, was eager to press on to his century.

14

'Better press on,' he said to Raffles, who had removed his batting-gloves and was swiftly going through Vilebastard's pockets. Dr Watson tugged at the back of W.G.'s sweater.

'Perhaps, Dr Grace, you could tell me the full story? I have this contact with the *Strand*. They pay quite well. Though since the demise of my colleague, I have been reduced to the occasional column giving medical advice. Warts, backache, congestion of the lungs and such. Clap.'

And as if on cue the crowd began to applaud ironically, and the Tavern folk commenced a ragged rendition of 'Why Are We Waiting?' in F.

'Play up, play up and play the Game!' heckled Henry Newbolt from the Long Room, and jotted the thought down on his scorecard. Just in case.

'We *must* get on.' W.G. turned impatiently on the Philadelphian captain. 'Have you a twenty-third man?' In fact, a new fielder was already running down the Pavilion steps past the corpse of the late Castor Vilebastard as it left the field held high on the shoulders of four of the Ground Staff.

'May I invite you to my Club for supper this evening, Dr Grace?' Watson worried at W.G.'s heels like the worst sort of retriever. 'You could reveal all then.' He was placing the arrow in his bag.

'Who's bowling now?' cried W.G., smacking bat against pad impatiently. Dr Watson would never surrender.

'Shall we say the Diogenes Club at Eight Thirty?'

'I would be delighted,' interposed Dr Jekyll, 'but a warm bed and a good muck-sweat are the best remedy for a man in my condition.'

The other doctors nodded in agreement. There was certainly no known cure for his ailment. Dr Jekyll sneezed again, with such vigour that for a second Watson thought Lord's had been cursed with a plague of Greenfly.

Watson turned once more to W.G. He scented Mystery and would not be denied.

'Very well.' said Dr Grace, 'Now go away. I want my hundred up before Luncheon.'

He was out next ball. It turned a good yard on the drying patch of the late Castor Vilebastard's life-blood and took the Champion of All-England's leg-stump.

'Even in death,' grumbled the Doctor as he stomped back to the Pavilion.

At eight o'clock that evening, Doctor Grace seethed in a hansom cab in the middle of Park Lane.

The black powder and the bodies had long been cleared from around the Marble Arch. The 'evil, ominous smells' no longer wafted up 'from the gratings of the cellars of some of the houses'. Mr Wells' 'spongy mass of dark red vegetation' still clogged the Regent's Canal however, as W.G. had observed when he drove by that morning. The 'Red Weed', as it was still popularly known, had also spread from the Serpentine and covered most of Hyde Park. Armies of those made redundant by the Second Great Fire of London and now employed by the London County Council were hacking away at it furiously round Speakers' Corner, uncovering the charred remains of orators who had thought misguidedly that the Martians would stop and listen. W.G. could see countless bonfires of Red Weed through the heavy pall of smoke that did nothing to help the visibility.

It might have crossed W.G.'s mind that some lesson was to be learned about Governments in general from the fact that, while on the very day the last Martian had keeled over and perished, battalions of workmen had already moved into 'the jagged ruins' of the palace of Westminster and begun the process of restoration, one could, on a clear day, still see 'the huge, gaping cavity' in the western side of the dome of St Paul's.

W.G.'s mind, however, was occupied by more pressing matters. He was trapped and steaming. He removed his bat from his cricket-bag and banged on the roof of the cab with the handle. The driver peered disconsolately down at him through the tiny aperture.

'Bang and seethe if you will, sir,' he proclaimed. 'There's bugger-all I can do about it.'

'How much longer, my good man, are we to remain sitting here?' Even his beard was soggy with perspiration.

'We're jammed up, sir. Bogged down, and that's the truth.'

Indeed, as far as the eye could see, which wasn't far in the ever-mounting pall of dust and smoke, stood carriages, coaches, omnibuses, drays, carts, broughams and hansoms. The noise

16

was intolerable. Wooden and metal wheels scraped and ground as horses fidgeted and pawed the uneven cobble. Drivers shouted, horses neighed — and the smell! How the Doctor hated London. His vast heart yearned for the Cotswolds. Instead of sitting in this magnified replica of F.R. Spofforth's jock-strap after a day's demon bowling on a Brisbane 'sticky', W.G. could have been somewhere on the Downs playing against XL One-Legged Men of Sussex. Though he was forced to admit to himself, as he shrugged off his damp blazer and heard the tinkling of coin from the pockets, that there were certain benefits to playing in the Metropolis.

'There's two dead 'orses, sir,' reported the driver — he had just received news from the front. 'Up by Londonderry 'Ouse. 'Em's the bastard, sir. Two dead 'orses.'

Moved by this sad news of former colleagues, his fat horse unleashed a Requiem in G Minor, a deep funereal sigh of flatulence that had Herr Richter yet come up with it, would certainly have registered heavily on his Scale. The darkest green it sounded. Like a thousand Venetian blinds going up in a Crematorium.

'That's it!' cried the Doctor, as the last vestiges of sky were blotted out. 'I'm walking!' and he stepped down from the cab, bag in hand, into the Matto Grosso of the horse's proximity.

'Eightpence from Lord's, sir,' said the cabbie.

'It would be cheaper, faster and a deal more exhilarating by hearse,' cried the Doctor, who could barely discern the baggy shape of the driver above him for murk.

'My word, sir,' riposted the cabbie, 'you are a caution, and that's not saying much.'

W.G. gave him back a penny from the change.

'Before you go, sir,' suddenly the cabbie was all unctuousness, a job applicant in a Funeral Parlour. 'I wonder if I might 'ave your autograph? Not for me, sir, but for my little girl. She's mad about you, sir. Backward she may be, but bright as a button. Cries out your name in her sleep, sir. I recognised you at once, of course, sir, when you got in. Lily, her name is, sir, as in what corpses pushes up. And the Prince of Wales for that matter, sir. My little joke.'

Whatever size it was wasted on the Doctor who had taken

17

out his fountain-pen, a gift from XXXIII Epileptic Sheep-Shearers from Wagga-Wagga, and was writing 'To Lily, Keep a straight bat, W.G. Grace' on a scorecard he had found in his pocket.

'There you are, my good man, and good day to you.'

'And good day to you, Mr Svengarlic!' the Cabbie cried after him, knowledgeably. The horse, by way of tribute, fired both barrels. Doctor Grace hurried south through the beastliness of London's traffic, treading with the care and precision of a born countryman in a cow-field.

The Cabbie gazed admiringly after his most recent fare until the large bearded gentleman had vanished into the haze. Well I never, he thought, wait until I tells Lily. He looked about him. At the present rate of progress, it could well be some days before he set eyes on his dreadful daughter. He heard a grunt from below him. His first thought was that it was the back of the horse again, but he was surprised to see four Red Indians hailing him. He recognised them at once for what they were from the posters for Buffalo Bill's Wild West Show and Exposition that were displayed all over Town.

'The Earls Court Pavilion, eh?' They grunted assent. ' 'Op in, gentlemen.' If he was going to sit here for an hour or two, then the meter might as well be ticking. No harm in taking money from foreigners, particularly half-naked ones with feathers in their heads.

He poked his face through the tiny window set in the roof of the cab.

'This'll interest you,' he said, 'being as 'ow you are in the same line of business, so to speak. Theatricals and that. Guess 'oo I just 'ad in the cab. You'll never bleeding guess.'

The Red Indians stared at him blankly.

'Sven-bleeding-garlic!' he roared triumphantly. The Red Indians were clearly not impressed.

'Svengarlic! Jesus, I'll spell it for you. S. F. E. N. Effin' N. *garlic*!' They began to make moves to leave. The Cabbie began desperately to mime Svengali's activities with vivid gesticulations and wild eye-boggling. The Red Indians clambered out briskly.

' 'Ere, I've got his signature!' The Cabbie waved the scorecard

18

at them. Their leader took it and peered at it closely. He gasped with astonishment.

'Grey Sea! Grey Sea!' he chanted, showing the others this seemingly holy relic. They took up the chant, prostrating themselves on the filthy cobbles of Park Lane. Having completed their devotions they rose lithely, grunted at the cabbie and loped off with his scorecard into the mists and smoke of Hyde Park.

' 'Ere!' said the Cabbie plaintively. ' 'Ere, what am I going to tell bleeding Lily?'

His horse discharged a further sympathetic gust, and the cabbie's head spun briefly under his bowler hat.

2 Strange Events at the Diogenes Club

W.G. had never previously entered the portals of the Diogenes Club. He stood in the echoing, domed vestibule, which lay, architecturally speaking, somewhere between the Pantheon and St Pancras Station. Physically speaking, it lay between Belcher's, a Club for retired white slave traders, and the offices of British Opium in Pall Mall.

An ancient porter with two finely carved peg-legs and an unlimited supply of opium had written down the Doctor's whispered name without a flicker of recognition, and had then set off in search of Dr Watson. That had been some twenty minutes ago, and the porter had still not reached the bottom of the staircase. It was a stately process, and worse than useless. A column of dust-filled light slanted through an upper window and stood in the middle of the marble-tiled floor like a Leaning Tower of Hock and Seltzer.

At that moment, some lunatic in a morning coat elected to leap ululating from a balcony two floors up to W.G.'s right and swinging from one chandelier to another to alight deftly on a balustraded landing above him to the left. He then vanished from view with a final whoop.

'Who on earth?' Dr Grace enquired of the tinkling, jostling chandeliers.

'Lord Greystoke,' said a voice behind him. It was Dr Watson. 'He's off to Africa. I've advised against it. His wife is in the family way, y'know, but he insists. I'm sorry I'm late but I've been doing a little investigating. Apache, you said?'

W.G. was still gazing heavenwards. He had never seen the like. He worried for the child.

'The arrow,' continued Watson. 'You said that it was an Apache arrow that did for poor Vilebastard. There are Apaches at the Earls Court Pavilion. Nightly. Twice on Saturdays.'

'Are there, by God?' boomed W.G., setting the chandeliers off again. 'It's a blooming small world and no mistake. I wonder.' And he wondered for a minute or two, while Dr Watson walked slowly around him twice, debating with himself as to

21

whether or not he could capture this bearded giant on paper without resorting to his Thesaurus.

'I detected an Apache hand in it,' Dr Grace went on. 'In the main, as I know only too well, the average Redskin is a pretty rotten shot with bow and arrow. Now, believe me, the shot that hit Vilebastard was a corker. Whoever fired it, Watson, had to be beyond the boundary. That's some seventy yards. Well, naturally, the first person I thought of was Gay Dog.'

'Gay Dog?' Watson had his faithful notebook out and was jotting the name down.

'In fact, his real name was something rather convoluted like Laughing-Dog-That-Bites-Your-Legs-By-The-Shores-of-Minnetonka; we all called him Gay Dog. It has to be him. After what happened. Out there.'

'Out where?' Dr Watson gasped for further information. He followed Dr Grace's steadfast gaze.

'Pall Mall?' he mooted. You had to start somewhere.

'The Wild West,' replied Dr Grace.

Dr Watson was not unnaturally agog. He could see the *Strand Magazine* paying through the nose for this one.

'Tell me more, Dr Grace, at once. Please.'

Dr Grace's stomach was groaning with hunger. He had enjoyed only a cold collation for lunch at Lord's and the Tea Interval had been spent shaking the collection out of the Treasurer. In Gloucestershire they are keenly aware of their priorities.

'Over dinner, Dr Watson, perhaps.'

'This way, this way,' and Dr Watson hustled the Great Cricketer towards the Dining Room. So swiftly that he failed to hear a despairing cry from the head of the stair that there was a Doctor Grace to see him. Nor did he hear the noise of the porter's subsequent fall. A staccato rattle as his finely carved peg-legs met bannister-rail after bannister-rail, like a child running sticks along a fence.

Dinner at the Diogenes was never a satisfying culinary experience, particularly if your host insisted on sticking tenaciously to the *Table d'Hôte* and would brook no trespassing into the more elaborate offerings *A La Carte*. Dr Grace, in truth, liked simple fare but not this Old School Fodder that seemed to delight the surrounding table-loads of lawyers, bankers, slave-traders, generals, admirals, bishops, captains of industry and the like. They trumpeted with pleasure as their plates were piled high with toad-in-the-hole and bread-and-butter pudding. Dr Grace, in a moment of rare fancifulness, attributable no doubt to malnutrition, idly imagined that a ferocious House Matron would soon appear and severely cuff a judge for not eating his cabbage. He was jolted back to reality by the sound of a ringing slap behind him. A meaty woman, starched till she crackled, was roundly buffeting a judge.

'Sir Horace!' she shrilled. 'Down the little red lane with *all* our greenstuffs!' The history of the English upper class could be written in starch.

Dr Watson had clearly enjoyed *his* toad-in-the-hole. He had announced contentedly that Mrs Hudson could have manufactured none better. He had then availed himself of further forkfuls of hard, round sprouts. Now, the bread pudding behind him, and with no little impatience, he produced his notebook and pencil.

'You were going to reveal all, Dr Grace,' he said.

Dr Grace's stomach growled. What was the toad up to now? Rudely exhumed from its batter sarcophagus, it was clearly eager to explore the mysteries of the small intestine.

'I had no idea,' prompted Watson, 'that you had visited the Americas.'

'Ever been yourself?' asked W.G., tapping his empty glass.

'Never. Holmes, my late partner, told me that he had once solved a case in the Lone Star State. That is Texas, I think. But no, not I. Why do you ask?'

'It is there, Watson, that you will find the reason for this afternoon's events. Rum, you said at the time. Inevitable, I think I replied, given the circumstances.'

Watson poured some wine into W.G.'s glass. He downed it in one. That might settle the toad's hash.

'I was there some years ago with the MCC, no less. I was skipper. The tour was intended as a short, flag-waving visit to Canada and some of the Eastern States of America. Despite the rise of baseball — and more and more are succumbing to the lure of the Horsehair, as they call it, there are still loyal pockets of cricket-players here and there in Boston, New York and Philadelphia. Lord's felt that they should be encouraged.'

'What is the lure of the Horsehair?' asked Watson.

'Oh, they like their games to have a result. Be over in an afternoon.' replied W.G. 'Bloody silly — what d'you do for the remaining two-and-a-half days?'

At this, the toad, suddenly doused with claret, emitted a hoarse gurgling cry that W.G. failed to entrap in his napkin. Dr Watson however missed this as he was unsuccessfully probing the end of a Corona Corona with a tablespoon.

'I must admit, Dr Grace, that I have never heard of this tour. I saw no mention in the *Morning Post*. Or *Strand*.' The cigar disintegrated in his hand. 'BY GOD!' he cried, and turned to marble.

W.G. leaned forward and said, 'You never will, Watson. There is no record of it. All hushed up. Lips were sealed.' He leaned further forward. Dr Watson's mind seemed to be elsewhere. W.G. stuck a fork in the back of Watson's hand.

'It was known only to a few as 'The Tour of Shame'!'

This startling revelation did not move his host one jot or tittle. It occurred to W.G. momentarily that Dr Watson might have died. He stuck the fork in again, this time more firmly. It bent.

'The TOUR OF SHAME, I said, Watson.' Nothing. He unloosed a whistling sigh as the toad executed a wild fandango. Watson blinked and shook his head. Vestiges of life seemed to be returning.

'Fellow at Lord's. Dead, wasn't he?' Watson was ashen. 'Three doctors, you, Doctor, I and that Jackal johnnie all pronounced him jolly dead. Didn't we?'

'Indeed we did,' replied Dr Grace in his best bedside manner, 'and so he was.'

Watson seized W.G.'s beard in both hands and tolled it.

'Then why, pray tell me, is he, deceased as was pronounced by as distinguished a trio of medical practitioners as you would find in Marylebone of a Saturday afternoon, sitting over there under the bust of Palmerston, wolfing asparagus? Eh?' He giggled nervously. W.G. gently prised Watson's fingers from his beard, and slowly turned to look.

'Ah,' he said. 'Now there's a thing.'

Watson stared at him, open-mouthed and blinking with

disbelief.

'Is that all you have to say? "Ah, now there's a thing." "Ah, now there's a thing." ' His voice rose to a porcine squeal. 'Holmes's brother, *Mycroft* Holmes, may be in the Library.'

'Another genius?' queried W.G.

'Yes, indeed, since you ask!'

'He'll probably fall off a shelf then.' The Toad joined him in a blast of laughter. Watson did not.

'This,' Watson waved at the butter-chinned corpse beneath the bust of Palmerston,' will interest *Mycroft*. This case will fascinate *him*. Man killed at Lord's of a morning, arrow in back, Apache to boot, dead as doornail, seen that evening sitting, bold as brass, in Diogenes Club. Wolfing asparagus. *You* may find that dull as ditchwater. *You* are probably wholly absorbed mentally in working out your batting average. Or inventing the Chinaman. But I, Dr Grace, am something of a criminologist and I certainly cannot rest until I find a solution to this most extraordinary of riddles.'

'Pollux,' said W.G. Grace.

'Owl-dung,' riposted Dr Watson gamely.

'Castor Vilebastard's twin,' explained W.G. to the puce-faced Watson.

'Ah, Pollux,' Watson nodded. 'It's uncanny. He's the living spit.'

'I can't place that red-eyed loony with him,' whispered W.G.

'Nor I.' Watson shook his head. The gentleman in question certainly seemed deranged. Apart from the wild red eyes, he had one black, bushy eyebrow that spread across his low forehead like a caterpillar poised to spring and vivid scarlet lips which, when peeled back to emit a chilling titter, revealed what appeared to be three rows of shark's teeth. He spotted Dr Watson and waved a hairy palm.

'What-fucking-ho, you camel-shagger!' he called cheerfully.

'The man *is* mad,' expostulated Watson, blushing furiously. Heads were turned, and such a slander tends to stick. Many of his fellow-members knew that he had spent some years in the foothills of Afghanistan, a thousand miles from the nearest woman. However, even as they considered whether or not Watson was, underneath it all, the sort of chap who would seek relief with a beast of burden, their attention was turned once again to the activities of the bushy-browed madman. He was prodding at the buttocks of a comely young waitress as she stooped over a trolley of bread-and-butter puddings. This in itself constituted no great crime at the Diogenes. What, after all, was the girl there for? She took home a good twenty pounds a year, less breakages, and one did not enter service in a male domain without expecting one's buttocks to be handled by Men of Distinction.

However, the tampering maniac swiftly moved beyond the Pale. With one movement he overturned his table, his chair, the trolley and the bust of Palmerston, and, throwing himself upon the squawking waitress, proceeded like a man possessed to tear away at her pinny. Pollux Vilebastard lay amidst the wreckage of the table, howling with glee.

Dr Grace proved himself, not for the first time, to be a Man of Action. While the judges and the waiters, the captains and the kings sat rooted, he strode across the dining room and broke a chair over the threshing lunatic's head.

'Turds in aspic, that's not nice!' The madman leaped to his feet and swung a wild blow at the Doctor who stepped back quickly, staying instantly the laughter on Pollux Vile-bastard's lips by treading on his neck. The Doctor then pushed the remains of the chair hard into the madman's waistcoat.

'Pull yourself together at once, man,' he commanded. 'There are men of the Cloth present.'

'Sons of Onan!' cried the Demented One, foaming at the mouth, 'Pud-pullers to a man!' And with this final blasphemy, he threw himself through the window behind him, scattering glass and wood, and landed heavily on the lawn a storey below. He was last seen limping and growling away into the night.

In the ensuing silence, the Head Waiter placed large, white-gloved hands over the waitress' naked breasts as impersonally as a man about to push an upright piano a foot or so, until she was spirited away towards the kitchens, swathed in table-cloths. In no time the Diogenes was itself again and waiters moved soundlessly and calmly among the wreckage, occasion-ally pausing to clear an ashtray or adjust a fork. Their proud boast was that for the entire duration of the War of the

Worlds, they had never closed.

Dr Grace picked the choking Vilebastard off the floor by his lapels.

'Who was that?' he boomed.

'He said he was a friend of yours,' Vilebastard wheezed, massaging his throat. 'A friend of yours and Dr Watson's.'

'Never,' said Watson stoutly.

'A Mr Edward Hyde?' gagged Vilebastard. Dr Grace returned him to the floor.

'I suggest,' suggested Watson, 'that we repair to my rooms in Baker Street. We can talk there about the — er — Tour of Shame, without further interruption'.

'*He* was there,' said W.G. pointing at the prostrate Vilebastard. 'He and his wretched brother.'

He bent over the juddering body. 'They'll get *you* next. Mark my words.' And he mimed the drawing of a bow, whistled the passage of an arrow, and poked his index finger sharply into the centre of Vilebastard's chest.

BUFFALO BILL'S (HON. W.F. CODY.) WILD WEST SHOW

EARLS COURT

3 Certain Substances at 22lb Baker Street

No sooner had Dr Grace sat down in the late Sherlock Holmes' old chair by the fire than he had fallen into a dreamless doze. It had been a long day. Watson, eager as he was to learn more, was not going to chance his arm by disturbing the snorting Champion. Instead he mooched about the room, looking at the collection of Holmesiana as if he had never seen it before.

The pile of unpaid bills impaled on the mantlepiece by a stiletto, the retorts, the hypodermics, the bust in the window. The skin of a boa-constrictor that hung down from the cornice to the coal-scuttle. The Persian Slipper. The Speckled Bandsman's Hat. Five Orange Pips shared a saucer with some hound's teeth from the Baskerville business. The Engineer's Thumb. The Blue Carbuncle. A Red Circle. A Cardboard Box. Lord, but life was empty without Holmes. That Music Hall number that Mrs Hudson gives so loudly in the lavatory, how does it go? After a moment's thought and in a most pleasing baritone, Watson sang:

Oh, we'll never look upon their like again
Because they've pulled down Memory Lane!

W.G. stirred, but mercifully did not awake. Perhaps fresh adventure lay ahead with this black-bearded giant, sitting there fast asleep in his red-and-yellow striped MCC blazer and matching cap. What was clear to Watson was that in this new partnership it was he who would carry the lion's share of the brain-work.

He reached into the Persian Slipper and, deep in thought, filled his pipe with some of the contents. He found Holmes' Mixture a deal more relaxing than his own. Stronger too, he admitted, as he puffed away and staggered slightly. Wisely, he sat down, and there he was sitting on the verandah of the Cricket Pavilion at Simla. The Regimental Band of the Duke of Relwick's Mounted Foot were playing The Greatest Hits of Gilbert and Sullivan. The Union Jack hung limp in the heat. So did he, even when a dusky *houri*, with a jewel in her nose and another in her navel, brought him a large brandy and soda. Fountains bubbled and a hoopoe sang. There were lips in his ear, and a low sweet voice murmured, 'Your hair is as the mustard-flower they sell in the shops; your moustaches as the Lotus Blossom; your eyes like pomegranates. I shall meet you in the Hanging Gardens of Rajpalitana at the Feast of the Bulbul. Come let us attempt the Congress of the Water Buffalo. Page eighty seven in the book I lent you'.

In the distance naked ladies played at cricket.

Their lips met and the earth moved slightly. A fine time, thought Watson, for a tremor. Mrs Hudson was tugging at his shoulder. Was there anything he wanted before she went to bed?

'Peace and quiet!' he heard himself shouting distantly. 'Go away, you silly woman! I am hullucinating.' He closed his eyes again. The nubile Lady Frances Carfax was going for a quick single, dugs bouncing merrily like racing piglets.

He was next awoken by the distant sounds of the door-bell and Mrs Hudson barking complaints at the late visitor. He heard heavy footsteps on the stair. How well he knew that elephantine tread.

'Come in, Inspector Lestrade,' he called thickly, before there had been time for that stout gentleman to knock. The Inspector entered briskly, then froze in his tracks, sniffing the air suspiciously.

'Funny haroma,' he said.

'It's Holmes' old shag,' laughed Watson.

Lestrade looked at Mrs Hudson and shook his head sadly.

No sooner had Dr Watson given a brief résumé of the day's events to the Inspector than, despite the lateness of the hour, he and W.G. found themselves bowling westwards in Lestrade's Police Wagon. An unprepossessing vehicle with small, barred windows and two hard wooden benches in the rear.

Lestrade looked at his watch by the one dim lamp.

'Show should just habout be finished now, gentlemen,' They were rattling west along the Old Brompton Road.

' 'Ard right 'ere, Charlie!' Lestrade called to the driver. The streets were now more crowded, evidence of a large audience dispersing.

'Give 'em the bell, Charles,' ordered Lestrade. They heard the furious clanging of a handbell above, and the carriage accelerated. W.G. could see men, women and children scattering in all directions.

'There are certain hadvantages to police work!' Lestrade guffawed and hung on for dear life.

The carriage did a sharp left.

'This'll do, Charlie!' shouted Lestrade and they ground to a halt. 'Hall hout!' Lestrade leaped through the doors at the rear. Watson and W.G. followed, Watson thinking to himself that this was far too early for a dénouement and W.G. that it was far too late for anything.

They were standing in the middle of a large back-stage area, a seething mass of properties and performers. There were mountainous rocks and forests of plaster and canvas, plains and hydraulically-operated waterfalls, stage-coaches and wagons, horses and horsemen of every description, Uhlans, Gauchos from the Pampas, Cossacks and Cowboys.

Every description save one, thought W.G. looking about. Nary a sign of an Apache. Odd.

'Haha!' exclaimed Lestrade. 'And 'ere, unless I am mistaken, comes your hactual Buffalo Billy.'

He was not at all mistaken. One was of course unlikely to meet a man in the Earls Court area wearing a pale tan beaver-skin hat with a brim as wide as his shoulders, a buckskin coat dotted with a kaleidoscope of coloured beads and dripping with thongs, thigh-length boots with silver spurs, flowing white hair with matching chef's beard and moustaches, who was *not* Buffalo Bill.

'Hinspector Lestrade of Scotland Yard,' announced the Inspector, as if embarking on an epic verse. 'This 'ere is Doctor Watson, brother-in-harms to the late Sherlock 'Olmes of 'om you have 'ave 'eard even in the far-flung reaches of the Hamericas. And this bearded gentleman is Doctor W.G. Grace, the world's greatest cricketer, 'oo will, of course, be quite hunknown to you.'

Colonel W.F. Cody hooked one thumb into his ornate belt from which hung elaborate holsters. The other thumb he placed thoughtfully between his moustaches and stroked

31

them away from his upper lip. Two stage-hands passed between Buffalo Bill and the Inspector carting a vast chunk of Monument Valley.

'And how, gentlemen,' enquired the buffaloes' worst enemy, 'can I be of assistance to you?'

Lestrade thrust an evening newspaper at him.

' 'Ave you clocked this, Colonel?'

The puzzled Cody studied the proffered Pink 'Un. W.G. glanced idly over his buckskin shoulder and saw that he was lost in Mrs Beeton's daily column. 'Today — How to Scald a Sucking-Pig'. There was, beside the article, rather a charming etching of the author. The Colonel smiled.

'Nope, Inspector, I have not — er — clocked this.' He looked back over his shoulder at W.G. and winked in a knowing manner. W.G. was quick to correct any misapprehension that the Colonel might be under.

'Nor I!' he boomed. 'Certainly not. Never. Not at all.' He was about to add that he was a married man, and Mrs Beeton a married woman as her name suggested, and anyway he was from Gloucestershire, and it was the Victorian Age, and apart from all that he had never met the woman — but he did not. This is just as well in the light of future events.

Lestrade seized the newspaper impatiently and shook it open to reveal a large etching of Lord's and under the banner headline — MURDER STOPS PLAY — the Cricket Correspondent's report.

'The harrow is the relevant bit,' the Inspector pointed out. 'The Hape Atchy harrow.'

Cody finished reading and handed the paper back to Lestrade. Without a word, he turned and walked quickly away.

'Follow 'im!' cried Lestrade, but they already were. Behind a number of covered wagons was a small office. Cody led them in and closed the door firmly behind them. The Great Buffalo Exterminator seemed agitated.

'By the Eternal Mongoose, gentlemen, I cannot allow one breath of scandal to permeate these halls. This show of mine, as you can well imagine, represents an extensive investment. A life's work is represented here. I have played host to Presidents, the Crowned Heads of Europe, your own

Gracious Queen — '

'One moment, Sir.' Inspector Lestrade pulled at his whiskers, as if applying brakes. Buffalo Bill's oration skidded to a full stop.

'When harrows are a-flying about the Metropolitan Area — Hape Atchy harrows — Hape Atchies not being hindigenous to my patch, it seems natural to commence hinvestigations 'ere, where your Hape Atchy would seem most at 'ome.'

Colonel Cody nodded briskly. 'I see that, Inspector. I follow your reasoning completely, but let me say this. These hostiles — these *Apaches* that I have imported to your shores are hand-picked. Only thoroughly dispirited, utterly beaten men are selected. They are not savages. Could I, Buffalo Bill Cody, exhibit *savages* to the King of Sweden? To the King of the Belgians? To the King of Saxony?' He shook his head till his hat fell off. 'No, gentlemen, I have a reputation to maintain. Pawnee Bill — now there is a fish from another bottle. He has Geronimo on his books. Armed guards, Inspector, surround *his* cage night and day.'

'Where,' enquired Lestrade, pencil at the ready, 'would I find this Pawnee Billy?'

'Buenos Aires,' replied Cody.

Lestrade rumbled like distant artillery, and savagely crossed out 'Jerry Nimmo.'

'Is there, by any chance, Colonel,' asked W.G. who had only recently stopped trying to think of further good reasons for not having taken advantage of Mrs Beeton, but was now concentrating afresh on the matter in hand, 'on your books an Apache by the name of Gay Dog or thereabouts?'

'Might well be, sir.' The Colonel looked hard at Doctor Grace, with a slight circular movement of the head, as a knife-thrower might look at his revolving partner prior to tossing a blade between her spread-eagled thighs. 'I would have to study those books.' He waved an intricately decorated glove at a filing-cabinet, covered in painted scenes of Pioneer Life in 1853.

'You used the phrase "utterly beaten men",' persisted W.G. 'Surely Gay Dog was never defeated?'

Watson was staring at his new-found friend in total amazement. Buffalo Bill opened the filing-cabinet and made an elaborate business of finding the only folder in an otherwise empty drawer. Then for a man who has performed before tens of thousands, not to mention Presidents and Crowned Heads, he gave an extraordinarily unconvincing performance of A Plainsman Astounded by Sudden Discovery.

'Well, bless me! I never knew!' He laughed nervously. Even his eyebrows appeared under-rehearsed. 'There he is! Gay Dog!' And he began to read a single sheet of foolscap to himself, complete with muttered exclamations of feigned surprise.

'Indeed an exceptional man, this Gay Dog.' He shook his head until his long white wig fell off. He swept it back on with one flowing movement. 'You are right, Doctor, undefeated to the end. A victory indeed, it says here, against the Seventh U.S. Cavalry no less at the so-called Battle of Large Rock.'

W.G. whooped with delight and Watson would have dearly loved to have enquired the reason, but Cody was reading on.

'This would explain why he is on our books, Inspector. He is no ordinary savage. He has been entertained at the White House to tea and cakes. The President himself presented him with a top hat and a Union Flag to drape about him. He is to be considered, and this comes from the Department of the Interior itself, as quite civilised. Grade IV, in fact.' He replaced the folder in the cabinet. 'I must speak to him.'

'So must I,' said Lestrade. '*Now* would be nice.'

'That will be impossible,' replied Cody quickly. 'He will have returned to his lodgings.'

'Where would they be, sir?' pressed Lestrade.

'Obviously I have no idea,' said Buffalo Bill. 'It is only in the last few minutes that I have discovered he was one of my Company.' He opened the office door and shouted, 'Seth still here?' There was a muffled negative and the suggestion that he had gone to see an elephant.

'These mountain-men!' laughed Cody, and hurried on before questions were asked about the elephant. 'Seth McGurk handles all matters concerning Injuns. He sure scalped plenty.'

'Perhaps,' said Lestrade, 'Mr McGurk could assemble 'is charges 'ere at 11 o'clock tomorrow morning. I would like to interview this Gay Dog. I shall 'ave the necessary warrants to hand. Tell 'im on no account to leave the Metropolitan Area.'

And with this he departed. W.G. and Watson raised their hats and made to follow him.

'Doctor Grace,' called Buffalo Bill. W.G. paused at the door. 'Is Gay Dog a friend of yours?'

Dr Grace smiled. 'He believes that I am God.'

4 High Noon
in Furnitureville

W.G. was famished. The toad had finally expired, leaving, as obituaries always insist, a gap seemingly impossible to fill. W.G. had promised Watson and Lestrade as they left Earls Court that he would tell them all about his dealings with Gay Dog over beer and sandwiches upon their return to Baker Street.

In the meantime he sat hunched in the police wagon thinking about Buffalo Bill. He had never actually met the gentleman before but it had seemed to W.G. when they toured America, and it had proved in the end to be an extensive tour — the Tour of Shame — that in every town that they visited, be it large or small, there was certain to be one of Colonel Cody's disgusting restaurants. Not of course that they were advertised as such; they were posted as 'BUFFALO BILL'S WILD WESTERN EATERIES' and housed in discarded railway-stock cheaply converted into covered wagons. Gas-lit 'flaming arrows' burnt in the canvas of the roof attracting custom. Beneath the name, they promised Pioneer Fare. The Menu, engraved with a branding-iron into a facsimile of a Boot Hill gravestone, contained such unappetising items as 'The Colonel's Hearty Buffalo Steaks Camp-fire-cooked with All the Salad You Kin Eat,' '57 Varieties of Pork'n'-Beans,' 'Hot Prairie Dogs,' 'Bisonburgers' and permanently etched above the door — the Chef's Special — 'Horse's Ass with Grits.' Quite often, alas, these were the only eating-places in town and the team was frequently obliged to eat at one of them. On occasion, an even more depressing event, they were entertained chez Buffalo Bill by local dignitaries.

W.G., to the great surprise of Watson and Lestrade, let out a sudden hiccough of laughter. He was thinking that, however beastly the Colonel's restaurants were, they were Cafés Royal compared to the place to which the Vilebastards conducted them on their first evening in America.

The MCC Touring Team had disembarked at New York's Pier A, with its pretty little clock-tower. They were damp, exhausted and storm-tossed after two harrowing weeks on the Atlantic, weak as chickens, mere shadows of the blazered Corinthians who had embarked at Southampton.

'It was one of those boats, Watson — ' W.G. stood in front of the fireplace at 221b Baker Street, idly toying with a bottle containing the Twisted Lip. (He was feeling a deal better for a beef sandwich and a bottle of Worthington.) 'One of those boats, half sail, half steam, so if you weren't covered in smuts, you were coated in sperm —'

'Spume?' suggested Watson.

'I'm not the Author,' snapped W.G.

God, it had been a terrible voyage, and now it appeared that no-one expected them. Certainly, the red carpet had not been unrolled.

'Aren't we being met?' asked Raffles.

'By the Vilebastard Twins,' replied the Doctor. 'Anyone know 'em?' No-one did. The general feeling was that they had only been selected because they were residing in the United States, thus saving the MCC two boat-fares.

'I hear one of them, Castor, I think, is quite quick,' said Raffles.

'Not this morning,' growled W.G. Their other advantage to the MCC was that they had volunteered to handle the team's transportation; baggage and the like. W.G. paced about angrily.

'Unless I'm seeing double, which is reasonable enough in the circumstances, I think,' said Raffles, 'that here come the sweaty pair.'

'Sorry we're late,' chorussed the twins.

'You must be the Vilebastards,' deduced W.G.

'Villibarts,' the pair barked.

The team was bundled unceremoniously into three waiting cabs, and instead of the eagerly anticipated hotel rooms and hot baths, were informed that their destination was Grand Central Station.

'I thought,' said W.G. referring to a piece of paper, 'that we were staying in New York for a few days and playing against a St George's Club XXII on the Hoboken Cricket Ground in New Jersey?'

'That's quite out of date now,' said a twin, taking the paper from W.G.'s hand and tossing it out of the cab window.

W.G. contented himself with frenzied glimpses of New York City. The cabs were travelling like the wind. Heaven knows how they avoided hitting the stalls and barrows packed on either side of the street. W.G. had never seen so many people. The streets seethed with them, as did the windows of the houses. No wonder, he thought, that the staircases are on the exterior. They must live on some rota system. Those inside coming out for a spell, while those on the street go indoors to put their feet up. He could not help but notice that many of the poor, huddled masses were clearly mad, shouting furiously at the moon. Barely a word of English was to be heard. What a place!

The cab swayed and tilted like the damnable boat. The streets seemed nothing more than thinly-coated field, untouched, probably, since the early New Amsterdam burgher had travelled up the Broad Way to sell cheese and clogs to the Algonquin. He was not sorry when they arrived at the Grand Central Station.

'And Grand it is,' said Raffles, gawping up at it.

The Vilebastards bustled them on to a train, and no sooner had they done so than whistles blew and they were travelling again. Raffles declared cheerfully that it came as something of a relief to be train-sick after what seemed like months of *mal-de-mer!* W.G. was more concerned about their destination. Castor Vilebastard at first simply said 'South' in an airy fashion, but when further pressed after two changes of train, said, 'I'll have Itineraries in your hands by the time we reach Philadelphia.'

'How far from New York is Philadelphia?' enquired W.G.

'This is a huge country, Doctor,' replied Pollux. 'Relax. You are in safe hands.'

By evening there were rumblings of discontent throughout the large open compartment, and the team was only slightly mollified when the train pulled into a small town and the Vilebastards announced that they would disembark and dine prior to catching the Midnight Flier.

'To Philadelphia?' asked W.G.

'Patience, doctor, patience,' was all he could elicit from Castor. Pollux did add that W.G. would be ready for anything after dinner at 'this little place we know.'

'Where are we now?' W.G. boomed after Pollux who was disappearing into the distance in the steps of his brother.

'Oh. Wheeling.' Pollux paused and waved about him vaguely.

'And where the blue blazes is Wheeling?' demanded W.G.

Pollux threw his arms outwards in desperation.

'On the way to bloody Philadelphia, isn't it?' he whinnied.

'I see,' said W.G. For some reason Pollux had made him feel somewhat foolish. He looked about. There was some sort of paper shop, but unfortunately closed.

'I must get a map,' he said.

Pollux was now gently patting him on the back and oozing charm.

'*You* must get some dinner inside you, old man,' he said, and off they all set into town.

The 'little place' known to the Vilebastards was a dreadful little place. It had obviously known better days.

It was called 'SCARLETT'S DINER'. Scarlett, they had deduced must be the 'Mrs S. Butler, Prop.' advertised over the door. There was an air of elegant decay about her. She wore an ancient ball-gown, layered in lace or cobwebs. The impression Raffles formed was of a woman who some years previously had attempted to jump out of a cake to enliven some evening at a Gentleman's Club, but had only succeeded in leaping about a foot-and-a-half and had then become permanently encased. She seemed to move on wheels. Faced with sudden and surprising custom she called out 'Rhett!', her rich Southern accent spinning the name into some eight or nine syllables. This was in fact to be the final words of the evening from her. From the moment that Rh-a-e-i-o-u-ett, clearly *Mr* Butler, emerged from the kitchen, she glared at him silently until the end of the evening.

Mine Host was a surly brute with a foul cigar jutting from his face. Give him his due, he essayed a welcoming smile, but as it crawled up one side of his head, it appeared to the casual observer that if his concentration lapsed he might well bite off one of his extremely large ears. The meal was as vile as the premises — greasy chicken coated in batter and dust, served up in cardboard boxes! There was talk of Mint Juleps, but all they received were glasses of dirty water. They eschewed the pudding and settled for coffee. Lukewarm and black and tasting of greasy chicken and dirty water.

At the precise moment that the bill arrived, the Vile-bastards leaped to their feet crying, 'By God! The Flier!' and ran off towards the station. W.G. settled the account and as the team left the diner, clutching their groaning stomachs and ravaged by wind, they heard behind them the sound of angry voices and breaking glass.

'Not a happy couple,' said W.G.

'Two more ill-fitting people glued together by circums-stance,' replied Raffles, the bachelor. 'Excuse me,' and he stepped quietly into a doorway.

W.G. was the only member of the team, apart from the Vilebastard twins, who was not racked by the dreadful after-effects of the diner. These, coupled with the rude facilities provided by the Railway Company, made for a most uncom-fortable night.

There was a brass travelling-clock sitting among the paraphen-alia on the mantlepiece. It was well past W.G.'s bed-time.

'The trains seemed to get smaller and smaller as the country got bigger. It's all bigger out there. The sun, the landscape, the weather. Nothing to do with Gloucestershire.' Perhaps he could round off the evening's play by describing how, after what they firmly believed to be a three-week train-ride to Philadelphia, they finally arrived in Furnitureville, Arizona. So he described the team alighting from the train on to the pile of sleepers that constituted Furnitureville Station and as they scratched their heads at what they took to be their first view of the great metropolis of Philadelphia, a single street with no sign of inhabitants, W.G. yawned hugely. He was going to add finally how happy he would be to get on to the subject of Gay Dog in the morning when he saw that both Watson and Lestrade were still sitting, notebooks ready, pencils poised, panting like thirsty Jack Russells.

W.G. helped himself to a large brandy and swooshed a fair amount of soda into the balloon. Another hour then, he thought.

'I can't rest without knowing more of Gay Dog,' said

41

Watson suddenly.

Two hours then thought W.G.

'He'll be hupon the scene in a moment, I fancy, eh, Doctor Grace?'

'Not by a long chalk, Inspector Lestrade.'

Lestrade pulled out a wicked-looking knife and began to sharpen his pencil.

'I shall need to know the relevant facts by eleven ho'clock tomorrow morning when I shall be hinterviewing one Gay Dog. This looks like being a long night.'

'I shall press on as quickly as I can,' said W.G. and drank deeply. *Three* hours, he thought.

'There was only the one street. A rough row of wooden buildings on either side of an uneven, earth thoroughfare. One side had a raised, covered pavement. Wooden, of course. Indeed most of the frontages — and they were only frontages, like stage scenery with ramshackle hutments or even marquees behind them — had some sort of crude verandah. I was reminded of the Palings in Tonbridge Wells, but not a great deal. I played there once against XXXIII Blind Men of Kent. Or were they Kentish Men? Blind as bats anyway. I made 307 not out and took all thirty-two wickets!' He finished the brandy and quickly refused another. For the moment. He was off the mark now to the tune of 'Clementine'. They never stopped singing that in Furnitureville. . . .

'If this is Philadelphia, W.G.,' said Raffles as they gazed down the Main Street, 'then I'm a Portugese flautist.'

A scrappy, little fellow in a peaked cap approached them.

'Welcome, gentlemen to Furnitureville,' he wheezed.

'Not Philadelphia?' said Raffles.

'Not unless he has an extraordinary speech impediment,' replied W.G. 'Where are those bloody Vilebastards?'

Raffles pointed down the street and there indeed were the twins bustling down the raised wooden walkway towards the tallest building in town. Doubtless in pursuit, he suggested, of a stiff drink. It seemed to be a hotel of sorts. A good number of horses were tethered outside and there was a distant sound of revelry. 'Thou art lost and gone forever' they sang. Very apt.

'Those two have landed us in it right up to here,' grumbled W.G. He looked around his team. They stood disconsolately among the array of baggage.

'My word, the lads look peaky.' There was only one cure for this in W.G.'s book: fresh air and exercise. The station master gladly volunteered his tiny hut as a changing-room.

'Into your kit, lads!' he cried. 'Full-scale practice at the end of the street there in ten minutes.' He pointed to a wooden platform-like structure that stood alone at the far end of town. 'I shall bat first', he further boomed.

Padded up and bat in hand, W.G. was the first to set off down the middle of the street. Still not a soul to be seen. He observed a small bank, a hat shop, Gatsby's General Sundries Store its frontage bedecked with rough canvas trousers ('De Nimes' said a poster), a barber, a saddlery, a livery stables. Quite the largest shop standing opposite the hotel was the Needle's Eye Emporium and Mayoral Parlour which sold furniture of every conceivable description.

W.G. could hear extraordinary noises coming from the hotel ('The Golden Camel' — a strange name): ladies whooping and screaming; gentlemen cheering and stamping; 'Clementine' in F; the occasional pistol shot.

'A Thé Dansant,' giggled the Reverend Studholme at his shoulder, and pointing excitedly.

'None of that,' said W.G. sharply. If this tour ever got under way, the Reverend Studholme had a good deal of bowling ahead of him. They were a little weak in that area, and W.G. did not wish him to over-exert himself in the tango or suchlike. Five or six of the team had stopped by the hotel and were peering in over the Double Swing-doors, hopping from one leg to the other and exchanging nudges.

'Come along, chaps,' commanded W.G. and began to chalk a wicket on the side of the structure. When the team had assembled reluctantly around him he delivered a short, sharp lecture on the Virtues of Abstinence, Moderation, Self-control, and the Constant Need to Practice. It proved very hard to keep their attention. The noise, if anything, was even louder.

'Come on, lads! Come on! It's weeks since anyone turned an arm.' W.G. was pacing out twenty-two yards from his chalked wicket. There he pushed a stump into the middle of

43

the street. As he set off back to his crease, he noticed with a slight shiver that he was stepping in the shadow of what was now clearly a gallows, that lay the length of the wicket. There was no rope attached. Not in use today then, he thought. He whacked a great ball of tumble-weed past square leg.

'Right, bowl up!' he called. Only the Reverend Studholme was at the bowler's end. The rest of the team had gathered outside the hotel again, forming a solid clump of fielders some thirty yards from the bat. W.G. was debating with himself how best to scatter this extraordinary field-setting when the job was done for him. There were a number of gun-shots and a crowd of disreputable-looking bar-flies in baggy hats erupted out of the saloon backwards, and froze in their tracks, obviously the better to witness the next bit. A gaggle of shrieking dancing-girls appeared on the balcony above. They, too, fell into anticipatory postures. A moment's still-ness and a further crowd of desperadoes, singing, shouting and discharging their pistols into the air came full-pelt into the street carrying head-high a badly frightened black-bearded man in a frock-coat.

'Unhand me!' he cried to no avail. 'Put me down!' he cried again, and this to some avail for they dropped him carelessly into a horse-trough. The crowd greeted his discomfiture with blasts of hard laughter, and their leader, a vicious-looking devil with one eye and a sombrero a good yard in diameter, seizing a length of rope from a passing saddle, marched a group of them towards the gallows. A chorus had started up of: 'Lynch him! Lynch him!' W.G. was slow to move, think-ing the cry was 'Lunch him! Lunch him!' Then it dawned.

Ah, *lynch* him! And this would seem to be the order of the day, as their leader had sprung up the stair to the plat-form and was affixing the rope to the gallows with the help of some inebriated confrères.

'Au quai!' roared the one-eyed fellow, illustrating at once, to anyone who was interested, that the phrase came originally from the docks in New Orleans.

'Bring the stinking Limey over here.' How they roared. 'We're gonna have us a neck-tie party!' W.G. had to laugh at the poetry of it all.

'The use of the word "Limey" is interesting too.' The Reverend Studholme was hiding behind the great bulk of W.G. 'To do with scurvy.'

'Quite,' said W.G. 'That chap they're hoiking out of the trough. He's an Englishman.' His grip tightened instinctively on his bat. There are, he thought, eleven of us — nine in truth, as there's no sign of the Vilebastards. Some forty-odd of them. They are armed with pistols and knives. We have three bats, eight balls and a healthy disregard for foreigners.

'My money's on our side, Padre,' whispered W.G. to the quivering cleric.

'Help! Help!' cried the Englishman as he was passed over the heads of the rabble and thrown up onto the platform.

'My name is Charles Dickens!' he screamed. 'Send for the British Consul!'

'The author — johnny!' cried Studholme.

'What to do?' whispered Raffles in W.G.'s ear.

'Follow me!' cried their Captain, and laid low a couple of cowboys with a square cut and a vigorous pull-shot. Studholme and Raffles followed W.G. up the steps and onto the platform.

'Confound it!' said W.G. and stopped dead in his tracks, for the one-eyed brigand was pointing a brace of pistols straight at his beard. Studholme it was, (never, W.G. had previously considered, among the front rank of England's fielders), who caught him clear between the eyes — well, the eye and the patch — with a ferocious throw. Even better, Raffles caught the rebound and instantly hurled the ball at another extremely ugly customer who was cocking a shot-gun. It caught him in the lower abdomen and such was his surprise that he discharged both barrels into the laughing faces below him as he fell. That should give them cause to pause, thought W.G., and threw Dickens over his shoulder.

'It usually goes so well,' moaned Dickens, sadly. 'I cannot understand the brutes.'

'Hang on, Mr Dickens!' cried W.G. and wielding King Willow with a will, cleared a path back down the steps. Cryer, a burly little Yorkshire professional was doing excellent work pirouetting at great speed, whirling his weighty cricket bag.

'They didn't want Little Nell to die,' sighed Dickens. W.G.

45

had not the slightest idea what he was talking about, nor, in all honesty, was he particularly interested. He was surrounded. He looked at the circle of angry, unshaven, purple faces pocked with shot. Then, sensing that a certain sobriety might be creeping over the gathering — a face full of shot after all, however irritating, can restore the senses as successfully as a bucket of cold water — W.G. shouted, 'Pax! Hold! Enough!'

His first thought was that it was his natural authority, that caused the grumbling mob to disperse at once. Not so, he discovered as he gently lowered the sodden author to the ground. Behind him stood a tall man in his fifties with a black frock-coat, a large hat, a silk waistcoat of many colours and a great blunderbuss with which he was shooing away stragglers.

'I would have been here sooner, gentlemen, but I have been attending to God's business.' He shook W.G.'s hand warmly. 'Furniture! That's God's business. Welcome to Furnitureville, Arizona, Future Furnishing Capital of the World. Praise the Lord!' He shook hands warmly with every member of the team. He seemed to be electioneering. 'Mayor Elmer Gatsby, Mayor of Furnitureville, Arizona. Or *Sheriff* Elmer Gatsby, if you prefer.' He chose to introduce himself thus while pumping Raffles' hand. 'Or indeed, Reverend,' and here he seized Studholme '*Pastor* Elmer Gatsby, a humble vicar of Jesus Christ the Carpenter. Jesus Christ the Worker in Wood. Jesus Christ the Furniture-maker!' He looked heavenwards, then addressed himself once more to the Marylebone Cricket Club. 'Perhaps the Elmer Gatsby you would most care to meet however is Elmer Gatsby, proprietor of the *Golden Camel*. Follow me!'

They were all gathered at the long bar enjoying drinks on the Mayor. His hotel was a great barn of a place. Indeed it appeared to have started its life as a great barn. The booths occupied by still seething locals might well previously have housed cattle. There were scattered card-tables. The vestiges of ancient green baize and the patches of dry wood reminded W.G. of some of the less prepossessing pitches he had played on. W.G. was most keen to find the Vilebastards; he wanted a word with them about the itinerary, but still not a sign. Cold beers and whiskies were ordered, and beefy girls in tinselly gowns and fishnet stockings draped themselves about the flanneled fools.

'A word in your ear.' The Reverend Studholme was tugging at W.G.'s blazer.

'Boys will be boys, padre,' said W.G., not that he altogether approved of this sort of thing. 'As long as no-one lets the side down.'

Studholme shook his head and pointed to Charles Dickens who was now clad in a gaudy silk dressing-gown belonging to the Mayor. What some of the dragons cavorting upon it were up to was nobody's business but theirs. Dr Grace had put him on a regimen of stiff brandies.

'Charles Dickens,' said Studholme, 'died in 1870.'

'I know,' replied W.G. He didn't, but firmly believed that leaders of men should never betray the slightest ignorance.

'Well, aren't you going to beard him?' Bloody stupid question, thought W.G. 'The good name of English literature,' persisted Studholme, 'is surely at risk? Doesn't look dead, does he?'

'I'll ask him about it,' said W.G. and beckoned to Charles Dickens, who disentangled himself from a particularly meaty 'danseuse' and scurried over.

'Doctor Grace,' he said, 'I have been slow, I fear, in expressing, my gratitude —' W.G. raised a massive hand.

'Are you or are you not the Author of *Robertson Crusoe?*'

'No.'

'Two Gentlemen of Venice?'

'No, I'm not.'

'Ginga Dung.'

Dickens shook his head vigorously.

'Gone with the Wind?' Thr Brothers-Kara whatnot?'

Dickens shook his head till his beard whistled.

'Then you are not *the* Dickens!' cried W.G. in triumph.

'I am *a* Dickens,' said a Dickens, 'but not, admittedly, *the* Dickens. Charles Dickens was my father.' W.G. was about to tell him how much he'd enjoyed the first few pages of *Treasure Island* when the swing-doors of the saloon plunked open and, bold as brass, in walked the Vilebastard twins.

'There you are!' W.G. pointed the finger at them across a crowded room. 'I want a word or two with you.'

The Vilebastards smiled at him in a somewhat patronising manner.

'This is not Philadelphia!' he roared.

'So we gather,' said Castor.

'Sorry,' said Pollux.

'Where were you two blighters when you were needed?'

'With the stationmaster,' said Castor, calmly.

'Sorting things out,' added Pollux, coolly.

'The devil!' cried Castor, pointing straight at Dickens.

'Sudden change of plan!' shouted Pollux.

And with a further plunk-plunk, plunk-plunk, they had vanished through the doors into Furnitureville again.

'What the —?' queried W.G.

'Follow me!' shouted Dickens and, pushing W.G. out of the way, was through the still-plunking doors and off down the street in pursuit. The Doctor was nimble and like many large men had an unexpected turn of speed. He had overtaken Dickens in the first twenty yards. There was no sign of the twins. The two pursuers slowed to a halt in the middle of the dusty street. W.G. was rather alarmed to see that the son of arguably England's Greatest Novelist was wielding a large pistol. Dickens pushed it away inside his frock-coat, and produced in its stead a card.

'Inspector Francis Dickens,' read W.G. 'North-West Mounted Police.'

Dickens bowed. The card gave Dickens' address as Fort Pitt, Moose Hills, Alberta, Canada.

'You're some distance,' said W.G. 'from your normal beat'.

'And I'm afraid, Doctor, well outside my jurisdiction,' replied Dickens, 'but as you may have heard, a Mountie always gets his man.' He looked up and down the empty street. 'Or men.'

'The twins?' W.G. scratched about under his cap. What on earth was going on? Members of the MCC being pursued by armed police? Somewhere in the middle of America?

'They won't get far,' said Dickens, and taking W.G. by the arm, propelled him back towards the Saloon. He suggested that they would both benefit from a large drink and an explanation. Plunk-plunk, plunk, plunk.

'It was an extraordinary tale he had to tell,' said W.G., and yawned and stretched.

'Hinspector *Dickens,* eh?' mused Lestrade, slowly turning a page of his notebook. He had taken copious notes. 'Dickens? The name rings a bell.'

'Of course it does,' said Watson, rather irritably.

'Just so,' said Lestrade. 'Now what precisely, Doctor, 'ad Hinspector Dickens against our friends?'

'Murder. Attempted murder. Assault and battery. The list was endless,' replied W.G.

'I was in command of Fort Pitt, a small outpost in the middle of Alberta. My garrison consisted of only twenty-three Mounted Policemen, and, by heck, we had had a very lucky escape. Chiefs Poundmaker and Big Bear of the Crees organised a Thirst Dance, an attempt to bring the various tribes together under their leadership, and cause a good deal of trouble for us. Their basic complaint was lack of food and blankets. A reasonable complaint in the event. It was getting damned crowded out there for the Indian. Apart from settlers, ever since Custer's defeat at the Little Big Horn, the U.S. Cavalry had been chasing Redskins over the border in ever-increasing numbers and the buffalo was rapidly approaching extinction. Now, unlike the American Army, we of the Mounted Police have always enjoyed very favourable relations with the Indians.'

Dickens pulled a piece of paper from his inside pocket and unfolded it on the table. 'An unsolicited testimonial,' he said.

W.G. read, 'Three years ago when the Mounted Police came to my country, I met and shook hands with Commissioner Macleod at the Belly River. Since that time he has made me many promises and has kept them all. Signed, Red Crow, Head Chief of the Blckfoot Nation.'

'Very nice,' said W.G.

Dickens replaced the paper, and looked very pleased with himself.

'Very nice,' repeated W.G.

'They had nothing but respect for the Great White Mother.'

'Nor should they,' said W.G. loyally.

'Someone was stirring them up though,' continued Dickens,

flicking beer froth from his beard. 'In my opinion it was a Métis, a half-breed, half French, half Indian, called Louis Riel. Big, handsome fellow, brilliant orator, but a religious maniac. Swore he could hear voices, like Joan of Arc. See visions, that sort of thing. Rumour had it he used to wander about stark naked, announcing to one and all that he was Jehovah. Nevertheless he was President of a provincial Métis Government for a while until Ottawa sent the Army in. He'd escaped to America, but I gathered from our sources that he was back. It had to be Riel.

'Anyway, one day there we are sitting quietly in Fort Pitt, when we're surrounded by 250 whooping indians shouting for food, blankets and weapons and eager to do for us. Now, thank the Lord, Big Bear and I had been quite chummy in the past — I had given him a blanket — and he smuggles in a note to me saying roughly, "My dear friend, always been friends . . . thanks for the blanket . . . Try and get away before this afternoon . . . hard to control my braves, etc."

'All we had was a boat with a hole in it, but that, in the circumstances, was good enough and come night-fall we were off down the Saskatchewan River, thirty below it was, and six days later we'd reached Fort Battleford. Naturally enough, when the Officer Commanding there heard what was going on, he said, "Grab a quick dinner, Dickens, saddle up, and go and arrest this Riel. The man's a trouble-maker." So here I am, do you see?'

'Not entirely,' said W.G. 'It doesn't explain why you're after the Vilebastards, whose only crime as far as I know is abysmal navigation and extremely poor taste in restaurants. I'll admit I don't care for them, but they are public-school men and members of the MCC.'

'Their crimes extend further than that,' replied Dickens. 'I lost Riel in the Yukon. I'd been told he was on a barn-storming tour of the tribes there, whipping them up into a full-scale rebellion. He wasn't in fact in that neck of the woods at all but I did discover that I wasn't the only one looking for him. Two chaps were asking questions and, from the condition of some of those interviewed, desperate for an answer. Clearly their informants were pointing them north in a bid to see the back of them, and I was simply trailing in their wake.

'Well, by the time I got to Dawson on the Alaska Border, signs were that I was nearly on top of them, and therefore close enough to Riel to call for reinforcements. So I borrowed a Constable from our small detachment there and a dog-sleigh and Mush! Mush! a couple of days later caught up with them at a frozen creek in the process of cutting an Eskimo about. I made the appropriate noises, in the name of the Law, Her Majesty the Queen, anything you say may be taken down, and got shot in the leg for my pains. They killed my Constable and my dogs, finished off the poor Eskimo and made their escape in a southerly direction, leaving me bleeding like a stuck pig.'

'Raffles used to stick pigs,' said W.G. This was all extraordinary stuff. He was most certainly viewing the Vilebastards in a new light. Lord's must be informed at once.

'I've trailed them for three years now,' sighed Dickens.

'How comes it,' enquired W.G. 'that you were here when we arrived?'

'At some stage,' said Dickens, 'I must have overtaken them.'

'They've been in New York,' said W.G.

'So have I,' replied Dickens. 'Wheeling?' asked W.G. thinking he might warn him against the restaurant there. 'All over I've been,' cried Dickens. And a despairing wave embraced the whole continent of North America and upset beer all over a porky girl with a heavy moustache and a dozen petticoats. The local denizen who had been entertaining her upon his knee immediately picked up a chair and broke it over Dickens' tired head. He was about to repeat his action with a card-table when there was a tremendous explosion from behind them and Dickens' assailant was suddenly no better than a bag of offal lying discarded in a corner some six or seven yards away from where he had previously been standing. There was a brief lull in the conversation, during which the fat girl, twittering obscenities, gathered up her petticoats and fled upstairs. The slam of a door aloft was the cue for merry-making to continue, and W.G. turned to see who had inflicted such rough and messy justice. It was Mine Host, Elmer Gatsby with his Sheriff's hat on and his great fowling-piece still belching smoke.

'More beer at this table,' he intoned towards the bar.

'You have just shot a man dead,' protested W.G. 'For-for- for breaking a chair!'

'Sacrilege! Blasphemy! The Devil's work!' said the Sheriff, now sporting his pastor's hat. 'Thou shalt not rend the temple in twain, nor any part or parcel thereof! Great is the wrath of God, the Creator of all Fine Furnishings, and vicious is his temper!'

W.G. had paused for effect and the drink he had been promised.

'Where are we now?' asked Watson quietly, blinking through his pince-nez.

'Is our Gay Dog related in any way to the late Heskimo?' Lestrade was helping himself to a brandy. He felt a solution looming. 'Are they not a sort of Reddish Hindian?' W.G. shook his head. 'Vengeance? Always a sound motive. Revenge.' W.G. shook his head again.

'No, we're not there yet, Inspector,' he said, and seeing Watson's face and pencil fall, added, 'Not by a long chalk.' Watson grimaced. This chalk was interminable!

'Anyway,' the Inspector picked up the telephone. 'I shall be on to our Canadian cousins in the morning. We 'ave one less man for the Mounties to get.' He laughed and belched into the mouthpiece. 'May I?' he asked of Watson, waving the instrument, and without waiting for a reply, started to dial Whitehall 1212. 'I'm going to 'ave all the Hamericans in the Greater Metropolitan Area brought in for questioning.' And he whistled 'I'm a Yankee-Doodle-Dandy' in F until there was a distant click, and he began to bark orders to some underling. W.G. looked at the carriage-clock and thought Anglo-American relations were due for another battering.

'Where are we now?' Watson enquired again.

'Still in Furnitureville, Arizona, Doctor,' answered W.G. 'But not for much longer and then once more we shall be "hitting the trail", as they have it.' Watson rose and poured himself a large drink.

'One thing still puzzles me, Doctor Grace,' Watson was chasing something around the surface of his whisky with his little finger. 'There is Dickens in Furnitureville, disguised as his father, a sensible disguise, for one imagines that news of his father's demise would not have reached these parts, but ' − it was a big "but" − BUT, how did he know the Vilebastards were coming? You were all meant to be in Philadelphia.'

'I had asked him that myself, if you remember, and he had skirted the issue − but, further pressed, he told me it was the Eskimo. After the Vilebastards had left him for dead in the snows south of Dawson, he had crawled over to his Constable to see if any vestiges of Life remained and finding none he had then checked on the Eskimo. Two words the poor fellow was able to muster prior to expiring: "Needle's Eye!" '

'Needle's Eye?' Watson wrote it down in capital letters. 'Rich men? Camels? Egyptians? Cleopatra's Needle? Nelson's Eye? I give up.'

'I told you,' said W.G. shortly. Watson slowly leaped back through his notes.

'The large Furniture Emporium in Furnitureville?' W.G. prompted.

Watson shook his head.

'It was called 'The Needle's Eye Emporium and Mayoral Parlour.'

'You *didn't* mention that.' Watson was quite petulant. Funny, thought W.G. He had walked past it in his mind and it had stood there as clearly as if it had been yesterday.

'Needle's Eye,' he told Watson, 'was the name of the town before it became Furnitureville. Not many people know that. That's why it took Dickens so long to find.'

'And why, Doctor, he was so certain when he got there!' Watson was out of his chair and tugging enthusiastically at his sleeve. A piece had fallen into place. The first one of the night. 'He had only to wait and his quarry would come to him!'

'How did the Eskimo know?' asked W.G. gently and watched Watson subside slowly in his chair again.

'Something he overheard?' Watson suggested weakly.

'In a sense,' said W.G. 'Do you believe that fact is stranger than fiction?'

'In the circumstances,' said Watson, 'that is a very difficult question to answer.'

'Sticky business for Hinspector Dickens!' Lestrade had finished barking and content that the night was now alive with policemen and irate 'Hamericans', was returning to the plot. 'Finally caught up with 'em and powerless to act.'

'The twins had recognised him. No doubt of that.' said W.G. 'Indeed Dickens was fairly certain that they had penetrated his disguise as soon as they had first entered the Saloon, and had immediately begun the heckling that almost culminated in his being hanged by the neck. He viewed his position as hopeless, and was thinking seriously of returning to Canada and handing in his resignation, having failed, as he considered, in his duty.'

Lestrade drew himself up to his full height and beamed hugely out of the window. ''Ighly commendable,' pronounced Lestrade, 'In the finest traditions of the Force.' He slow-marched proudly to the Decanters and poured himself a handsome measure to toast absent officers. ''E could, of course, 'ave shot the buggers prior to leaving.'

'He didn't leave,' said W.G. 'I pointed out to him that the team was due in Canada within a month or so. Once over the border, he could pounce. When precisely we would arrive in Canada at the then current rate of striking was another matter, but he brightened considerably. His plan was to leave town ostentatiously heading north. Then to double back and follow us at a sensible distance. Wherever our Itinerary, or the Vilebastards, took us.'

Dickens had gone upstairs to pack. W.G. sat with Raffles in a corner-booth, trying to put events into some order. Though A.J. Raffles represented much that the honest country doctor in W.G. found disagreeable, and he found urbanity and sophistication extremely irritating, particularly in one who had clearly never done a day's work in his life, nevertheless he was drawn to the fellow. The rest of the team, with the exception of the Reverend Studholme who was engaged in theological debate with Mine Host, were drunk as judges and behaving in that loud and oafish manner that distinguishes the Englishman Abroad. Not, thought W.G., that he would have turned to any of them anyway for a sensible word at the best of times. Whereas deep down,

Raffles was a practical cove.

'Relax, old chap,' Raffles was enjoying a cheap cigar and a glass of Red-eye. 'There's nothing we can do until the train arrives. The sins of the Vilebastards are not your concern, old boy, we simply wait until we cross into Canada, caps raised and flannels gleaming and to the sound of a distant bugle enter left at the gallop the North West Mounted Police. Curtain. Drink up, and I'll get you another.'

There was a burst of bestial laughter from the bar. The one-eyed desperado (with a vicious lump between eye and patch) and his cronies equally lumpy and shot-pocked were jeering and gesticulating at the staircase. Inspector Dickens was retreating in style. He stood at the head of the stair in full-dress uniform, the red jacket, the blue breeches with the broad yellow stripe, the brown boots and Sam Browne with a large holster on his hip, the pill-box cap set jauntily to one side of his head. Sensing possible unrest, Pastor Gatsby temporarily abandoned his theories concerning the theological importance of the dining-table and chairs used at the Last Supper, and Sheriff Gatsby moved to the bottom of the stairs.

'Goodbye to you, Mr Dickens,' he cried, 'Your bill has been attended to — I would not like you to leave Furnitureville with aught but the happiest of memories. God speed.' Dickens thanked him warmly, shook hands with Grace and Raffles and made for the doors as plunk! plunk! the Vilebastards entered.

They froze in their tracks, and might have made a dash for it had Dickens not quickly cried, 'Goodbye, Gentlemen. I have been recalled to Fort Pitt. Monsieur Riel's little rebellion is under way.' Plunk! He was gone. Plunk! Plunk! The twins sighed deeply and made for the bar.

Dr Grace flexed his shoulders and made for the twins.

Inspector Dickens mounted his horse and headed North ostentatiously.

5 Ambush on the Old Apache Trail

The days passed slowly in Furnitureville as they waited for their train. Doctor Grace led a vigorous practice session each morning at a half-past seven, but within two hours it was far too hot to continue, and any good achieved was swiftly dissipated by the side's immediate recourse to the Golden Camel for 'breakfast'.

W.G. would take a stiff constitutional around the town, 'Town' was a slight misnomer in his view. Two rows of buildings separated by a road that came from nowhere, could claim, he supposed, to be *somewhere,* albeit briefly as the road passed through; and then vanished into nowhere again. 'Very like life', he thought to himself one morning as he sat on a rock, surveying the landscape. He might have been on another planet. Furnitureville sat in the middle of the flat circular plain where the road crossed the single-track of the railway-line at a right angle. Smoke from cooking-stoves stood straight up in the hot, still air like ghosts at a picnic. Where he stood now, perhaps a mile from town, the land rose and would presumably have been hills had not Mother nature over several million years or so blown away the soil and left only the rocky roots.

'It must be quite like this under water,' thought W.G., though he had never been there, but when he had last toured Australia, a young Queenslander had sung to him the wonders of the Great Barrier Reef and W.G. imagined that it would not be unlike all this about him, if the plug were pulled out. He had only ever seen the like of these great rock formations in the Aquarium at London Zoo, which he had visited one day when rain stopped play at Lord's. He would not have been at all surprised if a goldfish had not floated around the corner of the orange rock he sat beneath. And then one did. But it was only the flash of Dickens' red tunic and brass buttons in the sun.

'Any news of your departure, Doctor?'

'Not yet,' replied W.G., throwing a stone at a lizard and

deliberately missing, for he bore it no malice.

'What was that train on Thursday?'

'The 3.10,' said W.G. 'To Yuma. No use to us.'

Dickens had abandoned his pill-box hat, and now wore rather a handsome round, brown Stetson that rose to four indentations and a point.

'Nice hat,' said W.G.

'Keeps the sun off,' said Dickens. 'Keep in touch,' and was gone.

W.G. arrived back at the Golden Camel about midday, when the town seemed empty. Siestas were not for him and it was his custom to sit in a rocking-chair outside the saloon and whittle. This was a popular local activity, and with a sharp knife loaned to him by the undertaker he had already reduced his least favourite bat to a foot-high statuette of a clean-shaven one-armed cricketer. It would have been of himself but a Vilebastard had crashed drunkenly through the doors behind him, plunk-plunk-plunk, and W.G.'s knife had severed the beard and the arm in one involuntary whittle.

The only other disadvantage to gently rocking and whittling was that you presented an easy target to Elmer Gatsby, who liked nothing more than to pull up a chair beside you and attempt to sell you the Resurrection, the Life and a cheap tallboy.

'One day, doctor, the trains will come through here regular as clockwork, Praise the Lord, and we shall be ready for the call. We shall furnish the West, in the name of Jesus. We shall furnish the East. And great shall be our rejoicing, Brother Grace, and manifold our blessings. Hallelujah!'

'Hallelujah!' echoed W.G. not knowing what else to say. He and the team had attended Matins in the Golden Camel one Sunday, and as Raffles had pointed out, the centre-piece of the service appeared to be the collection. The pastor seemed to enjoy an easy relationship with both God and Mammon.

'How did I first come here, Doctor?' The pastor appeared suddenly behind W.G. one morning with no warning plunk, and caused him so to start that he lopped the other arm off his rapidly diminishing cricketer. Unless Milo had an XI, he might as well start afresh on his second least-favourite bat.

'Good question,' continued the pastor. 'God sent me here.

Like those Three Men of the New Testament I was guided here by a wandering star. I was then but a simple preacher-man, an evangelist with a simple message. Come to Jesus, or He'll git you.' His voice rose dangerously as nostalgia gripped him.

'You're all damned to Hell, on the slippery slope to the Fiery Furnaces, the flames are a-lickin' at your boots. Sniff, brothers, sniff and tell me then that ain't the sulphurous stink of Satan risin' from the earth beneath you. Cain't you smell it, sinners? Ain't your quiverin' nostrils chokin' with the aroma of Beelzebub?' And the state of their souls was such that they would cry out as one man "Yeah! Yeah!" and "What can we do, Brother Gatsby, save us from the Wrath to come!"

'Doctor, I had congregations of two or three hundred down on their knees in a wet tent a-sniffin' and a 'wringin' their hands and a-shakin' with the fear of God Almighty!' His voice quavered and was racked with sobs, and the spittoon, which was a good four yards away, leaped a further five feet and fell off the verandah as a wedge of Almighty Gob struck it amid-ships like a cannon-ball.

' "How can we be saved?" ' they'd cry. ' "How can we be saved?" '

'And their eyes would roll and their teeth would gnash. And I'd fix them with my eye and cry, "How can ye be saved, you miserable bastards, how can ye be saved?" And I'd sell 'em bottles of Patent Holy Water and lay the hands on. Heck, I once raised a dead horse in Abilene. Thus I travelled, Doctor, exchanging the Word of the Lord for the Staff of Life. Then I thought, I must build me a Cathedral. And I came unto this Wilderness. And I was lost. And I thirsted. And my animals, also. And I lay in the shade of my wagon, and I lifted my eyes to the Lord, and I did pray. "Lord, I am lost, and Thou art not, send me a sign. And lo!" '

He paused dramatically. Everything he had was pointed heavenwards, and then with a great sweep was pointing in quite the opposite direction.

'And lo! Cool water gushed at my feet!' He opened up a trap-door in the verandah.

'Not since Moses struck his walking-stick against a rock,' intoned the Pastor. And W.G. gazed down through the trap and there was a hole shored up with timber, and water glistening some twenty feet below.

'And I said unto the Lord, "You have sent me a sign. I shall build my Cathedral here." And there came unto me a wagon-load of pilgrims, also lost and thirsty. A family of good people. And they said unto me, "Give unto us water, pray," and I said, "In exchange for a suitable donation to my Cathedral thou mayest fill thy barrels and thy bottles and go hence thy wagon swashing with the stuff." And they said, "We have no money, brother, take our furniture," and I spoke unto them, saying "That'll do." '

'And lo, more pilgrims came and unto them I sold water *and* furniture and my reputation grew, and so did the town about me, and I named it Needle's Eye. For, brother, this is a growing land and there ain't nobody comes here don't need a little Jesus and a lot of furniture. Praise the Lord! Jesus be praised! For Jesus was a Carpenter. He workethed with wood. Pine. Oak. The Cedar of Lebanon. The trees of the forest. The lilies of the field. And he sawethed. And it was good. And he chisellethed. And he brought forth in his father's house — furniture. Chairs and settles, tables and roll-top desks, great wardrobes, chaise-longues, beds and dressers. And in the fullness of time I renamed the town FURNITURE-VILLE for business reasons. And I built this Cathedral, the First Church of Jesus Christ the Carpenter! Behold!'

'It's a public house!' cried W.G., who would be damned if he was going to be born again on licensed premises.

'Not during the Holy Hour,' said Gatsby, looking at his watch. 'Whisky?' W.G. shook his head.

'Thank you no. I must go forth and see the Station-master.' It was catching.

The pastor blessed him, making an expansive cross. 'Go forth in the Lord! Rejoice in His joinery! Would you like to take home some book-shelves?'

The little station-master was sitting on the ground outside his hut trying without success to whittle an empty bottle. There were dreadful slashes in his trousers where his knife had skidded off the glass. It was readily apparent to W.G. that the bottle had only recently been emptied, and equally clear in which direction.

The station-master looked at him hard through one eye.

'Where wuz y'all, mishtah?'

He had wooden teeth; and they were rotting. (Gatsby had sold them to him. They had originally been genuine pieces of the True Cross.)

'When?' said W.G.

'When the train came in, came in. I shtopped it shpecial. Flares and flags and fireworksh. Regular Fourth of July.'

'The train?'

'Whatsh yer name?'

'Grace.'

'Any kin o' Zane Grace? Rode through here couple o' months ago — taking notes.'

'The train?' W.G. persisted. It was in his nature.

'I told 'em twinsh of yours. Five o'clock this mornin'. Train.' And he squealed with pain as he embedded his knife once more in his scrawny thigh. W.G. quietly removed the bottle from the station-master's hand and replaced it with the crippled cricketer.

'There was a train north at five o'clock this morning?' He wanted to get the facts straight before shouting at the Vilebastards.

'You mished it.' The station-master hiccoughed. 'Jeeshush! Look what I done whittled!' And he smiled triumphantly at the remains of the bat.

'When's the next one due?' W.G. could feel a foul temper bubbling within.

'Week or sho, I guess.' The station-master cut the cricketer's head off. 'That'sh better.' He waved it at W.G. 'That'sh my Grandad after the Comanches got him. A likenesh.'

A week or so! W.G. turned on his heel and set off at a brisk lope towards the Golden Camel, or the Cathedral, depending upon what time of day it was.

'Had I known then what I know now,' said W.G.

'Which is a deal more than we know yet,' mumbled Watson, ever-impatient.

'We should have waited for the train. We might have avoided the —' he sighed deeply, took a book from a shelf, opened and closed it without looking and dropped it into the fire distractedly. 'It might all have been so very different. Poor Charlie might be alive today —'

'Charlie?' enquired Watson. Fresh characters appearing every moment, and still not a whiff of Gay Dog.

'Charlie, yes. Mountain-Cat who Hates Tall Buildings was his proper name. We called him Charlie.' W.G. threw another book on the fire. The fire seemed to enjoy it. Watson himself had never cared for Sir Walter Scott. A reasonable quirk.

'Castor Vilebastard would most certainly —' W.G. paused.

'Be alive?' asked Watson.

W.G. nodded gravely.

'There'd have been none of that trouble with Pinkerton or the Statue of Liberty or Thomas Edison or Monsewer Eiffel or —'

'*OR* GAY DOG!!' screamed Watson. He hurled his pencil to the ground and pirouetting on his stiff leg ground it into the Wilton.

There was a long silence. Watson began to scrabble about on the carpet, retrieving bits of lead and wood. He was rather ashamed of himself.

W.G. finally spoke.

'Or indeed Gay Dog.'

Oh, the wretched past, he thought. You pack it all away neatly in the box-room of your brain, leaving it to gather dust, oh, you might pop up there and rummage about for some pleasant memento like the hundred before lunch at Old Trafford or the fat lunch in a friendly pub by the Avon, but then you bundle them away and . . . and get on with it. Then one day a typhoon takes the roof off or a gin-soaked Mrs Hudson goes berserk and attacks the baggage and there's the whole damnable issue splayed out all over the roof. Much as he liked him, he could not but wish that Gay Dog had kept his arrow to himself. That arrow had certainly released a sackful of cat.

He harumphed and shook himself like a damp bear. Enough of that sort of thing.

'Elvis Presley,' said a voice inside his head, and began to sing about wanting to be his Teddy Bear.

'Shut up, Charley,' smiled W.G. 'Right, gentlemen, onward.'

Watson and Lestrade huddled happily to each other, and

prepared to take notes.

When W.G. burst into the Saloon, plunk-plunk, plunk-plunk, plunk-plunk, he saw the Vilebastards, immediately. They were sitting either side of an extraordinary fly-blown figure. He looked like an ancient leathern bottle with a hat on. A leathern bottle so ancient that it had cracked in a good many places and thongs and feathers stiffened by age and dirt, hair and a rotting head stuck out at unlikely angles. Regardless of the cracks, the Vilebastards appeared to be re-charging the tatty vessel. Both held bottles of whisky and alternately filled the tiny glass that their companion was raising and lowering to and from the hole in his head with piston-like regularity. He gave off a pungent aroma, attractive to blow flies.

'Right you two,' roared W.G. They both paused and smiled at him in that bloody irritating manner of theirs. 'I have just spoken to the station-master here —'

'Worse than useless, isn't it?' Castor murmured sympathetically.

'Man has no idea,' added Pollux, and tut-tutted.

'He says there was a train last night —'

'Delirium tremens, wouldn't you say?' said Castor.

'You're the Doctor,' Pollux poured their friend another.

'He stopped it. It was there waiting for us. He spoke of flares, of fireworks —'

'Oh dear' sighed Pollux, 'Oh dear, oh dear.'

'The demon alcohol,' Castor shuddered. 'It can ruin a fellow,' and he poured another down the gaping man, ignoring the glass totally.

'You are saying, then, that there was no train last night? That —'

'No train last night, no.' Castor squeezed the bridge of his nose with thumb and forefinger. W.G. was clearly testing his patience, but, by God, he would be reasonable. 'No train last night. No train tonight. No train tomorrow. Or the day after tomorrow. No train in the immediate future. No flares. No whistles. No rockets or roman candles, no bursts of Handel on the Mighty Wonlitzer. Nothing, doctor, nothing.'

W.G.'s mouth opened to raise another boom, but Pollux outflanked him.

'Doctor, are we or are we not, in charge of transportation? We have a letter from the Committee of the MCC to that effect. To date, we admit, we have been very badly let down by a number of railway companies. The Baltimore & Ohio, the Southern Pacific, the Missouri Pacific, the Atchison, Topeka and Santa Fe, the Union Pacific, the Central Pacific, to name but a few. We have filed complaints with those companies. Remember, however, that this is a young country. It is highly unreasonable, even naive, to expect the sort of efficiency and service that one receives from, say, the Brighton line.'

'We are a long, long way from Brighton,' Castor too was standing. The bottle was empty. Not so the leathern one. Castor signalled to a serving-wench. W.G. was on the point of taxing them with the dead Eskimo, the rebellion in Canada, the whole Dickens' saga, but he remembered Raffles' words of caution. Castor was gazing deep into his eyes.

'Dickens, like his father before him, is a master of fiction.' There was a hint of menace in his voice.

Good God, thought W.G., they can read minds?

'Not as well as we would like,' smiled Castor.

'Practice makes perfect,' said Pollux.

W.G.'s temples hummed. The only idea formulating in his whirring brain was to bang their identical heads together, squeeze them until they were Siamese, but the Vilebastards, who were clearly reading the juddering ticker-tape of his mind, had moved swiftly out of range. They were interrupted by a sudden furore at the other end of the saloon. 'One-eye' Jack McSwine (for it was he), who had been playing at billiards at the table under the staircase, had, with an accusation of gross cheating, knocked his opponent off his horse with a vicious blow with the thick end of his cue. He had then broken the cue and leaning from his own horse held the jagged end at his victim's jugular. There was, W.G. observed at once, no sign, alas, of Sheriff Gatsby and his large gun.

The saloon was tense and still, like a nervous stomach. The Faro wheel stopped spinning. Dealers stopped dealing. McSwine was debating whether to go the whole hog. The only movement was from two bartenders, whose traditional duty at such moments was to take down the large mirror from behind the bar and stack it away safely under the counter.

In fact, so swift and unexpected was W.G.'s action that they dropped it; it broke into a thousand pieces. Not surprisingly, for W.G. burst across the saloon, seized One-eye's horse by one fore and one hind-leg and up-ended it, rider, billiard-table and all. It was only when the opponent crawled, gasping thanks from the ruins, that W.G. realised that it was A.J. Raffles.

'The sooner we leave this town, I think, W.G., the better,' Raffles dabbed his throat with a silk handkerchief.

'We are not exactly hitting it off with the locals,' agreed W.G. At that moment a stunned McSwine was groping about for his revolver and W.G. shifted the horse more athwart him to forestall any unpleasantness from that quarter.

In fact, that was the quarter from which the least unpleasantness was to come. The other three were full of McSwine's drunken supporters, all armed to the teeth. W.G. was aware that this was the second time they had crossed swords. Where was Gatsby the Sheriff? Even the Pastor or the Furniture Mogul would have sufficed. W.G. glanced towards the entrance. No Gatsby in sight, but he spotted the Vile-bastards slinking away, dragging their unconscious associate between them. Well, there was nothing he could do about that, he was surrounded again, and this time no King Willow to hand. Only a dazed A.J. Raffles.

W.G. closed his eyes to think. He usually found this a considerable help. Not, however, in this case. The noises off were far too disconcerting. The hoarse whispering of 'stranger' and 'lynch'; the hiss of an unsheathed knife, the unclipping of a holster, and the creak of leather as a pistol was tugged from a belt, the cocking of a fowling-piece. W.G. elected to keep his eyes shut for a little longer. Not that he thought that by doing so the troubles about him might disappear, but that his sudden rush for the exit with Raffles on his shoulder might come as rather more of a surprise.

Then plunk-plunk went the doors, there was a wild cry of 'Hi, ho, Silver!' which was taken up by the assembly, a great commotion and a deal of plunking and when he opened his eyes, he was alone in the saloon with Raffles. Raffles tugged his sleeve: 'Who was that mysterious masked stranger?'

'No idea,' said W.G. 'I wasn't looking.'

6 A Miracle on the Old Apache Trail

'Silver it was,' said W.G.

'Long John?' queried Watson. The cast was becoming bewildering. He guffawed and looked across at Lestrade in the hope that the Inspector would join in. His laugh was famous in the Force. In years to come, as a memorial to the great detective, the klaxon on police cars would imitate his rhythmic bray. Nothing was forthcoming now. The Inspector's face was twisted by deduction.

'Mind-reading,' he murmured, 'It keeps a-croppin' up. The Vilebastards we 'ave a-tamperin' with it. A-practisin' they said. The Heskimo. I fancy 'e was a dabbler. There's a deal of crime you could commit if you could read minds. It would 'elp a lot in the solvin' thereof.' And at this point he did omit a cheery hee-haw.

'I'd never thought of that,' admitted W.G. 'And there's more of it to come.'

'Aha!' repeated Watson, quickly writing down 'Mind-reading' which he had previously ignored.

'Silver, you said, Doctor Grace?' Lestrade was drawing out intricate diagrams in his notebook as he spoke.

'Yes, indeed,' replied W.G. He was slightly ashamed of himself for not having thought of this mind-reading business himself, but then so much had happened. 'Silver. Apparently, the moment the cry went up, the town emptied on every available horse, waggon, cart, and when those were exhausted, on foot and the entire population, bar-tenders, ostlers, strumpets, cowboys, undertakers, deputy sheriffs, shop-keepers, dancing girls, whatever, whatever, headed for the hills. By the time Raffles and I had helped ourselves to a quick one to steady the nerves and made our way into the street, there was not a local to be seen. All the shops and houses were shuttered, and apart from the odd dog, we were quite alone. We arranged rocking-chairs on the verandah and sat down with our drinks to think matters out. The remainder of the team appeared now and then, the Reverend Studholme had been butterfly-hunting, three or four of them had been upstairs sleeping off breakfast, Cryer and the others had been out in the desert shooting to no purpose. Cryer, in fact, bore a note for me from Dickens, who had obviously witnessed the general exodus. It read "Watch V's. Their chance to run. F.D." '

There was no sign of the Vilebastards. The last sign of them had been running. W.G. suggested to Raffles that they amble up to the station via the livery stables and see if there was any sign of life or indeed transport. W.G. mentioned casually to A.J. that Gatsby had been noticeable by his absence during the billiard-table furore, and he pointed over towards the Furniture Emporium and Mayoral Parlour and suggested that they look for him there.

'Though he's probably,' said Raffles 'taken to the hills.'

'Praise the Lord!' W.G. laughed, because Gatsby was a tedious blighter on the subjects of both God and Furniture.

As they approached the Emporium, a two-storey frontage hiding a hutment of inordinate length, there was a fearful caterwauling from within. They hopped up onto the board-walk and listened at the door. Someone or something was doing no good at all to a good deal of furniture. Raffles put his finger to his lips and gently pushed open the door. It said 'Closed' but this was a social call. Raffles was about to enter when the Station-master came scurrying out. The top of his cap had been severed and was flapping about as he ran. He was waving a piece of paper. In the middle of the street he paused to regain his breath. The effort caused him to fall over. He was still somewhat the worse for drink.

He took his cap off and pushed his hand through the hole.

'Look at that,' he cried, most aggrieved.

'There you see, my good man,' lectured W.G. 'the perils of whittling in an intoxicated condition.'

'Whistlin? Shit!' piped the little station-master. 'That's a goddam sabree!' And he swished the air with the paper. 'A goddam sabree!' Raffles and Grace looked anxiously towards the door.

'I just showed him this 'n' he went plumb crazee!' W.G. took the piece of paper. It was a wire from the main offices of the Southern Pacific Railroad Company. 'NO MORE TRAINS AS FROM THIS DATE' it read, 'FURNITURE-VILLE NOW RATED "GHOST TOWN".'

'That was quick,' said Raffles. The dust kicked up as the last citizens departed had barely settled on Main Street, Furnitureville.

'Same's Gold.' The stationmaster had seen it all in a long career with the railroad. 'News travels fast out hereaways.' And he spat a large gobbet some fifteen feet, as if to demonstrate the pace of communication where silver was concerned. This seemed to cue a further barrage of sound from within.

'I've seed the same in La Ventura, Cabezon, Loma Pardo, San Geronimo. Seen thrivin' towns, boomin' boomin' like Chloride and Mogollon, Old Oro Blanco, Twin Buttes, Contention City, Total Wreck and Cerro Colorado. They come, they go. There's a place y' know where you drank good whisky and whored till your pecker peeled, and played poker all night with blind-drunk miners and now it's a cemeeterry. Boom, boom, boom town. Boom, boom, Boot Hill.'

The stationmaster sank once more to the ground. The day's events had finally proved too much for him. The two Englishmen felt that the time had come to seek out Gatsby. They braced themselves and strode side by side into the Emporium.

They were greeted by a scene of total carnage. The air was thick with feathers and horse-hair and in the middle stood Gatsby like Custer at his last stand, sabre in hand, surrounded by dead furniture. He had disembowelled settees and armchairs and hacked chests and cupboards to ribbons. He had scalped bed-heads and skewered cushions. Unlike Custer, he was victorious, and he now stood, head bowed, sabre dangling, chest heaving with exhaustion in the middle of his Little Big Horn.

'Good day to you Sheriff Gatsby, Vicar!' W.G. hallooed.

'*Colonel* Gatsby! *Colonel*!' A whole new Gatsby was parading 'Of the Twentieth Virginians.'

'And a box of matches,' whispered Raffles.

It did not seem to be the thing to say at all. Slowly Gatsby's head raised. W.G. hadn't seen a face so out of sorts since F.R. Spofforth's in Adelaide that time he'd whacked him for a sixer over the Beer Tent. The sabre was rattling.

'Pray! Pray! Pray, you heathen bastards!' roared the Pastor 'Pray till your knees bleed!'

W.G. looked at A.J. A.J. looked at W.G. W.G. shrugged and they dropped to their knees. Just in time too, as the sabre hissed over their heads, and Gatsby staggered blindly between them, tripping on cushions and the remains of soft furnishings. They heard a crash, and when they turned Gatsby was on his knees too, supporting himself on the door-frame and glaring out into the street.

'Fornicators and furniture-makers! Cock-suckers and carpenters! Wherefore hast thou forsaken me, you two-timin' bastards? Is it not easier for a camel to pass through the asshole of a rich man, than for a poor man to shag the very udders off a sacred cow? Yeah, verily, verily, oh, my sacred vice and dove-tailed joints! I'm ruined!' He raised himself shakily to his feet and, dropping his sabre, ran like a frenzied old spinster into the bright street. He tripped over the station-master but hardly seemed to notice. 'Why me, Lord, Lord? Why me?' he shouted at Heaven. He scrambled away from them now as if the street were a cliff-face he was climbing. 'Why me? Why me?'

Bent double he never saw the stage-coach corner the Golden Camel at full belt. He was coming back now the way he had gone, his head jammed between the wooden spokes of the off-side back wheel and stuck firmly. The erratic movements of the wheel that spun him, and indeed the eccentric move-ments of the driver, caused the stage slowly to capsize, throwing the driver on top of the prone stationmaster. The mules reared but soon settled, gladly, probably, of the unexpected rest. Gatsby was not to be seen, he was under the coach, and no-one was in any great hurry to look.

All this had happened in less than half-a-minute and W.G. and Raffles still knelt in the doorway of the Emporium.

'Good Lord!' said W.G. 'What a surprising way to go,' and he described a series of circles in the air with a finger, shaking his great head the while.

'Ironic that,' murmured Raffles, 'Undone by woodwork in the end.'

Most of the MCC team had turned out and some of them were making half-hearted attempts to right the coach. W.C.

tore the embroidered cover off a sofa and made his way to the coach. En passant, he looked at the driver. It was the leathern bottle; he was in exactly the same shape as the stationmaster.

'Close your eyes,' he suggested to his team-mates, 'and lift'. When the remains of the late Elmer Gatsby were revealed, he threw the sofa-cover over them and pulled the body free.

'Right,' he cried, and the stage dropped back. There were aggrieved moans from within, the coach door opened upwards, and, as one, two pained and identical faces appeared.

I might have guessed it, thought W.G., the Vilebastards are back.

There was a flash of red by the hotel. Dickens was still on the job.

The entire population of Furnitureville was gathered in the saloon, all rather shaken by Gatsby's end, except, of course, for the Doctor who had seen men ploughed in half and scattered. The Vilebastards and their fly-blown driver sat alone in a corner resuscitating themselves. W.G. sat with the Stationmaster who seemed to be reviving. The Reverend Studholme had found a four for bridge and the rest of the team were either playing billiards or simply indulging in the free drink. Raffles had gone for a walk with a Gladstone bag.

The burial of Pastor Elmer Gatsby had been a brief but well-conducted affair. The Reverend Studholme had conducted the service, speaking of the many facets of the deceased and the rich variety of ways which God in his infinite wisdom has designed to strike us down. The corpse, suitably laid out in a wardrobe of his own manufacture, had been lowered into a deep hole on Boot Hill and they had raised a rude cross, fashioned from a pair of hat-racks and mounted in an elephant's foot umbrella stand. Into the Crucifix they screwed the brass plate from the door of the Emporium which simply stated, 'Elmer Gatsby. Mayor, Pastor, Sheriff and Maker of the World's Finest Furniture. Open All Day Saturday.'

W.G. stood up on a chair in the middle of the Saloon Bar and addressed the team.

'Gentlemen,' he said. 'We have now been here, where we

should not have been in the first place, for nearly two weeks. You have been most patient. The question you must be asking yourselves with ever-increasing urgency is —'

' 'Ow t'bloody 'Ell are we goin' to get out of 'ere?' Cryer was drinking warm champagne from the bottle.

'Good question,' pronounced the Doctor, 'and I feel that we should first look to those entrusted by Lord's with the responsibility of organising our transportation for an answer.'

All eyes turned towards the Vilebastards who were slapping their smelly friend into some semblance of sensibility.

'Well?' boomed Dr Grace.

Castor rose slowly and pointed to the leathern bottle.

'Our driver,' he announced. 'One Obadiah Hawkspit, a man with years of experience on the Oxbow Route. A trusted employee of Butterfields' Overland Mail and Express Stages. He will drive us East to El Paso in the morning. Thence we travel North by train and start to do what we came to do — to play cricket.'

'Cricket!' toasted the Reverend Studholme, raising his glass on high.

'Cricket!' roared the assembly, draining their glasses with a will.

'It was damned crowded, but no-one cared. We were returning to civilisation.' W.G. could see through the window that the sky was lightening. What the hell, he thought, no match today, and, to tell the truth, I'm enjoying myself.

'The eight smallest we packed inside the coach, the rest of us and our baggage went on the roof. I sat beside the driver, the aforementioned Hawkspit. I was prepared to tolerate his vile aroma. God only knows what foulness lurked in his buckskins but they had clearly not been removed for some years. I was happy to sit there beside him because of my life-long interest in coaches and carriages. Did you know that my grandfather drove from Gloucestershire to London in a carriage pulled by, and you'll find this hard to credit, pulled by a KITE?'

'No!' chorused Watson and Lestrade.

'He *did*!' said W.G. and disappeared into one of his reveries, accompanied only by a fresh whisky and water. Watson prepared drinks for Lestrade and himself. Lestrade was gazing out of the window at the new buildings that were going up the length of Baker Street.

'The terrace opposite was totally destroyed by their ray,' said Watson, handing Lestrade a glass. 'We were very lucky. There was only the one of them and the Royal Horse Artillery hit it with a lucky shot in Portman Square.'

'Bad Business,' said Lestrade, raised his whisky and with a whispered, 'Not on duty, sir, thank you very much, your good 'ealth,' poured it down his throat.

'What do you make of all this, Inspector?' asked Watson, gesturing towards the silent Champion.

'Patience, sir, is the key-word in matters of detection,' smiled Lestrade. 'The truth will out.'

'I suppose so,' replied Watson, who had found over the years that 'Incomprehension' was generally the keyword in matters of detection, but no matter.

'Where was I?' W.G. suddenly erupted again.

'Travelling east,' Watson replied, quickly darting for his notebook and pencil.

'Not at all,' said W.G. 'and here the mystery deepens. For after an hour or so I slowly realised that the stage-coach was travelling *west*!'

'Ah'm a-just-a-doin' what Ah just bin a-told to do, Doc.' Hawkspit transferred his whip from his right hand to his left and began to rummage about in the dark reaches of his buck-skin jacket. Even though they were travelling at a spanking trot, W.G. received the full benefit of Hawkspit's lack of personal hygiene, and found himself not looking forward to whatever was going to be produced from the driver's left armpit. Some flying insects seized the opportunity to escape, and they were followed by a mildewed sheet of paper which Hawkspit waved vigorously in front of the Doctor's face.

'Now look'ee here,' cried Hawkspit, 'Ah cain't read but Ah knows what Ah was told, and this be what that there Vilepart told me. 'An' that's why the charge was so high, 'cos Ah ain't drivin' no-one through this terrortory, for less'n five hundred dollars, no, sirree, dam 'n' blast it! They don't call this the Old Apachee Trail for nothin.' And he began to scan the horizon anxiously.

W.G. realised that he had been doing this ever since they set out from Furnitureville. He had put it down to perhaps a keen interest in the Wonders of Nature, though, admittedly, they had not see a living creature since their departure.

'I think,' pronounced W.G. 'that it would be best if we stopped.'

'Star-yopped?' screamed Hawkspit. 'Star-yopped!? *Out here*!?!'

'Yes,' said W.G., 'and sorted the whole business out.'

'Star-yopped?' whinnied Hawkspit again.

'Yes,' repeated W.G. and, seizing the reins from a gibbering Hawkspit, demonstrated another of his many talents by bringing the steaming team of horses to a perfectly judged halt. While the dust settled and sudden stillness fell upon them, Hawkspit reached under his seat and withdrew an ancient and villainous-looking shotgun. W.G.'s first thought was that this was intended for himself, and was about to protest, but Hawkspit lifted a ragged finger to his lips.

'Listen!' he whispered.

W.G. could hear nothing, except the Reverend Studholme rumbling on about *The Origin of Species*.

Hawspit cocked his piece.

W.G. wondered if he expected dinner in some form to come flying or hopping over the Horizon. 'It's too dang quiet,' whispered Hawkspit. Hawkspit suddenly stiffened like a pointer, nostrils quivering. He remained like this for a good minute.

Then 'Helldang blast it!' he cried, threw the gun to W.G., took up the reins and cracked the horses into an almost instant gallop.

'There's shells in mah pocket!' shouted Hawkspit, and hurled oaths like stones at the pounding buttocks ahead of him.

There was a whooping behind them. Raffles' head appeared at the window below W.G.

'What's up?' he shouted.

W.G. peered back along the dust-laden trail behind them. He saw distant figures on horseback. Whoever they were, they were the whoopers.

'Some people are following us,' he reported to Raffles, 'and whooping.'

Something whirred over his head.

'And throwing things at us,' he added, and conscious that the whooping was now louder —

'And getting closer.'

Dickens drew abreast, riding like a maniac, trousers awry, he had been attending to a clarion call of nature when the Apaches had swooped down upon him.

'Indians!' he bellowed. 'About forty of 'em. I think I winged one!' And he waved his revolver triumphantly. 'The varmints!' cried Old Hawkspit.

'Ought we not,' suggested W.G. 'to stop and reason with them?'

'Stop,' screeched Hawkspit, hitting a note that cannot be captured by block capitals, italics or any number of exclamation marks. Had there been bats in those parts, they would have been downed.

'Follow me!' cried Dickens and galloped off ahead.

An arrow passed through Hawkspit's hat, dislodging sleeping lice. Two more thwacked into the luggage. Anxious remarks were passed by those members of the team squatting on the stage-coach roof. The air was thick with orange dust, wild Hawkspit oaths and the ever more adjacent whooping. The stage-coach was clearly being taxed far beyond its limits. It swayed and bucked, and W.G. was convinced that any moment it would turn over.

'Shoot the bastards!' shouted Hawkspit.

'I am a Doctor,' said W.G. and unleashed both barrels into the air. 'Here, one of you chaps have a go!' he cried, passing the lethal weapon to a young Surrey fast bowler crouching behind a trunk. Then he realised that he would have to dip into the mush of Hawkspit's pocket for ammunition. Averting his eyes, with one movement he scooped some shells out of the grime and scattered them over the roof.

Ahead, Dickens was on a rise waving his hat.

'This way,' he called, and disappeared over the rise.

Hawkspit effected a terrifying right turn and the coach careered through brush and cactus up a slope. As they topped the rise they saw below them an open flat area surrounded by a circular outcrop of rocks. In the middle stood Dickens and his horse. In its last lunge for refuge the coach hit a rock and W.G.'s worst fears were realised. It turned over twice and the wheels fell off.

'That's torn it,' he thought, rolling away from the wreckage. As he rose slowly, dusting himself off with his cap, he noticed Dickens already hustling the team behind rocks. No-one seemed injured, but all were very frightened. Hawkspit and Dickens, the only armed members of the Company, took cover behind a couple of rocks. The Indians were now lined across the top of the escarpment, preparing to attack.

'What now, Dickens?' called W.G.

'A massacree!' shouted Hawkspit. 'A goddam massacree!'

'There's a lot of truth in that,' said Dickens, 'There's no escape. That's not my pal, Big Bear out there.'

'What were the Vilebastards doing during all this?' asked Watson, pencil poised.

'Nothing significant,' said W.G. 'but then it was scarcely the moment. My only memory of them at that time was fossicking about among the luggage: No idea why.' He stood up and stretched. He was a large man at best, but at full stretch, Watson thought, he seemed to fill the room. He noticed Lestrade press himself against a wall, as if in fear of being crushed. The Great Cricketer lumbered over to the door and idly fingered the V.R. that Holmes one dull evening had etched there with his revolver. He inserted his little finger in a full-stop.

'Dear old Holmes did that,' said Watson, smiling at the memory. 'Bang! Bang! Bang! Frightened the wits out of Mrs Hudson.'

'You probably thought it the work of patriotic wood-worm, Doctor Grace.' Lestrade liked his little joke, but very rarely anybody else's.

'Lets the draught in,' said W.G. His low opinion of genius would out.

'I wouldn't care to 'ave been in your boots, Doctor Grace,' said Lestrade. 'Surrounded and outnumbered by those naked heathens, no weapons to speak of and them with their bows and harrows and spears and knives and tommy-hawks. How come you are standing 'ere today 'ale and 'earty and playing better than ever, as I 'ear.'

W.G. smiled, shook his head and returned to the chair by the mantle. He slowly sipped his whisky.

W.G. was not going to sell his life cheaply. It was not in his nature. Not that he had ever contemplated a violent end. Spofforth at his quickest might have struck him on the heart or on the temple and ended it all, but he had never seriously contemplated that. While he had a bat in his hand he could defend himself. As the Apaches ululated in the distance preparing to attack, W.G. sought out his cricket bag, unbuttoned his trousers and thrust his Abdominal Protector, a massive cup of bamboo and weathered teak, into its voluminous woolly pouch. Seeking as much further bodily protection as he could he padded up, pulled on a thick MCC sweater and drew on his batting-gloves. Finally, he heaved from his bag his heaviest bat, a huge chunk of willow. Gilbert Jessop had laughingly remarked that it was in fact an entire willow tree stripped only of roots and branches, and W.G. felt as he whirled his bat above his head that it would have to be jolly swift arrow that could get past it. He strode through the gap between a protesting Dickens and a whimpering Hawkspit and marched boldly towards the enemy. He looked exactly as if he were emerging from the pavilion prior to engaging some Australians.

The first arrow he received stuck into the ground some two yards in front of him. He whacked it away one-handed as he passed, then quickly stepped back and with a solid backward defensive stroke took the second low-down on his bat. The third hummed harmlessly over his head, the fourth he edged past his left ear. Concentrate, Gilbert, concentrate, he whispered to himself and raked the opposition to see where the next would come from. He missed it completely. It caught him low down on his right pad. He pulled it out, broke it in half contemptuously and took guard once more. It was the last of the over that saved the side — and ultimately, of course, the World. He saw the fellow shoot it, and made to protect his chest but at the last split-second it dipped and thumped loudly into his crotch.

'I looked down and despite the tension of the moment I couldn't help but laugh. I've always worn an Abdominal Protector since, one time as a lad I was caught in the cluster while batting against XLIV Strapping Wenches from Budleigh Salterton.

'It was only a tennis ball, but, blow me, it hurt like Billy-oh! And now to see this arrow sticking out of my parts. Well, as I say, I could not help but laugh.'

W.G. had pushed the poker between two of his fly-buttons and stood guffawing in front of the fireplace.

'This is approximately the Spectacle that greeted the Apache. When I looked up at them, they had all dismounted and were face down in the dirt wailing like Burmese tomcats.

They clearly thought I was God. We were home by an innings.'

Watson and Lestrade stood speechless, their eyes pinned to the Champion of All England's crotch.

'Well, I never,' mumbled Lestrade.

'Do you still have the famous box?' asked Watson.

'Framed and mounted in my Surgery,' said W.G. 'It's a conversation-piece.'

Nothing was then too good for the Tourists. W.G. was mounted triumphantly on a mule and escorted with the rest of the team and their baggage back to the Apache Village. This transpired to be some forty miles away. From a distance it seemed to be just another remarkable lump of rock. But as they approached they could detect an entrance — a narrow pass which led into a circle of land about the size of a decent cricket ground totally surrounded by the high rock-wall. Here were wigwams and against the wall hutments. There was much rejoicing from the elders and the ladies of the tribe and the children at the return of Gay Dog and his band. And when he explained the position of W.G. the joy was unconfined.

The festivities started at once. 'The menu,' said W.G. 'was limited but edible. And they broached the fire-water. It was quite a night.'

'How did you communicate with them?' asked Watson. 'Did they speak English, any of them?'

'No,' said W.G. 'Gay Dog spoke a little Spanish, but none of us did. Quite rightly. Old Hawkspit knew a word or two of their tongue, but only sufficient as far as I could gather to obtain regular supplies of the fire-water, which was vicious stuff and obtainable at any Government Agency. No, funnily enough, it was old Raffles cracked the language barrier. He used to chat for hours with the Medicine Man.'

'Medicine Man?' asked Lestrade.

'Charlie. I mentioned him earlier. He was a sort of Witch Doctor, local padre. Plays a large part in the story — Charlie, the Medicine man! We ought to ask Raffles over to give us his end of it. I think he knows more of what went on there than anyone, with, of course, the exception of Castor and Pollux Vilebastard. I was very busy being God. "Grey Sea" they called me. "Grey Sea".'

'Is this where,' and Watson flicked back through his note-book until he found the gravy-stained page he had written on at the Diogenes — 'the Tour earned its name — the Tour of Shame? Where Vilebastard's demise became —' and he could barely read the word for custard, 'inevitable?'

'Oh, yes,' said W.G. 'Their behaviour was —' and he searched awhile for the word, abandoned the search and yawned instead. 'Bed,' he said.

'I'll send a lad round now to the Albany and ask Raffles to lunch tomorrow.'

'Send him in the morning, I would,' said W.G. 'I've popped round to see old Raffles after Middlesex-Gloucestershire games for a night-cap or a yarn. He's never in after dark. Funny fellow.' And he lumbered off to his room.

Morning had broken. The Red Weed glistened with dew.

7 Yankees at the Yard

Lestrade went straight to the Yard. There'd be no sleep for him this night. His men had collected a waiting-room full of Americans. Not a cheery room, either. Half dark-brown, the bottom half, with the remainder painted in a queasy cream. Not a cheery gathering either, thought Lestrade, as he glanced at them briefly through a spy-hole in the door. He recognised the painter Whistler. Was that his mother? This exercise was a very long shot, *that* he was prepared to admit. But at least the Commissioner would not be able in the morning to accuse him of leaving stones unturned. He beckoned to his assistant, Detective-Sergeant Chesterton, a morose giant with matching moustache.

'What 'ave we, then, Sergeant?' he enquired tenderly.

Chesterton handed him a sheaf of paper and forms covered in very large writing. His interviews had been slow and dull, but methodical. He was one of the new breed. A Cambridge graduate.

'He's the trouble-maker, Inspector,' he pointed at one of the sheets.

'James 'Enry,' the Inspector read out loud.

'That's Henry James, sir, you see on —'

''Enry James 'Oo?' asked Lestrade.

'Just Henry James, sir. You see on the form —'

'Form, Chesterton? 'As 'e got some form?'

'Not on this side of the Atlantic, sir.'

'That's nice. Lives in Rye. Lamb 'Ouse, Rye. A Cinque Port, Chesterton, no less. History. Where did you pick 'im up?'

'The Reform Club, sir. He has a room there.'

' "Author",' Lestrade continued his readings. 'Not a major crime. What did you mean precisely, Chesterton, by "trouble-maker"?'

'Oh, the usual, sir. All the other Americans were very co-operative in the circumstances, but he went on and on about Friends in High Places. The Prime Minister. The Home

The fingering of Henry James

Secretary, The American Ambassador. The President of the United States. A pompous poop sir, pardon my French.'

''E's never roamed the Prairies of the Wild West in Hamerica, 'as 'e, Chesterton? Never pursued the Hape Atchy across the plains of Harizona?'

'Says not, sir.'

'Best take 'im 'ome then.'

'To Rye, sir?'

'No, Chesterton, no. The Reform Club, and on the way oil the troubled waiters.'

Lestrade proceeded to leaf through the other products of Chesterton's scholarship. Mainly literary folk it seemed. Some artists. A sculptor. Three who had spent their formative years on the Frontier he put on his desk.

'Sir?'

'Chesterton? Back so soon.'

'Sir, Mr James was at Lord's yesterday morning.'

'Was he, by Thunder?' So! Lestrade heard distant bugles. So! Mister Henry James, ageing American author, with Friends in High Places, dowses the Great Novel roaring in his bosom, and comes all the way up from Rye to watch a game of cricket. So!

'An Hamerican at Lord's. Ho. Ho.'

'Odd, isn't it, sir?' Chesterton was suddenly less morose.

'Hodd enough, Chesterton!' Lestrade beamed. 'Wheel 'im in.'

He *was* a pompous poop. While Henry James threatened loudly and involved the names of further friends, Her Majesty the Queen no less, Bernard Shaw and H.G. Wells among others, Lestrade, deaf to all that, was making a mental note that Chesterton had a keen eye for human foibles. Bright lad.

'You was at the murder, sir,' he tossed into boiling air.

'My good man,' foamed Henry James, 'I have already informed your fellow here of the pertinencies —'

'An all-Hamerican murder, or so it seems.'

This cooled him down.

'In a sense, Inspector, though, of course, the victim was English-born, and the assailant, so far as I could gather, a savage from our more distant pastures.'

'A Hignorant savage, would you say, Mr James?'

'I would not employ those precise words, Inspector, but shall we say, a primitive certainly.'

'A primitive, Mr James, as would act upon 'is own hinitiative?'

'You suppose, Inspector, that he was a hireling, following the instructions of some —'

'Friends in 'Igh Places, Mr James? It's a theory, is it not?'

'I can recognise the logic —'

'Likes your cricket, does you, 'Enry?'

'I am most partial to the game. I have even played a little, but not of late. I often go to Lord's. I take a box.'

'Surely the chances, 'Enry, are a good million to one of you being struck in the bollocks —'

'A box, Inspector, in the stand, where one can entertain in some privacy.'

'Did you know the late Castor Vilebastard?'

'No.'

'Or 'is twin brother?'

'Oh, I may have met them briefly at some social occasion. As you are doubtless aware, they roomed for some little while in Washington Square.'

Lestrade could not believe his good fortune.

'Aha!' he said meaningfully. Over the years, he had found this a most successful ploy. 'Washington Square?' he added, and winked knowingly at Chesterton, who, bless him, picked up his cue and looked up at the ceiling and whistled.

Henry James was a very worried man.

'They — they came to visit me once at home,' he stammered. 'We all have skeletons in our cupboards, do we not, Inspector?'

Lestrade let that pass. He had an attic full of them, but there are certain things you do not mention to authors. Particularly novelists.

'They informed me that they were in urgent need of five hundred dollars. They showed me a brown envelope, the contents of which, they assured me, if shown to the public prints would ruin me, these are their very words, "both socially and professionally".'

'Five 'undred smackers does not seem excessive.'

'I think, Inspector, they knew their man. There was but one minor peccadillo that sprang to my mind. Minor, but in the hands of sensationalists of the type that produce certain of our New York journals, cause enough for deep embarrassment.'

'You forked out the necessary?'

'I did. To my bitter shame.'

'And what was in the brown envelope?'

'It was empty, Inspector, but the birds had flown.'

Motive too, thought Lestrade.

''Igh time, 'Enry James, author and admirer of our National Game, that you was in bed.'

'I *was* in bed,' Henry James complained.

'Chesterton,' Lestrade mimed the transporting of an author to a Club. 'And don't leave Town, will you, sir?'

Lestrade was very pleased with himself. Now for the three gentlemen who were no strangers to the Wilds. A Mr Bret

Harte, a Mr Samuel Clemens, and, Oh God, this one he had heard about, Mr Frank Harris. In a perfect world he'd have the lot for conspiracy by morning. Now was the moment to play the violin, if he had had one, and if he had had the remotest notion as to how.

'I'll see all three of 'em at once,' Lestrade beckoned to a constable. 'Send in Mr Bret Harte, Mr Samuel Clemens and —' he paused and sighed '— and Mr Frank Harris, God help me.'

He had Chesterton's interviews with them in front of him. It all seemed to fit. It could certainly be made to fit.

The Constable returned with one author and a handkerchief clasped to his nose.

'Mr Harris punched me on the nose, sir, and left, sir. He said we had interrupted him in the midst of pleasuring three Viennese ladies of distinction and that that was the action of the perfect varmint. Bang!'

'Only *three,* eh, Chesterton? Our Frank's slowing down in 'is old age.' He was secretly more than delighted not to have to lock horns with Harris. 'And who pray is this gentleman?'

'Bret Harte. Clemens is in the john,' growled this gentleman, turning a chair about and mounting it as one would a small horse. His white hair was parted down the middle, parted perhaps, it seemed to suggest, by a .45 'Peacemaker' percussion Colt. His moustache, if marketed, would have been described in the catalogue as 'The Wyatt Earp.'

'Mr B. Harte of 109, Lancaster Gate?'

'Yes.'

'A Menagerie à Trois unless I am mistaken. Could you go and bleed elsewhere, Chesterton?'

'You are mistaken, Inspector. *Mr* Van de Velde has passed on.'

'Another dead foreigner.' Lestrade made a note to check on that one. 'Your good lady and your children are in Hamerica?'

'They wouldn't like it here, Inspector.'

'Hi'd himagine not.' Lestrade found the whole arrangement rather too Continental for his taste. His eyes flicked down Harte's statement.

'You are the author of *A Night on the Divide? The Strange*

Experiences of Alkali Dick?'
'Yep.'
'An Hapostle of the Tules?'
'Yep.'
'The Luck of the Roaring Camp? The Outcast of Poker Flat?'
'Yep.'
Lestrade dropped the paper on the desk with a flicker of disgust. 'Oh dear, oh dear, oh dear. You were until recently Hamerican Consul in Glasgow?'
'Yep.' Harte shifted uneasily in the saddle. 'Until I was fired by Grover — Blast-his-Eyes — Cleveland.'
'The President of the United States, as was?'
'He read one of my stories and —' he cut his own throat with a finger — 'The bastard.'
'None too keen on dirty books then our Grover?'
Bret Harte rose in the stirrups and aimed a loaded finger straight at Lestrade's forehead.
'Hell and damnation, Inspector, these are rattling good yarns about Frontier life! How it was on the Sierras. The Great Outdoors! Clean as . . . Grover Cleveland began life as a Public Hangman! Did you know that?'
Lestrade fired from the hip.
'Meet a Gay Dog out there, did you?'
Harte fell back into the saddle.
'Who, Inspector?'
'Gay Dog, sir, a notorious Hape Atchy villain in 'is time.'
Harte seemed to rally. He could hear the Call of the Wilds.
'Hell, yes, we're blood brothers — we wrassled bah together many a time, Inspector.'
'Bah?' Lestrade was mystified. In this country, he thought, going three rounds with a sheep was a criminal offence. And rightly so, in his view.
'Bear, man, bear. We wrassled 'em from Mormon Gulch to Jackass Hill.' He leaned forward, 'And back, pilgrim.'
'You've wrassled bah with every bastard from Teddy Roosevelt to Wild Bill Hickock, to Sarah Bernhardt to Mrs Patrick Campbell, you lyin' son-of-a-bitch.'
Sam Clemens had entered, buttoning the fly of his disreputable white suit. He had white hair as well, and white

eyebrows and moustaches that broke like surf on the rocky foreshore of his face. The man was either as old as God, or had suffered a severe shock in the last twenty-four hours.

'You're a sham, Harte! You're shoddy. Your whole damn life is a dime novella with most of the pages missing!'

'You callin' me a liar, Clemens?' Harte was slowly dismounting.

Clemens ignored him and extended a lean, bony old hand to Lestrade.

'Sam Clemens, sir.'

'23 Tedworth Square, Chelsea,' replied Lestrade.

'The same.'

'He ain't Sam Clemens!' roared Bret Harte.

'Eh?' Lestrade made to pull at Clemen's false moustache.

'He's Mark dagnabbit Twain!'

'An alias, eh?' The moustache was real enough, what of the owner?

'He's also been, Inspector, one "Josh" of the *Territorial Enterprise*. A fairly clapped-out newspaper, I'd say, even by Virginia City's standards.'

The two old Westerners stared at each across Lestrade, breathing heavily. Lestrade felt he should say something.

'Mr Twain, sir, you are Sam Clemens?'

'Guilty on both counts,' smiled Sam/Mark.

'The author?'

Harte snorted.

'Best say "writer",' said Clemens, 'before Harte has an attack. Even, "journalist" which is what I became when I retired from prospectin' on the Comstock.'

'Prospectin'?' Lestrade heard another piece click into place 'Prospectin' for what precisely, sir?'

'Silver,' said Clemens. Click-click. Plunk-plunk, even, thought Lestrade.

''Ave you hever been to Furnitureville, Harizona?'

'Never bin that far south, Inspector. Bin to Hawaii. Bin to Australia.'

'Never met a Hindian named Gay Dog?'

'Nope.'

'Never hencountered the Vilebastard twins?'

Sam Clemens threw his head back with a hoot of laughter.

'That's one hell of a name, isn't it?'

'You know them, sir?'

'Nope.' Clemens was still shaking with mirth. 'Nope, can't say I do.'

Lestrade had the uneasy suspicion that his vein of good luck was running out.

'Thank you, sir.'

'My medicine man does though.'

'Who, sir? What? Knows the —?'

'Dr Jekyll,' smiled Sam, Mark or Josh.

Lestrade had great difficulty in hiding his emotions, even though he put his head in a desk-drawer. Chesterton returned, pale but interested.

Lestrade took a deep breath and emerged from his desk.

'Book 'em, Chesterton,' he pointed to Harte and Clemens. 'Haccessories to murder.' They were speechless.

'And bring in James 'Enry!'

8 A Strange View of the Shape of Things to Come

The one meal of the day that Mrs Hudson could handle with any degree of skill was the good solid English Breakfast, but then it is intended by nature to be filling and greasy. She loved to fry. She had fried eggs and bacon, tomatoes, mushrooms, potatoes, kidneys and great slabs of bread. All this, washed down with thick tea, she considered a fine start to any day.

Watson remarked, not for the first time, that he could not understand how the Frenchman could possibly get under way on buns and coffee. Lestrade, who had joined them for the feast, suggested that the coffee was invariably laced with some further stimulant, and added, with a wistful glance at the decanters on the sideboard, that this might help. Inwardly he bubbled with excitement, but for the moment he was keeping his coup at the Yard strictly to himself. W.G. who was not one for conversation at breakfast, merely mooted that it doubtless explained the Frenchies' appalling record at War and Plumbing, and returned to scanning the Sports Pages of Watson's *Sporting Chronicle*.

Watson was extremely excited. Not since Holmes' unfortunate demise had he felt like this. He ran his eye along the bound editions of the *Strand Magazine* that stood on 'his' shelf with *Gray's Anatomy* and his own treatise on the *Care and Breeding of Leeches*. None of the cases included there were any more fascinating than this one. How Holmes would have loved to have sunk his teeth into 'The Case of the Something Cricketer'! He would have to repair to *Roget* to find a single word that encompassed being laid low by an Apache arrow while bowling from the Pavilion End at Lords! 'Transfixed' wasn't it. 'Skewered' was something else entirely. He could perhaps approach the problem from another angle and call it 'A Study in White Flannel' or 'The Vilebastard Ritual'. Or even, and he sneaked a glance at the absorbed Grace, 'The Black-bearded League'!

His brain was saved from further exertion by Mrs Hudson's

knocking on the door and her announcement of the arrival of a Mr R.G. Ruggles. A.J. Raffles entered with a cheerful 'Good morning, one and all'. He was still dressed in top hat, white tie and tails and, propping an elegant cane against the sideboard, without further ado poured himself a healthy measure of 'Famous Grouse'. Watson knew all about A.J. Raffles. Raffles had once outwitted Sherlock Holmes, and for that reason Watson never mentioned him. Anyway he was no Moriarty. He was a gentleman and could therefore be forgiven much.

He raised his glass to Lestrade. 'Here's to Crime.' The Inspector raised his teacup in response. 'Lestrade', said Raffles, 'Do you know an Inspector Mackenzie also of the Yard?' He tossed his top hat onto the bust of Holmes that was on a table by the window. It pirouetted and sat at a rakish tilt.

'Ho, yes,' laughed Lestrade.

'Bane of my life,' said Raffles, and before the Inspector could reply that those were his own sentiments precisely Raffles had turned to W.G., whipped the *Sporting Chronicle* from his hands, screwed it into a ball and thrown it out of the window into Baker Street.

'What's up, Doc?' he enquired, beaming with pleasure at the Great Man's wrath.

'Great Powers, A.J.!' boomed W.G. 'Sometimes you go one too far. It'll be your downfall, mark my words.'

'They'll never catch me alive, said he,' said A.J. Raffles. 'When are we going to Australia again, my bearded bucko?'

'I am trying to relate to Dr Watson here —'

'Whom I have never had the pleasure of meeting,' interjected Raffles. Seizing Watson's limp hand he said, 'Hello, Doctor Watson, any friend of Sherlock Holmes is a friend of Sherlock Holmes. Did he ever find that Stradivarius he lost?'

It seemed an innocent enough enquiry, but it caused Watson's whole face to redden and twitch. He shook his head tautly, as if removing a wasp from his moustache with no hands.

'I am trying to relate to Dr Watson here,' W.G. continued, 'The extraordinary events that overtook us while in the hands of those Apaches insofar as they are relevant to the death of Castor Vilebastard.'

'Highly relevant,' said Raffles, pouring himself another

Scotch. 'It had to be old Gay Dog, didn't it? He was the only Apache we met who could despatch a quickish bowler in mid-run-up from seventy yards. On the whole, as we gathered at the time, your Red Indian is a pretty rotten shot. Except for the Chappie who hit you in the cod-piece, God.' Raffles roared with laughter and poked him in the parts with his cane.

'For heaven's sake, Raffles,' W.G. remonstrated, 'There are gentlemen present.'

'Sorry,' said Raffles. 'I'll be serious. Long night. Trifle light-headed.'

'I was telling them last night that you were the only member of our company who could communicate with the Apache. Particularly Mountain Cat Who Hates Tall Buildings, our old friend Charlie the Medicine Man —'

'Don't be confused by his title,' Raffles turned to Doctor Watson. 'He was more than your local GP. Much more. He could see into the future. He had the gift.'

'What could he see?' gasped an incredulous Watson.

Raffles strolled back to the sideboard, picked up a decanter and a glass and sat himself at the table with his back to the window. He tilted the chair back and elegantly placed his feet among the dirty crockery.

'Well, as far as I can gather, seeing into the future is a damned confusing business, particularly for a fellow who has a very limited view of the present. You get the images, but you don't know where you are or where they are. One of the first things he told me was that Gay Dog was one day to be portrayed in a Motion Picture by a Jeff Chandler. At the same time what on earth is a Motion Picture — what is a Jeff Chandler?'

'I knew an N.J. Chandler,' said W.G. 'Played for Somerset.'

'Charlie saw things flying in the sky full of people — but what or who or when — not a clue. Great earthquakes, cataclysms, wars, even the Martian Invasion, now I think back on it, but he couldn't put a date on them or any sort of geographical location. Bloody frustrating, really. I tried to squeeze the name of the next Derby winner out of him, but that was quite beyond him.'

' 'Ow *did* you communicate with the feller, sir?' asked Lestrade, finally getting a hand on the decanter.

'With a combination of sign language and good loud English, Inspector. That's all you need to communicate with any nationality under the sun. However primitive.' Something jogged in W.G.'s memory.

W.G. and Raffles and the wizened seer sat on the ground in the bright, hot sun enjoying a pipe. Suddenly the ancient Apache shuddered and moaned. His eyes shut tight.

'There goes something yet to come,' said Raffles.

Charlie's eyes opened again and he looked at the Doctor and winked.

'Paris,' he said and winked again.

'Paris,' said W.G. 'I've never been to Paris.'

'Of course you haven't. It hasn't happened yet,' explained Raffles. 'I told you. But it almost certainly will.'

'Paris,' repeated the ancient, and tapped the side of his nose and showed his few remaining teeth in a lascivious leer.

'What-about-Paris?' shouted W.G. slowly in English. 'Silly question,' said Raffles 'He doesn't know what Paris is.'

Charlie began to draw in the orange dust.

'What would that be when it's at home?' W.G. asked Raffles.

'It could be a large woman,' Raffles suggested.

'It looks more like the Oval with the field-placings for a bowler of my type. There are the gasometers.'

'It is almost certainly a large woman,' said Raffles, who knew about these things. 'With her leg in the air.'

W.G. looked closer.

'That's the Vauxhall Bridge.'

'That's her leg in the air.'

'There's the Pavilion.'

'No,' said Raffles. 'That is not the Pavilion.' He knew W.G. would be happier without the truth.

'Heaven help us,' said W.G., staring at the finished work, 'if that is the Shape of Things to Come.'

And Heaven would when they did, and shapely they would be.

The old Indian erased the picture with his stick, then closed his eyes again. He wasn't going to waste a pleasant afternoon in further explanations. Not with the visions he was getting.

Raffles and W.G. peered at him for some time in the hope

of other forecasts. He simply sat there, smiling and muttering. They only word they could make out, and he said it quite frequently, was 'Glue'.

'Glue?' said W.G.

'Glue,' repeated Raffles.

'Glue,' said the Medicine Man, and they could swear there was a stirring beneath his antique loin-cloth.

'Old Hawkspit,' said W.G., as Dr Watson wrote 'Glue' and 'Paris' in large block-capitals in his notebook and then drew rings around them and then stared blankly at them. 'Old Hawkspit rode off to get us some form of transport from El Paso.

'We never saw him again,' chuckled Raffles.

'Those Apaches were fascinated by our Cricket practice, which naturally God here insisted on.' said Raffles.

'They were a cheerful tribe and Gay Dog was a benevolent leader.' said W.G. 'It was a pleasure to live among them. That is, until the Vilebastards put up an ugly black.'

This is what Watson had waited what seemed days to hear. The nub. At last they had reached the nub.

'You were a terrifically good God, of course, W.G.,' Raffles patted him on the back on the way to the sideboard for another decanter. Once Lestrade had got his clutches on the previous one, he was not going to let go.

'Wasn't I, just?' beamed W.G. 'Did I tell you about my Living Image, Watson?'

'No,' said Watson glumly. He realised that the nub was going out of the window again.

'Well, the next morning, as I was saying,' the Doctor continued weightily, 'Charlie, the old medicine man, who was now in charge of worshipping me, led Gay Dog and me through a crack in the great wall of rock that surrounded the village into another circle of rock, somewhat smaller than the first. The rock, in fact, formed the figure "eight". Now in the middle of this second circle was a large stone pillar. A hundred and fifty or so feet high? Twenty feet round? The product obviously of some strange trick of the wind over a billion-odd years. This column of rock he sat us under in the shade. And there we sat. And waited. Unable to speak to each other, though Gay Dog would sometimes give me an encouraging nudge, there we sat. And waited. And then as the sun went down, the shadow of the column lengthened over the circle of ground and then began to creep up the wall of rock, and the little wizened old man began to point excitedly. And, lo and bloody behold, what did I see?'

'What did you see?' asked Watson, upon whom rhetoric was lost.

'What did I see? I saw the shadow of the pillar form a perfect silhouette of myself on the rock-face. I had one done on Brighton Pier one Sunday after playing against XXXIII Ear Nose and Throat Specialists of Worthing; so I know what I looked like sideways. Many don't, but I do. And there I was, and the Little Man and Gay Dog were prostrate again and praying happily.'

'Extraordinary, Doctor' said Lestrade. 'Whatever next?'

'Well, they wouldn't budge, so I picked them up and carried them back to the village, plonked them down on their faces again and told the lads to come and see what was going on next door. And they did and they were amazed as you, Inspector.'

'I gathered,' said Raffles 'that this monument was in their view the Centre of the Universe.'

'Their version of Piccadilly Circus,' said W.G.

'Canterbury Cathedral, pehaps,' said Raffles. 'Being a holy spot.'

'What was the Vilebastards' attitude to all this?' asked Watson, desperately.

'No idea,' said W.G. 'Any idea, A.J.?'

'Not a clue,' said Raffles.

9 The Battle of Large Rock

They had been living with the Apaches for about a week. W.G. had indeed become a splendid God. He had introduced the notion of being worshipped on Sundays only, (this was agreed as a lot less tiring), decent kneeling instead of prostration (so was this) and had taught them to sing most of 'To Be a Pilgrim' which had been one of his favourite hymns since childhood. One afternoon, leaving his team at practice with the braves of the village (cricket was now compulsory for all — as prescribed by the fourth of the New Ten Commandments which God was slowly coming up with) and passing Raffles and the Medicine Man deep into one of their discussions, shouting and gesticulating, W.G. wandered off into the Wildnerness.

'I want,' he had announced, 'to be alone.'

Grey Sea's wishes were their commands, though he had made certain that in his role as God he did not in anyway undermine the authority of their Chieftain, Gay Dog, or stamp on any of the mysterious ways of their Medicine Man. On the third day, Gay Dog had had some fingers broken by a sharply lifting ball from the Reverend Studholme, and while the Medicine Man had pranced about him howling remedial incantations and scattering the ground with dried buzzard entrails, W.G. had performed more orthodox surgery, making splints from a couple of bails. He now made it clear to Gay Dog that any resultant healing would owe as much to the dancing and the buzzard guts as his own modest efforts with the bails.

After strolling aimlessly for an hour he found himself sitting on a rock about a mile from the village admiring the scenery. He could have been on the surface of the Moon. Not that he ever would be, he thought (quite wrongly, as it happened), gazing upward into space.

Then the most extraordinary thing occurred. A voice, not his own, spoke to him inside his head. Naturally, this was not his first reading of the situation, and he imagined it was

101

someone behind him. He stood, rotated in a complete circle and could see no-one. He was quite alone. It then occurred to him that he had no idea what the voice had said.

'What?' he said, out loud.

'Return to village at once,' said the voice, quite obviously, he now realised, from the depths of his head.

'Who-are-you?' he articulated slowly and clearly.

'Shut up. Get move on,' said the voice rudely.

Better safe than sorry, he thought and set off at a trot towards the village.

As he neared the entrance of the pass he could see warriors blocking it with rocks and brushwood, while others climbed up its rocky walls seeking vantage points. Gay Dog was riding up and down, shouting orders. Dickens was secreting cricketers behind rocks and the womenfolk of the village stood in an anxious huddle in the middle of it all, their children clasped to them.

'What's going on?' W.G. called to Gay Dog, as he climbed over the barricade.

'Yellowlegs!' cried Gay Dog, which W.G. found strangely offensive. His flannels were certainly beginning to show signs of wear and tear, but that was a little strong.

Raffles appeared from behind a rock.

'Ah, good, you got the message,' he said.

'I heard a voice in my head, if that's what you mean. Bloody rude!'

'That was our old friend here,' said Raffles, pointing to the Medicine man who was beaming broadly. 'Another of his extraordinary gifts. Thought transference.'

'What's up then?' asked W.G. He would think about the thought transference after.

'The Cavalry is coming,' said Raffles.

'Oh good,' replied W.G. 'They'll know the way to the nearest railway station.'

'Not at all good, W.G.,' said Raffles. 'They have orders, apparently, to destroy the Apaches and this village.'

'When?'

'For heaven's sake, W.G. you know what he's like about dates.'

'He doesn't look very concerned himself.' The old fellow

was still beaming broadly, but had closed his eyes.

'He's probably elsewhere now,' said Raffles. 'He was very worried at the time.'

W.G. gave the ancient seer a prod.

'Piss off,' said a loud voice in his head. There was a distant bugle call.

'Are you saying,' Watson was unable to believe his ears, 'are you saying that this old savage could place thoughts in your head, in English, over the distance of one mile?'

'Yes,' chorussed Raffles and W.G.

'No trouble at all,' said W.G. 'He could handle longer distances than that, as we were later to discover. Dry work this story-telling.' Watson leapt to his feet and made for the sideboard.

'A glass of bottled ale will suffice,' said W.G. and Watson poured a bottle of bass into a silver tankard embossed with his old Regimental Crest.

'Are we?' asked Watson, as the froth settled 'any nearer to the Vilebastards — er — putting up of the — er — black?'

'This is it, doc,' said Raffles. 'All is about to be revealed.'

'New page,' said Watson, sitting down quickly and preparing his notebook for further excitement.

W.G. found himself behind the same rock as Castor Vile-bastard. This was as good a moment as any to settle a few outstanding matters.

'But for you, Vilebastard —' he began.

'Vilibart,' snapped Vilebastard.

'We would now,' continued Dr Grace, unabashed, 'be play-ing the Gentlemen of Virginia in Richmond, I think it was, wherever that is. We would most assuredly not be miles from anywhere in the middle of nowhere hiding behind a rock. Explain yourself.'

'Is it true, Doctor?'

'Is what true, Vilebastard?'

'Vilibart. Is it true that that little fellow with the hat with horns sticking out can telegraph thoughts mentally?'

It was absolutely typical of Vilebastard that he would change the subject like that.

'That has nothing to do with the appalling handling of our Team Transportation. If this had happened on the Australian Tour we would all now still be dancing a jamboree on top of Ayer's Rock.' True, of course, it's true, he was thinking.

'So is it *true,* Doctor?' said Vilebastard reading the previous thoughts.

'Yes,' shouted Grace, 'but that has nothing to do with the case. I demand answers. Why did you deliberately —?'

Vilebastard laid his hand on W.G.'s quivering shoulders.

'Excuse me, Doctor,' he murmured. 'Business.' And he was gone.

W.G. was about to pursue him and shake the truth out of him, when there was the most enormous explosion, blowing the barricade at the mouth of the pass to pieces.

A dust-covered Raffles appeared beside him, dropping a beaming Medicine Man.

'They've arrived,' said Raffles, 'as advertised.'

'Charlie, is certainly a remarkable little man,' said W.G., and would have begun to worry more about the Paris Glue, if another shell had not landed about ten yards away and he and Raffles had not been forced to hurry to another rock.

After ten minutes the shelling stopped. Apart from a few new holes in the ground and a wigwam that was burning merrily, as far as W.G. could see no harm had been done. He called a roll of his players and elicited that none was damaged. Gay Dog's lads were not in such good order. One brave had been killed and several injured at the barricade by the first shell, and the second had passed between a couple standing on a ledge above the pass, before exploding harmlessly in the middle of the village. The Chief rode up to W.G. and dismounted. He was clearly anxious about the cavalry's next move. He mimed a fierce charge and indicated that he was outnumbered and with the soldiers at the head of the pass, trapped.

Then he slid to his knees at Grace's feet and began to pray to him.

'Oh, God,' said W.G. attempting to shift the responsibility upstairs. He only had so many miracles in him and his trick with the box while eminently telling with an arrow would be stretched to its limits with a well aimed cannon-ball.

'What to do?' asked Raffles, rather unnecessarily in W.G.'s view.

'I could speak to them,' said W.G.

'I doubt that they would hear you,' replied Raffles.

Grey Sea's sudden flash of brilliance was inspired by the return of the Medicine Man to the land of the living. Charlie came out of his trance with a shrill cry and shook his head vigorously as if to clear it of another vision of beastliness to be. There was a thin veil of perspiration on his forehead. When his eyes opened they stared fixedly at W.G.

'Moon,' he said, and threw his buffalo-horned hat to the ground.

'One day,' said Raffles with a twinkle, 'the Moon is going to fall on your head.'

'And, it would seem, knock my cap off,' added W.G.

A bugle sounded from outside the pass. Gay Dog leapt to his feet and seized W.G. by the shoulders.

'Please, God,' he said. In English. 'Please, Grey Sea.'

'Right,' said W.G. and smiled reassuringly. He pointed at the Medicine Man. 'Charlie. Take a message.'

The officers and men of 'B' Company, Seventh Cavalry, were never to agree finally on what actually occurred at that moment. They were trotting forward in single line abreast, sabres at the ready, waiting for the call to charge into the pass. All eyes were on the Major and his bugler. They were a mixed bag of Irishmen, Scots, Germans, three Mexicans, a Dutchman and a Greek all gathered under the same flag. All experienced soldiers, all eager for the fray and all equally astounded when to a man they stopped, wheeled, turned tail and galloped away over the horizon.

At the Court Martial, several variations of the same extraordinary story were given, and pooh-poohed by the Prosecution.

'Are we seriously to believe, gentlemen,' he fixed his eye firmly on the General and the other senior officers who sat in judgement, 'that the voice of God was heard in Apache Valley? That an entire Company of Cavalry, trained men, conscious of their duty to the President and peoples of the

United States of America, that duty, as well you know, being to obliterate the constant threat of hostile savages from the North to the South from the East to the West of this Great Land? Are we to believe that they were dissuaded from that noble task by the Lord God in Heaven? Would He, capital "H",' he nodded towards the Clerk of the Court who was laboriously recording the proceedings, 'not rather have applauded our efforts? Would He not in His infinite wisdom, be the last person to scotch a potential wham-bang victory over the half-naked heathen? Does He say a word when you squash a cockroach in a cake?'

Trooper O'Toole was the next witness, the bugler, a sensitive soul from County Cork. He knew that God had spoken to him.

'How precisely, Trooper O'Toole, did God put His request? What were His exact words?'

'Well, sor,' Trooper O'Toole rotated his hat nervously in his hands, and wiped a wet palm on his dress trouser. 'The exact words and I would have written them down, sor, but for the lack of the ability, but they're still in my head, sor, and there they will remain there as clear as a bell and twice as loud were and here they are, sorrh, — "This is God speaking, hello," He said. In the head it was clear as a bell. "If you blighters," He said, sor, "do not," beggin' the Officers' pardon, his exact words — "Bugger off, great will be My wrath," he said, sor, and then He repeated; "I repeat, this is God." And He spelt it, I think, though I don't know. "And if you harm one hair on a head of your fellow creatures, the Apaches, I shall visit you with hailstones and coals of fire and chastise the arse off you".'

'That,' enquired the Prosecution, 'is what he said?'

'In those exact words, sor,' said Trooper O'Toole 'though he did add, sir, "Remember what happened to the Gyppos, shut up, Raffles. Message Ends. Yours sincerely, God".'

There was a heavy silence in Court.

'I never understood t'last bit, sor, and I may have made the odd error but I was riding like hell at the time, sir, pardon me for the use of the word "Hell", but that's the truth of it.'

'And you all heard this remarkable message from Above?'

'One or two did not, sor, but I don't tink that they're very receptive to the Voice of the Lord, or any sort of voices, sor!'

'So you blew retreat.'

'I did, sorrh. At His behest.'

As O'Toole scanned the row of officers presiding, he realised that not one believed a word he was saying. Ah well, he thought, all thoughts of promotion have vanished up the spout, but there's a very good chance of martyrdom, and if mother can get a letter off to the Pope, beatification. And he thought how pleased Granny would be.

'What a brilliant coup!' Watson applauded as if W.G.'s fifty were up.

'It was a long shot,' admitted W.G., 'but no more risky than putting on Newnes with his lob in the third over against XXXIII Apprentice Dentists of Ballarat. They didn't know what had hit them either.'

'Enter left the Vilebastards,' smiled Raffles.

Watson almost fell out of his chair at the news.

10   The Case of the Mutilated Medicine Man

The celebrations were short-lived. All the cricketers and Apaches and Dickens were jumping around and whooping and cheering. Only W.G. and Raffles and, of course, Charlie, knew why the cavalry had made a run for it, but run for it they had and Gay Dog and his tribe were delighted. Suddenly there was a single howl of such despair that W.G.'s first thought was that it must come from one of the squaws bemoaning the loss of her brave.

But it wasn't a bereaved squaw, it was a brave standing at the top of a slope of broken stone and pebble by a crack in the rock-wall. He had his hands over his eyes and he howled again.

W.G. was about to enquire what ailed him, when the Vilebastard Twins were pushed unceremoniously out of the crack by another brave, and a further shove sent them scrambling and tumbling down the escarpment pursued by an avalanche of gravel and small rocks. Both the braves were clearly distressed and gabbled away to Gay Dog whose face turned ashen. The Medicine Man spat furiously at the two Vilebastards.

W.G. gestured to Raffles to find out from Charlie what in Hades was going on. The old boy performed an angry and bizarre pantomine, which entailed frequent references to his seedy loin-cloth.

'It's not good, Doc,' said Raffles. 'It's a pretty awful show. The Vilebastards were discovered in a cave up there by those two braves who'd gone up to take cover.'

'We'd gone up there to take cover,' said Castor.

'It all seems quite above board so far,' said W.G., and he tried to look omniscient, as good Gods should. 'Gay Dog looks a bit upset.'

'Justifiably so,' said Raffles, 'that Cave is a sacred spot. Fact of the matter, old chap, the Vilebastards have pissed on his ancestors.'

'What?' W.G. was nonplussed. 'On their —er—tombs?'

'On their bones,' said Raffles.

'Obviously a misunderstanding,' said W.G.

'We were both extremely nervous,' said Pollux.

'The shelling,' said Castor.

'We thought it was a bear's lair or some such,' said Pollux.

'Good Lord, I'm God, I shall intercede on their behalf,' said W.G. 'Claim ignorance. Apologise.' He thrust his beard into Raffles' ear and lowered his voice. 'It could have been worse, eh?' And he whispered the unthinkable alternative to Raffles.

Raffles coughed nervously and pointed at the Medicine Man. He was squatting suggestively on the ground and making a noise like a wounded bison.

'Now that is going too far,' said W.G.

'Are we to understand,' enquired Watson, in the vague hope that he might, 'that Castor Vilebastard was shot by Gay Dog at Lord's for . . . for . . . for defiling his forbears?'

'Absolutely, old chap. There were other considerations, of course, but I think that was the main one. I mean they were going to spread the Vilebastards out in the sun and fry them up for the local buzzards there and then. It's fair to say that it was only your Divine Intervention that prevented that.'

'I promised Gay Dog that, in my position as God, as soon as we returned to England I would personally make certain that the Vilebastards were black-balled by the MCC. He seemed more than satisfied with that.'

'Quite frankly, W.G., I think your excellent mime suggested to Gay Dog a rather more painful exercise than you intended.'

Raffles gurgled with laughter. Inspector Lestrade rose slowly to his feet.

'Well, that's it then,' he announced. 'End of story. The jig is up. All that remains for me to do is slap the cuffs on G. Dog, Hesquire.'

W.G. and Raffles looked at each other helplessly.

'There is more,' said Raffles.

'No more for me, thank you, gentlemen, my file is bulging.' Lestrade made for the door. There he paused. 'Just one thing, Dr Grace, did you in your Wild Western Adventure meet a Mr Bret Harte?'

'No.'

'A Mr 'Enry James?'

110

'Met him once at Lords,' said Raffles. 'Yankee Chappie.'

'Never in America,' said W.G., 'I don't think so.'

'Well, I'll see myself out, Dr Watson, sir. Thank you for a most illuminating breakfast.'

As he left, Raffles was idly rifling a drawer in the sideboard. He found a napkin-ring with 'S.H.' engraved on it which he slipped into his pocket. It would make a suitable companion-piece to the famous fiddle.

Watson was terribly disappointed that the case was over. He had just been getting steam up. He flipped through his notes disconsolately. There was nothing here for *The Strand.* He looked at the bearded giant beside him. If, he thought, Dr Grace would give his permission and I could reveal all about the Tour of Shame then . . . . He looked at him again. Fat chance. And yet . . . and he whooped out loud with delight.

'I'm sorry, Dr Grace,' he said. 'I was imagining the sort of noise your friends the Apaches made.'

'That was very good,' applauded W.G.

'Excellent,' said Raffles.

'Well, I was just thinking,' said Watson, 'that all this,' and he waved his notes, 'will ultimately be revealed at Gay Dog's trial so would it be possible for me to have exclusive rights to the story now for publication in *The Strand*?'

Raffles took out his cigarette case and lit a cigarette. He carefully blew the smoke away from W.G.

'There won't be a trial,' he said.

'I don't understand,' said Watson. Blast, he'd said it again.

'Raffles is right,' said W.G. 'They'll never catch him, y'see. He's a sprightly devil. I should think he and his band are up in the Chilterns — and once they get on to the Moors I don't want you to think the story will never be told. We're not ashamed of our part in it. We just don't think it's over.'

'Come and have lunch at the Albany,' said Raffles. 'Bunny's out.'

'Thank God,' thought W.G. He was profoundly suspicious of men who smelt of anything but carbolic or honest sweat.

It was as W.G. and Raffles had suspected. When Lestrade arrived at the Earls Court Pavilion, the birds had flown.

'I told them you were coming to see them this morning,'

announced Buffalo Bill.

'Great,' said Lestrade.

'Taken their horses too,' said Cody, sadly. 'That means that tonight, the very night that our show is to be graced with the presence of King Thug of Belgravia no less,' he sighed deeply, 'the Wells Fargo Stage which I so daringly save from annihilation with my Rough Riders in the Finale will have to be attacked by elements of the Duke of Relwick's Mounted Foot. Shit, we'll say it's 1776 and pray for rain.'

'Did anyone see in which direction they rode?' asked Lestrade impatiently.

'No, Inspector, but follow me,' and he led Lestrade and his men out into the Warwick Road. Traffic was fortunately sparse as Buffalo Bill lay down and clapped an ear to the cobbles.

'Jesus, there's thousands of them,' said Buffalo Bill.

'That would be the District Railway sir, or possibly the Great Northern Piccadilly and Brompton. Both pass through Earls Court Station,' said Lestrade. Cody was already on his feet, crushing dry horse dung in his lean fingers and throwing it up into the wind.

'They went that-away!' he cried to Lestrade, who was pinching horse-matter out of his sidewhiskers — and pointed north to Kensington High Street. Lestrade despatched his mounted officers, truncheons drawn, in pursuit and followed in his police carriage. After a while the only sighting was a hansom cab travelling east towards Notting Hill. Lestrade drew up alongside.

'Have you seen any Indians, sir?' gasped Lestrade through the window.

'Millions of them,' replied K.S. Ranjitsinghi amiably.

Raffles had had a hamper of cold cuts, game pies and salads sent round to his rooms in the Albany from Fortnum and Mason's. They had also supplied some excellent champagne, and now, as they sat over coffee and Remy Martin, Watson felt the old excitement returning. W.G. and Raffles had promised 'more'. Perhaps this was not a simple case of revenge by a noble savage. Unwittingly he toyed with the Lestrade conspiracy theory. The Vilebastards had clearly been up to no good. The 'no good' up to which they had been might now be disclosed.

'See what you make of this, Watson,' said Dr Grace. 'It's a riddle that has long baffled Raffles here and myself. I had saved the Vilebastards' bacon. Not that they expressed any gratitude or indeed signs of relief. They just stood there, alone. The Apaches quite naturally didn't wish to go near them. And none of our own chaps was eager to socialise with them. So there they stood. Then I noticed Charlie.

'He was sitting with his eyes shut as he so often did. Occasionally emitting a gasp of alarm, sometimes a grunt of displeasure or a whistle of disbelief. He was off in the future somewhere, and he would be back soon, a little older but none the wiser.

'He returned suddenly, and sat there gasping for breath as though he had been underwater for some time. He looked up at Raffles and myself, and patted the ground beside him. We had learned how difficult it was to assess the full meaning of his gestures. Did he want us to sit down beside him? Was he drawing attention to the ground about him? Or the land in which he dwelt? Or was he thinking in terms of the entire Planet Earth that he was sitting on? Anyway we went for number one, and plonked ourselves down beside him.

'That was not what he meant. He pointed at the Vilebastards and again thumped the ground beside him. It was obvious from our expressions, I imagine, that we still weren't entirely with him. With a snort of frustration he picked up a stick, marched over to the Vilebastards and in the red earth drew a circle about them and looked at us meaningfully. We shook our heads again. So he drew another circle rather larger than the first, then another, then another.'

W.G. tailed off. For the first circle his finger had drawn a lower case 'o' in the air. For the second a capital. Now his arm was full-stretch and revolving like a propellor. He let it rotate eight or nine times then clapped his hand into his pocket as if to prevent any further movement. Then he stared out of the window as if the solution to the riddle lay in the well-tailored shadows of Savile Row. Henry Miller's great-uncle passed beneath them but they weren't to know that. He worked there as a lad.

'After about half-an-hour,' Raffles picked up the tale, 'he

was a good 400 yards away and still working hard at his ever-increasing circles like a man possessed.'

'Like a beaver,' interposed W.G., for no very good reason.

'Like a beaver possessed,' Raffles compromised.

'They never budged during all this, did they?' said W.G. 'The twins.'

'They seemed transfixed,' agreed Raffles.

'Perhaps they knew what he was talking about with his circles. We certainly didn't. We still don't. Any ideas, Watson?'

'None as yet,' said Watson, gamely. 'Then what?'

'Well,' said Raffles 'he stopped his circling. Tell the truth, his stick broke. And he began to rattle some bones and wail a good deal. Which he often did, admittedly.'

'He scattered some sort of powder too,' added W.G. 'I'd seen him do that before. It was a precautionary measure, we deduced, in case he felt Evil Spirits were adjacent.'

'Then,' said Raffles, 'and this part of the display I think he felt was the clincher, that — despite the fact that we had failed to latch on to date — would certainly make all plain. He picked up the branch of a tree and with the foliage began to erase the circles. Going round and round and round in the opposite direction.'

'I'll never forget that,' said W.G. 'Little feller with horns on his head running round and round and round — like a whirlwind! At his age. A tiny dust-storm.'

'Why?' asked Watson.

W.G. shook his head. 'No idea. No idea.'

Raffles stood up, 'My theory,' he said and looked doubtfully at W.G. who waved him on with a mumbled, 'no go on, it's a theory, A.J.'

'Well,' continued Raffles, 'my theory is that he was trying to demonstrate that the Vilebastards stood at the centre of the world in some way. That their future actions would at some time have world-wide repercussions.'

'In which case,' Watson was a little agitated, 'his *erasing* of the circles is somewhat alarming.' Since the Martian War the average Earthling was a little windy at the mention of words like 'repercussions.'

'Yes,' said Raffles. 'He could, could he not, have been foretelling the End of the World?'

114

'Agamemnon,' said W.G.

'Armageddon,' said Watson, helpfully. 'Well, we were precious close to it during the recent unpleasantness with our Martian visitors.'

'I don't think you can blame the Vilebastards for that,' said Raffles. 'They weren't in England at the time, as far as I know.'

'Where were they?' asked Watson.

'Rumour had it,' said W.G., 'that they were in South Africa.'

'South Africa? How —?' The plot is thickening like a pea-souper, thought Watson, and I can hardly see my nose in front of me.

'Gay Dog put them in a wigwam that night under guard, but they cut their way out and escaped. They took some of the horses and strangest of all, they took Charlie, the Medicine Man — we thought then — as a hostage. Gay Dog and his braves went off after them. So, of course, did Dickens in the finest traditions of the North-West Mounted. We bade them fond farewells. Gay Dog was particularly emotional, and spent some minutes on his knees in front of me. Then they were all gone.

'The team was alone. I led half the side on foot to find the stage and right it and Raffles took the rest off to recover the mules. This done, with myself in the driving-seat we set off in search of a railway-station. At one stage we were quite lost but put to rights by that Mister Theodore Roosevelt, after whom, of course, the bear is named.'

'Bear,' said Lestrade. Bears again. 'Did he wrestle this bear?'

'Not in my presence,' said W.G. 'He was hunting buffalo with friends.'

'Then one day,' W.G. took up the tale 'we were trotting along and a whole band of ruffians appeared from behind rocks, masked and pointing pistols. Naturally, I stopped. For a moment or two I thought that perhaps I would shortly be breathing my last. I think that was the general feeling.'

'I was none too optimistic, Doc,' Raffles nodded.

'Then one of the masked fellows whispered to another, and the whisper went the rounds and they were all pointing at me and I was firmly convinced that my end was nigh. Then the first fellow lowered his mask and said —

' "Stone the platypus, it's bloody W.G., goodonyermate,

saw yer at Sinney in '91!'' They were Australians!'

'The Sydney Ducks!' cried Raffles. 'They'd escaped from Tasmania, terrorised San Francisco and were heading East pursued by Vigilantes.'

'It's a small world, eh?' said W.G.

Watson could see further reminiscences blossoming. It was unbelievable. One minute they were within inches of the plot, and the next they were idly circling the prairies in the company of drunken Antipodean highwaymen.

'What' he implored 'of the Vilebastards?'

'Never saw either of them again until yesterday,' said W.G. 'Castor at the match. Pollux at your club. Nor I imagine did Gay Dog but he found one of them and he'll be looking for the other.'

'So should we!' cried Watson, rising, 'for he is at the heart of the matter, and we shan't be solving any riddles until we've wrung the truth out of Pollux Vilebastard.'

'He wasn't at the match yesterday.' Raffles was certain that had he been he would have run to his twin's side.

'But as Doctor Grace has mentioned, he was at the Diogenes last evening,' Watson said, 'with that Mr Hyde.'

'Hardly deep in mourning,' smiled Raffles.

'Dr Jekyll knows Pollux,' said W.G. 'It seems reasonable to believe that he might therefore know the whereabouts of both him and Mr Hyde.'

'Well, then,' Raffles jumped easily to his feet, 'let's go and ask him.'

This was voted the best idea yet and Watson set about finding Dr Jekyll's address in the Medical Register.

'Incidentally,' Watson looked up. 'Did you gather what happened to your Medicine Man?'

W.G. and Raffles looked at each other questioningly — W.G. nodded.

'Yes,' he said sadly. 'One last desperate cry for help. Raffles and I both heard it clear as a bell. It was some weeks later, we were in Canada, crossing for a second run on the County Ground at Calgary. It certainly stopped us dead in our tracks. Raffles, in fact, was run out. I wasn't. It must have been Charlie's last cry, for in the paper next day it said that the corpse of an Apache Medicine Man, badly beaten and mutilated had been found floating upside-down under the new Brooklyn Bridge.'

Watson found himself strangely moved.

'You're sure that that was . . . Charlie?'

'No doubt about it,' murmured Raffles. 'We both recognised the voice immediately, and the time given by the New York Police Department to the newspaper fitted perfectly.'

'I think he was calling out to his God. One final desperate plea,' W.G. sighed deeply and his beard rippled. 'And I was 3,000 miles away. Playing a game.'

'You made a bloody fine double century, Doc!' Raffles slapped him on the back.

'Yes, but my heart wasn't in it,' said the Great Man.

11 An Extraordinary Afternoon with Dr Jekyll

Dr Jekyll's house was the last in the square to enjoy single occupancy and clearly benefited therefrom. The rest of the fine old houses had fallen into some decay and been sub-divided into rooms and apartments for 'all sorts and conditions of men' as Mr Stevenson was to put it later, 'map-engravers, architects, shady lawyers and the agents of the obscure enter-prises.' Dr Watson would later wonder what Robert Louis had against map-engravers — he agreed about the rest — but he wasn't wondering about that now. Dr Watson knocked on Jekyll's front door. A well-dressed, elderly servant opened it.

W.G. was admiring the brass plate — Dr Henry JEKYLL MD DCL LLD FRS etc.'

'Good morning,' said Watson, 'Is Dr Jekyll at home?'

'Dr Jeekyll, sir,' corrected Poole, the well-dressed, elderly servant. 'He is to the best of my knowledge to be found in the old dissecting-room. He invariably is. Who shall I say — ?'

Dr Watson introduced himself and Dr Grace and Mr A.J. Raffles and they were ushered into a large, low-roofed, com-fortable hall, paved with flags, warmed by a bright, open fire, and furnished with costly cabinets of oak. Poole went off in search of his master. The two doctors thrust their behinds into the fireplace more from habit than necessity. Outside London boiled in a temperature well into the eighties. Raffles idly explored the 'costly cabinets'.

There was a rattle of footsteps and Dr Jekyll entered at the trot, hand extended.

'We met yesterday, of course, at Lord's,' he said. 'How good to see you, doctors.' He shook their hands warmly. 'And Mr Raffles, many's the time I have enjoyed your perfor-mances at the wicket.' Poole entered with coffee and dry biscuits on a tray.

'I imagine,' said Dr Jekyll, 'you have come about yesterday's extraordinary events.'

'Indeed,' said Dr Watson, 'for though we have solved the mystery of Castor Vilebastard's murder —'

Dr Jekyll's eyebrows rose raised questioningly.

W.G. responded quickly to their ascent. 'An Apache chief of my acquaintance struck him down,' he explained. He had been studying Dr Jekyll's eyebrows ever since his entry and had been idly wondering to himself whether or not they seemed a deal denser than on their meeting the previous day. Something else too. But what? Once again the doctor in him was out and running. Ah, yes.

'That rotten cold you had seems to have cleared up completely.'

'Completely,' replied Dr Jekyll.

All this seemed irrelevant to Watson who pressed on.

'We are now eager,' he pressed on, 'to contact his brother, Pollux.'

'There I am afraid I cannot help you,' replied Jekyll.

'I gained the impression yesterday,' said W.G., 'that you knew the twins.'

Jekyll opened a large silver cigarette box on the mantlepiece but Raffles had been there before him. There were no Whiffs in the humidor either.

'The Vilebastard twins approached me some months ago. They had heard somehow of my work and came here promising funds for its continuation.'

'May one enquire,' enquired Watson, 'What aspect of your work that might be?' His notebook was out again and more than ready.

'That I am afraid Dr Watson,' said Jekyll easily, 'I cannot divulge.'

'Not recta, anyway,' pronounced W.G. 'Schizo-thing, wasn't it?'

'Not schizophrenia, Dr Grace, though I am deeply involved in researches into that fascinating subject, which may I say that my friend Dr Lanyon, describes as "Scientific heresies". We shall see.'

'Not recta. Not schizophrenia,' mused Dr Watson. 'Do your researches take you below or above the waist?'

Jekyll laughed. 'I am afraid I can offer you no clues, Dr Watson. I am sworn to secrecy. It is part of my unwritten contract with the twins. Suffice to say that all will shortly be revealed.'

'Could you perhaps then furnish us with an address?' snapped Watson. He became quite tetchy when his pencil wasn't busy.

'There again I am afraid I must disappoint you. Funnily enough, I have no way of contacting them. They contact me when they deem it necessary, through an intermediary – an associate of mine.'

'Perhaps we might be allowed to speak with *him*,' pressed Watson.

Dr Jekyll went to a desk and from a drawer removed a white envelope which he gave to Watson.

'It would not be breaking my contract I fancy to issue this invitation to you.' Watson put it carefully into an inside pocket.

There was suddenly a violent banging on the door.

'Oh, my God,' whispered Poole, making for the door.

It was Lestrade.

'Dr 'Enry Jekyll?' he barked ignoring the others totally. 'Hinspector Lestrade. Scotland Yard. I understand that you would be cognisant of the whereabouts of one Mr Hedward 'Yde.'

W.G. had forgotten him. 'We'd like to know that too, Inspector.'

'Why?' Lestrade was in vigorous mood.

'He knows, if anyone does, where we can find Pollux Ville-bastard,' replied Watson.

'And vice-versa then,' cried Lestrade.

'Possibly,' said Watson.

'I'm bloody up to 'ere with bloody "possiblys," ' said Lestrade angrily, pointing at his wilting wing-collar. He sat down and fumed in a leather deep armchair. 'I am flummoxed on all fronts. Two different cases. Two different villains. One: our Mr Hedward 'Yde, who I am seeking in connection with the 'orrible murder of Sir Danvers Carew, MP. Two: our Mr G. Dog for the murder of C. Vilebastard. Both 'ave flown the coop.'

'And both are known,' said Watson, scribbling furiously, 'to Pollux.' 'Hinteresting that, eh?' Lestrade rose, marched over to Dr Jekyll and poked him in the waistcoat.

'Where is our Hedward, then?'

Dr Jekyll had turned a whiter shade of pale. He began to talk rapidly.

'I have no idea, Inspector. I have not seen him for some months. He is away. We argued. I'm sorry. Now I must ask you all to leave. Middle of an experiment.' He looked at his watch. 'It is bubbling away now.' He was backing away down the hall. Those eyebrows, thought W.G. have a life of their own.

'Poole will see you out,' cried Jekyll. 'Good day, gentle —' He was gone. They heard a door slam in the distance. Poole made to show them the door, but Lestrade placed his hand firmly on the butler's chest. He put a finger to his lips and listened.

Grotesque cries echoed through the house. Shrieks and groans of a horrifying nature. 'THE HOUND!!!' Watson was white as a sheet.

'What hound?' asked W.G., but answer came there none.

'Where is 'e?' demanded Lestrade.

'He set off towards the old dissecting-room, sir,' replied Poole nervously.

'Dissecting, is 'e?' Lestrade looked at the two doctors.

'Dissecting a gorilla, by the sound of it,' said Dr Grace.

'Without the benefit of anaesthetic,' added Dr Watson.

An anguished roar echoed from the distance.

'Follow me, gentlemen!' commanded Lestrade. 'And you, Poole,' and he lumbered off in the direction of the screams. They pursued him along corridors and down steep stone steps, two at a time until they fell upon him standing at a stout wooden door, studded with iron.

'Locked and bolted,' Lestrade rummaged about in the back of his trousers and finally produced an intricately carved truncheon, presented to him by his colleagues on completing twenty-five years of service, with which he beat a sharp tattoo on the door.

'Open up, Dr Jekyll, in the name of the Law!'

Silence reigned within. A tap dripped somewhere.

'Our friend the gorilla must 'ave got 'im,' Lestrade pronounced.

'The perils of vivisection,' muttered Watson, who would not harm a leech.

'Let me assure you, gentlemen,' said Poole 'Dr Jekyll has never performed experiments on live animals!'

''Ave you, friend Poole, another key?' asked Lestrade. Poole shook his head sadly.

'There is, sir, another door from the street behind the house!'

'Then let us take a butcher's,' said Lestrade. And off they set again at a rambling trot back towards the front door.

The rear entrance to the Jekyll residence was a wholly different proposition to the elegance of the front. A grim, windowless block it was, with a small door set into it, standing slightly ajar.

'I'll go in first,' announced Lestrade, clearly not savouring the notion.

'We'll be close behind you, Inspector,' Watson gestured with his walking-stick.

'Absolutely,' Raffles beamed happily as he revealed with a flourish that his silver-topped cane contained a vicious blade.

Somehow, W.G. who had said nothing, found himself at the head of the queue. He pushed the door open with a fore-finger and stode in.

'Woof! Woof!' he barked.

Instinct had suggested, and he relied heavily on it in every walk of his life and many a run, that the appearance of a large dog might give the gorilla more cause to pause than the appearance of several men in bowler-hats.

'Woof! Woof! Aaaaaarrgh!' he roared. Raffles stood beside him shaking with merriment.

'Bloody good, W.G.!' he laughed. 'Nary a sign of a gorilla! You've certainly seen it off!'

The laboratory was a shambles. Tables were overturned. Paper strewn everywhere. Racks of bottles and retorts lay broken on the floor. They crunched across broken glass to a single gas tap that burnt brightly. W.G. turned it off thought-fully. He was a tidy man and all this offended him.

A door creaked open behind them. W.G. began to bark again loudly; Raffles readied his sword-stick; Lestrade tight-ened his grip on his truncheon; Watson coughed anxiously and raised his stick.

A dishevelled Dr Jekyll reeled into the laboratory, dabbing

at his brow with a foul-looking cloth.

'My apologies, gentlemen,' he gasped, 'I was . . .'

'Cut short?' suggested Dr Watson

'Yes,' Dr Jekyll looked at him gratefully.

'When you've spent as many years as I on the Frontier,' nodded Watson, 'you know all there is to know about that sort of thing. Try *these*.' And he jotted down a prescription in his notebook, tore it out and pressed it into Dr Jekyll's trembling hand.

'The finest binder I know.' He smiled at W.G. professionally. 'Well, that would explain the mysterious noises we heard.'

'Rotten "do",' W.G. added a touch of his own bedside manner to the proceedings. Poole hovered, so Watson instructed him to put his master back into bed again and to have the prescription made up at once.

'Hold hard!' Lestrade raised a beefy hand. 'There are still one or two questions I would like to put to your patient.'

'Not now, Inspector,' said Watson. 'Let us return to Baker Street and pool our knowledge.' Poole led Jekyll away, cooing sympathy in strict tempo.

'It's all right for some,' Lestrade was peeved. 'I've got the Commissioner on my back.'

'I think,' said Watson, 'that we all realise now that there are greater issues at stake than the two murders you are currently investigating. Both of which, let it be said, you have solved, in that you know the perpetrators: Hyde and Gay Dog. We must look beyond these narrow horizons to find the Greater Truth. I mean no disrespect to my former colleague when I say that this mystery far transcends in its possible repercussions for, dare I say it, Mankind itself than any in which I engaged with Mr Sherlock Holmes.'

He looked round at their faces. He felt he could detect admiration. Sometimes he wished that *he* had a Boswell. Still he would put down the gist of his stirring address on the way to 221b. They followed him silently out through Jekyll's back door.

Only W.G. dawdled. He was catching some of Watson's investigative fervour. Questions were springing into his mind as he studied the wrecked laboratory. History kept repeating itself. This was the second laboratory he had seen in this condition since first encountering the Vilebastards. There was a question he wanted to put to Henry Jekyll and it went — 'Have you ever met, or better, *worked* with one Thomas Edison?'

As he closed the back door behind him, the others were a good hundred yards away and stepping out briskly. He was about to give chase when in a doorway across the street he caught a flash of scarlet.

He chuckled to himself. It must be.

'Dickens!' he hallooed, and so it was. The Lieutenant beckoned him over.

Then shook hands warmly, but swiftly skirted the other social niceties.

'Pollux was there last night. Hyde let him in through that door,' reported Dickens. 'I'm certain Hyde is still there. I'll swear it was him I saw about to leave when your gang came bursting round the corner. He nipped back in smartish.'

'We didn't see him,' said W.G. 'What of Pollux then?'

'He may have left through the front door. I can't watch both.'

'Borrow a man from Lestrade,' suggested W.G.

'I'm not meant to be here,' replied Dickens. 'I'm unofficial.'

'Isn't the uniform something of a give-away?' asked W.G. Dickens was in full-dress.

'The major problem,' Dickens looked about him anxiously, 'is the dogsleigh.'

'Mum's the word,' W.G. glanced up the street. No sign of the others. 'Watson may know of someone to watch the front. Stay here. We'll be in touch. By the way that laboratory's a dog's breakfast too.'

'All broken up?' enquired Dickens. 'I heard a lot of noise.'

'Just like —' W.G. started.

'We can't go on meeting like this,' smiled Dickens.

When W.G. finally got back to 221b Baker Street he found Watson, Raffles and Lestrade penning an enormous chart, headed in red ink 'EVENTS TO DATE'. W.G. took Watson aside and explained Dickens' predicament. Without hesitation, Watson suggested that he send boys of his acquaintance and Holmes' — the so-called Baker Street Irregulars — at once to

125

Jekyll's, to contact Dickens and keep an eye on the front door.

'Not a word of Dickens to Lestrade,' whispered W.G.

W.G. joined the other two at the chart. It seemed to consist mainly of question-marks. Single ones, of varying sizes, pairs of them here and there, and beside the words 'Thought-transference' three of them and an exclamation mark.

'*Two* wrecked laboratories,' corrected W.G., pointing to one of Lestrade's contributions in green ink which read: 'One wrecked laboratory' followed by a single question-mark.

'*Two*!!' Lestrade instantly amended this in red ink, and added another question-mark.

'Henry James!' shouted W.G. 'Of course!'

'There he blows,' Lestrade circled James's name which appeared under 'Arrested Americans' — not a happy description. He had explained to Watson about his arrests of Harte, Twain and James. Watson had approved wholeheartedly.

'I thought the name rang a bell,' W.G. banged his forehead with his palm as if to scare up further information. 'Henry James, unwittingly or no, financed the wrecking of the other laboratory.' And he sat down heavily in Holmes' old chair and closed his eyes.

Watson and Lestrade had learnt not to hurry the giant, but to bide their time.

After about five or so minutes, W.G.'s eyes opened. He blinked, clearly he had not expected to be where he was. Where, Watson, wondered, had he been?

'New York,' said W.G. He was getting more like Charlie by the minute.

'I told you that I had not clapped eyes on either Vilebastard since they had escaped from Gay Dog's encampment. Nevertheless I still fell foul of them in New York. They were there when we were, at the end of the Tour. They were trying to get me out of the way. Among other things.'

Lestrade turned to the Chart and wrote in block capitals OTHER THINGS. Here we go again, he thought.

12 Alarums at the Great Manhattan Gargantua Hotel

W.G. lay flat on his back in room 2502 of the Great Manhattan Gargantua Hotel, staring at the ceiling and thinking very slowly what an exhausting place New York was. Sore feet and vertigo, he thought, that's New York in my book. Outside the window it was growing dark. He rose painfully and limped across the room. Twelve floors below the gas lamps had been lit and to judge by the lights, the traffic seemed thick as ever. On the other side of the Avenue lay the vast black patch that was Central Park. They were lucky to have that, thought W.G. The odd lamp would glimmer in the darkness then vanish as its owner was either set upon by thieves or walked into one of the many lakes or ponds. Oh, to be in England, and soon they would be.

There was a single rap on the door. Probably one of the lads. 'Coming,' he called and hobbled over to the door. 'Raffles?' he guessed. But it wasn't Raffles at all. Standing outside was a man as large as himself in a white floor-length waterproof and a chocolate bowler hat. He sported a moustache that would have won plaudits in Walrus circles.

'Dr Grace?' the walrus rumbled. There was no sign of a mouth.

'The same,' said Dr Grace, graciously. The man was clearly a Yankee.

The stranger elbowed his way past him into the room peered anxiously out of the window, lowered the blind quickly and returning to the door, closed it and shot the bolt.

W.G. looked at him enquiringly. 'What?' he said, and 'Who?'

The large man tapped the side of his nose, and the moustache lifted at both ends in a smile — still no mouth.

'My card,' he said. (There must be a mouth, thought the Doctor, everybody has a mouth. Of sorts.)

'Where?' said W.G. as there was no evidence of it.

The large man removed his bowler and from it produced a printed card. 'Pinkerton', it said 'Detective Agency. Confidentiality a Premium.'

'Good Heavens,' said W.G. reading the card and hanging the hat politely on the hook behind the door.

Pinkerton snatched the card back, '*My* card,' he snarled.

Pinkerton groped about in his waterproof and produced a large pistol. He tapped the side of his nose again, this time with the barrel of his gun. With quite extraordinary agility for such a bulky detective he flew into the bathroom and out again, in and out the length of a hanging cupboard, and then vanishing briefly under the bed, reappeared at the other side and was on his feet again in one lithe movement.

'We are alone, Dr Grace,' he said.

'*I'm* not,' said W.G., rather tetchily. 'I *was*'. Perhaps, he thought, I should bang him on the nose. He felt this was the sort of language that Pinkerton would understand.

'Does the name Thomas Edison mean anything to you?' snapped Pinkerton.

'Short man with a goatee and a wooden leg,' replied W.G. briskly. 'Slow left arm, played for the Gentlemen of Brighton.'

Pinkerton rammed his pistol into the depths of the Doctor's beard.

'Or was it Hove?' W.G. continued pensively.

'Don't play games with me, Grace,' he snarled.

'Very well,' said the Doctor and banged him very hard on the nose. Pinkerton dropped his pistol and clapped both hands to his face.

'Jeeeesus!' he cried. 'Kee-rist!' he shouted.

Dr Grace kicked the pistol under the bed, and proffered Pinkerton a pillow to staunch the flow of blood.

'You ought to lie down really.' The medical man was out and about again and as some token gesture to the Hippocratic Oath he kicked Pinkerton's legs from under him. The bulky detective sat heavily on the floor.

'Something cold,' murmured the Doctor, his eyes flicking about his room, 'down the back of your neck.' He had ordered tea earlier and the tray was still on the dressing-table. Thoughtfully he poured the remaining contents of the silver tea-pot on Pinkerton's head. It was almost full, as they made undrinkable tea in the Doctor's view. He also poured what was left of his first cup. What on earth could old Tommy

Edison have done in or around distant Brighton (or was it Hove?) to cause an American detective to behave thus twelve storeys up in a highly respectable New York Hotel?

'Tommy Edison, I admit,' admitted W.G. to the groaning Pinkerton, 'was always known to be a bit of a lad. Particularly in his cups.' And he chuckled at a fleeting memory. Could it be the business of the policeman's helmet after the Gloucestershire/Sussex match? He bent over the recumbent detective.

'No, old man, you're up a blind alley there. He gave the blue-bottle his helmet back. Admittedly not until after he'd pissed in it, but that's ancient history now. Water under the bridge, so to speak. Your nose has stopped bleeding.' He helped Pinkerton to his feet. 'No hard feelings I trust?' he enquired, picking tea-leaves out of the drooping, bloodied moustache. Pinkerton shook his head and allowed himself to be sat down in the room's only armchair. W.G. went and fetched him a glass of water from a jug in the bathroom.

'Nog thag fuggig Togad Eddigug,' said the detective. 'Anugger fuggig Togad Eddigug.'

'Aha!' said W.G. Now all was made clear. No, it wasn't. 'I don't know any other Tommy Edison,' he said.

Pinkerton began to scramble painfully to his feet. He honked blood into the pillow-case, and inhaled deeply. 'There's something goddam odd going on here!' he snorted, shaking a finger under W.G.'s nose, and working his thumb like the hammer of a revolver. 'And I don't like it, dammit, I don't like it one little bit.' And then he looked hard at his finger and then his thumb, shook his head with disbelief, and dived once more under the bed in search of his weapon. He would have reached it too had W.G., no slouch when swift action was required, not stood firmly on Pinkerton's leg. W.G. pulled the sash beside his bed. A distant bell rang. There was an almost immediate knock on the door.

'Fetch me the Hotel Detective!' boomed W.G.

'Tell him to bring two pints of bourbon!' boomed Pinkerton from below. Footsteps ran off down the corridor.

'You're clearly deranged,' pronounced the Doctor, 'and in the wrong room.' He pulled out the other leg and tied the pair together with the sash. The bell began to jangle furiously.

'Keep still!' he ordered. The bell stopped. With furrowed brow he hobbled on his blistered feet to the other side of the bed and retrieved the pistol. Best to empty it, he thought. And seeing the detective's brown bowler swinging on the hook behind the door he fired the pistol at it. The first shot produced a startled cry from Pinkerton under the bed, clearly convinced his end was nigh. The bell began to toll furiously. The second elicited a female shriek from the corridor and the crash of broken glass. The third a bass-profundo shout of 'What the hell!' from further down the corridor. The fourth more screams from without and the slamming of doors. The fifth and sixth shot were met with a total silence from all quarters that lasted a good three-minutes until a red face appeared at the fan-light above the door. W.G. waved three fingers at it through the crown of the brown bowler.

'Three out of six,' he beamed. 'Not bad, eh?'

'What the hell!' said the red face. 'What the hell!'

W.G. was looking for traces of the missing trio. He opened the door, knocking a chair from under the red-faced man who hung desperately from the door-frame. A maid lay full-length on the carpet, two shattered bottles of bourbon at her feet. A number of white faces stared at him from the entrance to other rooms and vanished quickly. He heard bolts working. He put the chair back under the red-faced man, and knelt beside the maid.

A rough examination revealed that he hadn't winged her. Having opened her uniform he pressed an ear to her chest and listened. 'You swooned,' he said gently. 'Pity you dropped these bottles. A little drop would be just what the doctor ordered.'

'It was,' she said. 'You are Room 1225?'

'I am.'

'What the hell,' said the red-faced man. 'I am the House Detective, Flanagan.'

'Doctor Grace,' the doctor introduced himself, shaking Flanagan's fat hand. 'There is an armed madman in my room. Could he be moved?'

Flanagan looked extremely puzzled but slipped the fat hand into his coat and came out with a revolver very similar to Pinkerton's. The entire population of America from East to West thought W.G. is armed to the teeth.

'Follow me,' said Flanagan. They all entered Room 1225. Pinkerton had pulled the sash from the wall, and was sitting by the bed undoing the knot.

'There's your madman,' said W.G. 'Came at me with that,' he added and pointed to the empty pistol he had put on the tray with the tea-things.

'I don't believe it,' said Flanagan. 'Hell!' He put his pistol away and ferreting about in his jacket pulled out this time a large clasp-knife. He knelt at Pinkerton's feet and began to cut through the sash, apologising profusely as he did so.

'Mr Pinkerton. Mr Pinkerton. This is awful. Hell. I'm sorry. *We're* sorry.'

'*We're* not,' said W.G. 'What are you doing?'

'Please, let me help you up, Mr Pinkerton.' Flanagan was all over him like an alcohol rub. Pinkerton was standing now and Flanagan was brushing him down and sighting disapproval.

'Get some bourbon,' he ordered the maid.

'A pitcher of ale for me, please,' asked W.G. She smiled at him. No-one had ever said 'Please' to her before. She liked this large English doctor. She could still feel his beard upon her chest.

'Go on. Git!' shouted Flanagan mildly. She fled down the corridor.

'Look here,' said W.G.

'You,' said Flannagan, 'look'ee *here.* This here is Mr Pinkerton, the most famous detective in the world. More famous than your Sherlock Holmes.'

'Never heard of either of 'em,' said W.G. shaking his head.

Flanagan thrust his face into W.G.'s. He had breath like a septic tank.

'Who solved the Riddle of the Sands Hotel? Who cracked the Case of the Seven Strangled Dwarves? Who was summoned to the Little Big Horn to investigate into the death of General Custer?'

W.G. imagined a valley covered in the chalked outlines of the entire Seventh Cavalry.

'No idea,' he guessed.

'Him, that's who, and look what you done to him?' The aggrieved Flanagan pointed at Pinkerton, the Great Detective, bloody and tea-stained, hang-dog and shaking. Pinkerton was waving the tail of his rain-coat at W.G. There are two bullet-holes in it.

'Ah!' exclaimed W.G., peering about, 'Now. Where did the other feller go? Aha!'

There was a large hole in the ceiling. 'All accounted for. Shotgun's more my meat. Never shot one of these things. Damned inaccurate.'

The two detectives were whispering together. Flanagan appeared shocked to the core. Putting away his knife, he once again produced the revolver.

'Put your hands on your head, Doctor Grace, and do not move a muscle.'

The Doctor did so. Flanagan was too far away to be banged on the nose, and he obviously was not coming any closer. Doubtless, Pinkerton had warned him.

'Blackmail,' growled Flanagan, 'is an ugly word.'

'Blackpool,' replied Doctor Grace, 'is an ugly place.'

'Black*mail*,' hissed Pinkerton who, having retrieved his pistol from the tray, was loading it with bullets from a waist-coat pocket. 'I don't know just what your game is, Doctor, but, as I said before, I don't like it.'

From one of his voluminous raincoat pockets he pulled a tattered cracked leather loin-cloth that W.G. remembered well.

'Do you recognise this garment?'

'Oh, yes,' replied W.G.

'Murder One,' stated Pinkerton, and threw it on the bed.

From another pocket he produced a battered straw boater, which he handed to W.G.

'What about that?'

W.G. looked inside it.

'Herbert Johnson of Piccadilly,' he read, and then saw the initials embossed in gold 'A.J.R.'. There was a knock on the door.

'Who's there,' called W.G.

'Raffles,' answered Raffles.

'A.J. Raffles? asked Doctor Grace, still bemused.

'Of course it is, you daft old bugger. Let me in.'

'Very well,' said W.G. Flanagan forestalled him with a fat

palm in his chest, and made for the door himself. He wrenched it open and hoiked Raffles in by the tie. Raffles was remarkably civil in the circumstances and did not resist.

'I say, old chap!' was as far as he went, and then when he saw the pistols, 'So these are the buggers!'

'What buggers, A.J.?' W.G. was puzzled.

'I've been robbed, W.G.' said Raffles.

'These are not robbers, Raffles, these are detectives.'

'Not a great deal of difference is there, W.G.?'

'Not a lot,' laughed W.G.

'I see you've given that one a bloody nose.'

W.G. nodded, then seeing that Raffles was contemplating Flanagan's nose with considerable malice aforethought, quickly drew Raffles' attention to the sorry loin-cloth on the bed.

'Poor old Charlie,' said Raffles. 'You know who did this, don't you?' He waved the loin-cloth at Pinkerton, a visiting card fell from it.

'Sure,' said Pinkerton, picking the card off the floor and passing it to Raffles. 'He did.'

'Whose is that?' cried W.G. 'Bloody Vilebastard Brothers Limited?'

Raffles handed it to W.G.

'It's yours.'

'And this hat,'Pinkerton gave Raffles the boater, 'Is *yours.*'

'Got 'em!' said Flanagan, and slapped Pinkerton heartily on the back.

'Slap the cuffs on 'em, Flanagan,' growled Pinkerton.

W.G. drew himself to his full height. It was a fearsome sight to behold. Flanagan and Pinkerton seemed to shrink, as W.G.'s great frame slowly filled the room.

'May one enquire as to what charges you can possibly be pressing against two guests of your country?'

'Right,' said Pinkerton, as Flanagan handcuffed W.G.'s right wrist to Raffles' left. 'Try these for appetisers. Murder. Theft. Blackmail. Transvestism.'

'What on earth?' Raffles rose two feet as W.G. threw up his arms in total bewilderment.

'Dressing up as a woman, W.G.' he explained gently, as he descended.

'Dressing up as —'

'Assault. Battery.' Pinkerton droned on, 'and the unwonted destruction of a place of work, to wit, a scientific laboratory.'

'Who is bringing these charges?' asked Raffles. He felt he should take the lead as he was on ground more familiar to him than to W.G.

'Dressing up as —' W.G. was spouting like a whale, and quite useless.

'Mr Thomas Edison, who, as you know Doctor Grace, has a laboratory in Menlo Park, New Jersey. He is known as the Wizard of Menlo Park.' In W.G.'s book Thomas Edison had a semi-detached in Hove and was known as the One-Legged Wonder of Inkerman Terrace. He forebore to mention this. 'He is bringing all charges except the murder rap. That is a matter for the New York Police Department, who have already issued warrants for your arrest. I am therefore taking you to the 82nd Precinct where you will be formally —'

'This would be the murder of the previous occupant of this?' Raffles pointed with his free hand to the loin-cloth.

'The killing of an Apache may not be a crime out West where you've been, but it sure as Hell is in the middle of New York City!'

'Righty ho,' said Raffles cheerfully. 'Simply trying to clear the air. Now the other rather more bizarre charges, could you spare us a few more details before throwing us on the mercy of the local Peelers?'

Flanagan was obviously eager to have this pair of murdering perverts off the premises but W.G., still spluttering 'Women?' and the like, had somehow filled the door and even when prodded vigorously with a revolver, was not to be moved.

Pinkerton pulled out a notebook.

'Earlier this evening Thomas Edison was working in his laboratory when a woman, or what appeared to be a woman,' and here he eyed Raffles, 'of your size and description and wearing this straw hat burst in upon him, tore off a good deal of clothing, seized hold of Mr Edison and began to shout blue murder.'

'Were those her precise words?' asked Raffles, 'Blue murder?'

'No,' said Pinkerton.

'Just checking,' smiled Raffles.

'And began to shout,' corrected Pinkerton. 'In a French accent.'

'Oh. Oh. Ze Murdeur Bleu! Mon dieu! Comme ci, comme ca, Monsieur Pinkertong?' Raffles was a splendid mimic.

'Exactly comme ca,' rapped Pinkerton, and Raffles immediately regretted his frivolity. 'At which a large, black-bearded man in a small red-and-yellow striped cap entered with a camera, and took a picture of the scene, viz, Mr Edison struggling with a half-naked woman in his laboratory. The black-bearded accomplice then emerged from under the hood and said —' Pinkerton glanced down at his book, 'In an *English* accent — "So Mr Edison, you are now in our power" and waved the plate at him.'

'Gripping stuff,' said Raffles.

Pinkerton pointedly ignored him and continued.

'Mr Edison immediately made it clear to the blackmailing duo that they were astride a bum steer. Do you know what you get for rape and blue murder in New Jersey?'

'What *do* you get for rape and blue murder in New Jersey?' Raffles' hours at the Music Hall had not been wasted.

'The Keys of the City and a Big Parade.'

Flanagan bellowed with laughter.

'That's a joke,' explained Pinkerton, 'but it ain't so very far from the truth. The black-bearded man then threw the camera the length of a work-bench causing a great deal of damage. He told Mr Edison that unless he, Mr Edison, did precisely as they would instruct him, they would destroy the rest of his laboratory. Mr Edison replied that they could do what they liked, as he is leaving next week for Fort Myers in Florida to invent the electric light bulb. The "woman" and the black-bearded man then began systematically to break up the laboratory and its contents. When they had finished, seeing that this action had had no effect whatsoever on Mr Edison they walked out, leaving behind this straw hat. Mr Edison then telephoned me, as the New Jersey Police there are considerably more expensive, and it took me very little time to trace you two. Manhattan South have had you under surveillance since you arrived from Canada.'

137

'Me too,' said Flanagan proudly.

'What makes you deduce that the woman was a man?'

'Because this is *your* hat, Sonny Jim!' and Pinkerton placed it hard on Raffles' head. 'I was about to report its disappearance,' cried Raffles. 'Of course you were,' smiled Pinkerton.

'Didn't I say I had been robbed?'

There was a tentative knock at the door. Flanagan so startled the poor maid when he threw the door open, raised his revolver and shouted 'Freeze!' that for the second time she dropped her tray. The pitcher of ale, alas, went everywhere. The bottle of bourbon was saved, and Flanagan spared no time in pouring out drinks for himself and Pinkerton.

The maid scrabbled on the floor retrieving the pitcher, tankards and the tray, and apologising profusely.

'I'll get more beer,' she stammered.

'Just git!' said Flanagan rudely.

'That would be very kind,' said W.G. gently, 'but I think we are leaving in a moment.'

'Scram!' shouted Pinkerton.

'Thank you very much, anyway,' said W.G. She had never met a man like him in all her life. She returned his smile and scuttled away.

Pinkerton and Flanagan refilled their glasses.

'Would it not be a sound idea,' suggested W.G., a little happier now he had discovered that it was not he, but Raffles, who stood accused of dressing up as a woman, 'if we all went and saw Mr Edison?'

'Capital idea, W.G.!' said Raffles. 'He can see for himself that it wasn't us and clear up the whole damned business.'

The liberal use of bourbon seemed to have mollified Pinkerton somewhat and for the first time he seemed ready to compromise. Admittedly, it would cement his case were Edison to identify these two positively.

'OK' he said, using the modern spelling. 'Flanagan, get a cab.'

'Where to?' asked the dim Flanagan.

'Menlo Park, dummy,' hissed Pinkerton.

Raffles smiled and nudged W.G.

'We're off to see the Wizard,' he sang, but to a tune of his own.

It was a long and dreary drive to Menlo Park. It was hot and humid in the carriage, and both Pinkerton and Flanagan smoked beastly cheap cigars. Flanagan also spat a lot. They refused to open a window on the grounds of security, despite the fact that W.G. and Raffles were still handcuffed together, which added to their discomfiture. The Edison house seemed pleasant enough, but little did they see of it as they were bustled down a path at the side of it, across a sizeable garden and into a large shed with high windows many of which were broken.

The laboratory was in a dreadful state. Amidst the chaos stood a chunky figure in a stained cream suit with white hair chopped roughly to a forelock that sat on a large forehead. He recognised Pinkerton at once, but to W.G.'s intense relief, none of the rest of them. Flanagan was introduced, and with a whispered word of caution from Pinkerton, Edison walked twice around the two Englishmen.

'No, sir,' he announced firmly, 'these are not they. I told you, Pinkerton, that the woman was a shorter man.'

He suddenly kicked Raffles beneath the knee. Raffles yelped.

'With a wooden leg,' continued Edison. 'And that the beard —'

He tugged W.G.'s beard vigorously. W.G. hooted.

'Was false,' Edison apologised profusely to the two of them, and demanded that Pinkerton do likewise and also unlock the handcuffs. Edison was still fondling W.G.'s beard. Quickly and efficiently he plucked out four of five long hairs with a murmured, 'May I?'

'Feel free,' said W.G. Why not? He was extremely grateful to this Thomas Edison for clearing up the whole rotten business.

'I am having,' said Edison, testing the hairs as he might the strength of a piece of rope, 'a lot of trouble with the filament.'

Righting a bench and a couple of stools he invited them all to sit, and going to a cupboard hanging drunkenly from the wall, produced a bottle of clear liquid which he poured into an assortment of cups and beakers, the only ones he could find that were unbroken.

'It's all right,' he laughed, as Pinkerton sniffed suspiciously at his drink. 'It's gin.'

Pinkerton was disconsolate. Particularly when his hopes of salvaging the murder rap were dashed by the news that at the time of Charlie's demise the cricketers were cricketing in the middle of Canada.

'Damn it all to Hell,' he moaned. 'Back to Square One, and not a goddam thing to show for it.'

'I think,' said W.G., 'you need look no further than the Vilebastard twins.'

'I'll find 'em,' said Pinkerton.

'One thing,' said Raffles. 'If, as you say, the woman was shorter than the false-beard gentleman then it may well have been a woman.'

'I may have been too persuasive in my suggestion that we were looking for an English*man*,' Pinkerton admitted.

'Then it was a *French woman,*' said Edison. 'An actress, I'd say.'

'With a wooden leg,' added Pinkerton. 'A French actress with a wooden leg should not be hard to find.'

'The parts would,' laughed Raffles. 'There cannot be many roles for such a thespian.'

'Castor will have played me,' mumbled W.G. 'He did that rude impersonation of me on the train using that woman's dog as a beard.'

'I remember,' said Raffles. 'Pollux will have been outside keeping a look-out.' He glanced at Pinkerton. 'He smokes pink cigarettes.'

Pinkerton went to the door. Outside were the butts of four pink cigarettes, which he placed carefully in an envelope.

'Thanks,' he said, and the walrus stretched luxuriously into its first smile.

'You will find,' said W.G. 'That they are also responsible for the murder of the Medicine Man.' Good Lord! Dickens was at the window. W.G. was about to ask him in, but Dickens put a finger to his lips.

'And,' Raffles continued, 'further for trying to hoist the whole damn thing on us. Why?'

'Because we know too much?' suggested W.G. Dickens nodded.

'What *do* you know, sir?' Pinkerton leaned forward eagerly.

'Very little,' said W.G. Dickens waved 'goodbye' and was gone.

'Very little that makes any sort of sense.' Raffles then suggested that W.G. should give Pinkerton a résumé of their adventures in America to date, which, over further gins, he did.

Some two hours later, as he concluded, there was a knock at the door and an ancient maid entered, wrapped in a blanket and clasping her right ear.

'That damn telephone thing of yours went off!' she screeched. 'And it asked for a Mr Pinky, and I told it to shut its mouth, Mr Thomas, but it said it was a matter of life and death, so there.'

'Perhaps,' Edison smiled, 'you could show Mr Pinkerton here the whereabouts of the telephone.'

'One day,' she promised, 'I'll kill it, afore it kills me.'

She led Pinkerton away, and as Flanagan was asleep, Edison and the two Englishmen took their gins into the garden.

'What do you think, Mr Edison, that the Vilebastards were after?' enquired Raffles.

'No idea,' said the scientist, 'they never got that far'.

'They can read minds, y'know,' said W.G.

'Can they, by Jiminy?' cried Edison. 'Yes, yes, I think you're right. I was thinking of braining the woman with a pestle and mortar, and Black-beard said "Don't!" ' He shook his head in wonder. 'What did they want? They went to extraordinary lengths to obtain it.'

'Something perhaps in the electrical line?' mooted W.G.

'Possibly,' replied Edison. 'We are entering, gentlemen, the Age of Electricity, and the World will never be the same again. Until now the Human Race has been sustained by wood and coal and gas. Natural substances given to us by God. Now, with electricity, his work is finished. Oh, He can turn forests into coal over a few million years, but He couldn't invent a light-bulb. Man can. The Lord God can appear to us as a Burning Bush or a Pillar of Flame, but He'd be worse than useless on the telephone.'

A bell rang suddenly and W.G. and Raffles leapt to their feet.

That'll be him,' said Edison, running into the shed. Was that 'him' with a capital H? They followed nervously. W.G. contemplated kneeling.

Edison rummaged under a heap of broken glass and paper and retrieved a wooden instrument with an ear-piece and a speaking-tube.

'It's Pinkerton from the house,' he smiled. As Edison listened to Pinkerton's excited gabble, the smile vanished from his face. He replaced the ear-piece gravely.

'Quite extraordinary,' he said. 'Pinkerton had telephoned the 82nd Precinct to explain that all charges against you were to be dropped. He was informed that only moments previously you, Doctor, and Mr Raffles had shot to the top of the Ten Most Wanted list.'

'Congratulations!' beamed Pinkerton from the doorway.

'What have we done now?' Raffles sounded worn.

'Sufficient to have the whole of New York's finest combing the city for you.'

The walrus danced on Pinkerton's face. 'You know that fine statue the Frenchies have given us that's going up in New York Harbour?'

'Liberty,' replied Raffles. 'We caught a glimpse of the plinth on our arrival from Southampton.'

'Which seems as if it were years ago,' sighed W.G. 'We've stolen it, have we?'

'Only the face,' said Pinkerton, wiping tears of laughter from his eyes.

'The face?' W.G. seemed to be checking that his own was still present. 'I suppose we left clues at the scene of the crime.'

'A cap of yours,' said Pinkerton.

'We know they have one,' replied W.G.

'And a cane of mine, no doubt, with my initials on it,' said Raffles. 'That was taken from the hotel with my straw hat.' Pinkerton nodded. 'There was also a letter from you, Doctor.'

'Oh, good,' said W.G. 'And what did I have to say?'

'You put the screws on Monsieur Gustave Eiffel,' Pinkerton was reading from his notes.

'A good brain to pick,' said Edison. 'Brilliant engineer. The statue wouldn't stand up without him.'

W.G. was clearly out of his depth and floundering.

'Monsieur Eiffel,' continued Edison, 'is responsible for the iron skeleton that supports the lady. A Signor Bartholdi is responsible for the lady herself.'

'And he ain't none too pleased,' said Pinkerton. 'That was his mother's face you filched. And you know what Eyetalians are like about their mothers.'

'I cannot imagine,' said Edison, 'that Eiffel himself will be much affected by this. Signor Bartholdi can always do another face.'

'Mister Eiffel's very words,' said Pinkerton.

'Your friends, the twins, are having a hard time finding suitable subjects for blackmail over here,' smiled Edison. 'Eiffel, of course, is erecting this great tower for the Exposition in Paris in 1889. I'm meant to be taking my phonograph there for the American Pavilion. Bill Cody's coming too.'

'Not, I hope,' W.G. grimaced, 'with one of his disgusting restaurants.'

Edison laughed. 'No, I was simply wondering of what aspect of Eiffel's work they had hoped to take advantage.'

'What are those damned twins trying to do?' asked Raffles.

'Well,' replied Pinkerton, 'it would seem some large part of it is to blacken your good names. Even to have you put away for a long time. They must think you know something.'

'I know less and less by the minute,' said W.G.

'I heard talk of twins,' said Edison. 'I remember some twins. Bell and I were giving the first demonstration of the public telephone in New York. *His* telephone, I just did the transmitter. Oh, and I hit on the idea of saying "Hello" to it.'

'Bell's idea was to say "Ahoy".' Edison laughed.

'Ahoy,' said W.G.

'That would be 1876, we did that. Same year Custer was massacred. Centennial Year. I remember Bell and I thinking how differently things might have worked out for Custer if he'd been able to get to a telephone. Now, after the demonstration, we were subjected to a barrage of questioning. Bell was grabbed by these twins. They got him in a corner and set about him. I naturally went to the rescue. One of them had Bell by the lapels, and was shaking him and shouting — "How long-distance? How long a distance?" I'd forgotten that 'til now. Could be them.'

'Good God,' said W.G.

'There'll be less evidence of *Him* in the future,' said Edison. 'I reckon that e'en now he's packing his bags, and leaving a note on his desk for Mammon. Oh, the times they are a-changing. There'll be no more persuading the masses that a luxurious After-life will more than compensate them for a lousy life on earth. There seemed to be a natural order of things — not any more. It's started already. Anarchy. Revolution. God's on his way out — like Royalty.'

'It's a particularly disagreeable future you foresee,' said Raffles.

'At least when I've cracked the light bulb you'll be able to see it a whole heap clearer,' laughed Edison. 'No, I don't like it, but it's sure as Hell going to provide a deal more opportunities for the likes of your Vilebastards.'

'You think, therefore, that they are trying to pirate scientific knowledge?' asked Raffles.

'It'll be worth millions, mark my words,' said Edison. 'There's going to be a whole new Catalogue of Crime.'

This was sad news to a safe-cracker of the Old School.

13 Kidnapped on Primrose Hill

It is no great distance from 221b Baker Street to Primrose Hill, and after dinner the two Doctors, both sticklers for daily exercise, embarked on a brisk walk in that direction. W.G. was particularly keen to work off Mrs Hudson's attempts on a chicken. They stepped at Light Infantry pace through Regent's Park, where some progress had been made in clearing the Red Weed, past the silent, empty Zoological Gardens until they reached the top of Primrose Hill under the Martian War Memorial. They sat down on the grass.

'It is about time they did something about that dome,' Watson complained bitterly looking across at St Paul's. But as the doctors viewed the panorama of London laid out before them it was clear that there was much else to be done.

'Do you think,' asked W.G. 'that this Edward Hyde could be the Jack the Ripper?'

'No,' said Watson, 'Holmes actually solved the Ripper case faster than any other case in his career. Over a weekend, as I recall. Without going near Whitechapel. It was all a massive cover-up, of course. Free Masons to the Defence of the Realm! Well, you know what they're like at the best of times.' He looked anxiously at W.G. 'Oh, you're not a Mason yourself, are you?'

'Certainly not,' said W.G. 'All mumbo-jumbo and funny aprons.'

A memory of Holmes was always too much for Doctor Watson and he changed the subject. 'My cousin George was wiped out by one of those things,' and here he waved at the great War-Machine behind them. 'He was in the Royal Horse Artillery and they all went in the massacre of Woking. Where were you?'

'I was in Gloucestershire,' replied W.G. 'Not that we take kindly to strangers in those parts. We were advised to stay put. News filtered through, of course. Beastly business.'

'They made a terrible mess,' said Watson.

'Wrecked the pitch at Tunbridge Wells. Used to be a

batsman's paradise until the blasted Martians. Where were you?'

'Holmes and I were underground for the duration. In a great bunker under St James' Park. War-work. H.M.G. thought he could help.'

'Did he?' enquired W.G. who was laboriously clearing his fine beard of greenfly.

'Funnily enough,' said Watson, 'I, of all people, got nearest. They thought, I know, that I was a bit of a waste of space and rations down there. (Did you ever eat pemmican? Don't.) Huge place, the bunker. No-one knows it's there. I couldn't find it again. It's Uhlan-proof. What happened was that I suggested, trying to make a bit of a joke actually, one does in those circumstances, that our alien visitors might catch influenza and die. Holmes, bless him got very excited by this. Good old Watson, he cried, best of men! He was immediately all for collecting contaminated phlegm and such and hosing them down with it. The Top Brass pooh-poohed the idea. Holmes was always ahead of his times.' And back went Watson once again in his mind to the edge of the Reichenback Falls. 'A genius,' he murmured, 'but then so, in his own way, was Professor Moriarty.'

'He fell off the Thingyback Falls too, did he?' W.G. was a little vague about the incident, but it seemed a reasonable guess, genius being involved.

'Yes,' Watson gazed blankly down Primrose Hill.

They sat in silence. W.G. was quite keen to leave, as it was now dark and becoming chilly and his knee was stiffening, but Watson obviously needed these moments of blankness. Especially when he had been thinking. W.G. then began thinking, and was struck by a thought of such enormity that he stood up and made as if to seize the moon with both hands.

'What's up?' Watson was forcibly ejected from his reverie.

And W.G. would have told him there and then, and ultimately saved a good deal of time and no little trouble, but there was a jangle of harness from behind and a cough, something horsey like a whinney and the rattle of a number of rifle-bolts.

'Gentlemen,' said a voice, 'you are the Doctors Grace and Watson?'

'I are,' said Watson, in his confusion, and the two Doctors turned slowly. Around the Martian redoubt stood a troop of cavalry. A troop of carabiniers was Watson's guess, eyeing their weapons. Certainly not Lancers. Hussars perhaps. 'Captain Grimes,' said their officer, moving his horse forward and touching his shako with the guard of a drawn sabre. 'Duke of Relwick's Mounted Foot. Would you please be so good,' and pulling two large white handkerchiefs from a pouch on his saddle he threw them to W.G., 'as to blindfold yourselves?'

'I must insist —!' began Watson, foaming at the brim. The flat side of a sabre rapped him sharply on the bowler.

'No, you mustn't,' smiled Captain Grimes. 'Tie the hanky over your eyes, there's a good fellow.'

'Best do what they say, Watson,' said W.G., who for the life of him could not think of anything else to do. These fellows, after all, were British. One should be safe-ish.

'Good man!' said Captain Grimes and no sooner had they blindfolded themselves than they were led to and helped into some sort of carriage. They heard a bolt shot, orders being screamed, and then the carriage was moving at a sharp lick downhill and the noise of wheels and cavalry clattered and banged about them. Not, in fact a carriage but a stage-coach that had once belonged to the Wells Fargo Co, then to Buffalo Bill, but had been captured that evening at Earls Court by the Mounted Foot. The Rough Riders had suffered a massive defeat. Admittedly they did not have live ammunition.

'This is altogether a bit much,' W.G. heard Watson grumble.

'No talking, please, gentlemen!' That was Captain Grimes. This *was* a bit much.

'God's teeth!' boomed W.G. 'What the hell's afoot?'

'Shut up!' screamed Captain Grimes. 'Or I'll have your guts for gaiters!'

W.G. decided to lie low. Whatever was afoot, wherever they were going; why they would be wherever it was when they got there; all these things would become apparent in time, and therefore, he saw no good reason why he shouldn't drop off. And he would have done, had not there suddenly been the thunder of kettle-drums and the blast of brass.

'What the hell's that now?' he enquired.

149

'Something military,' said Watson. 'I can't place it.' There was something familiar in the jaunty march.

'What I meant, Watson, was why the band is playing in the middle of the night during what one would assume to be a clandestine operation?'

'Are you two talking?' It was Grimes again, clearly deafened by the march.

'No,' said W.G.

'Don't,' warned Grimes.

The band played on. I know it, I know it, I know it, thought Watson. If I relax my brain completely and think of nothing, thought Watson, it will come to me. Having turned his mind into a complete blank, there was a moment of drowning panic when he forgot what on earth he was trying to remember, when the Regimental March soared and there was the dusky houri with another brandy and soda, and there was the limp Union Jack, and there were the Duke of Relwick's Mounted Foot riding proudly past the Governor-General who was standing swaying slightly on a flower-decked dais outside the Old Red Fort, and there either side of the old piss-pot were, yes! the Vilebastards.

'Good Lord!' said Watson, right out loud.

'What is it?' whispered W.G.

'Say "Old Red Fort" to me later, and I will amaze you,' hissed Watson. I've just amazed myself, he thought and that's not easy.

'Old Red Fart?' cried W.G.

Mr Karl Marx, who was walking home after a long day at the British Museum, was also deafened by the band and fortunately unable to hear what he would clearly have taken as a vile slander. W.G. began to fear for Watson's sanity.

Lestrade was tired. He slowly lowered his aching body into his old chair at the Yard, and then rose at twenty-three times the speed as if he had sat on a hedgehog.

'Chesterton!' he cried, and as his young sergeant fell through the door, 'Wheel in 'Enry James! Wait!' Chesterton's face appeared again at the door. 'You can let Clemens and 'Arte go. Smile a lot.'

Washington had responded to his wire. Their news could

well provide the clincher. All he had to do now was finger the collars of Pollux Vilebastard, Edward Hyde, a French actress with a wooden leg and, of course, Gay Dog and his lads who wouldn't have collars.

Chesterton led in a dejected Henry James, dark-eyed and white-stubbled. James opened his mouth, probably to drop further names onto Lestrade's desk, but the Inspector quickly laid the Washington wire in front of him.

' 'Enry James,' he pronounced. 'Are you or are you not one of the James Gang? The brother of the notorious Frank James? The husband of Jessie? I imagine from your sound financial state that you are their leader. Come over 'ere in advance of the main party to scout out our railway system and prepare robberies of the sort in which you 'ave specialised in the Western Reaches of your Native Sod? Yes or no?'

'Certainly not!' shouted Henry James.

'Think about it,' suggested Lestrade coolly.

'Inspector, I have lived in this country for *fifteen* years −'

'And still not found a train worthy of your villainous intent?' Lestrade was not going to let go graciously.

'Inspector,' Henry James was too tired to give full vent to his feelings. He had also to be wary of his heart condition. American authors seemed to drop like flies in England.

'I have no brother Frank. Jesse is a famous outlaw, admittedly, a man, Inspector, to whom I am in no way related, not even by the bonds of matrimony. Your behaviour this night will be reported not only to the Commissioner, a personal friend, but to the House of Lords, to Number Ten, Downing Street, to Her Majesty herself. You are in a pretty pickle, Inspector Lestrade. I would now like to go to bed and prepare myself for a busy day devoted to your downfall and dismissal from the Force. Until I encountered your goodself I have constantly forwarded the proposition that your policemen were −' he sought a suitable word in the carpet, 'wonderful.' Not good, but it would suffice.

'Bugger,' said Lestrade softly.

'Shall I take Mr James home?' asked Chesterton. He had never seen his chief so low.

'One last question, Mr James.' Lestrade gritted his teeth.

'Prior to my leaving or prior to your seeking pastures new?'

Mr James turned the screw.

'Among your hextraordinary circle of acquaintances would there lurk a Mr Hedward 'Yde?'

'Of course,' said Henry James. 'I am a New Yorker.'

Bingo! thought Lestrade, his soul soared and he punched the air.

'Tell me more, Mr James.'

'Of Edward Hyde? Surely. Though what he has to do with the matter in question —'

'Let me be the judge of that!'

Henry James relaxed back in his chair and beamed fulsomely.

'Edward Hyde. Lord Cornbury, no less.* Governor of New York and a famous transvestite to boot. He would attire himself in his dear wife's dresses, coat his face in her rouge and other aids to feminine refinement, and mince and pout, as ladies do, upon the walls of the Residency. He would on occasion venture thus clad onto Broadway. He was, I believe on one occasion arrested for prostitution, but seized the ears of the officer and pulled them until he whimpered. He had a penchant for ears. His first speech upon taking office was at a banquet in his honour, and instead of addressing the assembled New Yorkers upon matters of moment and policy, he extolled at length the beauty of his wife's ears. He went so far as to invite male members of his audience to come up and fondle them, and verify for themselves, their delights . . . .'

Lestrade was beside himself with excitement.

'Had he a wooden leg?'

'He may well have —'

Lestrade's pencil was out and shaking.

'Could you give me an accurate description of him?'

'I could probably paint you an accurate picture of Edward Hyde in words, but this is fortunately rendered unnecessary by the fact that a portrait in oils exists of our friend, dressed, as I recall, as one of your former queens, Queen Anne, to whom he bore a marked likeness.'

'Where's the pic?'

'In New York, I suppose.'

'No matter,' said Lestrade 'Chesterton.'

*This is all true. So help me. Author.

152

'Sir?'

'Circulate a picture of Queen Hanne to all stations. I want 'er nicked in a trice. *She* is our man.'

Henry James gazed in awe at the sheer and luminous lunacy of the Inspector. He had more than sufficient ammunition to blast away this roaring madman.

'Would you care, Inspector, to be furnished with any appropriate dates?'

'DATES! DATES! A FINE TIME TO START WORRYING ABOUT *DATES*!! Chronological Horders!' He jumped up and down on them.

'This is murder, Mr James, not a bleedin' 'istory lesson.'

Henry James smiled. It was not for him to volunteer the information that these peculiar events took place between 1702 and 1708.

After about three-quarters of an hour there was a screamed order outside and with a final crash from the cymbals and booming 'Boom! Boom!' from the tympani, the band stopped playing, the Mounted Foot halted and the stage-coach pulled up. W.G. and Watson, still blindfolded were ushered out — onto paving-stone from the sound of it.

'Here we are then,' Grimes sounded pleased with himself.

'May we now remove our —?' Watson began.

'Not yet!' snapped Grimes, and a door was knocked and opened and they were pushed into an echoing hall-way or anti-chapel or coal-mine perhaps.

High-heeled shoes or boots approached. There was a strong whiff of scent. (Right, thought, W.G. we are indoors and being approached by an unmounted woman blessed with both feet. Not the Frenchwoman, therefore.)

The new person spoke in a badly cracked falsetto.

'For Heaven's sake, Captain, you didn't have to take the band!'

(The woman is a man, there is authority in the voice. It belongs to someone who is used to being obeyed without question, and to being given immediate answers to its questions, however stupid.)

'Yes, sir!' carolled Captain Grimes. 'Permission to correct you, sir!'

(Sir? Is the transvestite in stockinged feet? Perhaps a woman is with him in her high-heels and perfume?)

Grimes carried on, regardless. 'Marching with band playing, sir, by night! Regimental Battle Honour, sir, dating back to Quetta, sir, and the business with the elephants, sir! Purley and Beckenham, sir, have, I am proud to say been added to that list since our stand against the Martians, sir!'

The falsetto was raised indignantly, 'Don't call me *"Sir"*, for Heaven's sake! These very walls have ears.'

'Yes, sir,' Grimes sounded inconsolable. 'No, sir, sorry, sir, yes.'

'Stop it, you cretin! Now bundle these gentlemen into that room and offer them some refreshment — but, first, undo this damnable frock!'

There was a terrifying hissing sound from Grimes as his mouth wrestled with a fresh discipline.

'Unbutton me immediately and do *NOT* call me SIR!!'

(*What*? He *must* be on his own — or the woman could do that.)

Discipline was Grimes' undoing. His pack might well contain a Field Marshall's baton and a Manual of Military Law but he had not been issued with any other response to a sharp command in block letters with two exclamation marks than to crash his heels together and shout —

'Sir!!'

There was a whistle and a plummy squelch, a grunt, a fall and then a clack of high-heeled shoes and muttered falsetto cursing that disappeared quickly into the distance.

Wherever Watson and I are, thought W.G. we are now alone. He removed his blindfold and suggested to Watson that he do the same. They were not entirely alone. Grimes lay at their feet on black and white checked marble tiles, stiff as a ramrod, at attention and saluting. A nasty lump was rising in the middle of his forehead. A walking-stick lay beside him. He was still breathing, however, in the approved military manner.

They were standing in a large brightly-lit hall, with several highly-polished double-doors leading from it and a wide staircase at the end. W.G.'s first guess was Harley Street. Watson was thinking in terms of an Embassy.

'Well, here we are,' said W.G. 'Any idea where precisely?'

'Not a clue,' replied Watson. There was a semi-circular table standing against the wall, with a silver tray on it, but no letters or circulars that might have furnished an address.

W.G. moved to the front-door and peered out through the letter-box. Two burly figures loomed outside.

'We're prisoners, Watson,' he reported.

'So far,' Watson recapitulated, 'we have been kidnapped by a squadron of Mounted Foot and delivered into the hands of a screaming transvestite —'

'Or two,' interjected Dr Grace. He was still flirting with the stockinged-feet theory.

'One, or perhaps, one of *whom* has struck down our kidnapper, Captain Grimes with this stick and vanished upstairs in a frock, muttering oaths. Was that the voice, Doctor, of Pollux Vilebastard, for my instinct tells me that he has a hand in this ugly business?'

'No, too old,' said W.G. 'The Vilebastards sound more nasal, due probably to their time in the Americas. That voice had a sinister ring though, did you not think?'

'Far from trustworthy,' Watson nodded, 'but it spoke, did it not, of light refreshments?' He pointed towards one of the pairs of double-doors. It was half-open and the room was lit.

They were in a long high-ceilinged room, filled with an oblong table, some twenty-five to thirty feet long, surrounded by chairs. It was elaborately set for a buffet supper. The walls of the room were covered in portraits of what W.G. considered to be the gloomiest gang of old buffers he had ever seen outside the Long Room at Lords.

'Former clients, perhaps!' laughed Watson. 'Though one would expect them to look a deal more cheerful in such an establishment as this.'

'What?' Watson was clearly ahead of him in the game, thought W.G.

'Well,' said Watson. 'Unless my old eyes deceive me, this house is a disorderly one.'

'What?' To W.G. it seemed most orderly. The candlesticks on the table were immaculately dressed by the right, the cutlery and silverware aligned like grenadiers.

'A bordello, Dr Grace,' Watson could see that his companion

was quite mystified. 'A House of ill-repute. A *Maison de Convenance*. A whore-house. A knocking-shop. A brothel.'

'I can't help you there,' said W.G. quickly, having no practical experience of these matters.

'Nor can I,' replied Watson emphatically, 'though obviously as a Medical Practitioner in the Paddington District, and, of course, an old India-hand one has seen the darker side of life.'

'It all appears so eminently respectable.' W.G. would certainly have wagered a sovereign on this being the waiting-room of a successful dentist. Admittedly, there were no yellowing copies of that so-called humorous weekly, whose name he could never remember, or jokes comprehend.

'It would,' said Watson. 'Mark my words, they do. At this level.'

There was wine in abundance and buckets of champagne on ice. W.G. had found a cupboard full of decanters and glasses. He waved one at Watson.

'Whisky, doctor?'

'With a little water, please.' Watson had parted a curtain a fraction and was peeking at the street.

'The Mounted Foot are leaving.'

And so they were to the strains of 'I am a Gay Hussar' in F.

W.G. ran to the doors and looked into the hall. They had removed their Captain Grimes. The two heavy figures were still outside the front door, however, so the doctors sat at the long table, deep in thought, the decanter between them. Watson poured their second drinks.

'If,' said W.G., drinking deeply, 'we accept your hypothesis that this is, as you say, a — a —' He plucked a radish from a silver dish.

'A bawdy-house. A stew,' said Watson, boldly.

'If you like,' said W.G. 'I bow to your experience.'

'Don't,' said Watson. 'It is very limited.'

'Mine is nil,' said W.G., rather sadly, to his surprise. If pressed, he would have had to admit that there were stirrings within that he could not put a finger on. 'If you're correct, then surely at this hour of the night there would be more bustle, more activity? There is a banquet for some hundreds laid out on the table.'

Watson pushed his empty glass across the table.

'Much depends though, one imagines, on what is planned for *us*.'

W.G. nodded gravely. After two drinks he had begun to feel rather mellow. He must try and keep up with the plot.

'Blackmail.' Watson continued. 'As we already know from the cases of Thomas Edison and Monsieur Eiffel, it is a major weapon in the Vilebastard armoury. I imagine friend Pollux plans to capture us in compromising postures with a hidden camera or a lightening etching by some *Illustrated London News* wallah or such. The wine is most probably drugged. It was fortunate that we are whisky drinkers. It is always something of a compliment when the opposition is forced to take desperate measures.'

W.G. glanced anxiously at the doors in case the desperate measures were about to be taken. All was quiet, however. Too quiet, perhaps. Watson perceived his friend's anxiety.

'It's when the drums stop beating,' he smiled reassuringly, 'that you have to worry.'

'The drums *have* stopped beating,' replied W.G. and continued to worry. Watson watched the Great Cricketer brood gloomily for several minutes. His vast fingers drummed a rhythmless tattoo on the table, as if to forestall the worrying. Then with a deep, roaring intake of breath, he rose. Unless, which seemed most unlikely, the Doctor was passing the time with a lively impersonation of Krakatoa in bloom, then this could well be the cue for the action Watson craved.

'Watson,' boomed W.G. 'I cannot sit about twiddling my thumbs waiting upon the whim of others!'

'Hear, hear!' Watson rose as a man. This was more like it. The game was afoot!

'What is the best form of defence, Watson?'

'Attack!' cried the good Doctor. 'Up, Guards, and at 'em!'

'That's the spirit!' and with that W.G. divested himself of cap, blazer, tie, shirt, shoes, socks, flannels and sensible nether-wear and scattered them the length of the table. Glasses rattled and fell. Dishes flew.

'What are they expecting to find?' the huge nude enquired loudly of the boggling Watson. 'I will tell you. Two soberly-clad medical men, ill-at-ease and anxious to be elsewhere. Come, strip off, Watson, and what *will* they find: a brace of

157

customers, relaxed and full of drink, transparently eager for a night of slap and tickle!'

'Brilliant!' Watson cried, and in a flurry of tweed and wool was soon as pink and bare as The Naked Major.

'Now,' said W.G. advancing on the fireplace. 'We call the blighters' bluff.' And he pulled from the wall above the fire-irons a speaking tube and uncorked it.

'Call yourself a — a — a —?'

'Tarts' parlour,' prompted Watson.

'Tarts' parlour?' thundered W.G. into the mouth-piece. 'Here we have sat, the pair of us, for nigh on half-an-hour in the spartan fastness of your ante-rooms, with only a half-empty decanter of Scotch whisky and a lot of cold meat and puddings to while away the time. Is that why we are here? Never! Send down immediately a pair of your plumpest strumpets or we shall take our custom elsewhere!' And he banged the tube back into the wall.

'That should set the cat among the pygmies,' Watson guffawed. W.G. was circling the room briskly, turning out the lamps. The lamp nearest the doors he turned down until there was only the merest glimmer of light illuminating the entrance and the cheery puce of Watson's buttocks as he kept watch through a crack in the doors on the staircase outside. Watson poked his head back round the door.

'W.G.?' A most unpleasant thought had stuck him. 'What if it's that rum fellow in the frock?' W.G. had noticed that Watson was still wearing his brown bowler hat. Well, Old Watson's the man of the world, he thought. He has the know-ledge of onions, and he quickly retrieved his cap from the table.

'W.G.!!?' hissed Watson urgently, demanding an answer. It was slowly dawning on him where his duty lay and what England and W.G. expected of him. He set his hat more firmly on his head. Their plan was based on a reasonable supposition — that the last thing Pollux Vilebastard and his cronies would expect to see was two large naked revellers cavorting noisily with a couple of the house houris. It would give them cause to pause. 'Surprise,' W.G. had whispered, 'is of the essence.' And he had pointed to the success of Spofforth's slower ball. Watson was quite prepared to go so far, but would be most grateful for a ruling on the transvestite.

'W.G.!!??' Panic had him in its grip.

'We'll cross that bridge when we come to it,' said W.G. calmly.

Oh, bloody good, thought Watson. There was someone coming down the stairs. Watson didn't dare to look. He heard a swish of skirts.

'We do the necessary — well, you do — pay up — they fetch us a cab and off we go!'

'There's a lady approaching.'

'Not one imagines, Watson, a lady.'

'Well, a fat tart is coming,' Watson corrected himself. He felt desperately out of his depth.

'You know what to do, Watson.'

Swoon, thought Watson.

'I mean, you know better than I the sort of thing you should be doing. Two wives, India and Paddington, old soldier. You do it. I shall give you moral support.'

The doors opened, and one small plump strumpet, as ordered, was silhouetted against the lights of the hall. Watson stood like an unfinished statue. W.G. seized the small plump strumpet, whipped her skirts and petticoats over her head and with an easy movement laid her, legs waving in the air like a capsized tortoise on the table.

'Show us your meaty thighs, you saucy baggage!' he cried. 'We've paid a fat sum for this!' He waved Watson over the top. Watson stood transfixed.

'Set too, Sir Godfrey!' W.G. shouted, rather cleverly, in his view.

'Sir Godfrey?' queried Watson and found himself being propelled through the air by powerful hands and laid like a bloater on a fishmonger's slab upon the writhing doxy. His hands were suddenly packed with doughy woman. A vision of the dusky temptress from the foothills wafted before him. What he needed was a large brandy and soda. Two large brandies and soda. Correction. Three.

'Lie back,' he ordered, 'and think of India.'

'If you insist!' cried his victim.

'Bon voyage!' called W.G. as, with the deliberate movements of a cross-channel swimmer, Watson set off up the table into the darkness.

Someone else was approaching. The other half of the order? Pollux with photographic equipment? W.G. tightened his grip on the poker.

Some two hours later, though it seemed a lifetime, W.G. and Watson were alone again. Not, as they had feared, in a wet-walled dungeon in the Tower of London, but side by side in a large double bed. W.G. was motionless, his eyes wide open and unblinking. Watson was still shaking.

'What have I done?' he sobbed. 'W.G.? W.G.? What have I done?'

'Nothing I am sure, Watson, of which you need to feel ashamed. You did not, I imagine, go beyond the bounds of propriety. You dallied, perhaps, gaily flirted —'

'I don't know. I don't know, I tell you. The darkness, it was black as pitch. And the catering. There were legs of pork and napkins, boned capons, raised game pies and jellies in profusion. At no time could I tell whether I was feeling a trifle ... or ... or ... Oh, God!' he wailed and placed a pillow over his face.

'I was more fortunate,' said W.G. 'in that, as the second lady came through the door, I recognised her as Mrs Beeton at once from a recent photograph. 'How to Scald Suckling-Pig,' I cried. She was somewhat surprised at my appearance, but said that given the extraordinary circumstances of the evening, she imagined that I was undergoing some security procedure or medical examination. She, she said, had come to finish preparing a buffet supper for forty. I asked her where, in fact, we were. She replied that we were in, as we now know —'

There was a heart-rending groan from Watson's pillow.

'The Cabinet Room at Number Ten Downing Street. That we were *not* to know, Watson. We were *not* so informed. I was about to impart this startling twist in the case to you —'

Watson's anguished face appeared slowly from under his pillow.

'That ... that ... that ...' Watson quivered afresh.

'That, yes, Watson, was when the lights came on.' Did you see Gay Dog among the throng? White tie and tails and a most dashing feathered head-dress?' W.G. was confident that Watson could be jollied out of his manic melancholia.

'No, Doctor Grace, I did not see Gay Dog.' This sounded more like the old Watson.' I was rather too busy preserving my modesty with a Coquille St Jacques that fortunately came to hand.'

W.G. felt a great balloon of laughter rapidly inflating in his chest. It was the memory of Watson crouched on the table-top like Quasimodo at an Investiture. Out it came.

'W.G.!' cried Watson. 'Doctor Grace! How can you laugh at a time like this?'

'I'm sorry, Watson.' W.G. inhaled deeply. The lights had come on and framed in the doorway was a crowd of Crowned Heads and their escorts, jewellery and decorations shimmering, standing like a formal study taken after a Royal Wedding.

'I don't think you understand, Doctor Grace,' said Watson, hugging his pillow. 'It is quite probably not within your com-prehension, but I have done the vilest thing one can imagine —'

'She said "Whoopee, Dr Watson" as she left.' W.G. was determined to look on the bright side.

'I was not,' said Dr Watson, 'fishing for compliments.' There had been a polite ripple of white-gloved applause from the royalty as Her Majesty had silently and indeed regally pro-gressed to the doors. She had paused to re-adjust her tiara. 'Doctor Watson,' she had said in her strong, clear, voice.

'Whoopee!' repeated Watson sadly, now thrashing his pillow.

'Come along, old chap,' said W.G. sympathetically. 'Buck up.'

'I'll try,' said Watson. 'Oh dear, oh dear, oh dear.'

'It'll all seem better in the morning.' W.G. slid out of bed and after a quick glance down into an empty Downing Street, threw open the window and drew the curtains.

'Oh Doctor,' moaned Watson. 'I'd give my left buttock to be tucked up safe and sound in 221b, Baker Street.'

How very fortunate it was that he and Doctor Grace were not. For as he spoke Number 221b exploded, taking with it, of course, numbers 221a and 221c and not doing much good to numbers 219 or 223. Nothing remained of the building, which, incidentally, is why you cannot find it today.

Only Mrs Hudson survived. No-one knew how, except that the Mrs Hudsons of this world are not intended by nature to be blown apart by bombs. They live to a ripe old age, sustained by port and lemon and cats, and that is how it should be.

The Doctors were not to be informed of this latest development until the morning, which is why Doctor Grace fell asleep toying with the notion that the Prime Minister, for it must have been he in the frock and high-heeled shoes, was in the pay of Pollux Vilebastard. He would seem a laughably easy target for any blackmailer. Doctor Watson fell asleep toying with something else entirely. He was in love. He had found the Only Woman. Whoopee!

PALL MALL

14　The Plot Thickens at Number Ten

They were awoken by Lestrade of all people with two mugs of tea.

'I'm not 'ere,' he announced. 'Mum is the word.'

He looked out into the corridor and closed the door behind him.

'Something is up. I 'ave been summoned. I don't know you're 'ere, though.'

Watson's eyebrows were putting a number of questions.

'I saw your 'ats 'anging up downstairs. I asked a maid. I bribed the cook. The 'ole bleeding Himperial Security Hintelligence Service is 'ere.' Clearly he had no time for those gentlemen. The S's betrayed his feelings in that direction.

'I am the harbinger of evil tidings, Dr Watson. Baker Street's been blown to smithereens. 'Igh explosive. Boom!'

'Who? What?' gasped Watson.

'Pollux, I would 'azard,' replied Lestrade. 'nothing left except Mrs 'Udson and a dozen scrofulous Tom Moggies. She's gone to 'er sister in Tooting.'

'All Holmes's work gone. His experiments. His equipment. His books.

Watson sat miserably on a bed pulling on his trousers. 'My books. My —' and he began to rummage through his trouser pockets. 'My —' He was now searching through his jacket and waistcoat. 'Doctor Grace, check your blazer and flannels, my clothing has been ransacked.'

W.G. could find nothing in any of his pockets.

'What's up, Lestrade?' he enquired.

Lestrade went and checked the corridor again. He gathered the doctors to him and whispered urgently.

'I 'ave been instructed to call off my 'unt for Mr Gay Dog, to drop my investigations into the Vilebastard murder and to 'ave nothing further to do with you two gentlemen. That came from the Prime Minister, no less, I am 'owever still to 'unt down Mr Hedward 'Yde. Who is a transvestite. Go to that Party this evening. Forget I said that.'

'Party,' said Watson, 'Party? What Party?'

'I know nothing of any party. I am not 'ere!' And suddenly he wasn't.

There was a knock on the door, and a butler or some such (he wore a striped waistcoat and carried a rifle) beckoned them to follow him.

'Ours not to reason why,' shrugged Watson. So, he thought, it is to be a firing-squad. He thought it would have been more gentlemanly to have left a loaded Luger in the bathroom.

'Ours,' continued W.G., happy that for once a literary allusion was not lost upon him. 'Ours but to do or die,' and he wished with all his great heart that it *had* been lost upon him. The pace was getting a shade too hot in his view.

'Don't touch any thing, gentlemen,' the butler or some such warned, and when Watson had stumbled and grasped a bannister he had made much of wiping away the evidence with his sleeve. There seemed to be burly men in every shadow, who acknowledged the butler with a grunt.

He led them swiftly down some back stairs. He stopped them frequently, as if fearing ambush. Finally he directed them into a book-lined study. The door closed behind them, and a key turned in the lock. A Pearly King stood with his back to them gazing into the fireplace. 'The Pearly King, of Hackney' it read in black sequins on the rear of his sparkling jacket. He seemed quite unaware of their presence. W.G. coughed loudly.

'What cheer, mateys,' said the Pearly King of Hackney. 'Bet you don't know who Oi be, know what I mean, Cock. Trouble and strife. Apples and Pears. Knocked 'em down the Old Kent Road!'

'No,' said W.G., looking at Watson and shaking his head as if to indicate that the world had gone mad.

'Good. Good,' said the Pearly King of Hackney. 'One cannot be too careful.' The Prime Minister turned round and was obviously pleased that they were amazed and astonished at his deception.

'I am your Prime Minister. Lord Robert Arthur Talbot —'

'Honoured,' said W.G.

'I haven't finished,' snapped Lord Robert Arthur Talbot. 'Lord Robert Arthur Talbot Gascoyne-Cecil.'

'Proud,' said Watson. 'There is more yet,' shrilled the PM. 'Third Marquis of Salisbury.'

'I have been forced by circumstances,' continued the aforementioned, 'to become a Master of Disguise. Anarchy is at our very door.' He moved to the very door to check and then cautiously to the window, shooting an anxious glance around the curtain down into Downing Street. 'Sniper,' he said. 'Lunatic with fizzing bombs. One never knows.' He leapt away from the window and circumvented the study, hugging the books. 'One lunatic is enough,' he cried, and they were forced to agree.

'Four Heads of State assassinated this year,' he held up four fingers. 'There are assassins at every street-corner in Europe. The Intelligence Service insist that I am disguised from dawn to dusk. Yesterday, I was a Dowager Duchess. Damnably undignified, but I admit, effective. I survived the day. The King of Ruritania did not. Blown to pieces in the Cathedral at Strelsau alas. His lovely Queen was spared, thank God. She was here to represent her husband. She is below at this moment, breakfasting with the other Crowned Heads of Europe. Her Majesty summoned them to London for a conference. They are, after all, all relatives.'

At the mention of his noble Queen, Watson had blushed to deepest red. The Prime Minister noticed this and seemed to have some difficulty hiding a smile away in his bushy grey beard. He pushed an envelope across the desk towards Watson.

'A perfectly natural mistake, Doctor, could have happened to anyone. We were all a little squiffy. I was asked to give you this.'

Watson opened the envelope and extracted a weighty sheet of crested vellum. 'Good Lord,' he said, as he read. 'I've been invited to Windsor Castle for the weekend.' He felt a song coming on.

'I gather, Doctor, that you reminded Her Majesty forcibly of the late Prince Consort,' the Prime Minister smiled. 'Her Majesty has a heart every bit as big as her Dominions. Incidentally, you can have these things back.' The contents of their pockets were laid out on his blotter. 'I apologise for this, it was the work of the Marquis of Queensberry and his Imperial Security Intelligence Service. They were also responsible, I'm afraid, for your being brought here last night. Queensberry tends to over-dramatise, I fear.'

'You bastard!' said a voice from under the desk.

'Queensberry!' cried the Prime Minister springing back. 'What are you doing now? Come out, come out.'

A tall thin man with fierce whiskers rose from under the desk and laid his top hat and a large revolver on top of it.

'Did you think, Prime Minister, that you would be left alone with these two?' They could be Bulgars. Crazed Bosnians. Austro-Hungarians of unmentionable leanings. Bolsheviks. Anarchists. Serbian Revolutionaries of the worst type.'

The Prime Minister stamped his foot and marched to the window, hissing disapproval. Queensberry hurtled across the study, tackled him about the knees and bought him to the floor with a fearsome thud.

'And don't, with respect, Prime Minister, stand by that blasted window! How many times . . . ?' Queensberry had risen and was wagging a finger at the PM.

The Prime Minister's face had turned deep purple. Hell hath no fury like a small man who has just been knocked to the floor by a tall thin one. Queensberry's finger stopped wagging and he recoiled as his Prime Minister bounced back onto his feet and glared up at him. Queensberry paled, as any man might looking down into the crater of Vesuvius and realising that he was about to enjoy briefly a rare and intimate view of an eruption.

'OUTSIDE!' The PM erupted 'OUT!'

Queensberry, maddened, no doubt, by years in espionage, eschewed the door but threw open the window and leapt lithely onto the window-sill where he crouched glowering like some bird of prey. The Prime Minister slammed the window shut.

'Well might one ask, gentlemen,' he addressed the boggling doctors, 'who is in charge of this country? To be frank, I frequently ask myself that question and even after some years in high office, feel that I am no nearer the truth. Are you Masons?'

W.G. and Watson shook their heads.

'No matter.' The Prime Minister seeing Queensberry's ear

pressed to the window-pane, pulled the curtains to and lit a candle on his desk.

'We live, gentlemen, in perilous times. It would be no exaggeration to state that Revolution is but a hair's breadth away. Look at Europe. Cast your minds back to the riots in Trafalgar Square during the Ripper business. One would have thought civil disorder in the very heart of London unthinkable. But no longer. The recent War with the Martians has perhaps bought us a little time, but it has also greatly weakened the fabric of our society. And there are those out there only too eager to take advantage of that weakness. I can trust no-one. Who do you think, Doctor Watson, was responsible for the destruction of your rooms in Baker Street?'

'Dr Grace and I imagined that it was the work of one Pollux Vilebastard.'

'Ah yes,' the Prime Minister picked up a folder from his desk and tapped it knowingly. 'The Vilebastards. This is Queensberry's file on those two.' He quickly wiped the spot he had tapped with a handkerchief. 'Why do you think that Vilebastard was responsible?'

Watson was slowly filling his pipe. 'He seemed the obvious choice.'

'Obvious?' The Prime Minister glanced towards the curtained window, leant forward and whispered. 'Nothing, I fear, Doctor, is obvious where National Security is involved.'

Watson moved his chair closer to the desk. 'You don't believe it *was* Pollux Vilebastard, Prime Minister?'

'Quite frankly, no, Doctor Watson. My first guess was Queensberry, truth be known. He brought you here last night for reasons all his own, and what are you now? Angry, vengeful and of no fixed abode. Ideal material for his organisation. When I heard the news, I imagined that he was recruiting. He has men and indeed, women, all over Europe, nay, the World. If I could believe a word he said, it would be a most useful service.'

'It doesn't really matter, sir' said W.G. 'It's still Pollux we're after. I don't care who blew up Baker Street.'

'I do,' vouchsafed Watson. 'It was full of memories.'

'So is your head, Watson,' said W.G., 'and that is the best place for them.' W.G. had never been one to tolerate clutter.

'This Vilebastard,' said the Prime Minister, removing his pearl-buttoned cap and placing it on the adjacent bust of Pitt the Younger, 'Should he be . . . ' and he searched the ceiling for an appropriate euphemism, abandoned the hunt in the interests of clarity and said, 'killed?' in the same light tone he might have used for 'breakfasted?'

'This can most easily be arranged,' he continued quickly, seeing Watson's moustaches semaphoring grave doubts. 'It is well within my compass so to do. Queensberry is not the only one with a highly trained and discreet squadron of agents. Governments kill more people privately than you would imagine.'

'I *would* imagine,' said Watson 'that there must be times when such action is politic.'

'Poli*tics*,' emphasised the Prime Minister with such force that W.G. glanced anxiously around the room searching for a parrot with a time bomb up it.

There was a rattle on the window. Queensberry was tired, perhaps, of perching. The Prime Minister opened the Vilebastard File and took out a crumpled envelope that Watson recognised at once.

'That is the envelope Dr Jekyll gave me — it was in my —'

'My apologies Dr Watson, but needs must —'

'I'd forgotten about it.'

'It is an invitation.'

'Is it?'

'Read it,' the Prime Minister pushed, not the envelope, but a piece of paper towards Watson. 'This is a copy. We have stuck the envelope down again.' He wiped the envelope and put it back in the file.

Dr Henry Jekyll
and
The Brothers Vilebastard

[he read]

Invite you to witness
An Astonishing Medical Breakthrough!
A Miracle of Modern Chemistry!

There followed Jekyll's address and a date and a time.

'Good Lord!' said Watson, 'this very evening!'

'Precisely,' said the PM., and taking the paper he set fire to it with the candle and threw the blazing remains into the grate. There was a more violent banging at the window.

The Prime Minister flashed an anxious glance towards it, seized the doctors by their necks and pulled them to him. Beards, whiskers and moustaches mingled and danced in the candlelight.

'Queensberry has for some time been convinced that there is a conspiracy led by International Anarchists whose dastardly purpose, gentlemen, is nothing short of total World Domination, achieved by the use of the most modern scientific techniques, the creation of global revolt and public disorder, and ruthless political assasination. Of course, I thought him mad. I always have. Until yesterday afternoon when a great Apache Chief and several of his warriors appeared in Downing Street and surrendered to the Constable on the door.'

'Gay Dog!' cried W.G. 'I thought I saw him last night.'

'He insisted on being taken to our Leader,' the Prime Minister confirmed. 'The constable, by extraordinary good fortune possesses a smattering of Spanish, being married to an ex-Flamenco dancer (her family I believe have a Bodega in Battersea) and entirely on his own initiative and in the belief, a correct one in my view, that a Red Indian Chief, is as royal as an American can get, brought Gay Dog into the Cabinet Room where Her Majesty was opening the first session of the conference of Crowned Heads. I was summoned, and, roughly translated by the constable, out poured Gay Dog's story. It was greeted most sympathetically and I don't think there was a King, a Kaiser, an Archduke, what you will, in that room who did not agree that in the matter of Castor Vilebastard he would have acted in a similar fashion.

'Of course, out came the prophecies of his Medicine Man —'

'Charlie!' beamed W.G.

'Here's looking at *you*, kid,' said a voice inside his head. 'Good old Charlie!'

'These, albeit rather vague and in no particular order, fitted almost precisely the shreds of evidence that Queensberry had

171

culled from his sources in Canada, the United States, India, South Africa and Central Europe. The Vilebastards — or to be more precise since Castor's death — *Pollux* Vilebastard was our man. The head of the International Conspiracy.

'The case was at once taken out of the hands of Scotland Yard, and entrusted to the good offices of Queensberry out there. One moment, please!' he shouted at the rattling window.

'Her Majesty was of course aware of Mr Holmes' tragic death, Doctor, and she announced that in her view he alone could have found the missing Vilebastard. She could think of only one other man. She then mentioned your name, Doctor Watson. Gay Dog pronounced that Grey Sea was the only being who could undertake such a search successfully. He has a very high opinion of you, Doctor Grace. I immediately sent for you both.'

'We shall certainly continue to hunt for Pollux,' stated W.G.

'Most certainly,' agreed Watson. 'You have our word.'

'Then I shall let Queensberry in,' said the Prime Minister, but when he opened the curtain, the Head of the Imperial Security Intelligence Service had flown.

Raffles readily agreed to put the two doctors up in his Albany rooms. Bunny was now abroad. W.G. had breathed a huge sign of relief down the Downing Street telephone. It was lunch time as he and Watson strolled across St James' Park. The Park was full of top-hatted Foreign Office men pretending to blow ducks apart with their walking-sticks. Most of the Red Weed had been removed from the Lake, but few trees remained.

'Care for a light lunch on the way?' asked Watson.

'Good Idea,' said W.G. They had not been breakfasted. They had, however, had a cup of coffee in the garden after saying their farewells to the PM, squatting around the silver tray with Gay Dog and some Transylvanian Count who was eager to organise buffalo-hunting trips by night on the Apache Reservation. Gay Dog had been delighted to meet Grey Sea again and knelt for a good five minutes in prayer at his knee. In a corner of the garden W.G. saw a servant making a bonfire of what had clearly been their bedding the night before.

'The Diogenes?' suggested Watson.

'No,' said W.G. rather too sharply. He was thinking of the toad and the leaden sprouts, but he added quickly. 'Danger, Watson. Both Pollux and Hyde know you are a member and frequent visitor.'

'Good thinking, W.G.' Watson nodded. They walked across the Mall and picked their way up the remnants of the Duke of York's steps. Carlton House Terrace had taken a fearsome beating.

'When do you think Queensberry will make his move?' W.G. walked once round the base of the column upon which the Duke of York had so proudly stood until a passing Martian had rather frivolously picked him off. 'He could be anywhere.'

'That's what the PM said.' He and W.G. had agreed to know nothing of the Invitation until Queensberry or one of his agents approached them with it.

'He has his methods,' the PM had said, shaking his head sadly. They promised to report back to him secretly on their evening *chez* Jekyll.

'I feel I can trust you,' the Prime Minister had whispered as he shook their hands. W.G. could have sworn that there were tears in his eyes. Pathetic.

As they passed the empty shell of the Athenaeum Club, prior to crossing Pall Mall they were aware of a muffled drum-beat and the rattle of harness. Their first inclination was to run like billy-oh! It sounded omniously like the return of the Duke of Relwick's Mounted Foot, and they were not going to be surprised by *them* twice in twenty-four hours. W.G. had in fact set off towards the Park again, but Watson stayed a moment to check.

His laughing cry of 'Ha! Ha! It's a funeral!' caused a large number of the mourners to raise their heads as they followed the black-plumed horses and shrouded catafalque. Among the many veiled or black-betoppered faces registering distaste in his direction, Watson was surprised to see a good many Chinamen. Watson blushed deeply and removed his bowler hat. The procession stretched the length of Pall Mall. The only sounds were the muffled drum, the sniffing of female relatives and the echo of his merry laugh, which seemed to hover above the route like some gay demon, quite the reverse of Death doing whatever it was he did at the feast. He wished the happy noise would have the grace to turn right at the corner and vanish tittering away up St James'!

'And what, pray, brings you two gentlemen to pay your last respects to Sir Danvers Carew, MP?'

Lestrade was eyeing him keenly through a hole he had cut in a *Morning Post*.

'Just passing,' said Watson.

'Aren't we all, Doctor Watson — just a-passing. One moment we are a Member of Parliament, Chairman of British Hopium, a Member of Boodles, Whites and the Diogenes, A Pillar of the Rulin' Class, owner of Great 'Omes, wives, mistresses and slack-jawed progeny. The next, Dr Watson —' he waved at the coffin and flicked his fingers, 'Poof!'

'Thank you *very* much,' said Lord Alfred Douglas crossly. He was mincing by hot-foot for the Café Royal.

'I know that you and Doctor Grace are hengaged in more important affairs — Hinternational Conspiracies, World Domination and that hilk, stuff too 'eady for us at the Yard — but even 'umdrum day-to-day cases like mine have a hint of the hexotic.' Lestrade seemed bitter.

'Seen this man, 'ave you?' Lestrade proffered a picture of Queen Anne to Doctor Watson. Watson shook his head.

'Mr Hedward 'Yde, halias Queen Hanne. Murderers, I 'ave found often attend the funerals.'

'It's not a very good likeness, Inspector. Remember Dr Grace and I have briefly encountered this rogue,' and Watson pulled a pencil from his pocket and quickly filled in the thick, black slash of eyebrow and enlarged upon the lips.

'Very good,' murmured W.G., looking over his shoulder. 'The teeth were rather more jagged.' Watson began a ragged zig-zag below the upper lip. W.G. looked around for inspiration.

'There's a good likeness,' he pointed at the driver of the hearse. There indeed beneath the black chiffon-draped topper were the eyebrows, and there the lips and as the driver saw the three studying him, the beastly teeth.

'That's 'im!' cried Lestrade, pulling a huge Webley from his jacket.

At that moment through the black, white and grey of the funeral procession came a dash of red. A mad clatter of hooves, a hastily-requisitioned dray-horse, Lt Dickens up.

'There's your man!' he cried.

A shot banged down Pall Mall. The funeral cortège scattered like pigeons.

W.G. could scarce contain a cheer as Dickens of the Mounties charged.

''Oo the bloody hell's that?' mumbled Lestrade and shot the dray-horse between the eyes. As horse and rider fell, Hyde swung the hearse to the left and headed at a four-horse-power gallop north up Lower Regent Street for Piccadilly.

As W.G. effected brief introductions between Lestrade, Watson and the recumbent Dickens, Lestrade realised his folly.

'I am habject,' he moaned. 'I am an harse'ole.'

And briskly organising some uniformed men who had come running to the scene, set off on foot after the hearse.

'Pollux is in the coffin,' Dickens rubbed his head. 'The two of 'em came out of Jekyll's before dawn. I followed them to Codd's Funeral Parlour in Lambeth, and once I had deduced their purpose, I set about finding some form of transport. I am afraid Lestrade will find more corpses at Codd's than will be registered in their ledgers.'

He began slowly and painfully to climb to his feet. Both doctors had pronounced that no bones were broken. Watson did add however that Dickens would benefit from putting his feet up, and suggested Raffles' sofa for this purpose. He reckoned without Dickens' absurd sense of duty, and nothing the doctors could say would dissuade him from limping away in pursuit of the hearse. So, in fact, did the mourners and their vehicles.

Chinamen picked themselves from the gutters, or were thrown bodily out of the clubs into which, rather unwisely, they had run for shelter. Suddenly, it wasn't much of a funeral. All the neatness had gone out of it. The black was soiled and dirty; the white grey; and the grey black. Apart from which, the hearse had vanished. Those who weren't Chinese made for their Clubs. The Chinese set off after the hearse, unaware that the corpse of the late Sir Danvers stood rigidly upside-down in a dustbin at Codd's Funerarium. Perhaps the Orientals thought all this part of the British

Mourning Ritual. Perhaps they had nowhere else to go.

Watson and W.G. elected to go against the yellow tide and set off down Pall Mall towards St James', wondering whence Queensberry would spring. A bread-van stopped beside them in St James' Square, and they braced themselves. There was a nervous moment when they were separated by a platoon of Rabbis scurrying eastwards down Jermyn Street. They slipped into Piccadilly by the alley that runs along the side of St James' Church and would have aimed for the Burlington Arcade to their left thence to the Albany, had a quartet of young Guards Officers not burst out of Fortnum and Mason's and headed towards them, honking excitedly. The doctors crossed Piccadilly quickly and ran up Air Street towards a Regent Street that Nash himself would never have recognised since the carnage that the Martians had wrought upon it.

W.G. pulled Watson into a doorway.

'A thought,' he whispered. 'Why are we running away from our side viz Queensberry when he knows where we are going, anyway, as we left Raffles' address at Number Ten?'

'We like it that way,' said a voice. 'Come in, gentlemen, show's on now.'

It was the Marquis himself, strangely attired in a powdered periwig, and the Regency dress still affected by footmen. He led them down a dingy stair into a damp basement. It was dark after the brightness of the day, and the carpet squished wetly beneath their feet. Queensberry rapped out a rhythmic tattoo on a door, which opened revealing an exotic cellar furnished wall-to-wall in the Turkish manner. So were the ladies who removed their hats. They were thinly veiled, with rubies twinkling in their navels. The doctors were ushered to a richly-curtained booth lit by brass lamps. There Queensberry sat down on a sprawled heap of cushions and signalled that the doctors should do likewise. Damned uncomfortable, thought W.G. as he tried desperately to find a position in which his right knee could find some ease. The dusky houris brought champagne and drapped themselves over the remaining cushions.

'We can talk here,' said Queensberry. 'The gels are deaf-mutes. No customers will arrive for at least an hour.'

'Where on earth are we now?' asked W.G.

'In a building owned, in fact, by the Foreign Office, Doctor Grace,' replied Queensberry. 'We use it, among other things, for the entertainment of foreign dignitaries. The evenings can be very lively here.' He possessed a disgusting laugh.

'Is this,' pressed W.G., 'a — a — knocking shop?'

'Not in so many words,' answered Queensberry smoothly. 'There would be questions in the house.' From his livery he pulled the envelope.

'For some reason, Doctor Watson, you have not opened this.' He passed it over. 'Good Lord,' said Watson. 'Forgotten all about it. That Doctor-fellow — what *was* his name, W.G.? — Jackal? Jellicoe?'

'*Jee*kyll, Dr Watson,' smiled Queensberry.

'Jekyll,' corrected W.G. swiftly.

'It's an invitation!' Watson was performing surprisingly well in the circumstances. 'To some demonstration of a medical nature.'

'Haemorrhoids, isn't it?' W.G. played along.

'No idea,' said Watson. 'Anyway, it's for this evening.'

'Do you think Pollux Vilebastard will be there?' enquired Queensberry.

'Who?' Watson tried to look innocent, but succeeded in looking criminally inane.

'Castor's brother?' W.G. came to the rescue. 'I don't know, I imagine from what I know of him — and I've played cricket with the man after all — that, knowing how close he was to Castor, he would think it bally bad form to be seen at any sort of party so soon after his brother's death. Quite frankly.'

Queensberry sprang easily to his feet.

'You would be well advised, gentlemen, not to play silly-buggers with me. I've kept an eye clapped on the Vilebastards since their sudden farewell to Eton. I thought them likely lads for the Service. They were totally unscrupulous, and keen on foreign travel. However, they preferred careers in crime, and very successful they were. It became more and more apparent to me as my Department collated information over the years that the trail of theft, murder, blackmail (in which, as such, I had no interest whatever, for I am in the business of National Security) that the trail led towards some

177

greater purpose, some *Inter*national ambition that could well fall under my auspice. It has become increasingly clear to me of late that that purpose, whatever it is, and here I must confess to an alarming ignorance of its precise nature, is approaching fulfilment.'

W.G. suddenly saw in his mind Charlie, the Medicine Man, running like a hairy goat around and around the bewildered twins. What was the little fellow trying to say?

'The Medicine Man —' he started to say.

'Oh, we know all about that. We received a full report from our man in the MCC. He was on the — er — Tour of Shame.'

'Who was that?' W.G. felt rather betrayed. But not greatly.

Queensberry thought of not telling him. He believed firmly in the Public's Right Not to Know.

'This is strictly classified information, but as the person in question is dead — I see no real harm. He was a man of the cloth —'

'I had no idea Studholme was dead,' said W.G. 'Good Lord, still in his prime. What —?'

'He was working for us in Paris. We hadn't heard a word from him for all of a month. Then his body was found in a hotel in the Rue Morgue. The Hotel Paradise.'

'How did he die?'

'He was torn apart by a great ape.'

'What a surprising end!' gasped Watson. 'In Paris of all places —'

'Poor old Studholme — not a great fielder but a bowler of imagination and a sturdy enough if unexciting bat — no match though for a gorilla — a French gorilla at that.' W.G. sighed deeply.

'And you've no idea, my Lord, on what business he was engaged?'

'Oh, yes,' said Queensberry. 'He was pursuing the Vilebastards.'

W.G. rose this time, rather more slowly and certainly more stiffly than the Marquis.

'One more good reason,' boomed W.G. 'for settling Pollux's hash.'

Watson stood up, and waved the invitation.

'We'll start the hunt here.'

'Let me know what happens,' commanded Queensberry 'and not a word to you-know-who.'

Now he must go and lie to the Prime Minister.

'I feel I can trust you!' he shouted after them.

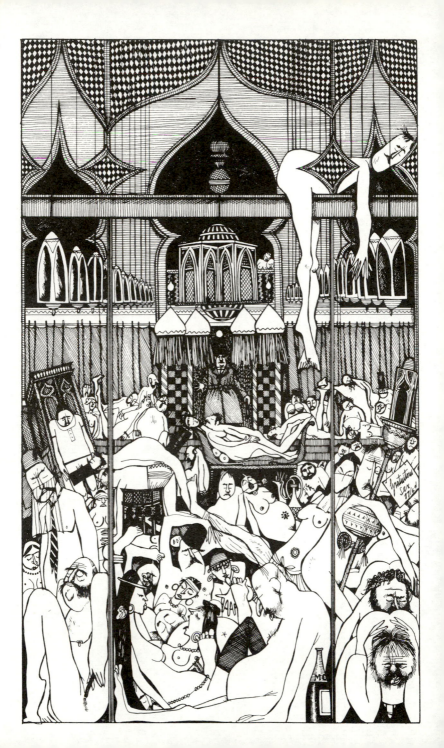

15 An Extraordinary Evening with Dr Jekyll

Poole, the well-dressed, elderly servant, opened the door to them. He recognised them at once and this time led them upstairs to a large pleasant L-shaped drawing room lit by two french windows with balconies overlooking the square. They were clearly the last to arrive, for, having announced them, Poole closed the doors and moved to a table with several carafes of a green drink upon it and a large collection of rummers.

Watson recognised a few of the guests, all obviously medical men, Sir Patrick Cullen, Sir Colenso Ridgeon, Cutler Walpole, Sir Ralph Bloomfield Bonington yet, two fellow GP's of his acquaintance, and the Medical Correspondent of *The Times*, a sickly-looking fellow with a vicious facial tic. There must have been another forty-five to fifty more that he did not know. W.G. only recognised one, a Welsh leg-spinner and chestman he had met when playing against XVIII Inebriated Heart Specialists of Cardiff.

Dr Jekyll, having heard their names announced, pushed his way through the sherry-swilling throng to greet them.

'Upon my word, what would doctors do without their drink?' he laughed.

Watson agreed heartily, seizing a passing Bristol Cream but W.G. stood hypnotised by Jekyll's eyebrows. They had changed shape yet again! This surely could not be the medical breakthrough they had been invited to celebrate.

He had asked Raffles before they came what he thought the party might be about. Watson had repaired to the lavatory for an hour with an encyclopedia. Raffles had seemed far more interested in the Foreign Office's bizarre 'House' in Air Street. Pressed further, however, by W.G., Raffles did point out the similarities between this case and Thomas Edison's. The New Crime. The stealing of scientific knowledge. Jekyll has come up with something, and Pollux intends to make a great deal of money out of it.

What, mused W.G., would be the greatest scientific discovery of our age?

'What about the Cure for the Common Cold?' suggested Raffles.

'Bullseye!' cried W.G. 'He could well be working on that. He had a stinker at Lord's the afternoon of Castor's death — next day, quite cleared up! That's what I was thinking on Primrose Hill when we were seized by the cavalry. Well done, Raffles!' He had thought more than that, but blowed if he could remember what.

'Would Pollux be interested, though?'

'Lord, yes, big financial rewards for that one. The bottles of medicine, the pills that could be sold. Everyone gets a cold, shouts for a cure. Oh, yes, if Pollux captured the rights to that, he would be rich as —'

'Right,' said Raffles. 'A Hypothesis: all having gone to plan, the Vilebastards have disposed of Jekyll, they hold the sole rights to "Vilebastard's Patent Cold Remedy". It is known internationally as the only cure for the sniffles, the honking nose, the rasping cough, the running eye, the feeling of death. They are rich as Croesus, they live the life of Riley, in Cannes, say, or Torquay with yachts full of fat Turkish boys or whatever — now, apart from Dr Jekyll, who will not be receiving his just desserts — what harm will they be doing the rest of the human race? The only thing not to have gone exactly to plan, is that Castor is no longer in it. But what harm can Pollux do? Perhaps Charlie could explain, if he were still with us?'

W.G. had listened inside his head but Charlie was out. It was certainly a puzzle. After W.G. and Watson had left the Albany, a chuckling Raffles summoned a lad to take a note around to Scotland Yard. He felt they needed stirring up.

'So,' W.G. patted Dr Jekyll on the back, and took a swig of sherry. 'You have cured the Common Cold.'

Jekyll turned white as a sheet, and placed a large cold palm over W.G.'s lips.

'Who told you that? How do you know?'

His eyes darted about the room.

'He'll kill me,' he whispered hoarsely.

'Pollux Vilebastard will kill you?' Watson was in, like flint.

'He made me swear — otherwise —' Dr Jekyll was floundering. W.G. put him out of his misery.

'Just a guess,' he said. 'An inspired guess. I happened to notice that the severe cold you had at Lord's had quite gone when we met here the next day.'

Jekyll heaved a great sigh of relief. He seized W.G. by the side-whiskers and shook them with glee.

'Praise be,' he laughed. 'Praise be,' and waved to a waiter, an orange-haired hunchback with extraordinary front teeth, for further sherries. For a fleeting second, Watson thought that Edward Hyde was back, but this fellow was smaller. Equally grotesque, but definitely smaller. Perhaps a relative of Poole's.

'I think, gentlemen, the moment has arrived,' Jekyll clapped his hands and shouting, 'Quiet please, gentlemen!' made his way to the table at which Poole was pouring the green concoction into rummers. Jekyll picked up a glass and held it aloft.

'Gentlemen, you are looking at Medical History in the making. I am happy to have noted that several of you are suffering from colds and summer chills — and like all your fellow-sufferers you are grinning and bearing it until Mother Nature takes her course. No more. Quite by chance, in the course of another experiment entirely, the purpose of which I cannot divulge to you, I struck upon the answer to a question that has preyed upon medical minds since Hippocrates composed his Oath.'

'You have found the Secret of Perpetual Youth,' Sir Ralph Bloomfield Bonington rolled with merriment.

'Eternal *Life*, eh, Jekyll,' scoffed a senior consultant from Barts. 'Last thing we want. No more grateful widows.' The room roared with laughter.

'Sir Ralph,' said Jekyll calmly, 'You are wrestling manfully with a rotten cold, which seven sherries have done nothing to alleviate.'

'I say, steady on, old chap,' said Sir Ralph.

'Come and enjoy a glass of this,' said Jekyll, proffering a rummer full to the brim with the green liquid.

'Work a miracle, will it, Jekyll?' He smiled around the room. It was obviously on his side. Doctors tend to scoff at the new.

'See for yourself.'

'Well' beamed Sir Ralph, taking the glass and raising it to the room. 'Let us see,' and he drank a good half of the mixture. He smacked his lips and pronounced it 'palatable'.

'Drink up,' said Jekyll, sharply.

Sir Ralph finished the glass, and belched loudly.

'Feeling better?' called a GP.

'He's still alive!' quipped another.

'Good Lord,' said Sir Ralph, clutching his forehead, and the general ribaldry ceased.

'I do feel better. It's — it's gone.' His fingers explored the glands in his neck, he felt his pulse, he breathed in and out quite freely, he shook Jekyll's hand.

'You've done it, by George, you've done it! Bravo, Jekyll!'

Jekyll raised his hand to stay the cheering of the doctors.

'Would all those with any sort of chill or cold, please come and try the mixture? I guarantee that one draught will banish all symptoms almost immediately.' Several doctors made their way to the table.

Sir Ralph still stood there, staring intently into his empty green-stained rummer, shaking his head in disbelief.

'You were right, Jekyll, quite right. You said 'Miracle' and I thought you exaggerated. Not so. If anything you undervalue your contribution to medical science. How soon, may I ask, will this be available for the use of our patients?'

'That side of the business, Sir Ralph, I leave to my partner, who alas, for personal reasons, the recent death, in fact of his twin brother, cannot be here today to share these historical moments.' The ten or so doctors who had come forward, thick with phlegm, now whistled and sang with pleasure.

'May I add,' cried Dr Jekyll to the rest of the assembly, 'that this medicine also works as a pick-me-up. Do please indulge.'

'It's quite delicious,' laughed Sir Ralph to the company. 'Fruity sort of thing.'

'I'll give it a try,' said Watson. 'I've been feeling a little dicky.'

The party was becoming very loud, Watson returned with his green drink.

'Sure you won't?'

W.G. shook his head firmly, and Watson downed the dose in one.

'Very agreeable,' he reported.

W.G. grunted. Sir Ralph seemed to be undergoing some sort of relapse. His face was strangely contorted and he was scratching the back of his right hand furiously. So, indeed, were some of the other doctors. Some were tearing at their collars, others rubbing their foreheads. Dr Jekyll seemed quite oblivious to all this, and was still shaking hands contentedly with a host of new admirers, who lavished praise upon him. Even one or two of these lurched out of the circle and clung to a chair or table to steady themselves.

Sir Ralph suddenly roared like some great ape. How the gathering enjoyed that, a good percentage imitating the savage noise.

'Watson,' said W.G. but Watson was scratching the back of *his* right hand vigorously and was lost to the world.

'Watson!' repeated W.G. giving him a good shake. He looked at Watson in astonishment. He had surely never enjoyed such eyebrows previously. The good doctor rolled his reddening eyes.

'Hello, bushy-faced Bill,' he croaked in a voice that Dr Grace barely recognised. The noise about them had become quite zoo-like. Watson's neat moustaches were spreading across his face like rogue ivy. Behind Watson, the Cardiff heart-man was tearing a sofa apart with his bare hands. Bare, thought W.G. but a deal hairier than I recall. A tiny obstetrician was scrambling up a curtain and howling like a banshee.

'Let's do something really vile, Bill,' rasped Watson, his lips peeling back to reveal teeth pointed like an unsprung mantrap. 'Bill,' he went on (more than anything else W.G. hated to be called 'Bill'). 'Bill, come on, Bill,' Watson's eyes glowed like coals through the surrounding facial hair. 'Let's get bleeding pissed and jump about on some jolly fat whores and . . .'

'Doctor Watson!' W.G. cuffed him sharply. 'Can I believe my ears? Is this Doctor Watson speaking?'

'Of course not, you buttock-faced fart-arse,' screeched Watson. 'I'm Edward Hyde!'

'So am I,' cried Sir Ralph, leaping onto the table and braining poor Poole with an empty carafe.

'Edward Hyde?' shouted Paddy Cullen, ripping with his nails into a Queen Anne table-top.

'Did you call?' replied a fourth, his mouth full of aspidistra.

Although to W.G.'s knowledge Dr Jekyll had not touched a drop of the offending liquid, he too seemed to be on the turn. W.G. scrambled towards him. Kicking aside a number of Edward Hydes, each engaged in some extremely doubtful activity, W.G. realised with sudden certainty that Darwin was spot on.

'Jekyll! Jekyll!' W.G. grasped him by the shoulder. 'These drinks have been — doctored, doctor!'

Jekyll shook his hirsute head sadly, 'Vilebastard did it. Vilebastard. He overdid the — the measure. Vilebastard.' And he let out a howl of such pain and anguish that had he been a horse, W.G. would have shot him then and there, screens or no. As it was, Jekyll emitted a ghastly laugh, and set off across the room in an anthropoid crouch. The room was now entirely peopled by Edward Hydes. Evil-looking fellows too, thought W.G. Eyebrows, teeth and halitosis. He must somehow extricate Watson and report back first to 10 Downing Street, and then to Queensberry. Poole was in no position to help. He was trouserless now and suffering appalling indignities at the hands of a couple of Hydes.

Where the hell was Watson? Could that be he ripping asunder a pleasing view of Salisbury Cathedral by Mr Constable?

'Watson!!!' roared W.G. Then he recognised familiar tweeds on a pine-desk by a window.

'Watson! Control yourself!' W.G. was then temporarily inconvenienced by a sharp rap on the head from Jekyll's carafe. He sank into an armchair.

'Come on lads!' cried Watson hoarsely. 'Let's go to Town!' and he leaped from the balcony into the garden below, closely followed by half-a-hundred Hydes. When W.G. recovered his senses the room was empty, save for a moaning Poole. W.G. ran to the window and saw the last of the Hydes vanishing at a swift lope round the corner, heading towards Town. W.G. was in no mood to pursue them. He set off for Downing Street, unaware that the red-haired, hunch-backed waiter was watching him from a balcony.

'You're next, Doctor Grace!' he hissed, hurling the ginger

wig into the street.

'You are "Espéce de sheet", Pollux!' whispered a wooden-legged Frenchwoman, who had hopped elegantly to his side.

Lestrade was exhausted. They had found the hearse, abandoned in Cambridge Circus and no sign of corpse or driver. He now sat in his office at Scotland Yard trying to close his ears to the sounds from the room below.

'Oh say, can you see by the Dawn's early light?' they sang. (In F.)

Lestrade banged his feet on the floor angrily. They would not be silenced.

'Chesterton!' Chesterton's head appeared at the door. 'All that bleedin' fuss from Queensberry's mob about taking over the Vilebastard affair. "Too sophistacerhated for your plodding minds at the Yard", said he. Hinternational himplications, Crowned 'Eads and Hanarchists. We shall send around for the evidence, he said, see that it is ready. Bollocks, I say, Chesterton. The hevidence is seething about in the room below, several of them, like your James 'Enry, like to 'ave an 'eart attack before those bastards get 'ere. The files are gathering dust. What's that bloody great box, Chesterton?'

'Their *Collected Works*, sir. You asked for them.'

'Literary coves, aren't they?' Lestrade picked up several leather-bound books weighed them in his hand and dropped them back in the packing-case. 'I henjoys a good read, Chesterton, but I think we'll let the Himperial Security Hintelligence bleeding Service work their way through that lot. Give 'em something to do. We 'ave more pressing business to 'and. Mr Hedward 'Yde. His apprehension would be a feather in the hat. Any news on that front, Chesterton?'

'Well, sir, yes and no.'

'Anything will do, Chesterton.'

'An anonymous message, sir, suggesting that Mr Hyde might well be found enjoying himself at the El Turco, a nightery in Air Street. The problem, sir, is that we have no such nightery on our books.'

'All the more reason, Chesterton, to hinvestigate, to probe, to swoop. Order up a brace of wagons packed with the

Metropolitan's finest. Cry 'Avoc, Chesterton! Hair Street and step on it!'

The Prime Minister and Dr W.G. Grace sat in the garden of Number Ten, sipping gins. It was a balmy evening, warm and still. No sniper peering through the sights at the garden would have recognised either of the two white-flannelled gentlemen with gaily striped blazers as the Prime Minister. One he might have recognised from his great beard as the Champion of All-England but he would have been hard-pressed indeed to have put a name to the blackface minstrel sitting beside him.

'They tell me this black stuff comes off,' said the PM, through whited painted lips. 'Your news, doctor, is very confusing. Queensberry is never here when you want him. He might have some theory. Have you?'

'I can only think, Mr Prime Minister, that Vilebastard is intent on creating perhaps an army of Edward Hydes. To what end, I cannot imagine. They're vicious brutes, though.'

'Oh Dr Grace, these are difficult times. The recent business with the Mars people. The Boers buggering about. The Germans up to no good at all. The French ever stirring up the pot. Central Europe fizzing like an unexploded bomb. I wouldn't recommend this job to my worst enemy. Though ironically there are three of those in the Cabinet and they all want it. I'm only here because my wife insisted. That's probably true of most politicians I know. Quiet, unassuming men, who'd far rather be at home tending their vast acres, shooting fish or hosing down the peacocks. But no, their wives pushed and pushed. Bloody women! Nothing better to do but try and run the country. One day they'll get into politics proper and then God help us all, doctor.'

'God help us all, Mr Prime Minister.'

'The female of the species is a political animal,' pronounced the Prime Minister.

A white-faced *aide* in morning coat and striped trousers was scuttling across the grass towards them. W.G. rather hoped this might be news of Watson. W.G. naturally felt anxious about Watson, but consoled himself with the thought that he was an old campaigner and when the effects of the green liquid wore off would be more than capable of looking after himself. Wherever he was. After all, a week ago W.G. would not have been asked to his funeral. One can only worry so much about people.

The *aide* was whispering in the Prime Minister's ear. The Prime Minister leapt to his feet and began to shake. Doubtless he had paled but not visibly as his face was coated in black boot polish and white grease paint.

'Inside at once, Dr Grace!' cried the Prime Minister. 'The Revolution has begun! Bar the windows! Call out the militia! Seal off Whitehall! I want the Royal Horse Artillery in Parliament Square, the Coldstreamers in Downing Street, the

Mediterranean Fleet in the Thames. And get a Scottish Regiment out here in the garden, Jock stands no nonsense. Quickly, quickly, inside!' And W.G. found himself following the Prime Minister into the cellars at a hot lick.

They were in a cellar with a rounded roof. It was gloomy but W.G. could detect a couple of long settle tables surrounded by chairs and at the end a large map of London. A number of senior Military and Naval Officers were engaged in shifting variously coloured flags on the map.

A general glanced up at the Prime Minister. A junior officer took the Prime Minister's banjo.

'They're in Piccadilly now, sir,' snapped the General, pointing to fifty clustered yellow flags. 'Fifty of 'em, making a hell of a din, raping and pillaging as they go. They have already routed a small force of constables at the entrance to Green Park. Have I your permission, sir, to send in the Mounted Foot?'

'Are the anarchists armed?' asked the Prime Minister.

'Some have stout walking-sticks, sir, but no weapons as such. Their bare hands seem more than adequate. They tore one young officer's leg off.'

'Good God,' said the Prime Minister, and waved to his *aide*. 'The usual letter.' It was this sort of attention to detail that his wife insisted upon. Good to receive a letter from the Prime Minister's Office saying, 'My Wife and I were most distressed to hear about your leg. Remember that no limb given for your country is wasted. It went in a good cause. One should always remember that. Patriotism demands Sacrifice. Sacrifice demand the odd life or limb. Well done! My Wife and I are in excellent health, we hope we find you so. Yours etc.'

'Sir,' the general cried. 'The Mounted Foot are positioned for the charge. Shall I let them rip? I have a man on the roof with flags ready to signal your permission.'

'Unleash the Mounted Foot!' ordered the Prime Minister. 'Best to quash this uprising as swiftly as we can.'

A sergeant major ran to the door and shouted to the roof.

'A good firm nipping in the bud, General, will be a fine example to any others who may contemplate public disorder and outrage.'

190

'A few deaths then, sir, of a salutary nature.'

The Prime Minister nodded. 'A short, sharp shock.'

The general nodded to the sergeant major.

The sergeant major bellowed a postscript to his previous shriek.

Dusk settled reluctantly on a still humid London. Outside Swan & Edgar, the Duke of Relwick's Mounted Foot waited eagerly for the signal, sabres drawn. They were strung across Piccadilly Circus line abreast. A hundred yards away the Hydes had ransacked Fortnum's and were now picnicking by lamplight in the middle of the road on port and crystallised fruits, sinking their jagged teeth into hams and succulent pies. The noise alone was vomit-making, like a thousand hogs nuzzling for slops in a septic tank.

'The signal, sir!' Flags were waving on a roof in St James'.

Captain Grimes, head bandaged beneath his helmet, raised his sabre.

'B Squadron of the Mounted Foot, in single line abreast, at the trot, Forward!'

'This,' added Grimes to his second-in-command, 'will be a walk-over.'

At Grimes' signal the bugler sounded the charge.

The Hydes looked up from their repast, and grunted, as one beast.

Lestrade was first upon the scene of the massacre. Groaning cavalry-men and horses lay among the broken bottles and ham-bones. Captain Grimes, still mounted, lay in the window of Fortnums where he had been casually tossed by an Edward Hyde.

'Who did this?' asked Lestrade gently, easing one of Grimes' feet from the stirrup of his dead horse. The other leg had gone completely.

'They were worse than animals,' gasped Grimes. 'There was no killing them. They tackled the horses and broke their necks. They stamped on the faces of our lads 'till they were quite flat. They —' he sobbed with pain and memories.

'Who?'

Grimes tried to raise his head. His helmet had a deep dent in it where a passing Hyde had kicked him.

191

'I heard a name,' he whispered.

'A name?' Lestrade folded his waterproof under Grimes' head.

'Edward Hyde,' breathed Grimes. Lestrade was about to show him a portrait of Queen Anne for identification when Grimes passed out for the second time in twenty-four hours. Lestrade looked around at the debris that had once been 'B' Squadron, pride of the Mounted Foot. It was dark now and Lestrade gathered his dozen men under a lamp outside the Royal Academy.

'Hedward 'Yde,' he pronounced, ''as gone too bleeding' far this time.'

His sergeant spoke up. 'The anarchists was seen entering El Turco's, sir, a place of entertainment in Air Street. They 'ave not come out.'

A nervous young constable raised his hand. He was only too aware of the ambulances and the stretcher-parties behind him.

'Are we still swooping, sir?'

Lestrade braced himself and set his bowler more firmly on his head.

'Is that not why we are 'ere? Among the hanarchists his Mr Hedward 'Yde.'

Her sergeant coughed politely and touched his helmet. 'There are but a dozen of us, sir.'

'Chesterton's around somewhere,' said Lestrade cheerfully.

'Thirteen, sir?' The sergeant shook his head sadly. Superstition apart, that did not seem the ideal number to feel the collars of fifty raw-horse-eating hooligans.

'Follow me, lads,' said Lestrade, and pulled his truncheon from his trousers.

In the bunker under Number Ten, gloom pervaded. The Mounted Foot had been routed, the Marquis of Queensberry had disappeared. So had the Revolution. Watson too, thought W.G. Can he still be with the Hydes, wherever they may be? If he is, how long will he be a Hyde? The effects of the cure had better wear off quickly; Watson was weekending at Windsor.

'Where is the Revolution now?' The PM was extremely irked.

The General waved vaguely at the map of London. 'Picca-dilly, sir. Last sighting — Air Street, sir.'

It was slowly dawning on W.G. that the so-called Revolution that the Prime Minister was so keen to put down summarily could well be Dr Jekyll's party. In which case, this beverage of Jekyll's was extraordinary stuff, and Watson was in grave danger. Piccadilly? Air Street? That pit of Queensberry's would be the very sort of place that a number of raving medical men, under the influence of God-knows-what, would congregate. Champagne and belly-dancers? Good Lord, even he, a pillar of rectitude, had felt Mother Nature's warm hand upon his privates. He blurted out his theory to the War Room and, within minutes, surrounded by a Squadron of Household Cavalry and a troop of Royal House Artillery, W.G. was being driven in the Prime Minister's personal carriage towards Piccadilly.

As Lestrade and his men turned the corner of Air Street, Chesterton stepped out of the shadows.

'They're all in there, sir,' he nodded towards the door in which Queensberry had lurked that very afternoon. 'Are we waiting for reinforcements?'

'My job, Chesterton, is to happrehend one Hedward 'Yde. 'E is within. The rest is hirrelevant. 'Ave you clapped eyes on Mr 'Yde?'

'Yes, sir,' Chesterton was uncertain as to how to phrase the next bit. 'Fifty of him, sir. All mad as hatters.'

'Fifty of them, Chesterton? Fifty Hedward 'Ydes?'

'I heard them all, sir, as they entered El Turco — they all signed in as "Edward Hyde" — the young lady on the door, to whom incidentally, such is the long arm of coincidence, I am engaged — though I thought she worked at the Foreign Office — Miss Henrietta Lumley, sir, was not going to argue, indeed she was in no position to, when I pulled two of the brutes off her and sent her home in a hansom.'

'They seems to be henjoying themselves, Chesterton.'

'It's not as noisy as it was, sir.'

'They've 'ad a tiring evening.' Lestrade peered down the ill-lit stair. 'Our Hedward is throwing up a smoke-screen. 'Oping to 'ide 'imself among a crowd of paid haccomplices. What 'e does not know, Chesterton, 'is that thanks to Dr Watson's rude penmanship I 'as 'is likeness.' And he proudly thrust the rearranged features of the late Queen Anne in front of Chesterton's nose.

'Got 'im! Right, lads, watch these doors. I ham going in.'

'Alone, sir?'

'Im my hexperience, Chesterton, over the years I 'ave observed that an ugly crowd is more likely to bend to the sensible cautions of one policeman than whole regiments of Militia. Hobserve!' And in he went. Chesterton removed his hat and whispered a prayer for those in peril in a damp basement.

Watson was beginning to feel himself again. It had been a frightening experience, his previous hallucinations in Baker Street had all been jolly affairs, this had been dark and terrifying. It was certainly the last time he would accept any green drinks from Dr Jekyll. Where was he? Ah, El Turco's no less. Or what remained of it. He had a sudden flash of the awful Captain Grimes galloping straight at him, sabre pointed at his breast, and he, Watson, seizing the horse by the neck and with the action of a hammer-thrower revolving thrice and tossing the whole caboodle through a window of Fortnum and Mason's. Nightmare-ish, that was the word. And he would use it. This story might be a little heady for the *Strand* but he knew other publishers who would leap at it.

What he would have to describe here was a scene not witnessed perhaps since Caligula was struck off the social list. It was the morning after the night before in Nero's Bathroom. A sea of exhausted pink flesh with the wreckage floating on top of it. Broken screens and coffee-tables, torn curtains and rugs, shattered glass and used food. The smell was appalling. He would certainly never find his tweeds again in that lot, so moving with great difficulty, he draped his soggy body in a length of Persian Carpet and began to pick his way through the human jetsam towards the exit. These did not consist solely of Edward Hydes and belly-dancers; there was also the regular clientelle who had gone down in the first wave. Several politicians he recognised frozen in postures of abandon, two Dukes, a Bishop, three judges welded together in a sticky pile. It came as no surprise therefore when he found himself standing on the face of the Marquis of Queensberry. He opened one of the Marquis's eyes with a toe.

'Doctor Watson?' Queensberry had no idea where he was. There was a moment of panic as his eye skidded over the surrounding mayhem. 'My God' he enquired pathetically. 'What happened?'

'A number of medical men, maddened by certain substances, fell upon this den of iniquity in the night, and here we see the results.'

'There are Kings here, Watson, and Archdukes. I was asked to "entertain" many of the Crowned Heads who are, as you know, guests of . . . our Queen, our Government, oh, my God!' and he clasped his head and groaned.

'Right!' the voice of authority barked from the door, 'Nobody moves!' It was Lestrade, and he was absolutely right. 'I am Hinspector Lestrade of Scotland Yard, and you are all under harrest!' Nobody moved. 'Stand up, Mr Hedward 'Yde, and make yourself known to me.'

'Is there another exit?' Watson whispered to Queensberry.

'Of course there is. Place like this. There are twelve to my certain knowledge.'

Reasonable trepidation kept Lestrade at the door, he liked to feel the stairs were behind him and at the first sign of trouble, he could beat a tactical retreat. It was all too quiet.

'Mr Hedward 'Yde! I 'ave 'ere a Warrant for your Harrest. Hi will not 'ang about much longer!'

Queensberry and Watson were crawling away over damp hillocks of breast and buttock towards the kitchens. Slumped across the bottom of the double-doors, preventing their movement lay Dr Jekyll. He was trouserless, but otherwise correct. Watson pushed him out of the way and he and Queensberry dived into the kitchen — Squeak! Squeak! Clunk! Clunk!

Hyde was making his move! Lestrade blew three shrill, loud blasts on his whistle.

'Stay where you are!' he shrieked as Chesterton and the small force tumbled towards him down the stair. What had been a still pond of pink had suddenly erupted into a whirl-pool of puce.

Queensberry bolted the kitchen doors behind the three of them.

'Bit unfair,' said Watson.

Queensberry winked, and they ran out into an alley and the arms of W.G. who bundled them into the PM's carriage. 'Albany!' he cried.

Meanwhile in 'El Turco' — 'Right!' beamed Lestrade. 'You are all nicked! Get the cuffs on this lot, lads, and round to Savile Row — they'll be up before the beak by nine o'clock.' A good night's work — he thought proudly to himself — there'll be promotion in this and no mistake. He pushed his way through the crowd, blind and deaf to protest and bribe. He felt warmly smug. Suddenly he was face to face with a face he knew. A desperate face, an anxious face.

'Dr Jekyll,' he said, 'And naked to boot.'

'Trouserless perhaps, Inspector Lestrade,' said Jekyll 'I am as you can see a victim of circumstance.'

'Enough said,' said Lestrade, who fancied himself as a judge of human behaviour. ''Ome you go, sir. Chesterton, lend Dr Jekyll your coat and hail him an 'ansom.'

Compassion, as well. What a good night's work. Now to find our Hedward.

W.G. was gazing up Savile Row out of Raffle's drawing-room window. In the distance more than a hundred shackled nudes were being pushed out of police-wagons and into the station. Lestrade, he could see, strolling about smoking a large cigar and issuing the occasional order. He was casually juggling with three confiscated rubies. Behind W.G., Queensberry sat stark naked, save for his shoes and gartered socks, (obviously he was not the sort of man who removes them even for an orgy), smoking a cheroot and staring silently into the empty grate. Heads were going to roll after this night, and unless the grate had any bright ideas, his would seem to be first up on the platter. Watson was having a bath and a serious thought about Social Diseases. Heaven knows what had befallen him at El Turco's — he certainly had no memory of events there — but had the very worst befallen him and with Windsor looming — it did not bear thinking about. He ignored the loofah, this was a job for the pumice. Raffles was out.

Some dogs were barking furiously in the street below.

'It's the sight of all that fresh meat,' laughed Queensberry. Not that he was one to talk. W.G. had met many men like him over the years in changing-rooms. W.G. looked down at the dogs. What was that they were tied to? Some sort of sledge-like object — Dickens!

There was a knock at the door and there *was* the splendid Mountie with an ancient Porter.

'Gentleman 'ere,' sniffed the porter, who trusted no-one, 'says as 'ow 'e is an acquaintinance of Mr Raffles. Who are you?'

'I am Dr W.G. Grace. I have known Mr Raffles for many a moon. We are fellow-cricketers. This gentleman is Lieutenant Dickens of the Canadian Police. Yes, indeed, he knows Mr Raffles.'

The porter looked him up and down slowly.

'It's 'ighly suspicious, sir. Mr Raffles, goes out every night about his lawful business. Well, unless Mr Bunny is 'ere — no-one else is. And now all of a sudden foreign policemen in fancy dress, great bearded men and who the bloody hell is that — a nudist of disgusting proportions! I for one, sir, am shouting "'elp" and running for the constabulary! That is my sworn duty sir, the reason for my salary and brass buttons!'

'Here is a guinea, my good man,' said W.G.

'Oh, sir. Now I am torn between greed and duty. One half of me cries out "Shame upon you, sir!" but the other is thinking imagine the cost of a Home Secretary or a Chief Constable in similar circumstances. Astrobleedinomical.'

'Two guineas?'

'It would be unpatriotic, sir, not to recognise the English art of compromise when you see it. Be as nude as you like, sir. Entertain as many as you wish. Burgle the premises — let there be cakes full of women —'

'We have no intention of behaving so!' said W.G. sharply.

'That, sir, is the great beauty of it,' replied the porter. 'But I find myself richer by two guineas. God bless you, gentlemen.' And he lumbered off in search of fresh game.

'Straight from Dickens, eh?' laughed Queensberry.

'So am I,' said the Unmounted Policeman.

W.G. made the necessary introductions. Queensberry joked lightly about the disadvantages of having a famous father.

'I have news,' said Dickens. 'I know where Pollux Vilebastard is, though I cannot imagine why he is there.'

Watson emerged from the bathroom, wrapped in a towel. 'Where? Where?' he said, thrusting his backside into the unlit fireplace.

Dickens lowered himself into an armchair, and gratefully accepted a drink from W.G.

'Let me begin at the beginning,' he said.

On my sainted aunt, groaned Watson inwardly, another of them. Everybody wants to be an author. Why can't he simply say, 'Potter's Bar' or 'Zanzibar' or 'The Bar at the Folies Bergères' (which in fact was precisely where Pollux was, rolling his eyes at a square-jawed blonde barmaid.) He's going to take hours, reaching for adverbs, plucking adjectives. He seriously contemplated not fetching his notebook from his jacket pocket as some sort of protest.

'Have any of you in the course of this case crossed the path of a French actress with a wooden leg?'

'We have never met on the path,' replied W.G., 'but one has been aware of such a person lurking in the adjacent shrubbery.'

Dickens smiled. Get a bloody move on, thought Watson. W.G.'s caught it now.

'The Divine Sarah, they call her,' announced Dickens.

'True. True. Bloody true,' cried Queensberry and had the decency to seize a towel to wrap around his waist and face the mantlepiece. This left Watson naked and pink in a public place for the third day running. 'I've seen her. I can vouch for her divinity. What part has she to play in all this?'

'A reluctant one,' said Dickens. 'She is I fear another victim of the Vilebastard genius for conjuring skeletons from cupboards. While she was at the Comédie Francaise she had a mild, but ultimately tragic affair with a Communard, one Jacques Vernet.'

'Any relation,' cried Watson, 'to Vernet the painter?' Damn, *he* was doing it now. 'It's just,' he mumbled, 'that Holmes was related to a painter called Vernet.'

'Very interesting,' said W.G. pleasantly.

'No, it isn't,' said Watson. 'Let's get on with it.'

'She used to go to see Alfred Stevens. Friend of Degas — handsome Belgian. Had a studio in the Rue des Martyrs. Very fashionable. Baudelaire was often there. Alexandre Dumas *fils*. There she met Vernet. One thing led to the other. There were pictures. Somehow the Vilebastards laid hands on one and, of course, the Divine Sarah would not want her involvement with the Communards published today.'

Watson sighed. 'That a life can be manipulated by dirty post-cards.'

'Dirty great oil-paintings,' said Dickens.

'The brutes,' said Watson. 'Innocent gel like that.'

'Not so innocent,' replied Dickens. 'But not so guilty.'

'Where did you meet her?' asked Watson. His initial resentment was past, now he felt that old surge of excitement again. The chase was on again.

'At Jekyll's house,' answered Dickens. 'Once I'd lost the hearse. I returned there. I'd left the dogs behind, anyway. Those young lads of Dr Watson's were watching the front of the house, so I went to my usual spot at the rear. Naturally, one of the lads came and told me there was some sort of party going on. I still couldn't see Pollux using the front door, so I stayed where I was. I missed the sudden exodus of the guests though it was reported to me and some of the lads set off in pursuit. Well, nothing happened for about an hour and then I see that backdoor to the laboratory opening, but it's only a waiter going home. A hunchback —'

'Met him,' said W.G. 'Thought he might be a relative of Poole's.'

'Then five minutes later out came this woman, middle-aged but striking with a pronounced limp.'

'How pronounced?' asked Dr Watson.

'Leemp,' replied Dickens. 'She was a Frenchwoman and most forthcoming. Of course, she knew Pollux Vilebastard. Had I not seen him leave with a cushion up the back of him? Too late to follow him, so I asked her if she knew where he was going. *Mais oui*, she laughs, and I am going there myself *ce soir*, she says, to play Napoleon's son.'

'His *son*?' Dr Watson scratched the back of his neck.

'I've seen her Hamlet,' said Queensberry. 'Splendid legs.

Leg anyway.'

'Hamlet?' Watson pondered where all this would end. He thought of asking if she had ever essayed Long John Silver, but decided not to.

'You're not going anywhere, Mademoiselle, I said.' said Dickens, 'and made to apprehend her. That's when I discovered about the wooden leg. Her shin caught me right in the Orchestras.' He rubbed the aching region.

'Where was she going to?' asked W.G.

'Paris,' replied Dickens.

'Paris?' mused W.G.

'Glue,' said Watson, peering into his notebook.

'Glue?' queried W.G.

'Paris. Glue,' read Dr Watson and showed him the illuminated page.

'Oh, my God,' said W.G. remembering. 'Paris, Glue'.

And Charlie chortled in his head.

16   An Eventful Night at the Hotel Paradiso

Watson and W.G. were alone in Watson's room at the Hotel Paradiso in the Rue Morgue, and quite content so to be. Queensberry's last words as their train pulled out of Victoria Station had been — 'Don't worry, you're not alone! My man in Paris will be in touch. You'll recognise him. Oh, yes, you'll recognise him.'

A strange young English artist had insisted on carrying their bags at the Gare du Nord. But they had not recognised him.

'This,' said W.G. sipping a glass of excellent wine, 'is the very room in which they found poor Studholme.' He looked all round it carefully as if some torn morsel of the Reverend might have been overlooked.

'The window is certainly large enough for a great ape to enter by,' noted Watson. 'Quite a sizeable gorilla could get through there. Without much difficulty.'

He looked out into the garden below. 'No, no difficulty at all.' He poured them another glass of wine apiece. W.G.'s mind seemed to be on other things.

'I was saying,' said Watson, 'that it would be the simplest thing in the world for an enormous anthropoid to shin up here, burst through the window and tear the occupant of this room limb from limb —'

W.G. nodded, 'Yes, indeed,' he said, in a thoroughly off-hand manner.

'From limb from limb,' continued Watson uneasily, and ferreted about in his valise for his faithful old service revolver.

'I was thinking,' erupted W.G. 'about this Great Ape.'

'I was just *talking* about it,' Watson complained. 'You could have saved yourself a good deal of brain-strain.'

'I very much doubt that it was a great ape,' said W.G. 'My theory would be that it was more of an Edward Hyde. Pollux perhaps imbibed a little of the green liquid and — well, one of the Hydes, I read, threw a man and a horse through a shop window.'

Watson blushed deeply. This was, however, not the time

to tell his friend the truth of that incident.

'If,' W.G. wagged his finger dramatically, he was beginning to enjoy detection, 'Pollux was not Hyde, then Lestrade will only have to check at Boulogne as to who accompanied Pollux to France. That will be Edward Hyde.'

What a pity that the doctors forgot this fascinating deduction in the excitement of the next few days. It would have saved Lestrade weeks of interviewing the most unlikely candidates all huddled in the same room at the Yard, that had only recently been vacated by London's American population. It was, in fact to prove the last investigation of his not unsuccessful career.

'Bed, I think,' said W.G., rising, 'and tomorrow we begin the hunt for Pollux.'

'Yes, we must find him before he does whatever it is

that he intends to do.'

'Perhaps Queensberry's man will prove to be of some assistance, whoever he may be.'

'And wherever,' replied Watson, taking another anxious peek out of the window. Whoever and wherever — he was out there somewhere.

Sleep does not come easily to guests at the Hotel Paradiso, as W.G. soon discovered to his cost. As his head touched the pillow his wardrobe burst open and a trouserless Captain of Zouaves, moustaches reading ten minutes past eight, burst forth and, throwing a bunch of roses at W.G. with a cry of 'Hortense, je t'adore!', disappeared through one of the room's seven doors, as another burst open and a bearded nun rushed in, leaped across W.G.'s recumbent form and vanished through the French windows. To some extent W.G. blamed himself for being something of a fresh-air fiend and being unable to sleep without windows and curtains open. The room was bathed with light from a lamp outside. There was knocking at three doors simultaneously.

'What?' cried W.G.

The three doors opened as one, and in sprang a waiter, a porter and clearly an upstairs maid.

The waiter and the porter kissed vigorously, their moustaches becoming inextricably entwined in passion.

'Jean-Paul! Maurice!' cried the upstairs maid, and bursting into floods of tears, pursued them from the room. Half-a-dozen gendarmes entered at the trot, apologised, and left through the door by which they had entered. W.G. lay as still as possible watching the dancing reflections on the ceiling. The bearded nun reappeared at the window and was chased from the room by a dozen 'pompiers' with brass helmets and gleaming axes. A bowler-hatted gentleman danced in with a lady in a delicious, flowered hat and petticoats. Hot on their heels came a fat, red-faced top-hatted johnnie in a morning coat who discharged a double-barrelled shotgun into the ceiling and ran into the bathroom, whence startled squeals proclaimed that he had interrupted the ablutions of a number of ladies that W.G. was perfectly certain had not been there when he had cleaned his teeth. A *chef*'s cheerful head appeared round a door, but the smile disappeared when he saw W.G.

'What have you done with Hortense?' he raged.

All one needs now, thought W.G. blearily, is the bloody great ape.

All seven doors opened at once, disgorging into the room thirty-eight matelots; the trouserless Captain of Zouaves; eight bearded nuns; waiters; porters; maids from every direction; six gendarmes; the bowler-hatted gentleman; his friend in the delicious hat; the fat man in the topper blazing away; a good dozen schoolgirls; a quartet of gypsy violinists playing like furies; three straw-hatted life-guards; a post-impressionist, a juggler, balls and all; three Bankers wrapped in eiderdowns, and an old lady with a candle calling 'Raoul!' in a plaintive contralto.

W.G. rose in his bed like the ghost at the end of Act One and roared his protest.

'Out! Out! Allez! Allez! This is mon rume! I am not Hortense! Bugger off! I wish to dormitoir.'

Slowly the room cleared. It was a long business, but in the end he was at last alone.

'Not quite, monsieur,' sang a lilting voice from the bed. 'Hortense est ici.'

'Oh God,' whispered Dr Grace. He could make out a frilly figure in the bed — a delicious flowered hat. 'Venez ici, Monsieur Feydeau.' Watson would know what to do. One of these doors leads to Watson. There. There's Watson, fast asleep, despite evidence all over his room of heavy traffic. He could sleep through anything. W.G. thought of waking him, but decided that the shock might prove too much. A sudden beard in the night — he might well think the great ape was back, and do something desperate with the enormous pistol he was clutching under the pillow.

Ah, well, thought W.G. I'd best deal with Hortense alone. He buttoned his night-shirt to the throat and adjusted it to cover his knees. No need to inflame the baggage with unnecessary glimpses. He squared his shoulders and entered his room again. His bed was empty. She had gone.

Gratefully he bolted the seven doors, and retired.

Outside in the corridor, the bangs and crashes of doors and shot-guns slowly died. W.G.'s last thought before wild dreams set in was that this all seemed typically French to him.

W.G. was next awoken by the strangest of sounds. It was to some extent musical but not a tune he knew. A door creaking on unoiled hinges? Too relentless. A large wasp or bee perhaps peculiar to Paris? Not relentless enough. He groped under the bed for his cricket-bag and felt for the handle of his faithful willow. The noise continued unabated and he could now detect a hissing sound as well. This could all, he reasoned, be a further lamentable example of your Frenchman's inability to cope with the most elementary aspects of modern plumbing. He might well have turned over and gone to sleep, never, in fact, to wake again, had not the moon reappeared from behind a cloud. The hissing was instantly explained.

Not the plumbing, but erect at the end of the bed and eyeing him far too closely for comfort was some sort of large snake. Seizing his bat, W.G. stood up in bed and prepared for the worst. The music ceased and with a sudden, darting movement the snake attacked. It came at him with the speed of one of Tom Richardson's shooters. Faster by far off the pitch than through the air, it would have been a close LBW decision had he missed, but W.G., despite the poor light, struck it on the rise and the snake flew like a jet of tobacco-juice across the room, smacked against the wall and dribbled down it into a dark corner.

'Watson!' boomed Grace, 'Watson!' and was quite astonished when the honest physician rushed through his door and discharged three shots from his service revolver into the wriggling cobra's head.

'Definitely a cobra,' said the old India-hand, and darted out of the room again returning almost at once waving a round wicker-basket with a small round hole at the top.

'Damned nearly fell over this in the corridor,' he complained.

'Bit on the small side for laundry isn't it?' said W.G.

'Snake basket, in fact,' replied Watson, authoritatively. 'I've encountered these things before. Snake in basket, little chap with pipe would lure it out with a bit of music. All over India you'd find 'em. Popular turn. Rather dull, I thought. Rope-trick, now you're talking. And gingerly he picked up the snake and dropped it into the basket, stuffing the hole with a towel.

'Nasty business,' he said 'Damned careless, too. I suggest we go down and tear a strip or two of Monsieur le Manager.'

'I did hear some sort of music,' said W.G.

'Sort of whiny, wailing, nasal sort of Indian Music?'

'Yes. Creaking door, only longer. Thought it might be the plumbing.'

'That's the noise those little chaps come up with in the bazaars.' And Watson held his nose, and whined and wailed in a none too musical manner.

'Precisely so,' said W.G.

'Then that snake was deliberate,' cried Watson. 'Old Red Fort', he added.

W.G. vaguely remembered some mention of this before.

Watson sat himself on the end of W.G.'s bed, and removed his night-cap.

'In that coach, on the way to what transpired to be Downing Street I asked you to remind me.' He forgave W.G. with a quick smile. 'It was when the band started up, it all flooded back. They were playing the Regimental March of the Duke of Relwick's Mounted Foot, and there I was back at this parade in Delhi, standing on a dais in front of the Old Red Fort, and there was the Governor-General standing in front of me taking the salute. Swaying a little, which is why I was there, the sun and drink had got him. He was off to Old Blighty within the month. I was there for purely medical reasons, in case he fell over. Now, and I can't imagine how I'd forgotten this, also standing on that dais were those Vile-bastards. Fact is, I'm not even certain they called themselves that, they were known as the Toupés. Some wag said they were as alike as toupés in a pod and it sort of stuck. The Toupé Twins. Not that they hadn't got their own hair. They were on some kind of attachment to the Bengal Lancers. Vets or Engineers, I don't know. Probably they were on the Governor-General's staff, that would explain their presence on the dais. I'm afraid I'm pretty vague about all that. What I do remember is that they were drummed out of India.'

'Good Lord!' said W.G. 'They certainly left their mark wherever they went!'

'What I don't remember,' continued Watson, 'is *why* they were given the old heave-ho.' He began to read his brow in braille. 'Something to do with a Holy Man, a mystic — some sort of swami or fakir or whatever, one of those chaps who lies on beds of nails, y'know, sticks knitting-needles through his tongue and that sort of malarkey. Now how the Toupés got involved I have no idea, but this feller was found face-down on a bed of hot coals. Dead, of course, and not a pretty sight. I don't think anything was proved against the Vile-bastards, but Home they were sent.'

'Could he read minds or such?' W.G. was thinking of the Eskimo and Charlie.

'Via South Africa!' Watson wasn't. Watson was padding off back to his room. W.G. shouted after him.

'Could he read minds?'

'No. Don't think so.' Watson was looking for something. 'He could die when he wanted to. Not that he did. Ah!' Watson had found something and was padding back with a pink folder marked, 'Most Secret. I.S.I.S.' By the light of a candle, he beban to rifle through it.

'Queensberry gave me this. It's the Vilebastards File. Thought it might help.' And he pulled out a tattered postcard with several views of Table Mountain on the front in sepia.

'South Africa!' he turned the PC over and began to read.

'It's addressed to the Marquess of Queensberry, c/o The Imperial Security Intelligence Service, Whitehall, London. It says "Confidential" in the top left corner. And "TOP SECRET".'

'Not too loud, then,' smiled W.G.

Watson refused to see the humour of it. He proceeded to read.

'V's back from Zululand or thereabouts. No sign of Mjanji. They deny all knowledge. Balls, of course. They've killed the old bitch. Cetshwayo bloody furious. War looms. Must dash. R. Haggard.'

'Who's Mjanji?' W.G. ran his fingers thoughtfully through his beard, found a cockroach and flicked it with a casual movement into the snake-basket.

Watson found a Memo in Queenberry's erratic hand. 'Mjanji,' it said, 'Chieftainess of Bapedis. Queen of the Locusts. Colour: Black as your Hat. Special Peculiarities: One: 4 bloody great Tits. Two: Ability to conjure up floods or droughts or plagues of locusts to confound her enemies.'

'Another mystic bites the dust at the hands of the Vile-bastards,' mused W.G.

'Jolly bad luck on her being dead.' Watson was reading on. 'She was said to be immortal.'

'What the hell were they up to?' W.G. got up and walked over to the window. He breathed in deeply. Paris air was not the freshest. Garlic, and poor drains are not the healthiest of ingredients, he thought.

'At one moment,' said W.G., 'our twins were tinkering with the most sophisticated modern inventions and discoveries, electricity and the like. The next, they're wiping out the purveyors of ancient, nay, prehistoric beliefs and practices. What's up Watson?'

'Perhaps Queensberry's man will enlighten us.' He held up another sheet of paper. 'They were in Ramsgate the night that The Great Ralpho (He Hypnotises! He Reads Minds! He will Amaze you!) and Wanda were discovered on the beach, drowned.'

They sat in silence, contemplating the Vilebastards' distressing and bewildering record.

'Best to sleep on it, old chap,' Watson rose. 'All may be clearer in the morning.'

'I very much doubt it,' said W.G., but Morpheus beckoned. 'Don't forget the snake,' he added to the departing Watson.

'I don't want it,' said Watson, 'give it to the chambermaid!'

'You misunderstand me,' said W.G. 'I meant that the presence of the snake indicates that Pollux knows we are here, a fact that we must not now forget.'

'Oh Lord,' Watson whispered, 'I hadn't thought of that.'

W.G. slipped out of bed and firmly bolted the French windows against any further incursions from the Rue Morgue.

Next morning over a particularly shoddy French breakfast, W.G. and Watson decided that their first priority was to contact Queensberry's man in Paris, although their confidence in him had been slightly tempered by the apparent idiocy of Queensberry's man in Capetown.

'You, Watson, watch here at the Hotel with your service revolver. Pollux knows we are here, but so does Queensberry. I cannot imagine that Pollux will chance his arm during the daylight hours, however, Queensberry's man may well. Best we are ready.'

'What are you going to do?' asked Watson, thinking that the last place he wanted to spend a day alone was the Hotel Paradiso.

'I am going to walk about,' announced W.G.

'Very nice too,' said a disgruntled Watson, 'lovely day for a stroll along the boulevards. Paris, I hear, is particularly lovely at this time of year. The blooms. The cherry blossom. The Seine a-twinkle. Perfect day not to be locked in a hotel room, all hot and bothered, besieged by burly cleaning women with mops and towels, not to mention possible visitations by great apes and snake-charmers, spies and assassins. Going to walk about are you?' He stared disconsolately down at the Rue Morgue. 'Have a nice day.'

'I'm sorry Watson, I've been skippering far too long. I'm afraid I naturally seized the reins — would *you* like to go and walk about? I simply thought that Queensberry's man might more easily recognise *me*. A large, black-bearded fellow with a red-and-yellow striped blazer and matching cap presents perhaps a larger target than, shall we say, a distinguished looking medical man in a pleasing tweed suit and a brown bowler hat.'

'With a limp,' said Watson. 'I am quite recognisable. I am not unknown.'

W.G. put his arm round Watson's shoulder.

'Watson, I am an arrogant fool. So far on this case it is upon your experience with Mr Hume —'

'Holmes.'

'Holmes, that's right, fellow who fell off a cliff. It is upon your experience with him in matters of deduction that we have leaned. You are the reason we are here now so near to ending the matter.'

Watson cheered up visibly. 'Thank you, W.G., that's damned polite of you. But in fairness, I owe a good deal to your natural intuition. Have we not worked jolly well to date — as a team?'

'Team-work! You've said it, Watson. That has been the essence of our success. Let us do things the British Way. We shall *both* sit here, you with your pistol, I with my bat, and await events.'

All day, they stoutly withstood the siege of the cleaning-ladies. The keys constantly rattling at the lock, the angry knocking, the banging of buckets, the whispering in the corridor. At one point some managerial figure called to them in French. 'Non, merci' replied Watson firmly. 'Pas today.' There was a furious conference outside. W.G. whose ear was clapped to the keyhole, whispered to Watson, 'What is La Vice Anglaise?'

'The English *Avis*,' replied Watson. 'Notice, I think, the English notice.'

W.G. searched the back of the door. 'There isn't one,' he said. There were Fire Regulations, but they were Greek to him.

It was intensely hot with all the windows closed and they moved restlessly to and fro from one room to another, seeking.

'If we let those harridans in,' said Watson. 'We're a sitting bull.'

It was growing darker outside. W.G. went around their rooms drawing the curtains. Tell the truth, he was bloody hungry. If, however, they sent down for something from the Hotel kitchens, such are the excesses of French cuisine, that there'd be no telling if the stuff contained some drug or poisons until it was far too late.

'Hang on, W.G., said Watson. 'I fancy someone or other will make a move very shortly.' He cocked his pistol. There were too many doors for safety, in his view, but he had found a piano-stool in W.G.'s bathroom and was revolving slowly, covering all the entrances.

There was not a sound for a good hour. Then footsteps and two men laughing together. Snatches of French. 'Les deux gentilhommes Anglais,' followed by that strange French laugh that sounds like the last farewell of bathwater vanishing down the plug-hole.

'Zere is a man over at ze Bar du Gros Nez who would like to meet those two.' Watson and W.G. exchanged pregnant glances. More French including the word 'pédéraste'.

'Pédéraste?' mouthed W.G.

Watson shook his head.

''Oneymoon,' he understood.

'What?' he barked.

'Ah, Monsieur,' called a voice from the corridor, 'I was saying how much a gentleman over at ze Bar zere would enjoy meeting you two.' There was giggling.

'It's very hard to spot irony, however heavy, when delivered in a foreign tongue,' said Watson, 'But I fancy I spotted it there. What are they suggesting?'

It was W.G.'s turn to shake his head. 'I don't know' he said, marching off into his room and taking his cap off a hook. 'But I feel one of us should go and see if this man exists.'

'You say "one of us" ' said Watson, nodding at W.G.'s cap.

'I thought you might prefer to remain here with your pistol.'

'I might well prefer to remain here with my pistol but I would like to be consulted first. Is that asking too much?'

W.G. went to a window and counted ten very slowly. Watson could be vastly irritating. He idly wondered how Mr Shylock Haynes had coped with his peevishness. Through a crack in the curtain he could see the bar. It was a small dark building, the upper rooms shuttered. On the pavement, under a glass canopy (the word 'Nez' was just decipherable through the encrusted bird-lime,) were scattered assorted tables and chairs, intermingled with pots of diseased plant-life. The clientèle sat as if for a group portrait. Not, thought W.G., a picture one would have up on the wall, certainly not next to the Famous Box. There was a movement. From behind a shaggy piece of hedge a statuesque figure with a long oval face framed by flowing locks and a saucily perched black topper, was waving a yellow glove. W.G. closed the curtain quickly and made for the door.

'We may have made contact, Watson. I was waved to from the bar. Big fellow, top hat.' Watson dashed to the window for a look.

'Keep an eye on him,' cried W.G., and was gone.

As W.G. crossed the road outside the Hotel Paradiso the only sound coming from the Bar was the lilt of Irish laughter. Ignoring the sensible advice of his father, 'When Irish eyes are smiling, run like a hairy goat,' he passed between two tubs of bush and sat himself at the only empty table on the pavement. The lilt of Irish laughter came from within. W.G. was staying without. He was aware of a presence behind him, the musky tang of some exotic ungent.

'Sure,' said a lilting Irish voice, 'and is it not the Greatest Cricket Player in all the World?'

A green drink was placed before him and the presence sat beside him sipping at another. It was the Waver. Queensberry had forecast that his man would be recognisable. He was.

'Wilde, O.F.O.W.,' breathed W.G. A yellow-gloved hand was laid on his lips 'Melmoth,' cried Oscar. 'Sebastian Melmoth. We played cricket together some summers ago on Prince's Ground, in what is now, alas, Hans Place. I walked sadly round it, the night they swooped at the Cadogan Hotel.'

'I always find it hard to imagine,' said W.G., 'your sort playing the Noble Game.'

'There is only the one team and that's in Limerick,' laughed the huge Paddy, 'and didn't they come third in the All-Ireland Championship?'

'Damned fairies,' said W.G.

'Damned *leprechauns,*' replied Oscar, quick as Spofforth.

'Spofforth,' said W.G., quite irrelevantly, 'was almost certainly the quickest I ever faced, though there was a Philadelphian, Newhall, who was as swift as any I have faced.'

Oscar gazed at him, lost for words. Never let it be said, thought W.G. that I can't bandy words with a master of badinage. Oscar pulled himself together.

'Let's get out of here, Gracie. We must talk.'

Rather ostentatiously, W.G. poured his green drink into a flower-pot. No green drinks for him. Oscar threw some *sous* onto the disgusting tablecloth.

'Follow me, Gracie,' said Oscar. 'I know a place.'

W.G. glanced up at the Paradiso and there was Watson

signalling something from his balcony. Had he been an umpire, he would have been signalling a boundary four. His hands extended in front of him, palms down, he was doing a swift breast-stroke at waist level. Now he was cutting his throat with his right hand. Now he was shaking his head from side to side. Any scorer would be totally bemused. Was he trying to suggest the venture best abandoned? Possibility of death of some sort? Danger? Oscar and W.G. stood at the entrance to the bar both fascinated by Watson's pantomime.

'Pay no heed to the daft old bastard!'

The Irishman was now tugging impatiently at W.G.'s sleeve. Queensberry's man? Ha! Bloody unlikely. Queensberry would hardly be likely to employ a man who had gone well beyond the pale with a member of his family. W.G. brought his flannelled knee up sharply into Wilde's velvety groin. He moved quickly, however, for an overweightish wicket-keeper.

'Try that again, you bushy-faced barbarian,' hissed Oscar, his green carnation quivering in W.G.'s nostril, 'and I'll scream my head off!' Never one to give up W.G. had another crack. He missed by a yard.

'Let me bed you *again, tonight,* you beautiful beaver!' shouted Wilde, at the very top of his voice. Heads turned. There was a general buzz. A waiter whistled and made a crude gesture at the starry, starry night.

'Come with me, my pretty,' cooed Oscar, and seizing W.G. by the beard-end, swept him round a corner into an ill-lit alley. His large hands flew about W.G.'s flannels.

'A deal less of that!' screamed W.G. in an alarming falsetto.

'I'm only frisking you,' said Wilde. 'You are wholly safe in my hands, you delicious animal.'

'I think,' said W.G. checking his essentials, 'that you owe me some sort of explanation.'

'Your place or mine?' smiled Oscar.

Oscar Wilde was slumped heavily in an armchair in Watson's room at the Hotel Paradiso. Watson staunchly refused, despite W.G.'s protestations, to lower his revolver and kept it trained on Wilde's midriff.

'With all due respect, Dr Grace,' said Watson. 'while I bow to your opinion on such matters as the Chinese cut, the use of the heavy roller, bad light, Spofforth's speed, and How to Handle the Grubber, in matters such as espionage, detection, intrigue and conspiracy you are an innocent. When faced with an evil genius, a Moriarty, a Fu Manchu, a Vilebastard you cannot change the bowling, more long leg round a bit, hit him back over his head —'

'Bravely said, Jolly Jack Watson,' Oscar applauded heartily and then sank back in the chair. 'But believe me, boyo, I'm on your side, though 'tis sand-blasted that I am, worn to a frazzle. Pour us a tooth-mug of that Calvados there, and I'll tell you a thing, that I will.'

W.G. poured a good half of the bottle into a white-flecked tumbler and handed it to him.

'God bless you, massive Sir,' beamed the poet, running a hand through his long, greying hair and downing the Calvados in one. He belched happily and threw the tumbler at W.G. who caught it adroitly, and poured the remains of the bottle into it.

'They'll kill you soon as look at you — Governments!' Wilde smiled as Watson pocketed his revolver. Clearly he had come to a decision. 'Queensberry wanted a man in Paris. The Brits think the next war could be with the French. I've worked on and off for Irish Intelligence.' He looked keenly at the pair of them. The contradiction was wasted on them.

'This man,' said Queensberry, 'should be furnished with good reason for hating the British, so that the French would take him to their bosom.' In my view he overdid it, but, Jesus, it worked.' And he tittered helplessly and sipped at his drink.

'You mean,' said Watson, 'that the accusations of sodomy, the Court Cases, the ostlers, Lord Alfred Douglas — all that was Queensberry's fabrication?'

'Well, not all of it,' admitted Oscar. 'But I don't suppose I've had more of my share of the Uranian delights than most.' He looked at W.G.

'Don't look at me,' said W.G. He looked at Watson.

Watson was strangely silent.

'Is that a blush I see crawling like the dawn across your varicose cheek?' Oscar winked at W.G., and pointed with his glass at Watson.

'Well,' said Watson, and breathed in deeply. 'Not since school.'

W.G. inspected the ceiling. Wilde's full red lips worked as if he were about to spit out a bitter pill. He was obviously controlling a great bubble of laughter.

'Oho, what will you be doing after the show, Johnny?'

Watson was somewhat bemused by this invitation.

'What show, Mr Wilde?'

'The show that I'll be taking you both to tonight, Dr Watson.'

'Show?' queried W.G.

'The Moulin Rouge. I think you'll find it to your taste.'

'Really, Mr Wilde,' W.G. protested. 'We are not here on pleasure bent.'

'Don't you want to see the Can-Can, then?'

'Certainly not,' said W.G.

'Whatever it is,' added Watson, loyally.

'Don't you want to see Pollux?'

The doctors ran for their hats.

17 The Beginning of the End at the Moulin Rouge

When W.G. entered the Moulin Rouge with Watson and a rather inebriated S. Melmoth, *alias* Oscar Wilde, he underwent a startling religious experience. He had a vision as clear as any enjoyed on the Damascus Road or the Arc By-pass of what Hell was like. Boiling hot and humid, packing with humanity, sweat, the air heavy with garlic and cigar-smoke, cheap scent and armpits, and the noise. The deafening sound of raucous modern music, screaming women, cursing waiters, customers shouting for service, the crash of glass and crockery — W.G.'s head began to throb to the beat of Offenbach.

It took this small party a good ten minutes to squeeze through twenty feet of damp throng to the comparative peace of a small alcove with a table in it, but nowhere to sit. Monsieur Melmoth was obviously known here — a bottle of warm champagne arrived at once.

'The Can-Can!' Wilde shouted in W.G.'s ear and pointed through the murk. In the distance W.G. could see petticoats whirling. Those must be the screaming women. The audience seemed to enjoy it. This was the old Camel's Eye Saloon multiplied ten-thousand fold!

'Any sign of Pollux?' he bellowed into Oscar's ear. Oscar shook his head.

'J'accuse!' shouted Emile Zola *en passant*.

'I know no-one of that name,' replied W.G. loudly. 'Though there was a *Jim* Hughes who opened the bowling for the XXXIII Chartered Surveyors of Hertfordshire.' But Zola was gone. So were the can-can dancers, to be replaced by a mou-stachioed gentleman in frock-coat and black breeches who, to a swiftly hushed Moulin, proceeded to fart 'God Save the Queen' in F.

'A tribute to you, Billy-boy, I think!' laughed Oscar. More and more champagne kept arriving and W.G. had to admit that he was rather enjoying himself. At one stage he found himself *smoking a cigar*! Another glass of champagne, and he was beginning to warm towards the French. Perhaps, he thought, that's the necessary antidote — one bottle of sparkling wine. The farting man was most droll, there was an atmosphere of cheerful licence. Young cavalry officers thrust their hands down the front of laughing ladies' bodices, while the ladies filled their boots with sparkling wine. Old men in top hats dangled trinkets before excited young biddies' eyes. Young men in rakish bowlers introduced their new moustaches to the wet, white necks of their more experienced escorts. The farter had crouched again after the success of 'The Queen', and was now piping between his musical buttocks a jaunty arrangement of 'Greensleeves'.

The only dissenting note struck during this sensitive performance was by a lean monocled English *Milord*, who stood not five yards from W.G. and had been whinnying unpleasantries at the ladies ever since he arrived. Now he was objecting to traditional English pieces being rasped through the rear of an 'Obscene Frog'! as he shouted.

'I'd like to see Dr Guillotine work on your haemorrhoids!' he heckled toothily.

'Greensleeves' thwarped to a halt. Le Petomane (for it was he) straightened angrily and, as Frenchmen will when words fail them, waved his arms about.

All eyes were now on the Englishman.

'Do you know him?' W.G. asked Wilde. He had met his type, of course, on the Hill at the Sydney Oval. Wilde shook his head. 'Whoever he is, he is barking mad!'

'By God! It's him!' cried Watson suddenly and vanished into the crowd at pace towards the banacker.

'Your sphincter would make a bloody good repository for that awful Eiffel Tower!' shouted the Milord, and cackled happily. 'Aha!' he cried, as Watson sprang from the crowd about him, 'Don't I know you?' and rapped him to the ground with a sharp blow of his cane.

It was at that moment that W.G. fell in love for the first time in his life, hopelessly and helplessly. Later he would blame it on the effects of the champagne, Paris, the heat, the roaring excitement of the moment, but in fact the simple reason was that for the first time in his life the Man of Action met a Woman of Action. Opposites attract one another, perhaps, but not with the immediacy of Highly Adjacents.

The press around the Milord parted and through it strode a woman with a dancer's swagger that caused W.G.'s senses to lurch. She wore the highest heels he had ever seen, laced boots that extended up to a shapely black-stockinged calf, a flash of lace petticoats and a bodice that struggled to contain a most sporting bosom. She had powerful shoulders and a pretty enough face, from which her hair was pulled back and tied into a thick top-knot.

'What a spanker!' hallooed the Milord. 'Whoopee! I'd like to spank you black and blue! Spank! Spank! Then you —' his lewd ambitions were never declared. The lady in question laid him low with a vicious uppercut. As he rose she lifted her right leg till it sat straight and tight against her shoulder. Then released it with a crack like a rat trap — breaking his nose with her pointed toe. W.G. led the applause. She was tremendous. W.G. followed Oscar towards her. Despite the crush, he arrived first. Perhaps he flew.

'Vous êtes magnifique,' he beamed.

'You are standing on your friend,' she smilingly replied. W.G. stepped off the prostrate Watson, but paid him no further heed.

'De la Musique!' she cried, for the Moulin Rouge was unnaturally silent. Le Pétomane crouched again and led the orchestra into a rollicking polka.

'We dance!' she commanded, and marched W.G. to the floor. His feet never touched the ground. Her skin was un-blemished, slightly yellow and with a sheen of perspiration. Where she touched him, he sizzled. The polka worked him into a fine lather. He felt as exhilarated as if he had swam the Bristol Channel. The orchestra having sailed into the calmer waters of the waltz — it was now possible to speak.

'What is your name, dear lady?' He shouted slowly in case her English was none too hot.

'Zey call me La Goulue,' she tossed her head and laughed prettily. A rough-looking oaf in a beret grasped her by the arm and whispered something in her ear. With a balletic movement she spun, pirouetted twice and with a high kick between the legs lifted him a good three feet into the air. He crawled away squealing through the waltzing couples. What a woman! La Glue, eh?! La Glue!

'Glue,' he said. 'Paris. Glue. Paris.'

'Remember! You read it here first!' said a voice in his head, and Charlie gurgled with pleasure.

The wonderful woman had now put both arms around his neck and pillowed her head upon his beard. Oh, this is as it was writ. You can't fight Fate. W.G. clasped her in a mighty bear-hug. She growled with pleasure.

What about Mrs Grace? he shouted to himself, and none too soon. My wife? A personal friend of mine and known to half the county as the sort of woman who would not be married to a man who after only hours in Paris had fallen madly in love with a woman young enough to be a dancer. Could any self-respect be salvaged from the memory of Mrs Grace at the wicket-gate, (for he had gone home to pack) bidding farewell and stating unequivocally that the idea of a visit to Paris was nauseating and that he would in all probability despite his protestations be visiting low haunts and indulging in unbridled behaviour with foreign dancing-girls? No. He could offer no defence on that score, though he doubted if there was a Judge in the land who wouldn't pat him on the back and say, 'Bloody good luck to you!'

She was cooing sweet nothings up his nose in a foreign tongue. Probably French. Definitely a French tongue, he thought, as it traversed his lower lip.

Oscar Wilde was at his back. God, he was surrounded.

'For Christ's sake, Gracie, these are perilous times, this is no time for idle dalliance. I'd like you to meet my French counterpart.'

'Where?' W.G. looked about.

' 'Allo,' said a voice from below.

'Ou?' W.G. had a smattering of the language. La Goulue had a hand inside his blazer and was tickling his stomach.

'Ici, you preek!' said the irritable little voice beneath.

He looked down at the top of a shiny black topper.

'Count Henri de Toulouse-Lautrec,' Wilde effected the introductions. 'Doctor W.G. Grace and vice-versa.'

'Sod zem,' whispered La Goulue, and pressed her lips to Dr Grace's.

'Doctor Watson,' said the tiny Count, ' 'as bin took to Ze 'Otel Paradiso. E 'as ze mild concussion.'

'Ahg' mumbled W.G. His mouth was full. The little fellow he diagnosed quickly was drunk as a Milord.

'That English bastard was spirited away in the excitement. It wasn't Pollux now, was it?' shouted Oscar.

' 'Oo 'all?' W.G. gestured height. He wished she would stop. No, he didn't. Now she was running a finger round the top of his trousers. Terrific!

'You must return at once to ze Paradiso and luke ufter Le Docteur.' This Toulouse-Lautrec was an officious little bastard. 'Demain, you and I will go and look at an 'ouse in ze Bois de Boulogne. I sink your Pollux is zere. I will come to ze 'Otel. Alors!' And he was gone.

'Do that, Gracey. I'll see you in the mornin'. Duty calls.' And Wilde was away, and apart from several hundred French persons, he and la Goulue were alone.

It was pitch dark in W.G.'s room. They fell on his bed, laughing like hyenas. Their naked bodies clasped together. My word, thought W.G. this isn't the act as laid down under conjugal rights. Mrs Grace and he had an almost military order to the business. On their honeymoon, he had briefly hoped that it would be the Trooping of the Colour but it had evolved into a joyless process not unlike a Royal Funeral. As W.G.'s eyes became more accustomed to the gloom he caught at glimpse of what was going on in a large mirror set into the wardrobe. It reminded him vividly of some postal cards he had once come across in Raffles' cricket-bag.

Where had she gone now? What was she doing down there? Mrs Grace to his certain knowledge had never *seen* that bit, let alone — he unleashed a who-ho-ho of bliss. He couldn't understand a word she was saying and not only because of the language barrier, nevertheless, she made her intentions splendidly apparent, and, by Jove, he would follow her anywhere. Onwards, onwards, upwards and sideways, she knew every crevice, every foothold, every fissure, every cleft. It was becoming eminently transparent that they were nearing the peak. A fine time, he thought, to mix metaphors, but as La Goulue, bless her, bounded towards the summit with the *savoir faire* and abandon one associates with a mountain-goat, he could only see himself as an overturned turtle, a creature rarely found at such altitudes. He was, in fairness, giving a very reasonable impersonation of such a beast, floundering and waving, and beating vigorous tattoos on the mattress with his heels. The only difference being that instead of wearing an expression of high anxiety, understandable in a sea-tortoise that discovers itself capsized on the giddy heights of Olympia, W.G. was smiling uncontrollably.

What now? The turtle was being turned. A swirl of vertigo as he contemplated the drop, but no, he was on soft, yielding sand, waves rippled beneath him, gently at first, but the fifth and sixth were more robust and then, he tolled Quasimodo — like on her top-knot — the seventh! And La Goulue emitted a deep throated battle-cry and W.G. found himself singing a succession of songs many of which had not yet been written. And then La Goulue screamed a fearsome sound — and leapt out of the bed. W.G. groped for a match and with a shaking hand lit a candle.

'Good Lord!' he said. Dr Watson had been delivered to the wrong bed. He was sitting bolt upright, stark naked, head bandaged like a turban, gibbering in Urdu. Or something like it, thought W.G., or nothing like it perhaps. In fact it was beginning to sound like the endless repetition of, 'Moriarty alive and kicking. Moriarty alive and kicking.'

'Bed for you, old fellow,' said W.G. and gently led Watson to his room.

As they neared Watson's bed, the two naked gentlemen fell over the piano-stool. The resultant noise and lamentation coupled with the screaming and the song confirmed the management's worst suspicions as he crouched at the keyhole. La Goulue collected her clothing and slipped away into the night. Naked ladies clasping clothing are quite acceptable in the corridors of the Hotel Paradiso, the management told himself, but those two English persons have gone too far. He returned to his own bed to think seriously about the Act II Curtain.

When W.G. awoke he felt very Gilbert. Strangely out of control, a yawning vacuum where his bowels usually set, regular as clockwork. He had not felt like this since Mother (a hard woman, his father had said that you could fell a tree

224

with her) had screamed at the infant Gilbert for tickling outside the off-stump. The Doctor in him rejected the obvious possibility. Not food-poisoning. Certainly, not the clap, Paris' other traditional offering to the unwary visitor. Not yet, at any rate. You might point to the tap water, but no Englishman would let it near his lips. The doctor cleaned his teeth with an emeryboard, carved in the shape of a bat, given to him for playing against a team of XLIV One-eyed Warwickshire Dentists.

Watson was still asleep. W.G. immersed himself in an icy-cold bath for half-an-hour. Drying himself off with a rough towel he realised he was in love. He looked at his tongue. That was in love, and ready for anything. He did press-ups until his arms ached. He rubbed embrocation all over himself. That cured most ills. He drank a wine-glassful and hoped for the best. His pulse was all over the place. His sturdy heart raced.

La Goulue, thought the Doctor.

La Gooooooooo-loooooooooo! he sang. Shall I compare thee to a Summer's Day? — God, poetry now. And yet, all the good things that had ever happened to him had happened on a summer's day. Shall I compare thee to my first fifty? Oh no, my first century. Better yet, my first two hundred. Smack through the covers! Whack past square leg! Bang up La Goulue! Summer's Day? She was all winter's night. She'd probably never seen daylight. He couldn't imagine that it would flatter her to the same extent as gaslight or candle.

'La-la-la-la-la- Goulue,' he sang again, even louder.

'What?' said Watson, waking suddenly.

'Nothing at all, old fellow,' replied W.G.

'Thought you said "Glue" ' mumbled Watson dozily.

W.G. got back into the cold bath and attacked his mighty Wurlitzer with a scrubbing-brush.

Breakfast was bought up to Watson's room with a note from the management stating that it was with regret, blind eyes and deaf ears being the watch-words of the Hotel Paradiso, that it must be insisted that Dr Watson and Dr Grace vacate their rooms by noon, and never darken the corridors of the Hotel again.

'A rotten hotel at best,' grumbled W.G.

'Baedeker gives it two stars,' said Watson, and scoffed.

At that, there was a knock at the door and Henri de Toulouse-Lautrec entered, looking even grimmer than W.G. remembered. He clambered up into a chair and eyed the two doctors.

'We must be close, gentlemen. Zey are resorting to desperate measures. Monsieur Wilde, poor Oscar, was shot through the lunks last night when he returned to the Hotel d'Alsace. Naturally, we are putting it about that he has been taken ill. One does not wish to cause public alarm. It is serious, though. He is doing jokes about Dess.'

'How terrible,' said Watson.

'Damned unsporting,' added W.G.

'It's Moriarty,' said Watson. 'I thought him dead, but that was him last night at the Moulin Rouge. I'd know him anywhere.'

'So,' said Henri. 'Ze Napoleon of Crime, he works for Pollux.'

'It looks very like it,' said Watson. 'That puts Pollux Vilebastard in a class of his own.'

'I will see Dr Watson is moved to new rooms' said Toulouse-Lautrec.

'I'm fit as a fiddle,' protested Watson. 'Eager for the fray.'

'Another day in bed for you, John,' said Doctor Grace, realising that he had never called Watson that before, and indeed, that 'Watson' suited him much better. 'We don't want to lose you, Watson.'

'Very well,' replied a morose Watson.

'Stay here, Dr Watson,' said Toulouse-Lautrec. 'My man will come for you. You, Dr Grace, will accompany me to the Bois de Boulogne. I have reason to believe that Pollux has a villa there, near Longchamps.'

'Right,' said W.G. and took a bat and a ball from his bag. 'We can play at a little cricket while we —'

'*I* can't,' Toulouse-Lautrec was purple with anger.

'Well, what can we do in the Bois in the early morning?'

'Fight a duel,' replied Toulouse-Lautrec. 'Most natural thing in the world. We shall not warrant a second glance. Come!'

'Won't we be rather conspicuous, Mr Lautrec. Ought we not perhaps to disguise ourselves?'

'What as?' queried Toulouse-Lautrec. 'A bearded nanny

pushing a pram containing a bearded bébé? One and half *matelots*?' He scoffed at the notion.

'Holmes was a master of disguise,' said Watson, eager to be of assistance. 'What he could do to his nose with glazier's putty. I have seen him masquerading as a plumber with a rising business, a loafer, an old salt, a drunken groom, an amicable and simple-minded nonconformist clergyman, an opium addict, a venerable Italian priest, a crippled bookseller, an unshaven French *ouvrier* in a blue blouse, a workman looking for a job and an old woman.'

'Your amnesia is better,' said W.G. cheerfully.

'He also made a fine coalman.'

'Coalman?' W.G. liked that. 'Anyone know the French for coal?'

'I do, of course,' snapped Henri de Toulouse-Lautrec. 'But I do not know ze English for it. What is zis *cole*?'

'Duellists, then,' agreed W.G. 'What are we fighting over, may I ask?'

'I do not know, Dr Grace,' smiled little Henri. 'Perhaps ze hand of La Goulue!' W.G. blushed crimson.

'More Glue,' murmured Watson, and fell asleep. W.G. and Henri tiptoed forth.

18 As I Walked along the Bois de Boulogne

Even the Bois de Boulogne was crowded, but W.G.'s heart, already happy as a meadow-lark's, was further stirred by having grass beneath his feet and trees about him. There seemed to be a painter or a pair of lovers under every elm, and the path abounded with cyclists, particularly ladies showing at least half their legs in knee-length bicycling bloomers. One thought nagged however.

'Henry,' he said. 'Isn't it a bit chock-a-block for a duel?'

'Oh, we can look as though we are sinking of a duel, and then agree that it would be *dangéreux* and not do it. It allows us, zough, to have a pistol apiece.' Toulouse-Lautrec patted the wooden box he carried. 'Remember poor Oscar! We are dealing with ruseless men.'

They stopped near the Chalet du Cycle, a rustic café dedicated to the sport. A painter was capturing the scene on canvas (Jean Béraud in fact).

'Bit avant-garde for my taste,' whispered W.G. 'Do *you* paint?'

Henri smiled for the first time. 'Un peu.'

'I dabble,' said W.G., rather surprisingly.

'Zere is ze 'ouse.' Henri pointed through the gates of the Chalet and over a fence and a wealth of bushes, W.G. could see a modest two-storey residence tucked among some trees. Many of the windows were broken. 'I followed 'im ere from ze Jablockhof in ze Jardin de Paris, the first night 'e was 'ere.'

'What's the plan then?' asked W.G. 'Find out where he goes from here? Follow him, see what he's up to?'

Henri nodded, and led W.G. to an open space with a clear view of the house. He opened his box. Two duelling pistols glamed within.

'Peek your weapong.'

W.G. took the nearest.

'Alors, now we stand back-to-back, walk fifteen paces, turn and have a heated discussion about ze *danger* to ze publique and keep an eye on ze 'ouse of Monsieur Pollux.'

'Right,' said W.G. 'This thing *is* perfectly safe, is it?' He waved the pistol.

Henri smiled again and nodded.

W.G. beamed back and pulled the trigger. There was a violent explosion and a tinkle of glass from the direction of the Maison Vilebastard.

'Oh, sheet,' whispered Henri.

'Sorry,' said W.G. replacing the smoking pistol in the box carefully.

The windows of the house were now full of the faces of desperate men.

Pollux himself appeared on the upstairs balcony. He pointed straight at W.G. They heard his shrill order of, 'Get them!' quite distinctly.

'Do you cycle?' W.G. enquired of Toulouse-Lautrec.

'My legs, zey are too brief.'

'Not to worry,' and seizing a bicycle from a fat-bottomed lovely in flowered hat and acres of bloomer, W.G. popped the little fellow on the handlebars, mounted the machine and began to pedal away like a manic hamster on its wheel. Desperate men, a good dozen of them, in berets and hooped jerseys, were sprinting from the house in pursuit.

'Apaches!' shouted Toulouse-Lautrec, referring to the denizens of the Paris Underworld rather than the Indians of the Plain.

W.G. thought of enlightening him. He knew *his* Apache and lightning doesn't strike twice.

'Doesn't look too good,' gasped W.G. who was experiencing a great deal of difficulty in the handling of this machine. It was when he remembered that he had never previously ridden one that he fell off. The desperadoes were alarmingly close as he tried to disentangle Henri from the front wheel.

'Au secours!' cried the elfin Count, and a dozen Impressionists threw down their brushes, rose from their works and charged the approaching villains. W.G. and Toulouse-Lautrec took cover behind a tree.

'Allez, les Impressionists!' shouted Henri, waving his little stick, and then unscrewing the silver knob and refreshing himself from it.

'Who?' asked W.G.

Henri's private army looked jolly game, but the average age must be well into the sixties. White beards flashed as they set about the *Apaches* with canes and easels.

'Zey are Impressionists,' Henri's tiny chest swelled visibly with pride.

'Bit long in the tooth, aren't they?' suggested W.G., feeling it was time that he joined in the fracas. Toulouse-Lautrec grasped him firmly by the lapels of his blazer.

'Zese men do not know ze meaning of ze word *défaite*.'

'Nor do I,' replied W.G. in all honesty.

Toulouse-Lautrec shook him vigorously. Not an easy task.

'You sank your Gird zat zis is not ze 'Yde Park, and we only 'as ze Pre-Raphaelites between uz and certain dess.'

The old boys were doing rather well.

'Luke at Degas!' cried Henri. 'Allez, Edgar! He's almost blind, you know,' he added as an aside to W.G.

A funny little man, well into his sixties, a furious face with white beard and moustaches had pinned an Apache to the ground with his easel and was kicking his head, slowly but with great precision.

'If you 'ad spent your yuice around ze ballet,' cried Degas, pausing to rest his leg, 'you would wear ze steel toe-cap, and know where to poot it.' He roared with laughter took a deep breath, and went back to his kicking. For some reason this was the last civil word he said to a fellow-impressionist. He found them dull company after this and went off and died a lonely, angry old man.

A frightfully handsome old fellow with a huge beard and a Tyrolean hat was working a large paint-brush up the nostril of a screaming Apache.

'Ah Henri, if only Vincent was a life, eh?'

'And if only Gaugin wasn't in Tahiti screwing ze arse off zose *belles Tahitiennes*,' responded Henri, ''E would 'ave made *ratatouille* of zese *espèces de merdes*.'

'That's Claude Monet!', said Henri, 'and there's Vuillard. Poussez, Edouard!' And Edouard Vuillard, who had skilfully trapped his opponent's *stiletto* in his palette, drove his shooting-stick further into the fellow's navel.

'Bravo, Edouard!' shouted Henri. 'We 'ave ze same dealer —

Le Barc de Bouteville in the Rue Le Petelier. And what about old Renoir there — arthritique but toff as sheet.' The two Bonnards were being threatened by a knife-wielding assassin of immense proportions. Pierre Bonnard fell over backwards and Emile Bonnard swiftly tore off his canvas jacket, wrapped it in one matador-like sweep around the weapon and drove his boot into the groin of his adversary.

Toulouse-Lautrec laughed uproariously. 'He was a good friend of Vincent's *and* Gauguin's — *sans doute* zat is where he learnt zat leetle treek!'

There was a crash beside them, and they turned and saw poor Monet sitting holding a red and white spotted handkerchief to his bleeding nose.

'You are doing well, Claude,' Henri applauded. Monet took a deep breath.

''Ave we not always taken ze bastards on?' snorted Monet. Henri introduced him to W.G. 'Ah, Docteur, sank you for ze lovely bettle.'

'When Claude was a student of Gleyne,' said Henri, 'who was one of ze old school — ze ballsaching bourgeois — 'e told Monet one day, "Is not a bad picture, but ze breasts zey are too big, ze shoulder is grotesque, ze foot is, 'ow you say, too much," and Monet said modestly, "I paint what I see". And Gleyre said, "To create ze masterpieces you must imitate ze great artists of antiquity — take ze foot from one model, ze titties of another, ze shoulders of someone else together — zis way lies perfection, Monet. You must always sink of ze great classical works — ze Greeks etc. etcetera." And Monet gets hold of Renoir and Alfred Sisley and says, "Let's get the folk out of 'ere. Zis place is unhelsie. Zere is no sincirity." '

Monet and Henri roared with merriment. W.G. looked rather puzzled. A stiletto quivered in the tree by Henri's head. Monet sat on the perpetrator and began to squeeze tubes of oil-paint up his nostrils. 'You would not comprehend, Monsieur,' said Monet, 'what we have been up against here for years. Do you know what Ze Count de Nieuwerkerke, so-called Imperial Director des Beaux-Arts said about us? "Zis", he said, and Monet put on a strange squawking voice, "Zis is ze painting of democrats, of those men who do not change their linen and who want to thrust themselves on mundane people: zis art displeases and disgusts me." Beaux-Arts, pah! Academicians, pah! The Salon! Yut! Zey wear top hats and frock coats to paint. Critics! Critics? Pah! pah!pah! Theophile Gautier, pah! He said Courbet slandered nature horribly — realism was precision and polish.' An Apache ran towards them. 'Va-t-en' snapped Monet and he spun him through a hundred and eighty degrees on the spot and pushed him into the arms of Bonnard and Bernard, who turned him upside down in a bucket of turpentine.

'How are we doing?' asked Henri, peering around the tree.

'All zey wanted, Monsieur,' said Monet, pulling the Apache with the multi-coloured face to his feet, giving him a fierce butt and sending him on his giddy way. 'was a sunset over a nude goatherd with nymphs and satyrs pissing about in ze shade of a Grecian temple. If he's focking Venus, zat's all right too. Arsehols!'

Palette knives flashed and blood-stained easels rose and fell.

'I sink we are winning' said Henri.

'Where is Cézanne?' asked Monet 'He's good at zis. He is always bloody late.'

''Oo is always bloody late?' A tough little old man in a sawn-off bowler, with a short dagger of a white beard and aggressive moustaches was leaning against the tree. 'I'm a fucking recluse.'

'Ah, Paul,' said Henri. 'It is good of you to come, but ze *bataille* she is over, I sink.'

'It's a bloody long way from Aix, it was good of me to come. Still, zere is one of zem still standing over zere,' said Cézanne. 'Un moment.' And he strolled over to an Apache blinded with paint and felled him in one with a massive blow of his large pine paint-box. He wandered back to the tree.

'What did you say, Paul,' asked Monet, 'to zat *stupide* who asked why you did not belong to the Salon?'

Cézanne chuckled. 'I said I paint as I see, as I feel, and I have very strong sensations! Those Salon bastards feel and see as I do, but zey *dare* not. "I dare, sir," I said, "I dare". I have the courage of my convictions — and he who laughs longest laughs last!'

The artists began to laugh loud and last. 'I can't complain,' said Cézanne. 'Vollard is giving me retrospective. Thirty pictures!' The other impressionists had now gathered at the tree and were passing bottles of wine around, and congratulating themselves on a job well done. W.G. was still watching the house. The vanquished Apaches were limping back towards it, but a pony and trap were leaving and it looked like Pollux sitting beside the driver.

'Vilebastard's getting away!' he shouted.

The only route the trap could take was straight through the cheerful gathering of artists. The Impressionists scattered as it careered between them. Two shots rang out and the driver fell from his seat at W.G.'s feet. As the trap disappeared at the gallop down the path, W.G. could see Pollux taking up the reins. Pollux turned and baring his teeth, waved a fist.

'We've lost him,' W.G. sighed deeply and kicked the body at his feet petulantly. The body groaned disapproval.

'Sorry,' said W.G. 'I thought you were dead.' He did the decent thing. He knelt down and inspected the wounds in the invalid's chest. 'Well I'm afraid you're as good as,' he said. He had never believed in hiding the truth from a patient, however bad the news.

'Good Lord,' he added. 'You were at the Moulin Rouge last night. The English fellow who heckled. And, indeed, gave Watson a very nasty bang.'

'Good Old Watson,' coughed the English fellow. 'He recognised me. I am Moriarty. You, of course, are Doctor Grace. I have seen you playing many times. May I say . . . ?'

'No, you may not,' said W.G. 'With your dying breath perhaps you could clear up some of the mystery surrounding the activities of Pollux Vilebastard.'

Moriarty chuckled and gurgled. 'It is the big one, Doctor Grace. World Domination. The man is an evil genius. On a par, dare I say it, with myself.'

'What's he up to, for God's sake!' W.G. was growing impatient.

Moriarty underwent a series of ghastly coughs. Blood dribbled from his whitening lips.

'Eiffel Tower,' he whispered. 'The Moon.' Now he was coughing his last.

'They're coming,' he added.

'Who?' asked W.G. but Moriarty's dying brain was skidding. A brief thought flashed through that he would have liked Watson to know that Sherlock Holmes was alive and living somewhere near Shangri-La for reasons best known to Sherlock Holmes. But he could think of no way of condensing that information into Last Words.

Then his head rose slightly and he grabbed W.G. by the lapel. There was one thing he *had* to know before he — it is natural to want to go in some style.

'Who . . . shot . . . me?' he pleaded.

'I don't know,' said W.G. and looking up, called to Toulouse-Lautrec.

'Who shot him?' An armed artist was a fearsome prospect.

''Oo shot heem?' cried Toulouse-Lautrec.

A short, barrel-chested young gnome with black hair cut like a bad wig was pushed forward. He was holding a small pistol.

'Aha,' said Toulouse-Lautrec 'Young Picasso!' He clapped the squat Spaniard on the back.

'He carries zat damn' Browning everywhere,' said Utrillo, pissed again. ''E likes to wake ze neighbours with it at night

235

on his way back from the *Lapin* to the Rue Ravignan.'

W.G. leant close to Moriarty.

'Mr Picasso shot you,' he reported. 'A Mr Picasso.'

Moriarty's head fell back.

'Shit. Shit. Shit,' were his Famous Penultimate Words. 'Shot by a nobody,' were his last.

W.G. and Toulouse-Lautrec's cab slewed to a halt outside the Hotel d'Alsace where Watson had been taken from the Paradiso. A scrawny, wiry man, out of Rozinante by Don Quixote, dressed in blue velvet jacket, flowing foulard and nonsensically large beret, thrust his military moustaches into the window and demanded, 'Who goes there?'

'It is I, Henri,' said Henri.

'Ah, Henri!' cried the other Henri. 'And who is your burly friend with the thundercloud of a beard?'

'Zis is Doctor Grace,' replied Henri. 'Doctor Grace, Henri Rousseau — le Douanier —'

The artist quivered to attention like an arrow whacking into a barrel.

'How went ze Battle?'

'We won, Rousseau, we put them to the sword.'

He relaxed briefly as he opened the cab door. 'As instructed, I have kept watch upon this door. No man has entered since I have stood here. I was in the Army, you know.' He crashed to attention and saluted. 'Before I was in the Octboi Service in Paris, I fought for Napoleon III in Mexico, I fought the Prussian in 1870. Such experience has not been wasted today. They have not passed.'

'Well done, Rousseau,' said Toulouse-Lautrec as he and W.G. alighted. 'What news of Monsieur Wilde?'

Rousseau shook his head sadly.

'Not good. Not good. Were there casualties in the Bois?'

'Not on our side,' replied Henri. 'But young Picasso shot dead one of their leaders.'

'My excellent Picasso!' cried Rousseau. 'He and I are quite the best. I in my modern style, and he in his Egyptian manner. Bravo, Pablo!' He turned to W.G. 'I am not, sir, of the Impressionist School. I belong to Les Indépendants.'

Leaving Rousseau marching stiff-legged to and fro on the

pavement — singing a little thing of his own.*

W.G. and Toulouse-Lautrec walked up to Watson's room. The bed was empty. The room, indeed, was empty.

'He may be in with Oscar,' suggested W.G. and they tip-toed into the adjoining room. Oscar was lying neatly on his back, dozing quietly. He opened an eye.

'Have you seen Watson?' whispered W.G.

'Ah, Gracie, darling,' croaked Oscar. 'No, there's not been a squeak from Jolly Jack. I think he disapproves. Reggie and Robert have been ministering to my needs.'

---

*   Poor dead Vincent will slit his wrists
    And distant Gauguin shout 'Huzza!'
    When they hear how the Impressionists
    Did battle in the Bois.

W.G. could smell death in the room. He'd smelt it countless times before.

'You need some air,' he said, and opened a window.

"E is dying,' whispered Toulouse-Lautrec, 'but zen so am I.'

'So are we all,' said W.G. philosophically.

'Not as quickly as Oscar and I,' snapped Henri.

'That depends,' replied W.G., 'on what Pollux is up to.'

'Could you lend us a sou or two, Harry, for a glass of something unhealthy?' Henri threw some money on to the bed.

'And for the love of God could you close the window?'

'Come along,' said W.G. 'We must find Watson. He may have been abducted!'

The concierge had not seen Watson leave but had a purple envelope for W.G. that smelt strongly of his lodestar. He tore it open, while Henri limped away to talk to Rousseau.

'Watson went out an hour ago!' cried Toulouse-Lautrec from the door.

'Why didn't Rissole say so?' barked W.G.

Rousseau leapt to attention, steadied himself and cried, 'I was told to keep ze peoples *out*, not ze peoples *in!*'

'Where did he go?'

Rousseau shrugged.

'Blast!' said W.G. and read the note again. Toulouse-Lautrec sniffed the envelope and smiled.

'Ah, La Goulue, n'est-ce-pas? Does she say zat she is steel plocking ze pieces of your beard from between her teeths? Zat ze memory of last night cause 'er to larzer and frothe?'

'How would I know?' W.G. was in no mood for frivol. 'The thing's in bloody French.' He thrust the offending note at Henri.

'You do not lack to be moked,' Henri read the note. 'No mention of your beard, or her teeths or the frothering. *But* she wants you to go to 'er.'

'Now?'

'*Maintenant*,' Toulouse-Lautrec nodded. 'She says *'vite'*.

'That means "quickly",' said W.G. proudly.

'I sink so,' Toulouse-Lautrec started to walk slowly and painfully upstairs. 'I don't feel so good. I shall lie down on Watson's bed. Bonne chance, mon brave.'

'Where *is* bloody Watson?' shouted W.G., running past Rousseau for the street and La Goulue.

Watson was in Wonderland!

A fat woman had waddled into his room shortly after his arrival and begun idly to dust about him, singing some sad song of a thoroughly French nature; probably on the theme of the wretched life she was forced to lead, reduced to dusting about bed-ridden Englishmen when one could be in a sun-splashed field near Amiens, drinking wine and swatting butterflies. To still this turgid outpouring Watson had thumbed quickly through his Anglo-French phrase-book and enquired with great deliberation, 'Pourquoi-Paris-est-elle-si-pleine-de-personnes?' He was not at his peak. He had spent a most disturbed night. Extraordinary dreams about W.G. mingled with nightmares about Moriarty. Moriarty? Alive? Watson had seen him vanish over the Falls. And now he was in league with Pollux.

The fat woman looked at him contemptuously; he might have just puked in her handbag. She shuffled out of the room and returned five minutes later with a glossy booklet which she threw at him unceremoniously. It was the Official Guide Book of the Universal Exhibition, a lavishly illustrated catalogue of the joys that awaited the visitor on the banks of the Seine in the shadows of the Eiffel Tower.

'Ah, merci,' smiled Watson.

'Cochon!' replied the fat woman and, having made her contribution to History, gallumphed away unnoticed by Watson, who was staring at the guide book, transfixed, burbling, 'Elementary, my dear Watson,' to himself, over and over again.

He knew exactly why Pollux and Moriarty were in Paris and had a very good idea as to what they were up to. Slowly and painfully he got out of bed.

And now he stood in the middle of Wonderland, surrounded by people and cheerfully ejaculating fountains, staring at the Great Central Power House, the Palace of Electricity, which he was certain ever since he had come across a photograph of it (taken incidentally by Emile Zola) in the guide-book, would provide the solution to this Mystery of Mysteries.

'Palace' was the word for it, thought Watson. You might well be looking at an Opera House, a Cathedral even, if it wasn't for the smoke billowing from its chimneys and the rumbling and grumbling from the great dynamos inside. Mounted on top of the white plaster edifice (Watson had variously described it in his notebook as 'enormous birthday-cake' which he had crossed out as being unoriginal, and 'Giant's *pissoir*' which he'd also erased as being unnecessarily rude) was a Boadicea-like figure in a chariot of fire, not wielding a spear of burning gold, but gaily scattering bolts of light. She, apparently, was the Spirit of Electricity. Watson wondered idly what foul designs Pollux Vilebastard had upon her. That they involved great danger to the World he did not doubt, and the World was here in Paris with his wife. So, Watson had deduced, Pollux and his friend, Moriarty, were going to do something fiendish and electrical to the World, as represented, by their Pavilions at the Exposition, using this massive source. Something that might well lead, given the volatile nature of current international relationships into a War to end all Wars. A *World* War? Watson had coined another phrase.

The 'War of the Worlds' was bad enough in all conscience, though in truth it was the South-Western Counties of England versus Mars, but a *World* War, with Pollux and Moriarty waiting to take over at the end of it? Watson's head was beginning to ache beneath the bandage. He wandered down the Rue des Nations towards the Eiffel Tower and the huge Globe at its base. Pavilions of all nations jostled for Watson's attention like blousy tarts. He had a cup of tea under some roaring dragons with the Chinese. He had a filthy dirt-filled cup of coffee with the Turks in their Moorish Castle. He looked in on the Australian pavilion, but the sheep-shearer was not performing for an hour. The tiny American building seemed to be devoted to office furniture. He sat in a railway-carriage in the enormous Russian pavilion while mountains and steppes flashed by on a circular backcloth. He avoided entering the equally enormous German offering, but paused to admire the great lighthouse set on the roof. The millions of coloured lights were being switched on now. Watson had never seen the like. The water, the gilt, the myriads of mirrors picked up the frenzied reflections of the lights, and he was almost overwhelmed by the dazzling brightness and the giddy-making noise of people, underground railways, overground railways, moving pavements, automobiles, merry-go-rounds, brass bands, electronic devices whirring and cracking — and when the German lighthouse flashed its first massive beam of the night he fled for the peace and gentility of the British pavilion — an Elizabethan manor house designed by Sir Edward Lutyens. There, in the sudden coolness, he sneezed and the last piece in the puzzle fell into place. He began to run towards the Eiffel Tower.

W.G. ran up the stairs two at a time. He had shaken off the thundering old bore in the vestibule — a large fat bearded Englishman with a top hat perched on his egg-shaped head. 'Like your blazer. You're looking well. Small world. Long way from Lord's. On the razzle, eh?' This was no time for signing autographs or reliving another's memory of your hundred at Cheltenham in '82. He was right, though, he thought, I am well — I'm in first-rate condition for a man of my age and stature. He arrived on the Cinquiéme Etage in precisely the same state as when he embarked on the ascent. His breathing was as steady, his pulse as normal. Not a muscle protested, there was not a bead of sweat upon his brow. He straightened his red and yellow tie and made for Room 507.

Room 507! There she lay — La Goulue! All mine! All woman! Ripe as a decent plum. The colour of a haystack. Silky smooth and slightly damp. Good Lord, he could move the ball both ways on the likes of her. His breathing unsteady, his pulse leapt. A muscle in his leg twitched like a catapult, Sweat gathered on his forehead like small pearls. He quickened his stride. Something in his baggy flannels was alive and kicking. There was a crash and rattle of iron to his left. The lift-gates were open and that bloody man was standing by a pot-plant, raising his topper.

'May I join you, sir?' he enquired. His voice had a faintly Teutonic ring. His face was alarmingly familiar.

'Join me, sir?' queried W.G.

'You are, I gather, about to pay your respects to Mademoiselle Weber?'

'Weber?'

'Mademoiselle *Louise* Weber?' The top hat was replaced.

'Louise?' W.G. shook his head. The man was deranged.

'The Glutton, I think they call her.'

W.G. shook his head again.

'La Goulue?'

W.G. finally nodded. This fellow clearly knew her well.

'Then may I join you, sir?'

'You may not,' replied W.G. 'Get back in that lift. Press the button marked 'R de C' which is Frenchy for 'Ground Floor' and be gone. I pray that our paths never cross again. You are dull. You are pompous. You are a poop. An ass. I like you not.'

'*I* am,' the fat man drew himself to his full height, 'Edward, Prince of Wales, you blasted idiot. And when I, the Prince of Wales, *we*, if you wish to be formal, when *we* politely moot that *we* join you, *we* bleeding join you, Doctor W.G. sodding Grace.'

'After you, your Highness,' said W.G. He was not going to apologise. If Princes of Wales chose to roam incognito about the corridors of second-rate Paris Hotels, then they must expect short shrift. La Goulue will bite his silver-plated goolies off, he thought cheerfully.

They entered the first pair of double-doors side by side.

They tossed their cards simultaneously onto a silver tray that stood in the tiny ante-room.

His read 'E. Cornwall. Royal Personage Travelling Incognito,' W.G.'s was simpler: 'W.G. Grace. Physician, Surgeon and Champion of All-England.' Through the second pair of doors they dived as one, and as one halted, frozen to the carpet. There lay the object of their respective lusts, but there alas lay another. A weasley-looking cove with a wizened arm.

'Willie!' cried Edward 'It is you!'

'Bertie!' cried Willie.

W.G. could not help but notice that the weasel's moustache was upside-down.

'Chérie!' cried La Goulue.

'Miss Weber!' cried W.G., with all the formality he could muster.

There followed a good minute's silence, broken only by

the sound of heavy breathing.

The Prince of Wales performed the introductions.

'Kaiser William — Doctor Grace. Doctor Grace — Kaiser William.'

They bowed with difficulty, and silence fell again.

'The Germans,' said the Prince of Wales, amiably, 'Call cricket "Fachsprachen".' He beamed happily.

'Why?' asked W.G.

'I've no idea,' replied the Prince of Wales. 'I don't even know why they mention it.'

Further silence.

'Ve met first, Frau Weber und I, during ze Franco-Prussian War,' announced the Kaiser proudly, sliding lithely from the bed and revealing that he was clad only in an Iron Cross (First Class) and shiny, black jackboots. 'She vos most infentive durink ze Ziege von Paris. You may haf heard of Ze Pétomane?'

'Chappie who drinks buckets of water and farts like a barrel-organ. Moulin Rouge. I know him.' Edward, Prince of Wales seemed to know the most extraordinary people. Ask him who the current Foreign Secretary is, thought W.G., and he would in all probability not have the least notion.

'Jawohl, mein Bertie!' beamed the Kaiser. 'Ze same. He vould blast forth in vindy morse code ze little pieces of information so vital to ze Prussian Intelligence. Ze Goolie vould zen transmit zese gobbets to our lines mit ze Pigeon Act she zen hat at ze *Moulin de la Galette.*'

Edward seemed visibly shaken by the news of La Goulue's duplicity, and asked her how long she had been involved in espionage against her fellow-countrymen. La Goulue shrieked with laughter, and smacked the Kaiser on a shroud-white buttock.

'Ah! Bertie!' she cooed in those delicious tones that caused W.G.'s beard to crawl with pleasure. ''Ow could you sink zat I vould betray my country? We gave zem *absolument* ze most useless sinks. All lies. For a month or two we sent ze pigeons and took zeir money, but zen ze food she run out, and we 'ad to curry ze pigeons. Poor Pétomane, he 'ad one of ze birds with me, very 'ot, very, 'ow you say, a l'indienne. 'E was unable to risk ze 'Marseillaise' in F for two weeks.

She went off again into peals of laughter, during which her
'peignoir' slipped from her shoulder, exposing a magnificent
breast. While the Prince and Emperor barked insults at each
other, W.G. sat down on the end of the bed and simply
enjoyed the view. He felt not a pang of jealousy, no indigna-
tion toward her promiscuous behaviour. She, thought W.G.,
is a Frenchwoman and a dancer, I am an Englishman and can
hardly dance a step. We are as different as chalk and quite
a number of cheeses, not *that* many admittedly, but then I
must admit I'm none too fond of cheese. Gloucester, of
course, is fine. I would no sooner lecture her on the pro-
prieties than expect her to tutor me on the finer points of
the lob. She winked at W.G. who smiled back. He felt rather
pleased with himself. The Royal Cousins were now rolling
about on the floor, bellowing in their native tongues and
hitting at each other.

If ever, W.G. thought, war should break out, Heaven
forbid! between our two great nations, I shall remember the
occasion in La Goulue's boudoir and wonder.

W.G. and La Goulue left them to it. La Goulue wrapped an
eiderdown about her and led him down the corridor to
another identical room, the door of which was ajar. The
room was empty. La Goulue sat W.G. on the bed. The
urgency mentioned in the note seemed not to be of a sexual
nature. W.G. was rather disappointed. He had never done that
sort of thing in the daylight hours. But then again, probably
La Goulue was not in full working-order until the moon came
up. He was about to speak but she laid a hot finger on his
lips. He bit it, and giggled.

'Un moment, Guillame,' she paused.

Not time enough for a cold bath then. There was someone limping down the corridor. Watson? The door opened
quickly. Watson, if it was he, had changed sex. He was now a
striking looking woman in full military ceremonial — a high-
collar, medals, knee-breeches and a sabre. Not Watson, of
course, this would be the Divine Sarah.

'I have come directly from the theatre,' she explained. 'I
am playing the Duc de Reichstadt, the doomed son of
Napoléon. It is a great personal success for me. The horse
has had to go, though. You cannot have a horse making the

244

A Gilbert
Bras d'amour
Sarah

'coup de vent' when I cry 'Vive L'Empéreur!' During this informative preamble La Goulue had sat her down and poured a glass of wine.

W.G. suggested cheerfully that the horse might be offered employment at the Moulin Rouge performing duets with Le Pétomane. The Divine Sarah laughed copiously.

'Who is your friend, Louise?' she cried in her wondrous voice. 'I like him.'

'You cannot have him,' replied La Goulue. 'He is mine. He is the World's Greatest Croquet player.' W.G. did not correct her, indeed there was some truth in it. He was, after all President of the All-England Croquet and Tennis Club at Wimbledon. 'Tell him your news, Madame Sarah.'

'I do not fully understand,' said Madame Bernhardt,

adjusting her sabre more comfortably, 'why the greatest croquet player in the world would be interested in my news.' She looked puzzled, as well she might. 'There will be no more croquet admittedly, but then there will be no more anything else.'

W.G. jumped off the bed and knelt at the Divine Sarah's side. He felt that it was a fitting posture, even if it played hell with the old right knee.

'If, Madame, your news concerns one Pollux Vilebastard, then it is of great interest to me. I have been engaged by the British Government, the Marquess of Queensberry no less, to apprehend the bugger.'

'Oh, la, la, the Marquess of Queenberry!' Sarah made a gallic gesture, shaking her right hand vigorously from the wrist as if she had just burnt it leaning on a stove.

'If you can tell me where he is, Madame Bernhardt, I can set the wheels of Justice in motion.' He was not certain that 'the wheels of Justice' was the phrase he was looking for, but it seemed to ring a dramatic chord with Sarah, and to loosely describe his team, viz. one giant Irish poet (half-dead), one French dwarf (dying of drink), one lame English Doctor (concussed and missing).

The Divine Sarah laid a pale hand on W.G.'s cheek. La Goulue knelt beside him and laid a yellow-ish hand on his thigh. W.G. fought hard to concentrate, making a mental note that the bathroom was some distance down the corridor.

'Monsieur, it does concern Pollux Vilebastard, I was with him last night in the Bois. Alas, he has me in his power, I am —'

'The Vernet business?' W.G. nodded sympathetically.

'Oh, magnifique!' she cried. 'Tout le bloody monde sait ca! Ha!'

'Sorry,' said W.G. 'Naturally, my lips are sealed.'

'He was very drunken when I arrived, and very excitable. It was late, I had been playing in *L'Aiglon*. He said we must eat, drink and be merry for tomorrow the old world dies.'

'That's today,' breathed W.G. The toad was back. Or a relation.

'I asked what did he mean, but he just laughed and poured more champagne. This is the Duchess of Richmond's Ball, he said, tomorrow sees the start of the last great battle. Tonight, he shouted, and then he made a list of the things he would be doing to me to relax him. I do not think I would have survived past the half-way mark. He is a cruel and disgusting lover, Mister Grace. His bedroom is like a torture-chamber.'

'The swine,' muttered W.G. politely.

'My leg drives him mad. He had removed my clothing with a rhinoceros hide whip and was about to lash me to a table with leather thongs and ropes all the while biting chips out of my leg, when there was a terrible clatter from downstairs. He ran out of the room, and I could hear a lot of shouting and arguing. I dressed quickly and tippy-toed out on to the landing. A gentleman in evening-dress was lying on the floor of the hall with a very bloody nose. Pollux was kicking him and calling him all sorts of names. I heard "Watson" and "Morrie Something".'

'Moriarty,' W.G. said. 'Evil genius. Mr Picasso shot him this morning.'

Sarah looked quite pleased.

'Perhaps you can explain their conversation. It went like this.' She placed the back of her hand to her brow and closed her eyes in deepest concentration. 'I have total recall', she whispered. 'It is useful in my line of work.

"I told you to come straight here, you festering ox-dropping, not bugger about in a dance-hall. Call yourself an evil genius. Tomorrow is the big one, the World is ours, and you are lying on the floor with your nose bleeding and your belly full of cognac."

"I'm sorry, Vilebastard, the crossing was extremely rough."

"If you put a foot wrong tomorrow night, Moriarty, a finger, breathe a breath unless I so order it, I shall throw you off the Tower."

"You have no worries about tomorrow, Vilebastard. But I bring you disturbing news from London."

"What news, you crushed pillock? London? London is of little interest to me. I shall rule from Monte Carlo probably. The Casino shall be my office. News from up there is what I await!" And he pointed to the Heavens.

"Jekyll is dead," said the Moriarty person —'

'Jekyll is dead,' said W.G.

'That is what he said,' replied the Divine Sarah. 'Jekyll is dead,' and Pollux let out such a howl of anguish that the chandelier rattled. He began to smash everything in sight. I have never heard such rage. I left quickly by a back-stair, and ran through the Bois until I could no longer hear his demented cries.'

La Goulue's hand tightened on his thigh.

'Madame Bernhardt contacted me because she thought that I knew people in the Government. Well, I once nearly killed a President, President Fauré, in fact, he died next night as a result of his Number One mistress, Madame Stenheil, who killed her mother and her husband and got off and married a Scottish Milord. It did a lot for Fauré's popularity though.'

W.G. wasn't listening. He said 'Jekyll' several times to himself. 'Tower.' Whispered 'Hyde' twice, mimed a sneeze, pointed towards the Heavens, then snapped his fingers.

'Got it!' he cried. Coincidentally at precisely the same moment as Watson sneezed. W.G. kissed both the ladies fulsomely and set off to Save the World.

19   Dénouement sur la Tour Eiffel

W.G. had picked Toulouse-Lautrec up at the Alsace and although he seemed far from well he was glad he had done so when they arrived at the Porte Binet, a palatial Gatehouse off the Place de la Concorde with over fifty ticket-booths to the Exposition. A fair amount of translation was necessary. The Exposition had come as something of a shock to W.G., as this was the first evidence of it that he had detected. He put it down to inexperience. Nor had Toulouse-Lautrec previously noticed it. As a result of a severe drinking-bout he had also completely missed the Paris Exposition of 1889, and had indeed screamed and fallen over on first seeing the Eiffel Tower in 1894.

'Zey should warn you of zese sings!' he complained to W.G. as they set off as fast as they could to the new Pont Alexandre III which would take them across the Seine to the southern bank of the Exposition and the Eiffel Tower.

'It's an enormous fairground!' cried W.G. to the panting painter. 'I've never seen the like. The size, the brightness, the crush!'

Toulouse-Lautrec cursed all three roundly in his native tongue.

'The fireworks, Henri! The music!'

'My legs 'urt.'

'These Pavilions are like . . . wedding-cakes.'

'Zey are like piles of encrusted bird sheet.'

He was slowing down with every step and pallid and sweating. The bridge stretched away before them like the Golden Road to Samarkand. Toulouse-Lautrec sighed so deeply that W.G. thought he might be giving up the ghost. There was only one thing to be done. He lifted Henri, placed him upon his shoulders and with a cheerful, 'Off we go then,' set off across the Seine. It was a hot, humid evening, and by the time W.G. had reached the Left Bank, what with the constant jostling of the crowd and Henri's ceaseless shifting as he emptied his cane, he had decided to establish some sort of

Base Camp and rest up for a moment, before beginning the Assault. Behind a pavilion to his right (the Italian Pavilion one gathered from the garlands of pasta, salami and Chianti bottles surrounding the entrance) was perhaps the last remaining piece of the Champ-de-Mars to remain remotely champ-like. A small copse still remained with an empty seat in it, shaded and cool. W.G. entered this oasis and lowered Henri gently onto the seat beside him.

'You go on,' Henri was in a terrible condition. 'I will wait 'ere.'

'Nonsense,' said W.G. 'A brief breather will do us both the world of good.' It was not to be so. Two of Pollux's Apaches, built like beef mountains, stood over them. One was matted with hair; it covered his arms and palms, it curled thickly from the collar of his blue and white striped jersey and mingled with the shiny blue stubble of his lower face; his eyebrows met above his nose; it flowed from his ears and nostrils; there was a clump on either cheek; he appeared to have cut his forehead shaving for there was a livid scar across his brow. The other was an albino; white and hairless as an ostrich egg, with vicious pink eyes. He scratched a good deal. They both carried bright, shiny butcher's cleavers. Knocking their heads together, thought W.G., would be the act of a desperate man. With great presence of mind, Dr Grace seized the tiny Impressionist by the stiff-collar and planted him on his knee. He cleared his throat several times, but could think of nothing to say.

Henri was as swift in his reaction as the Great Man, and as the Doctor fixed a startling grin to his beard, Henri quickly responded.

'Je gésire une gouteille de gière!' he said.

'You le Docteur Grice?' said the hirsute Apache, testing the sharpness of his cleaver.

'Non. Ce n'est pas moi,' said Henri. 'Je suis Gilberto — le ventriloque célèbre.'

The ugly duo circled them scratching their chins. Then the hirsute one thrust his face into W.G.'s. ''Ave you nussing to sigh?' W.G. was well nigh asphyxiated by his sty-like breath.

'Il ne parle pas francais,' announced his dummy.

W.G. grunted and shook his head vigorously.

252

' 'E is deaf and dumb,' continued Henri.

W.G. nodded and pointed at his open mouth.

'Aaaaaaaaah!' he said, and from force of habit almost added 'Ninety-nine'.

The duo scratched their chins again, and weighed their cleavers, and retired a pace to mutter together.

'That's good,' said the albino.

'Deaf and dumb ventriloquist,' added the hirsute one, shaking his head appreciatively.

'No wonder 'e is famous,' said the albino.

' 'E 'as played before ze Crowned 'Eads of Europe,' declared Henri piously.

W.G. had no idea what they were saying, but nodded affably.

The albino seemed particularly fascinated by the workmanship on Henri's head. W.G. mimed hours of whittling.

The albino began to stretch Toulouse-Lautrec's already lengthy nose.

'Ah! Aha!' W.G. saw the problem. Wood would not do that. He quickly laid the albino's suspicions with an impersonation of a potter at his wheel, and then pulled Henri's nose sharply.

'Gon't goo gat!' snorted his dummy, and stuck his finger in W.G.'s eye rather painfully. W.G. handed Henri to the albino, waving with one hand that the albino might like to try his hand with the puppet, while with the other he groped in his blazer pocket for a handkerchief. The albino with a merry whoop threw down his cleaver and made a vigorous attempt to put his hand up the back of Henri Toulouse-Lautrec, whose immediate reaction was to thrust two fingers into the vicious pink-eyes and twist. The albino dropped Henri like a stone and sank whimpering to the ground. This left the hirsute one in two minds, which was stretching what little mind he had to spare too far, and clearly causing it intense pain. This was further accentuated when he unleashed a loud groan and clasped his head in both hands, forgetting that the right one held a cleaver and inflicting a very nasty wound to the top of his head.

'Sod the Hippocratic Oath!' cried Doctor Grace and he tucked a very poorly Henri under his arm and left the maimed

Apaches to their own dark devices.

Watson was feeling none too well. His head was spinning and his stomach deeply unsettled. This he blamed as much on vertigo, as the nasty crack in the 'Moulin'. He had been to the Third Level of the Tower, and the view while breath-taking was also bowel-curdling and knee-watering. He was decidedly shaky, but at least now only a minute or so from *terra firma.* He had favoured the Otis Lift, the American system; that took him straight down from the second platform to the ground via the North Pier. Doubtless Messrs Roux, Combaluzia and Lepage were the *crème de la crème* in Elevator Circles, but they were French and you had to change twice. The Otis bumped quietly to a stop. As he stepped out, blowing his cheeks with relief, the first person he saw was W.G. and he felt a surge of intense well-being.

'W.G.!' he cried. 'I've solved the bugger!'

'So have I, Watson,' replied a smiling W.G. and they shook hands and almost danced.

'I know where Pollux is,' said Watson. 'I've just seen him.' He was shaking all over. 'I was going to fetch a policeman.'

'It's all right, Watson,' W.G. pointed to the prostrate Toulouse-Lautrec. '*We* are here.'

'We could do with a squadron or two of the Mounted Foot,' sighed Watson and lay down on the grass beside Henri.

'Where is Pollux?'

'When I last saw him he was going up the circular stairway from the second level to the third. He was alone.'

'What's up there, do you know?'

'An observation platform, much favoured by suicides, but that's being over-optimistic and I believe that Monsieur Eiffel has some sort of office or workshop up there. Otherwise, no idea. I can pose the question at altitude, but I find it very difficult to concentrate on the answer.'

'You've done bloody well, Watson, bloody well.' And W.G. sat down beside Watson and looked up at the intricate mass of ironwork above them.

'So Pollux is going to signal in some way to the Martians, give them the good news that the cold that laid them low last time is now curable and they can come when they like.'

'Something like that,' agreed Watson. 'Long way to signal — Mars.'

'They're on the Moon,' said W.G. 'Or some of them at any rate.'

'How will he signal?'

'Well, I'm not much good at electricals, but I'd say there were quite a few options open to him here —'

'There's the Palace of Electricity, and a bloody great German Lighthouse.'

'The Tower itself has a great beacon on top that can reach 120 miles. Not to mention spotlights scattered here and there, properly wired, or improperly wired, more likely. Isn't there something called a short-circus?'

'Short-circuit,' Watson said. 'Dangerous business, causes sparks, fires.'

'That would be it then — Martians on Q.V. for big flash, followed by large fire — then, Righty ho, chaps, into the canisters and off we go!'

The Exposition was closing. Uniformed attendants marched about with whistles, hurrying stragglers homewards.

'I'd best go and stop him' said W.G. rising. The lifts had stopped and it looked a long walk.

'I'll come with you,' said Watson, getting up with enormous difficulty. 'The thought of those dreadful machines again, operated by beastly little Martians full of Jekyll's green drink. It hardly bears thinking —'

'But your head,' protested W.G. 'Your old leg. Your —'

Watson raised a stiff arm to stem the flow of handicaps.

'While there is breath in my body, Doctor Grace, while there is movement in my limbs, I shall limp, crawl or slither towards the sound of cannon-fire when Duty calls.'

'I can't carry *you*,' complained W.G., tucking Henri under a bush. He was fast asleep, his breathing perilously erratic.

'I have no desire to be carried,' snapped Watson. 'You go first. I shall not be far behind.'

'I'm glad you're coming,' said W.G. 'Your country needs you. I need you.'

'I know,' replied Watson. 'I'm a dab hand at dénouements.'

It took them a good fifty minutes to reach the second level.

Watson seemed to be growing stronger as they neared their quarry.

'Last lap,' Watson smiled grimly, and checked the workings of his faithful pistol.

'Last lap,' nodded W.G. 'Unless of course we're too late.' He looked anxiously aloft. There was a light on the third level.

'We've done our best,' said Watson. 'If we fail, then I feel that is God's intention. He may not consider the World worth saving. Time, perhaps, for another Great Flood or Plague of something.'

They were now climbing a spiral stairway, breathing heavily and trying hard not to clatter on the iron steps. They were aware of cable and wire dangling from above. These seemed to have nothing to do with the illuminations. Obviously Pollux and his men had secreted them carefully up to the second level, but were now past caring. At last, W.G. surfaced at the third level. He carefully raised his head until he could see over the top step. There was the office, up some steps, the door open and, one of Pollux's men guarding it. He could hear Pollux's voice from inside. That suggested three people. W.G. beckoned to Watson who ascended slowly and crouched on the stair beside him. He was trying very hard not to look at the lights of Paris flickering miles below them.

'Shoot that bugger, I would,' whispered W.G.

'Dead?' said Watson.

'In the leg, say, slow him down. I shall charge.' W.G. braced himself, and on his word, Watson shot the Apache in the knee, almost at the moment that W.G. leaped over his falling body up the steps and burst into Mr Eiffel's small *appartement*. Womp! He punched another henchman on the ear and he sank like a stone. There was Pollux standing amidst an array of electrical equipment and switches.

'Aha!' cried W.G. and realising that he was unarmed, pointed at Pollux dramatically, 'The jig is up!' Pollux, alas, *was* armed, and, as Watson came hopping through the door, Pollux shouted to him to drop his pistol at once or he would shoot Doctor Grace through the beard. Watson dropped his pistol and he and W.G. at a wave from Pollux sat obediently on a couple of chairs beneath a window. He appeared to be extremely drunk and raving.

'Woo! Hoo!' said Pollux. 'Look at all those moons! Come for the whopping great bang! Sod 'Em!'

'You prize Cad,' replied W.G.

Pollux shook with laughter and pulled out his gold hunter. He had difficulty focusing.

'Fifteen minutes,' he said grimly, and looked out of the window as if to check that the moon was still there. 'All there!' He studied W.G. and Watson closely, then roared again his disgusting laugh. 'And that's as long as you two have got! Fifteen minutes.' His behaviour seemed highly erratic. His mood would change in a second.

'The man's a maniac,' said W.G.

'Mad as a hatter,' agreed Watson. 'Should, by rights, be in a padded cell.'

'Oh, gentlemen,' sighed Pollux sadly. 'Are you the best the world could come up with? All they could pit against an evil genius of my calibre? I suppose I admire your bovine persistence. You did after all arrive on the scene of the crime with quarter of an hour to spare. But oh, deary, deary me!'

'We should have brought troops,' said Watson. 'A Scottish Regiment' and went to sleep.

'To little purpose,' Pollux fingered a switch. 'The staircases are all mined. I shan't be using them. My balloon awaits. I let you two come up. I thought you deserved to be in at the finish.' He looked at his hunter again. His two apaches, one with a shirt-tail bandaging his knee, now stood over the two doctors with revolvers.

Pollux was sweating. He *was* in a most unstable condition. He opened a window and gazed out at Paris. Occasionally he banged his head against the window — perhaps this was an aid to concentration.

'It began a long time ago in the Klondike, soon after Castor and I were expelled from Eton — oh, not for interfering with the delicate sons of gentlefolk. Oh dear me, no, Castor and I were always perverse. We preferred the fleshy delights with gels, Doctor. Thick shop-assistants from Windsor and Slough; the chaplain's daughter; the housemaster's wife; even the Captain of Cricket's mother, as I recall. All part of a decent education, in our view. They discovered us in a Fives Court à trois with a barmaid from Maidenhead of all places. Family distraught, of course. The Vilebastard name. The blot on the escutcheon. Father cut us off with the proverbial and took to the bottle. Mother died of grief. Sister Emily became a Carmelite. Castor and I went to Oxford. There we were sent down almost instantly for buggery. Should have gone to Cambridge. Then we went to the Klondike.

'We weren't *born* criminals, Watson. Indeed we were prepared to be honest as the day was long provided that the Klondike made us rich. Alas, the best laid plans, *NOT* the Land of Opportunity the Klondike, very crowded, and it was not long, I fear, before temptation overcame us. We turned to theft, to fraud, blackmail, extortion, at which we were rather good, and ultimately I fear to murder most foul. Unfortunately, even after running the gamut we were still little better off.

'Then came that once-in-a-life time opportunity that one must seize with both hands or goodbye, cakes and ale. There's a moral there for you, Gilbert, if you were looking for one.

'One winter, we were evading the Mounties — we had "taken to the hills" — and bless me — we met a Martian. Yuk! Have *you* ever met one, my darlings? Well, this one was dying, so it was even more nauseating. A nasty ball of a thing like a distended head. Ugly little mouth with tentacles round it. It gave us a very nasty turn. We didn't know what it was. Castor said that whatever it was its remains might well be worth a bit, as it was undoubtedly rare. Of course, we never imagined it was a Martian, until Castor and I looked at each other and said in unison, "He's a Martian," and we suddenly both knew that he was on a reconnaissance mission ahead of a main invasion force. This was alarming news, but Castor's first thought, bless him, was that there might be something in it for us. Then we found its craft — a cylinder much smaller than the ones used by the main party later. You will remember them. He'd brought his lunch — we found humanish creatures, about three of them, tall biped sponges. He would have lived on their blood but they were dead. Castor shot a bear, and this sustained him for a while.

'He told us that the cylinder had gone off course. It was intended to land in Kent but had swerved towards Canada, hit the Rockies and been terminally damaged. Any sort of communication with Mars was out of the question. There seemed to be some sort of apparatus inside that might have achieved this, but it was wrecked. He was doubtless trained to transmit any sort of message with his mind, but he was now too weak so to do. He could reach *us* with this thoughts, however, I gather that twins *are* particularly receptive. If we could get a message to Mars somehow, Mars would be very grateful — said our friend. Tell them not to come, he said. Apparently it wasn't the crash that had cut him down, it was a French trapper he had eaten. The Froggie had violently disagreed with him. He must in his prime have been a hard, round ball of matter, but now he was deflating slowly, the tissue was collapsing, he was sneezing and dribbling and coughing.

'I said I knew it sounded silly but he seemed to be suffering from a very nasty head cold. Then, he said, that *that* therefore is what they must be warned against. Was there no-one on Earth with the necessary power? He was going fast. We promised to try and find someone. He gave us a small machine which when warmed emitted a high pitched "Ulla!-Ulla!-Ulla!-" that almost burst our ear-drums. This was our means of contacting the Martians should they come to Earth. To contact them on Mars we needed a scientific genius or a mystic of sorts. We also needed a cure. Well, the scientists we approached over the years were worse than useless and *Mystics*! Really you have never come across a profession so full of charlatans! We were told of a man called Riel, and trailed him for a thousand miles across Canada. Oh, he had visions but that was a far as he went. We found an Eskimo, Dickens will have told you. He could only *receive* messages. We tried fortune-tellers, gurus, swamis, witch-doctors, four-titted black women, mind-readers, star-gazers, mediums, Tibetan monks, a coven of warlocks and witches in Chelmsford. We covered five continents. In Australia we found a very promising Abo but he proved too backward, and then in New York we heard about an Apache. That part of the saga you know.

'I think your friend Charlie came very close before his untimely. He didn't stop them coming, of course, which was our intention, but he certainly must have performed an introduction.'

W.G. nodded.

Charlie unleashed a series of curses that would not come into vogue until the height of the Second World War.

'Suffice to say, they did not seem surprised to meet us when they finally arrived some fifteen or so years later. We *were* in South Africa, but when we read of activity on Mars, we headed home. When the Martians landed in Surrey we were, in fact at the Diogenes and very comfortable too. The staff were still all there, they had been ordered to remain, and we were the only members resident. We put the Ululator on the roof and when the War Machines got a bit close for comfort, we warmed it, and retired to the Library to await events. It is, by the by, entirely thanks to us and the Martian noise-maker that the Diogenes and the neighbouring buildings survived the Holocaust. Quite frankly, I think Castor and I deserve a plaque, in the Library perhaps, over Mycroft's chair. What a delightful room that is when Mycroft bloody Holmes is not fulminating in the corner.

'One morning, we knew they were close. Castor and I received the summons. *Mentally,* gentlemen, they did not present themselves at the Porter's Desk. Would we be so good as to step outside? With some trepidation we went downstairs. There were two of their great fighting-machines parked outside. At the bottom of the steps of the Club stood one of our round friends, looking quite as seedy as his *confrère* in the Yukon. We explained about the dangers of the Common Cold, but they had already diagnosed the complaint and reported back to Mars. No more cylinders were being propelled from there for the moment.

'We told him that after searching for nearly twenty years, we had high hopes of finding a cure in the very near future. Upon our arrival at Tilbury, both suffering acutely from a year among the Boers, the most turgid of men, we had repaired at once to a low haunt in Limehouse for a little unhealthy entertainment. There we had fallen in with a Mr Edward Hyde, who swore that he had never had a cold in his life. He owed this all to a concoction, whose only side-effects as far as he could gauge were brief periods of intense boredom, but that he would introduce us to its inventor. This he had not yet done as the Invasion then took place, but, we told the poor

260

fellow, we had an address. They assured us that the building and any occupants would be spared.

'Given that, replied our friend, then Mars would move a large number of cylinders to the dark side of the Moon, as Mars itself would obviously be observed particularly when in conjunction with Earth. They would invade from there, unless we signalled to them that we had failed in our mission. They promised considerable rewards. Castor said, I think in jest though it was always difficult to tell, that he had ever had a yen to live in Vatican City. Could they spare it? Of course, said Mars. You can see why we considered it the Big One.'

'So there they are on the moon, waiting for the signal that we have found the necessary cure. And we did — we bloody did!'

His whole body began to shudder uncontrollably. He took a great swig from his hip flask.

'Oh, God!' he cried, in an hysterical screech. 'Oh, God!' W.G. was astonished. The man was now blubbing. Time for some amateur psychology.

'You don't want to go through with this, do you, Pollux?' he said gently. 'It's not too late, you know, to recant. We'll speak up for you. Say you saw the light in time. We'll see you don't hang. Come along, Pollux, pack up your electrical equipment, and let's all go and have a jolly good drink downstairs.'

Watson woke up with a start. 'What?' he said and then, 'Oh, Christ!' when he remembered where he was.

'All's well, Watson. Pollux is relenting,' said W.G. 'Under it all, an Englishman. Tempted perhaps, as any of us might be at the prospect of World Domination, he has wrestled with Satan, and ... and ... and ... *won*!' W.G. clapped his hands together, and stood up. 'Well done!' he said, World saved, go and have a drink. A good evening's work.

'Sit down, you great hairy testicle!' screamed Pollux, his pistol to W.G.'s nose. 'In four minutes. This whole lot goes up. There are charges under each of the four columns at ground level, the Tower will fall into the Exposition. Up will go most of fucking gay Paree! And you! You, you smug, self-satisfied bastard, up will go you and shit-brain here! I despise human life!' And to prove his point he shot the two apaches, one in the head and one in the body. 'Effing frogs! Don't want them in my nice balloon. Nasty little creatures,' he smiled, then screamed. 'Don't move!' and he lurched out of the door. At once W.G. launched himself for the equipment. Perhaps, if he could pull out a wire or two. He broke as much as he could.

'I can *see* you!' cried Pollux and a bullet whacked into the wall beside his head. He laughed that terrible laugh again. His head poked round the door. 'Incidentally, the actual switch is out here. Up there. Near my balloon. That's Mr Eiffel's impedimenta you have just kicked to death. Goodbye, gentlemen, we shall not meet again.' He closed the door. They heard him running for the staircase.

'Come on Watson,' W.G. cried. 'If we charge at him together, he may not hit both of us.' He gripped Watson's hand. 'It's a chance we must take.'

'Right, W.G.,' said Watson. 'Good luck. It's been the grandest of adventures.'

'Oh yes,' said W.G. And they opened the door and charged.

To tell the truth both Watson and W.G. had their eyes firmly closed as they reached the stair — squeezed tight against sudden death. W.G. had planned to attack the anticipated banging. He would, he imagined, be a hard man to bring down. Watson was hopping in circles on his good leg scything about with his stout walking stick. W.G. stopped groping. Watson ceased his pirouette. There was only a light wind faintly whistling. The huge Tricolor above them flapping. No explosions. They opened their eyes simultaneously. They were alone.

'What?' said Watson.

W.G. shrugged, then pointed. The balloon was away. Watson set off as fast as he could for his pistol which was somewhere below on the office floor.

'Wait!' hissed W.G. Somebody or bodies was descending from the observation turret at the very top of the Tower. It was Dickens! And behind him a smiling Gay Dog!

'Grey Sea!' saluted the genuine Apache, and sank to his knees.

'Good Lord!' whispered W.G.

'Got here in the nick!' smiled Dickens. He was replacing

his pistol in its leather holster. Gay Dog was in full war-paint with bow and arrow. 'Got my man finally, W.G. Leastways, our friend here did.' Gay Dog beamed with pleasure.

Watson was looking about and pulling his moustache.

'Where is he?' he finally enquired.

'Old Pollux?' laughed Dickens, nudging Gay Dog. 'You know what happened? He missed. On the hour every hour in the Canadian Pavilion, he shoots a cigar out of my mouth at twenty paces. Well, he nicked my nose one evening, but Pollux he missed by a yard. Pollux was so surprised – he fell over.'

'Fell over?' said Watson.

'Fell over the edge,' explained Dickens.

W.G. looked hard at Watson.

'I don't trust that Vilebastard one inch,' and he and Watson set off again, downstairs this time, with all the speed they could muster.

A light flashed on the Moon, but no-one noticed.

Pollux Vilebastard was dying. This is, of course, was not surprising in a man who has fallen off the top of the Eiffel Tower. There are a number of good medical reasons for this, indeed most medical prognosis would point to such a person being dead already. The surprise was that he was still alive. There certainly wasn't an unbroken bone in his body – but Pollux could still hear. There is an interesting fact – falling One Thousand Feet off the Eiffel Tower does not necessarily cause deafness. Death, perhaps, but not deafness. He could hear the pitter-patter and rattle of Watson and W.G. approaching down the iron stairs. They were laughing and singing and congratulating themselves loudly on saving the World.

Other conditions, thought Pollux, not brought about by falling off the top of the Eiffel Tower – laughing, singing and self-congratulation for a start – then whooping-cough, arthritis, writers' cramp, obesity, bankruptcy, acne, varicose veins, bronchitis, clap. He would have come up with more but the necessary information was filed in those grey cells that were dribbling like porridge out of his left ear. His was a highly precarious hold on life.

Funny old world, Watson, he could hear the distant boom of W.G. Why were their voices growing fainter the nearer they came?

'We met, Watson, over the simplest diagnosis, one dead Vilebastard, arrow in back. And now here we are with another simple case. Another dead Vilebastard. Precipitation, I would say, from a great height, wouldn't you? Shall I pronounce death?'

'After you, Doctor Grace.'

'No, no, after you, Doctor Watson.'

'Pray be my guest, Doctor Grace.'

A huge beard settled on his chest like a friendly wombat.

'Another dead Vilebastard,' rumbled the beard. 'Well, there's a thing.'

'You bloody fools!' gasped Pollux.

The huge beard retreated at pace.

'Fuckpigs! Perfect turds!' screamed Pollux with one of his last few breaths.

'Steady, the Buffs!' said Watson. 'There's no need for that. We were obliged to stop you. Duty y'know. Save the World and all that.'

'You're too fucking early,' hissed Pollux. Another breath gone.

'*Early*?!' W.G. exploded. 'What do you mean by that? Too late, possibly, though I very much doubt it. This is another rotten trick of yours, Vilebastard.'

'Villibart,' hissed Pollux. He was now reduced by circumstances to one painful word at a time. 'Early.'

'Early.'

'Jekyll.'

'Dead.'

'His.'

'Mixture.'

'Kills.'

'We.'

'Failed.'

'Martians.'

'Coming.'

One great deep breath. 'I . . . was . . . going . . . to . . . tell . . . them . . . not . . . to . . .'

'Oh, bugger,' said W.G.

'I'm dead now,' said Pollux, and he was.
'Oh, bugger,' repeated W.G.
'What?' said Watson.

20   The British Expedition to the Moon

Dr Watson and Dr Grace stepped on to the surface of the Moon with deeply mixed emotions. Of course, it was rather splendid to be the First Men on the Moon, but, as W.G. had pointed out, they had had very little to do with the achievement. No more, W.G. had said, than a bullet that hits a target. They had been fired at the Moon by American artillerymen from the largest gun ever created, the huge barrel buried deep in the East Coast of Florida.

'Well, here we are,' cried W.G., kicking a pebble a good hundred yards, and falling over backwards very slowly, bouncing, floating a while and then settling gently in the green dust. 'I'm light as a feather,' he giggled.

'One small step for —' prompted Charlie from somewhere in the future.

'God, I wish I was home in bed,' croaked Watson.

Charlie gave up. Some people have no sense of occasion.

'So much,' gasped W.G., staggering to his feet with difficulty, 'for H.G. bloody Wells. For one thing, there's not a trace of vegetation or any evidence of moon-cows — for another, you can't breathe.'

'I'd be the last to know,' snorted Watson, 'with this rotten cold.' He looked up at Earth and suffered a major attack of vertigo. To shake this off, he embarked on a brisk walk and discovered for himself the joys of weightlessness. W.G. watched with fascination as Watson circled about him at a slow, bounding lope, covering a good five yards with every step. This cheerful progress even brought a smile to Watson's lips. Gay Dog joined him in a single leap from the steps to the machine and together they cavorted balletically.

W.G. found himself gazing at the bright blue and white Earth. It looks very beautiful from a distance, he thought, and eminently worth saving.

'I expect,' said Lestrade, bouncing up behind him, 'that you thought a good 'alf of it would be painted red!'

Raffles was standing at the door of the machine, peering

with obvious distaste at the landscape.

'I doubt we'll have much trouble with your Martians,' he said. 'I would imagine they've died of boredom. What do you do in a place like this?'

'Firstly,' ordered W.G. 'we get back in the machine and don our helmets and air-bags — it is extremely stuffy up here.' And he caught Watson by a passing leg and led him back to the steps of the machine.

Lestrade sniffed. 'No air,' he said, 'but a fine haroma.'

'I think Mrs Hudson is frying something up,' said Dickens.

'We shall have lunch,' said W.G. 'Then put on our equipment, unload our tackle and go and deal with Johnny Martian.'

He ushered the others back into the Machine and slammed the door tight behind them.

The British and French governments had been forced to put their heads together, over the potential Martian Invasion. The British had first mooted that the Moon should be shelled, even destroyed, but the French had pointed out that this would only bring about an earlier Martian attack. 'La Surprise' was of the essence. The British Prime Minister had then suggested, as he would on every occasion that he was contradicted by his opposite number, that the simple answer was to set fire to Paris, upon seeing which the Martians believing it to be the Vilebastard signal would, as arranged, pack up and go home. This always sent the French into a rare Paddy, which pleased him enormously. While they waved their arms about and thumped the table, he would proffer the only other viable solution in his view — an Invasion of the Moon. The landing of a small party — British Grenadiers would be most suitable — armed with bacteria-grenades or such — British made — the whole enterprise to be master-minded by a forward-looking, scientific genius of British extraction, such as H.G. Wells.

The only matter upon which the two sides were agreed was that whatever enterprise they finally elected to embark on, it must be shrouded in the utmost secrecy. Both countries had brought the minimum number of representatives to the conference table. A Prime Minister, a Foreign Secretary, a Security Chief and the necessary interpreter. The meetings were held, and it had taken a good month to agree a suitable venue, in a French battleship off Gibraltar.

After some six weeks, thanks to the ruthless diplomacy of the PM and possibly the suggestion that, in the final resort, the Royal Navy would steam up the Seine (those that fitted) and set light to both Banks, the French capitulated. A decision was reached.

The British, having after all weathered the first invasion alone, and discovered about the possibility of a second, would be allowed first crack, though there must be some French representation in the Moon-party. The PM was cock-a-hoop, until H.G. Wells was summoned to the conference to expound his theories on Moon-Travel and, after keeping his end up highly satisfactorily against stiff French interrogation, was obliged finally to confess, under pressure, that his fuel, Cavorite, was in fact, fiction. Indeed, he further admitted that he was only halfway through *The First Men on the Moon*. It was then that the French produced their trump-card — Monsieur Jules Verne.

The old man came to Gibraltar with his cousin Henri Garcet, a famous cosmographer and mathematician, as Technical Adviser, a role he had filled in the writing of Verne's books. Together they explained that as long ago as 1865 they had established the correct trajectories for the trip, and the height and weight of the aluminium space-vehicle. They had devised a sophisticated system of air regeneration. Admittedly they had not at that stage found fuels suitable to combat excessive velocity during the launching and over-heating due to friction. H.G. Wells smiled knowingly and felt a lot better. For this reason, their rocket had not landed on the Moon. The only fuels available in those days had been far too heavy for sufficient to be carried to (a) decelerate on landing or, (b) more important yet, to provide sufficient thrust for blast-off from the Moon's surface. At the end of *From the Earth to the Moon,* copies of which were passed around the table, the rocket had been orbiting around the Moon, unable to land, and also in grave danger, according to the Director of the Observatory at Cambridge, of either being attracted by the Moon's gravity and crashing thereon or indeed careering into space and orbiting forever. The PM shivered at the thought. H.G. Wells was preening himself.

Five years later, after considerable research, the two cousins had their travellers splash down safely off the coast of Florida.

'So,' cried H.G. Wells, triumphantly, '*you* have never succeeded in *landing* on the Moon! And if you did, you could never get off it. This does not bode well for our invasion force, should they succeed.'

The PM touched his sleeve and whispered, 'Their return is irrelevant, Wells. We only require that enough survive the landing.'

'Then perhaps the French should provide the party as well, Prime Minister, as the rocket.'

'I would like to see some British representation.'

'Who?' Wells was more than a little anxious.

'I was thinking of —' and he jerked a surreptitious thumb towards the Marquess of Queensberry. 'Some lips need sealing.' He tapped the side of his nose.

Henri Garcet was now standing and between savage sucks on a fat yellow cigarette, which coated his lips in paper and produced voluminous clouds of smoke, he was theorising that science had come a long way in the last thirty years and there was almost certainly now an answer to their fuel problem.

Even the French were looking somewhat dubious about the whole business.

'There's electricity now.' Garcet belched fog, and looked anxiously at Jules Verne.

'*Certainement*!' nodded the great man.

'There you are,' said Garcet. 'Leave it to us. We will come up with something, believe me.'

'Done!' cried the PM to everyone's surprise. 'That's good enough for me! You chappies make the rocket — we, *les Anglais,* shall provide the invasion force, which will be commanded by no less a person than —' and he might have been introducing the top of the bill at the Gaiety — 'The Marquess of Queensberry!'

The Marquess paled visibly as the British rose to congratulate him, and the French to cheer and kiss each other.

W.G. and Watson were sitting in Queensberry's office. A handsome room behind the Treasury.

'Doctors!' said the Marquess of Queensberry. 'The Prime Minister is most insistent that the British Expedition should consist only of those who know of the Vilebastard's plot. He does not want anyone further to know of it or of our forth-coming trip. All Government files have been destroyed. There is no record whatsoever of your adventures.'

Watson looked at the ceiling and puffed on his pipe.

'I have this for you, Dr Watson,' said Queensberry, handing him the empty covers of his faithful note-book. 'My apologies, but it was necessary.'

'You broke into my rooms?' cried Watson.

'Oh, yes!' replied Queensberry. 'While you were away on the Isle of Wight.' Watson blushed furiously. 'Now to important matters. Who are we taking on our voyage to the Moon?'

Watson had only just returned from his fortnight at Osborne.

'You have made an old woman very happy,' she had said, adjusting her lace cap in front of the mirror.

Watson hopped in from the bathroom, trying to force his game leg into a particularly skittish pair of trousers.

'I wish, Ma'am, that I could have brought you happier news of the Paris business.'

'You did your best, Dr Watson. Sherlock Holmes himself could have done no better.'

'Your Majesty, you could pay me no higher compliment.' He attempted to bow, and fell forward on his face. The tussle with the trouser was escalating into a brawl.

'Stay still, Dr Watson,' she ordered, and kneeling she tender-ly took his leg in her cool hands and gathered the elusive tweed about it.

'You damaged that leg in our service, Doctor?'

'At Maiwand, Ma'am.'

'Did you sustain any other damage in our service, Doctor?'

'A stiff arm, Ma'am.'

'A stiff leg, Doctor? A stiff arm?' His trousers were coming off again. And the memory of her happy, regal laughter washed over him as he sat and fumed at Queensberry.

Watson had returned from Paris almost immediately and reported the bad news to the PM. W.G. had dallied. Henri had gone south to die. Oscar remained in his rooms at the

Alsace with the same intention. W.G. had visited him once but found it a depressing half-hour. For a doctor, he was surprisingly intolerant of the sick. He remembered Oscar as a booming, boisterous man, he would prefer to remember him that way. Also, he had nothing to say to his strange companions. What time he could spend with La Goulue, he spent with La Goulue. He felt like a child that has run away to the Circus. Suddenly, he was an aerialist, an acrobat, a juggler, a tight-rope walker, he could somersault backwards, balance a billiard-cue on his nose, leap a thousand feet into a bucket of water. He never used a safety-net. It was a fearful disappointment when Watson's letter arrived stressing that it was of the utmost importance that he return to London forthwith — England Expects! The Goodbye was better than the Hello.

'Zat,' said La Goulue, 'is 'ow eet is meant to be. 'Ere's to ze next 'Ello.'

'How about another Goodbye?' whispered Dr Grace. 'I would like to die of you,' he had said. 'Burst in your bed of an excess of you, La Glue.'

'Doctors!' Queensberry banged his fist on his desk, and W.G. and Watson returned to Earth with a bump. 'I was wondering who shall accompany us on this jaunt?'

Watson looked at W.G. anxiously. 'What?'

'Jaunt,' W.G. mouthed.

Watson shook his head.

'Excuse me, My Lord, did I hear you mention a jaunt earlier?' W.G. enquired.

'Weren't you listening?' snapped Queensberry.

'No, I'm afraid not,' replied W.G. amiably.

'Watson, will you tell your friend what I have been saying?'

'What?'

'Gentlemen, this is a briefing and I am talking to myself. We are being fired at the moon in a vehicle currently being designed and made in France. On the Moon we shall be attacking the Martian base with bacteria and such. Who shall we take with us?'

Watson rose slowly to his feet.

'I wonder, sir, if you could give us a simple resumé of what you have said to date. I'm afraid that I am rather confused.'

'We are going to the Moon,' Queensberry's face was

blood-red and steaming. 'WE ARE GOING TO THE MOON!!!'

'Bloody dangerous,' said W.G. 'Stiff with nasty little Martians.'

Queensberry clutched at and hugged a bust of Walpole.

'*I* don't want to go,' he shrieked. 'I don't want to go! I've no head for heights! I suffer from acute claustrophobia! It's my time of the month!' He sank to his knees, still hanging on grimly to the marble plinth. Walpole wobbled. Queensberry gibbered. The doctors made to leave.

'One moment,' said W.G. and picked a piece of paper off Queensberry's desk.

'He has already picked his team,' said W.G. reading. ' "Myself (Captain); Dr Grace; Dr Watson; Inspector Lestrade of Scotland Yard; Inspector Dickens of the North-West Mounted Police; Detective Sergeant Chesterton; Gay Dog, Apache Chief; and A.J. Raffles, Gentleman".'

'A good team, too,' said Watson.

'I shall have to do all the bowling,' complained W.G. 'Do you turn your arm?'

'Not since Maiwand,' said Watson, stiffly.

'Gay Dog could be useful,' W.G. mused.

'We're going to the Moon,' Watson cried. 'Not bloody Lord's.'

'That's different,' said W.G., nodding. 'Still a good team, though.'

'Who will handle the catering?' asked Watson.

'Good question,' replied W.G. scanning the list. Raffles had once whipped him up an appalling omelette at the Albany.

'I shall propose Mrs Hudson,' proposed Watson. 'She needs to be busy.'

'I shall second that proposal,' said W.G. in a spirit of self-sacrifice.

The door crashed open and a mounted Major of the Life Guards, helmet, sabre and breast plate gleaming, horse snorting, burst into the room.

'The PM wants you at Number Ten post-haste. Come, gentlemen.'

'What?' said Watson, carefully evading the back of the clattering stallion.

'There are spare horses in the ante-chamber,' cried the

273

Major, and they left Queensberry where he knelt, licking a plinth and moaning.

It would have been quicker to walk, thought W.G., by the time they had negotiated the two flights of stairs down from Queensberry's office and ridden round the corner to Downing Street.

The Prime Minister appeared to have come as Fagin. He wore a wide black hat and floor-length coat, his beard and eyebrows had been blackened and his nose lengthened with glazier's putty. He waved his arms about a good deal whenever he passed a window.

'Fagin!' cried Watson, 'as I live and breathe.'

'No,' said Fagin. 'It is I, your Prime Minister!'

The two Doctors feigned disbelief.

'Look out there,' said the Prime Minister, his nose bending double against the window-pane. 'That ragged woman and her dirty child, not a shoe between them. That's not right, is it?'

'No,' said W.G.

'Absolutely not,' said Watson.

The Prime Minister hastily closed the curtains.

'Well, don't look at me! There's damm-all I can do about it. In my position you can't afford to care. If I went to bed worrying about that woman and her filthy babe and the millions like her, I'd get no sleep. A Prime Minister must be oblivious to the condition of the lower classes, or he would go mad. Fortunately, one gains strength from being surrounded by callous bastards and those who have no idea. Do you know what I do before I go to bed?'

The doctors shook their heads.

'I worry about the Turks. They are not a major worry, being Turkish. So I ask myself — "why worry about the Turks?" And I sleep like a log. Why am I telling you all this? (Because I shall not be seeing them again? No.) Because I am sending you on an extraordinary mission to save the World, and, let's be frank, you may not return. Now you might well think that such a thought would give me sleepless nights, but now you can rejoice in the knowledge that that will not be so.'

'I fancy the Marquess of Queensberry will not be leading the party,' said Watson.

'I gather not,' replied the PM glancing at a paper on his desk. 'He had undergone a personal collapse. He is at this moment in a private room at St Thomas'. (There he will have his brain removed. No-one will notice. One down and, he counted the names remaining on the List, *seven* to go. Then no-one will ever know.)'

'No-one will ever know,' he said, 'the enormous debt this country owes that great man. Amen.'

'Amen,' agreed the doctors.

'You, Doctor Grace, shall be captain of the saintly band and you shall want for nothing. Your slightest whim is our command.'

'We thought Mrs Hudson, Watson's old housekeeper, could handle the catering.'

'Done!' said the Prime Minister. 'And she will be amply rewarded upon her return to Earth. We shall also provide hampers from Fortnum's.'

'How kind,' said Watson.

'The plan seems simple enough,' said the PM, re-arranging his errant nose. 'Land on the Moon, attack the Martian redoubt with bacteria-bombs, and come home to a Hero's Welcome.' He lied, easily. 'Are you happy with your party, Doctor Grace?'

'All good fellows,' replied the Doctor.

'One thing,' Watson interjected. 'While Mrs Hudson can handle the cooking and light dusting, I think we owe it to her lumbago to provide some sort of back-up for her.'

The PM examined another paper. 'What about Poole, the late Dr Jekyll's butler, he must now be unemployed?'

He was, in fact, pencilled in for an 'accident' that afternoon, he was listed as a possible loophole. The PM ate the piece of paper and rang a bell. It was answered by a small gentleman in a bowler-hat.

'Poole,' said the PM, 'is now going to the Moon.'

''Nuf said, sir,' said the hired assassin. 'I shall cancel the — er — Butt of Malmsey. They both tapped the sides of their noses; the PM's nose came out of it very badly.

'Well done', said the PM. 'You two had best get to France and subject yourselves to a crash-course from this Verne fellow.'

'Vernet?' asked Watson.

275

'No, just *Verne*,' replied the PM. He was peeling off the ruined nose entirely now. 'Good luck!' he smiled, and shook their hands warmly. As they left, he began to set fire to all the papers on his desk.

Number 44, Boulevard de Longueville, Amiens, was a large house covered in ivy. Watson and W.G. passed through the wrought-iron gate and crossed the courtyard towards the front door.

'How do you feel about all this, Watson?' asked W.G. as he rang the bell.

'Proud,' said Watson, chest swelling 'and funnily enough — free. This is, at last, an area in to which Holmes never ventured. He had no interest in a knowledge of the Coepernica Theory, or indeed astronomy in general. I recorded a conversation with him about it in "A Study in Scarlet"!'

W.G. shook his head. Watson lived in hope.

'He said "The World can go round the Moon for all I care" or words to that effect.'

At this, the door opened, and they were ushered into a cool, dark hall by a maid. A large, white-bearded old boy emerged from a book-filled room and embraced them heartily.

'I have great admiration, gentlemen, for the English and their way of life. Your Blackwall Tunnel. "The Great Eastern". Your energy, your determination. Your logicality in pursuit of apparently irrational and unconventional deeds and forms of behaviour. Did I see you in "Macbeth" at the Princess Royal?'

'No,' said Dr Grace.

'Wonderful. Wonderful. I congratulate you. You are at the same time a cruel people, perhaps. I disapprove heartily of some of your ruthless profit-seeking. And those high-born gentry of yours destined to become perfect imbeciles, albeit of perfect breeding.' He roared with laughter, and the two doctors smiled politely.

'Come into my study. You would like to see what you are going up in. You have an engineer in your party? A scientist?'

'We have a butler,' said Watson, hesitantly, 'who worked for a man who had a laboratory.'

'That will do nicely,' said Jules Verne. 'It is to him that I shall address the *Book of Instructions*. Getting you there will be no trouble at all.' He pulled out a roll of diagrams and blue-prints.

'There is your rocket, gentlemen.' He spread it before them.

'It looks very comfortable,' said Watson. There were plenty of good, deep armchairs and bags of brasswork. The interior design seemed to be based loosely on that of a Royal Train.

'The Kitchens,' said Verne, 'are well to the rear.'

'As to the technicalities —' he continued.

'Spare us those,' said W.G.

'I'm afraid they would fall upon deaf ears,' laughed Watson.

'So be it,' said Verne.

'Could my bed be rather larger?' asked W.G.

'But, of course,' said the old man, sharpening a pencil with some difficulty, as he was a martyr to writer's cramp.

'Allow me,' said Watson, taking the pencil and the knife.

'Writer's cramp,' explained the great author.

'I know,' sympathised the other great author.

'Bring wine!' shouted Monsieur Verne, and they set to studying his plans.

After they had taken their leave and were strolling through Amiens towards the station, Watson said, 'You seem very confident, W.G. I must confess to being a sack of panic. The whole venture fills me with apprehension. Monsieur Verne is a charming man admittedly, but a *novelist*! Did you not hear him say "*Getting you there* will be no trouble at all!" Did you hear any mention of our *return*? Did you?'

They walked on a while in silence. Then W.G. stopped.

'Watson, I have the advantage of you, and it's an unfair advantage. I haven't told you this before but I am the recipient of . . . of . . . messages from the Beyond . . . .'

'Beyond what, old chap?'

'Beyond the Beyond, Watson. The After-life, The Grave. Charlie speaks to me. The Medicine Man, you remember him?'

'Yes.'

'He was killed some years ago, but has . . . stayed in touch.'

'Would you like to sit down, W.G.?'

'Yes, and have a large drink.' There was a bar handy. 'Second best thing about France,' said W.G.

Watson laughed. 'And the first?'

'Glue,' said W.G.

Watson stopped laughing. Sometimes W.G.'s joke went miles over his head. Over yellow drinks, W.G. explained about Charlie's occasional appearances in his head with bewildering news from the future.

'It would explain your long silences and sudden smiles and, perhaps, some of your jokes,' said Watson.

W.G. finished his yellow drink and smiled.

'The future sounds most confusing,' said Watson.

W.G. rubbed his forehead. 'I'm not certain how much more of it I can stand.' He stoop up and clapped Watson on the shoulder. 'Anyway, good news from the front. *We get back*! Doesn't that make *you* feel *confident*? Eh?'

'All of us?' asked Watson.

'Well,' said W.G. 'To tell the truth he said "You get back". I like to think he meant all of us. He speaks very highly of Monsieur Verne. From what I can gather in the —er— After-Life he has become very close to Hereward the Wake, who has become something of an expert on late Twentieth Century Space Travel —'

'He speaks English now — your friend Charlie?'

'A sort of English — with a heavy Anglo-Saxon accent. Wessex, perhaps. Or Mercia. Suffice to say, Verne has cracked it on almost all counts, the ascent from Florida, the orbitting, the height and weight of the vehicle, the aluminium casing, all this and the landing in the water off Florida, all this is absolutely correct and how they will do when they do it.'

'When will they do it?'

'Great powers, Watson, you expect a lot. Can you imagine how long it took to extract *that* information? My head ached for days. The good news is that —'

'*You* get back,' said Watson, and draining his glass, banged it down on the table and strode out of the bar into Amiens. It was raining. Bloody Man! thought W.G. He'll be difficult to the last, the cantankerous old fool! He threw money down on the table sighed deeply and set off after his friend at the gallop. Watson had the umbrella.

'Are you coming to the moon then, you obdurate old bugger?' asked W.G.

'Of course I am!' cried Watson.

'To whack the Martians?'

'Absolutely, old chap! What an adventure!' Watson stopped. 'Was I peevish in that bar?'

'A little,' said W.G. 'But understandably so.'

'I blame that yellow drink,' said Watson. And they strode out against the driving rain, singing cheerfully.

> Upward, Christian Soldiers,
> Au Clair de la lune,
> In a French contraption
> Destination Moon!

21 The War of the Worlds Part Two

After lunch, the British Expeditionary Force set out to find the Martians. They left Poole on guard with a large goose-shooter, while Mrs Hudson swept the steps. They did not take long to find them. The carefully modified diving-helmets and large air-bags hardly restricted their movements at all as they bounded lightly across the surface of the Moon. They were nearing the top of a rise when W.G. signalled them to stop. He pointed over the lip and when they crawled forward and looked down into the large crater, there was the Martian redoubt. Two dozen canisters were sunk into the grey dust, ready for launching, obviously sufficient, in their view, for the conquest of Earth, and dozens of little round Martians bustled about like globs of Mercury on a plate.

Watson pulled a pad and pencil from his great-coat pocket and wrote carefully — 'WE'VE GOT THEM CORNERED.'

'SO TO SPEAK' wrote W.G. and then he wrote: 'PREPARE BACTERIA-BOMBS AND PHLEGM-GRENADES', and this was passed around the party, who unstrapped the flaps of the stout Army packs with which they had been issued. Gay Dog unslung his bow and inserted an arrow.

'GRAVITY AND SURPRISE ARE ON OUR SIDE', wrote W.G. This too was passed around. Morale seemed high. Raffles gave W.G. the thumbs up and Lestrade waved cheerfully.

W.G. signalled his team to surround the Martians and Dickens, Lestrade, Chesterton and Gay Dog set off for the other side of the crater.

'TEN MINUTES', wrote W.G. to Raffles and Watson. Watson's helmet shook from side to side. W.G. peered in through the circular glass window.

Watson't face was strangely contorted. His moustache seemed to be attacking his face.

'SNEEZ', he wrote before W.G. tore the pad from his hand.

A Watson sneeze up here, thought W.G. rapidly, and the Martians with their extraordinarily sensitive hearing —

'CHARGE!' he wrote, and sprang into the crater.

It was a massacre.

Watson fired the first shot. He opened the window on his helmet and unleashed a fearsome sneeze that scythed across the crater and closed the eye of a startled Martian, while the recoil threw Watson a good thirty yards backwards against the wall of the crater. From this he ricochetted back towards the redoubt, crying 'Weybridge is avenged!' and sneezing again with such velocity that two Martians were bowled away into the distance.

The Martians were not armed. Their dreadful weapons of destruction lay in the canisters, unassembled. W.G. and Raffles were throwing their deadly grenades with that accuracy that comes from happy hours of fielding. They were exploding all around the ululating Martians. Lestrade, Chesterton and Dickens came down the side of the crater like spring-heeled Jacks and joined in the rout. Gay Dog remained at the rim of the crater, and once he had realised that he had to aim off considerably for gravity was popping Martians like balloons. It was a messy business, and they were glad when it was over.

'WELL DONE,' wrote W.G. and then composed a note to Dickens.

'WOULD YOU FETCH POOLE AND MRS HUDSON? WE SHOULD TIDY UP BEFORE WE LEAVE.'

It was good to get back to the vehicle and remove the helmets and air-bags.

'Not much left,' said Watson, tossing his almost empty air-bag aside and shrugging off his great-coat. Poole had a good fire going.

'Cold out,' said Raffles, clapping his hands together.

Poole broached the champagne, and the party toasted itself and the Queen, and W.G. congratulated them on a job well done. Mrs Hudson was prevailed upon to sit at the piano and sing 'Rule Britannia' in her rich contralto.

'There'll be Knighthoods in this!' cried Raffles, who would not of course be the first, or indeed last, professional criminal to be so honoured.

'We'll be Hearls!' cried Lestrade. 'Lord Lestrade of Scotland Yard!'

Euphoria reigned in the Stateroom of the Moon-vehicle.

'There had to be some good reason for the Common Cold,' said W.G. 'God's no man's fool. Not in the long run. To every thing there is a thing.'

'Purpose,' said Watson, mopping away at the nose that had helped save Earth from extinction.

'Home?' asked Dickens, pouring more 'bubbly' down a gurgling Mrs Hudson.

'No hurry,' replied W.G. 'It's Winter there. And I'm not touring.'

'I wouldn't say that,' said Dickens, and they all laughed like drains.

'Absolutely right,' said W.G. 'Let's go home.'

'What to do?' asked Raffles, half-way up the circular iron stair that led to the Bridge.

'There's a button, sir,' said Poole, 'marked "START". One simply presses it and away we soar. I think, gentlemen, we should all be seated for the launching. Mrs Hudson will clear away the glasses. Perhaps you would fasten your safety-belts, and Dr Watson would knock out his pipe. I'll put the guard over the fire, and strap down the cats.'

A tiredness and a peace fell over them as, they sat there waiting for the boom and the roar that spelt 'England' and home again.

'What an adventure!' crooned Watson 'What an adventure.'

Raffles was standing half-way down the stair.

'I say, A.J.' cried W.G. 'Press the tit and let's be off.'

Raffles shook his head.

'I did. Some twenty-seven times. It's dead as a doornail.'

Watson looked hard at W.G.

'Well, so much for Charlie,' he grunted crossly.

'Perhaps,' said W.G. 'a wire is loose. Or something. Poole, would you have a look, there's a good fellow?'

'Certainly, sir,' and Poole moved up to the front.

'More champagne, Watson?' asked W.G.

'No, thank you,' replied Watson, gloomily. He was looking out of the window at Earth and thinking what a very long way he was from Harrods.

'What about a sing-song?' W.G. felt that morale needed boosting. 'Mrs Hudson could you give us some help at the piano?'

'No, sir.' She and her cats too were gazing morosely up at Earth.

Poole was still crashing and banging about upstairs.

'Lestrade,' W.G. was determined not to show any signs of alarm. 'What will you be doing upon your return to Earth?'

Lestrade seemed quite cheerful. Perhaps the full impact of their plight had not yet struck him.

'If spared, I shall compose my Memoirs. Hinspector Dickens 'as hoffered 'is hassistance.'

'Jolly good!' cried W.G.

'Not,' said Dickens, 'until I have finished my first novel. A Gothic Horror Story of Satanism in the Yukon.'

'Got a title for it?' asked W.G.

'I thought "Rose Marie's Baby" had a certain ring to it.'

'Poole!?' shouted W.G.

'Won't be long, sir.' Bang, Crash.

Silence reigned again.

'Has it occurred to anyone,' Raffles was still standing half-way down the stair, his thin moustache furrowed, 'that this is intentional? That they don't want us back? That they want the whole bloody business hushed-up and this is their way of seeing to it?'

'Oh, come on now, A.J.' said W.G. 'Prime Ministers don't —'

'Yes, they do,' cried Watson. 'Like you, I never thought they did, but I am certain now that Raffles is perfectly correct. That bastard's done for us.'

'I can't believe it,' said W.G. 'He's an Englishman and a gentleman.'

There was the clank of a footstep at the top of the stair. Poole was descending, his face as white as a sheet. Raffles leant back to let him pass. No-one liked to pose the obvious question.

'Well, Poole,' said W.G. quietly. 'Any news?'

'The fuel tank is empty, sir.' Poole steadied himself against the mantelpiece. 'The fuel-gauge reads "Half", ample for our return, but the tank is empty.'

'There is a spare tank is there not,' cried Watson, 'under the Library?'

'That is empty too, sir.'

284

'That two-faced bastard!' W.G. was up and fuming, 'If I ever see that smug little politician's hairy visage again, I shall . . . operate on it.'

'I hate to say "I told you so",' said Raffles.

'So do I,' said Watson. 'But there it is and here we are.'

'How much air do we have?' asked Dickens.

'Enough for about a week, sir' replied Poole, 'if we do not over-exert ourselves. As to provender —'

'You're not eating my moggies,' shrilled Mrs Hudson.

'Certainly not, Mrs Hudson,' smiled W.G. 'We certainly have sufficient hampers for . . . a week. God, I'm sorry about this, chaps. It was all going so well.'

'Luck of the draw, old fruit,' drawled Raffles.

'Champagne!' shouted Lestrade. 'I for one intend to get hextremely hinebriated!' The saloon filled with laughter.

Stout lads, thought W.G.

Epilogue

W.G. was sitting alone on the Bridge filling in the log. At least, some time later in the twentieth century some voyager might discover their remains, and History could then judge the devious machinations of that bloody little man in Number Ten. From below he could hear Lestrade singing 'If I had the Wings of a Dove I'd fly' which seemed in doubtful taste given the circumstances. At last, Charlie got through. Interference had been appalling. Chiefly Watson who would not stop talking despite protestations about the conservation of air.

'Hello!' said Charlie in his head.

'Hello, Charlie!' thought W.G. I have a bone to pick with this little fellow.

'You get back.'

'Oh, yes,' replied W.G. sarcastically.

'Fly Martian!' said Charlie.

'What?' thought W.G. 'What?'

'Fly Martian.'

'Of course,' thought W.G.

'Of course!' boomed W.G., out loud.

'There are two dozen canisters out there all set on a course to some destination on Planet Earth. Charlie, *you* are a genius!' His brain was spinning.

'Hereward Wake, tell truth.'

W.G. was about to fly down the stair with the good news, when a further sobering thought struck him.

'How do you work them?' he thought. Sophisticated machines. An alien culture.

'Simple. Where want go?'

'Home.'

'Third canister from left. Pull lever. It say "Lord's Crickey Place, Wood of Saint Joan, London!"'

'LORD'S?' thought W.G.

'Best we can do,' said Charlie.

'It's perfect. Thank you, Charlie, and — er — thank *you* Hereward.'

He jumped twice in the air with excitement, and made for the staircase, thinking, it'll play merry hell with the wicket, but ultimately, so what?